BODY LANGUAGE

Other novels by James W. Hall

Red Sky at Night (1997)

Buzz Cut (1996)

Gone Wild (1995)

Mean High Tide (1994)

Hard Aground (1993)

Bones of Coral (1992)

Tropical Freeze (1990)

Under Cover of Daylight (1987)

James W. Hall

BODY LANGUAGE

ST. MARTIN'S PRESS
NEW YORK

Design by Kathryn Parise

ISBN 0-312-19243-6

First Edition: September 1998
10 9 8 7 6 5 4 3 2 1

For Evelyn, maker of vivid memories

A special thanks to Rick Badali, Sylvia Romans, and Lazaro Fernandez of the Miami Police Department and to Dr. Bruce Lenes and Michael Carroll for their technical assistance. And my deepest thanks to John Boisonault, Bill Beesting, Joe Wisdom, Les Standiford, and Mary Jane Elkins for reading, listening, and offering excellent suggestions. And to Richard Pine for crucial editorial and emotional support that was above and beyond the call.

O! It comes over my memory
as doth the raven over the infected house,
boding to all . . .

—SHAKESPEARE, *Othello*

To look back is to relax one's vigil.

—BETTE DAVIS, *The Lonely Life*

BODY LANGUAGE

PROLOGUE

Her memory of that day never lost clarity. Eighteen years later, it was still there, every odor, every word and image, the exact heft of the pistol, each decibel of the explosion detonating again and again in the soft tissues of memory.

The loop of tape replayed unexpectedly, while she was driving the car, drifting off to sleep, in the middle of conversation: seeing again the boy sprawled on his bedroom floor, his face blown away, hearing the deafening echo.

Like transparencies overlaid, that time and this one continually mingled. The terrified girl she'd been and the resolute woman she had become, inhabiting, forever, the same body.

Alexandra Collins aimed the .38 Smith & Wesson revolver at the rear window of her parents' bedroom. Eleven years old, a tall, thin child with straight black hair and bangs that brushed her eyebrows. The revolver belonged to her father. It had a four-inch barrel and was too heavy for her to hold in a shooting position for very long. After only a few seconds, her arm began to droop. Not long enough to take careful aim.

The fifth of September. Her father was mowing grass down by the canal where their small wooden fishing boat was moored against the seawall. As she lowered the pistol and held it loosely at her side, Alex watched her father work in the Miami sun, shirtless and sweating heavily. He was an inch over six feet tall, with muscular shoulders and a tight waist. His hair was black and wavy and he wore it longer than most men. When he grew out his mustache, people said he looked like Clark Gable. Alexandra could tell that other women found him attractive from the way they smiled with their eyes and followed his movements even when Alexandra's mother was watching.

At that moment, her mother, Grace Collins, was at the grocery store and wouldn't be home for at least another hour. Alexandra was alone in the house. She could hear a drone that sounded like a bumblebee trapped in a glass bottle. It was louder than the lawn mower.

Turning from the rear window, she lifted the pistol again and this time aimed across her father's bureau out the side window of her parents' bedroom. The gauzy curtains were open a few inches and she could see the side of the Flints' house and, off in the far corner of their yard, a plywood playhouse painted white with red trim. It had a single window and a flower box with some plastic roses poking out. Mr. Flint had built the house and positioned it beneath a jacaranda tree. It was the neighborhood hangout, where the Flint girls, Molly and Millie, and their kid brother, J.D., and Alexandra played with Barbies until last week, when Alexandra decided she was too old for dolls. That was right after Darnel Flint raped her.

On television she'd seen men holding pistols with both hands. She tried to remember how it was done. She found a comfortable grip on the .38, then tried to locate the best place for her left hand. After some experimenting, she discovered that by cradling her right wrist, she could hold the pistol steady for maybe half a minute. Long enough to scare him.

The buzzing sound was changing, growing more impatient. It sounded like it was coming from somewhere deep inside her flesh.

Through her parents' window she watched the Flints' station wagon back out their driveway, the kids and parents going off to do their weekly grocery shopping. Only Darnel allowed to stay home.

Darnel Flint was seventeen, a senior in high school. He had long fingers and broken nails and he lisped certain words. He didn't play sports and he didn't have a car or a part-time job, and his clothes were always wrinkled. His skin was pale and his mustache was so blond, it was nearly invisible. Darnel's father was a burly, flat-faced man who drove a Coca-Cola truck for a living. He was extremely religious and he filled his house with wood plaques and metalwork and mirrors with Old Testament quotations that he had hand-painted on them. While he was at work, Mrs. Flint drank whiskey from iced-tea glasses and sat in her Florida room in her pink housecoat, talking on the telephone.

The month before the rape had been the happiest time in Alexandra's life. She and her parents had vacationed in North Florida at a beachfront village named Seagrove, where there were dunes and sea oats and miles of white sand. For the whole month of August, her father rented a wood house with a tin roof and a wraparound porch just across from the beach. The house was painted pale yellow and had white trim. The days were long and hot and she and her dad spent several hours each day building a sand castle beside the still waters of the Gulf.

While her mother looked on, the two of them constructed it on a part of the beach where hardly anyone walked, far enough from the gentle slap of the surf so that her father claimed the castle would survive at least a thousand years. They worked on it all month—minarets and moats and towers, and a complex system of escape tunnels beneath the castle walls. She collected twisted pieces of driftwood to use as barricades and placed them strategically just beyond the moats. Her father christened Alexandra "Princess of the Sugary Sands" and declared the sand castle her official palace.

In the cool of the late afternoons, her parents took long walks down the beach, holding hands, leaving her to add new features to the sand castle. The morning they were to depart Seagrove, her father assured her that her creation would always be there, forever in the same place, exactly as they'd left it. And someday they would return and resume their building project.

Then just a week ago, on the first Saturday after the start of the new school year, Darnel came into the playhouse holding a bowl of ice cream and he told his sisters and kid brother to scram. J.D., a cute kid of five with dark hair, demanded to stay, but Darnel punched him in the chest and he ran off, wailing. As Molly and Millie marched away, they gave Alexandra superior smiles, as if they both knew exactly what was in store for her and didn't much care.

"The dog goes, too," Darnel said as he dumped Pugsy, Alexandra's boxer, outside the door.

While Pugsy scratched at the plywood door, Darnel held out the dish of Neapolitan ice cream to Alexandra. The dish was green. Reluctantly, she took it and ate a few bites; then Darnel unzipped himself.

"This is for you. I've been saving it."

Alexandra stared at his erect penis, then dropped the dish and sprang for the door, but Darnel was quick and got a hand over her mouth. While he clamped her mouth shut with one hand, he dragged down the elastic band of her white shorts and shoved his rough hand between her legs.

As he wedged himself inside her, Alexandra opened her mouth against Darnel's hand and bit deep into one of his fingers, wrenching her head to the side, trying to strip flesh from the bone. She tasted the tang of his blood, and Darnel cried out, but he did not stop.

The rest of it was fast and clumsy and it hurt at first; then she was numb. The ice cream dish was broken on the plywood floor and a puddle of ice cream melted next to her head the whole time. As Darnel rose up on straightened arms and began to groan, she turned her head to the side and her gaze fell on the playhouse mirror, where she and the Flint sisters had made their first experiments with makeup. Mr. Flint had inscribed a passage from the Twenty-third Psalm across the top of the mirror. With her eyes blurred, Alexandra stared at the mirror, and for a second she thought she saw the outline of someone's face. But when she blinked her eyes, the apparition had vanished.

As Darnel worked to his climax, she turned her head away and let the Scripture run through her mind, a quieting refrain. "Yea, though I walk through the valley of the shadow of death, I will fear no evil."

Finally, Darnel rolled away and lay panting for several moments. Then he told her that from this moment onward he and Alexandra were engaged, which meant he had the right to kill her if she violated their sacred oath of silence.

She said nothing to her parents. Her father was a police officer and she was afraid he would explode and kill someone. Her mother taught high school and had a very stern manner. Several times, she had told Alexandra that girls who misbehaved with boys had only themselves to blame. Girls were in charge. They simply had to be strong and prudent and exercise good judgment about what gestures of affection they gave to their male friends. Flirting could lead to trouble, she said. Be vigilant.

For the next few nights after the rape, Darnel tapped on her bedroom window and stood with a bowl of ice cream in his hand. Ashamed she'd provoked him to such an emotional pitch, Alexandra trembled and fought back tears. She peeked around the edge of the curtains but wouldn't show herself.

Even after he gave up and stalked away, she couldn't sleep. Each time her eyes began to drift closed, she felt again Darnel Flint's suffocating weight against her chest, and she jerked awake.

Then last night, Darnel Flint had been at the window again and his hair was slicked back and he wore a new shirt and was holding a rose. Through the glass she told him to leave her alone. She never wanted to see him again. He was disgusting and mean and he had hurt her.

"I love you and you love me. This is the way love works."

"I don't love you. I hate you."

"Be careful what you say," he hissed at her. "If you reject me, I might go crazy and kill your entire family."

She shut her curtains against him.

The next morning when her father went out for the paper, he found Pugsy lying on the sidewalk. His neck was broken and his hips were crushed as if he'd been run over by a car and had dragged himself into their yard to die. Alexandra sobbed but was too frightened to tell her parents what she suspected.

After they buried the dog down by the canal, Alexandra lay all morning in her room and thought of the summer on the beach, trying to revive the feelings she'd had just a few weeks earlier. How every morning she woke to the pleasant mumble of the surf, then right after breakfast ran across the empty roadway to check her sand castle. Dolphins rolled past in groups of three and four; the Gulf changed colors all day, from blue to emerald green, and then to silvery red. Each night, the sunsets turned the sky into immense paintings that the three of them would try to interpret. At lunch, they had lemonade and sandwiches on the screened porch with the radio playing country music, the paddle fans circling. Lazy lizards climbed the screens, puffing out the orange disks at their throats. The air was rich with honeysuckle and coconut suntan oil. Her mother and father were quietly in love. Alexandra was tanned and healthy, Princess of the Sugary Sands.

But recalling it didn't help. She was no longer that girl. Last week, after Darnel raped her, Alexandra had risen out of her body, and now she hovered above herself like a shadowy haze. She looked down at the little girl with the pistol that was too heavy. Floating near the ceiling, she watched the girl open the cylinder of the .38 and look at the bullets, spin the cylinder as she'd seen her father do, then click it closed.

Alexandra wasn't afraid of guns. She'd been around them since she was little. Her father had shown her how to clean them, how to put the safety on and take it off. He had pistols and rifles and shotguns around the house and he said it was important that she knew how to handle them responsibly.

Alexandra listened to her father pushing the lawn mower through the brittle September weeds. She felt dizzy and far away. She had been forced out of her body by Darnel Flint and she doubted she would ever be able to return. She would have to live in exile for the rest of her days, forever homesick, forever banished from her own flesh.

The Flints' front door was unlocked, as it always was. When Alexandra pushed it open and stepped into the house, she heard one of Darnel's heavy-metal albums playing from his bedroom stereo.

She shut the front door and stepped into the Flints' living room. Mr. Flint's Old Testament verses crowded the walls and shelves and mantel. Women's magazines littered the floor; ashtrays overflowed. There was the smell of stale cigarettes tinged with Mr. Flint's English Leather cologne.

She walked down the hallway to Darnel's room and pushed open the door.

He was propped against his pillows, still in his pajamas. J.D.'s twin bed was neatly made beside his. It took Darnel a few seconds to look up from his *Penthouse* magazine. When he saw her, he grinned. His cheeks were puffy and white, and as always they seemed to be printed with circles of rouge.

"Well, well, well, look who came for a visit. My little fiancée. Couldn't stay away, could you?"

He set the magazine aside and started to get up. Then he saw the pistol and his grin crumpled.

"You killed Pugsy," she said.

She watched herself from above, a girl in pink shorts and a

yellow top, white Keds, holding a .38 Smith & Wesson down by her side. She felt giddy and breathless from being so far outside her body.

"Jesus Christ! What do you think you're doing with that gun?"

He was kneeling in the center of the unmade bed.

"You killed my dog, Darnel. Admit what you did." She lifted the gun a few inches but didn't point it at him.

"Okay, okay, I killed the damn dog. He was getting old anyway. He was a pest."

She took a deep breath and blew it out.

"You shoot me, they'll send you to the electric chair. You'll get fried."

"You're going to stop bothering me, Darnel."

"Yeah, yeah. Sure. Whatever you say."

"You're going to stop coming to my window and you aren't ever going to touch me again, either."

"All right, all right," he said, staring at the gun. "I won't ever bother you again. Okay? Now get out of here."

"You've got to swear on a Bible."

She kept the pistol at her side.

He looked wildly around the room.

"This will do." He leaned over to his bedside table and picked up one of his schoolbooks—twelfth-grade civics.

"And swear you'll never tell anyone what you did to me, either."

"Okay, yeah. I swear. I swear. All of it. Every single word you just said." He pressed the civics text against his heart.

"I don't believe you."

"Goddamn it, I swore, didn't I? You and me, it's finished. I got another girlfriend anyway. I'm not interested in you anymore, you little shrimp."

"You'll never stand outside my window again. Say it."

"Okay, okay, never in a million years will I stand outside your window."

"All right," she said. "Now when your parents get home, you're going to tell them what you did to Pugsy."

"Christ," he said. "I can't do that. My dad'll kill me."

She raised the pistol, supported it with her left hand, cocked the hammer with her thumb, and aimed at the wall a couple of feet beside him.

She heard her father's lawn mower sputter and die out. She heard him trying to start it. Pulling the cord, pulling it again.

She was very calm, floating high, watching herself, that little girl.

"All right, all right, goddamn it." He put his hands up beside his shoulders. "I'll tell my dad about your stupid dog. Okay? Now get the hell out of my room."

Alexandra took a deep breath and let it go. She was lowering the pistol when behind her she heard the surge and flutter of water—a toilet flushing.

She swung around and peered down the hall toward the Flints' single bathroom. As she waited for the bathroom door to open, she heard Darnel fling his civics book aside, then heard the screech of the bedsprings.

She spun back and glimpsed his snarling face, his hands clawing the air as he leapt at her. Jerking away, she slammed against the door, stumbled, and fell to the floor. On her way down, the pistol fired.

Darnel was flung backward against the edge of the bed. After hanging there a moment, he spilled to the floor and came to rest in a sitting position, his legs stretched across the rattan rug, his back propped against the side of the mattress. He was motionless except for his right arm, which twitched.

The bullet had struck him in the jaw and had torn away his right cheek. His bedspread was covered with blood and the spatter of his skull. She watched Darnel's arm quiver for a few moments. It was as if he was trying to shake loose something stuck to his fingers. Gradually, the arm went dead. And at the same time, the buzzing beneath her skin eased.

She got back on her feet. She felt nauseated and empty and even farther away from her body than she'd been before—up above the ceiling, beyond the roof, way up in the air and the high, streaming clouds. But she couldn't stop staring at Darnel, at the open place where his jaw had been. In her hand, the pistol hung heavy, tilting her sideways. She saw the blood running down his hairless chest, the angle of his neck as it hung to the side. Her eyes burned from staring, but she could not pull away.

Then she was crying, dragging in gulps of air between sobs, but at the same time she floated high up in the air like a peaceful mist, looking down at the girl who sobbed and was frozen in place, a gun in her hand.

In the Flints' hallway, there were heavy steps. She stopped crying, but Alexandra didn't move, didn't turn from the faceless thing before her. Her eyes ached, but she continued to stare at the dead boy.

"Oh, sweet Jesus." Her father, Lawton, was behind her, breathing hard. He smelled of cut grass and sweat. "Christ Almighty."

He stood unmoving for a few moments; then his hands were gentle but commanding as he drew Alexandra into the hallway and pried the pistol from her hand and ordered her to stay put, not to move. He sprinted down the hallway and out the back door of the Flints' house.

Alexandra wiped her nose and stared at a rectangle of copper that sat on the hallway bookshelf. Etched into it was a quote from Ecclesiastes: "One generation passeth away, and another generation cometh: but the earth abideth for ever."

She looked at the words from the Bible, read them over and over to herself for whatever comfort they might provide, but she had no idea what they meant. She was cold and vacant and the buzzing had completely ceased.

When her father returned, he was carrying a plastic sandwich bag filled with white powder. He held it inside a blue bandanna.

"You stay here," he said.

He went into Darnel's room, and Alexandra moved to the doorway to see.

She watched him step around the widening circle of blood and stoop over Darnel and dump the powdery dust across his shirt. He stood up and dropped the empty bag near his lifeless hand.

"What's that?"

"A drug," he said. "An illegal substance."

"Why do you have it?"

"For emergencies," he said, "occasions like this."

He stared down at the body, the sweat sheening his face.

"Daddy," she said. "Don't you want to know what happened?"

"I don't need to hear it, sweetheart. I can see."

"I just wanted to scare him. That's all."

"I know, I know. It's all right. We'll fix this. We will."

"He killed Pugsy, Dad. He murdered the dog."

Her father stepped over to Darnel's dresser and, using the blue bandanna, opened each of the drawers and dumped them onto the floor.

"But it wasn't just about Pugsy," she said. "It was about me."

Her father drew a long breath and stared at the dead boy.

"Did he touch you, Alexandra?" he asked quietly, his eyes hidden from her. "Did he hurt you?"

"Yes."

Her father tried to say something, but the words failed in his throat and he swallowed hard.

"Am I going to the electric chair?"

He shook his head and stepped over to her and squatted down to look squarely into her eyes.

"No," he said. "Not if I have anything to say about it."

She hugged him and he patted her back as she wept. Finally, he rose and took her by the arm, then drew her away and guided her out of the room, down the hallway and toward the back door.

At the door, she halted.

"There's somebody else in the house."

Her father turned and knelt down to peer into her eyes. His

eyes were bruised and misty. She had never seen him look so naked before.

"I heard a toilet flush," she said. "There's someone else here."

Her father gazed past her, down the hallway, and swallowed hard. Then he rose, walked down the hallway, opened the bathroom door, and went inside. He came back out a few moments later. Next, he went into the Flints' bedroom, then the girls' room. When he came back down the hall, he was shaking his head.

"There's no one here."

"You're sure?"

"Alexandra, listen to me. Nothing happened here. It's all going to go away and we'll forget it and things will be the way they were before. I promise you that. Exactly the way they were. This didn't happen, Alex. This simply didn't occur."

They walked back to their yard and Alexandra sat in the shade of a mango tree, and through the blur of her tears she watched her father finish mowing the grass. Her body felt heavy and old, as if the part of her that had been floating above had stolen all the buoyancy from her flesh.

She watched him, shirtless in the sun, a scattering of gray hairs showing among the dense forest on his chest. He pushed the mower through the tall grass by the canal. And she thought about men, how they could do such terrible things, then go right back to eating ice cream, mowing the grass. She watched her father and tried to picture herself as a grown woman married to a man like him, someone strong and sheltering.

The flesh of her face felt heavy. She couldn't imagine laughing again, or even smiling. It was the first time in her life she had noticed the dreadful pull of gravity.

A half hour later when the Flints returned home, the twins ran over to Alexandra and began to chatter while they ate their raspberry Popsicles. Alex tried to act natural, listening and nodding. Molly asked her about her reddened eyes, and Alexandra said her allergies were acting up. A few minutes later, Mrs. Flint screamed and screamed again, and the girls went flying into their house.

Then the police arrived, and while Darnel's body was wheeled away, one of the plainclothes detectives spoke with her father on the sidewalk. Alexandra watched from the living room window.

"Are you all right, sweet pea?" Her mother put an arm over her shoulder and tried to turn her away from the activity in the street. But Alexandra told her she wanted to watch. She didn't say it, but she was afraid this would be the last moment she would see her father outside of a jail cell.

A short while later, the police left. Her father spent the rest of the afternoon clipping the hedges, and Alexandra lay in her bed and watched the curtains swell and fall and listened to the snip of her father's blade.

That evening, Mrs. Flint wailed on her back porch and she broke glass after glass against the cement floor. It was that noise Alexandra would hear forever, the crash and clatter whenever she began to drift off to sleep. The beginning of a lifetime of insomnia.

By Christmas, the Flints had moved away. Alex decided that the flushing toilet had been in her imagination, a product of her panic, or maybe just some peculiarity of the Flints' plumbing, something she didn't understand.

Her father never spoke of the event again, and though once or twice in the weeks that followed Alexandra was on the verge of confessing to her mother, she never found a way to begin. Apparently, her mother didn't know. She continued to refer to Darnel's death as "a drug deal gone bad," saying it was a lesson about the effects of heavy-metal music and shiftlessness.

ONE

Alexandra began shooting at fifty yards. She worked slowly toward the four-story building, taking several wide-angle shots of the whole structure. A stucco apartment building with red tile roof and dark green stairways and landings, here and there a coral rock facade. In that part of Coconut Grove, two bedrooms started at eight hundred a month. Sporty compacts filled the parking lot, owned by the young lawyers and stockbrokers who populated these buildings, twenty-something singles with more expendable income than Alexandra had take-home pay.

She got a wide-angle shot of the cars. You never knew when a perp might leave his vehicle behind. Car trouble, panic, even arrogance. A year earlier, after studying hundreds of photos of two different murder scenes, Alexandra had spotted the same car parked at both, a fact that broke the case.

It took her four shots to get all the cars near the apartment. The Minolta 700 SI she was using was motor-driven, had an autofocus, auto everything. Nearly impossible to make a mistake.

Alexandra Rafferty was an ID tech with the Miami PD, photographic specialist. Not being a sworn police officer meant, among other things, that she wasn't authorized to carry a gun. Which was fine by her. She'd had more than enough of guns. Her only weapon was the telescoping baton she carried on her belt. Her counterparts with Metro-Dade, the county ID techs, were sworn officers, and they were paid even more than the detectives. They carried the latest Glocks, ran the crime scene, bossed the homicide guys around. But not the City of Miami PD. Exactly the same job, only Alexandra and her colleagues were considered technicians, bottom of the totem.

Night after night, she ghosted through rooms, took her shots, and when she was finished, she moved on to the next scene. Hardly noticed. Which was fine. She had no aspiration to run things. That wasn't her. She had her attitude, her opinion. Had no problem speaking up if one of the homicide guys missed something or asked for her view. But she didn't aspire to run the show or get involved with the daily dick measuring that went on all around her. She took her rolls of film, sent them to processing, got them back, arranged them, put together her files, and then moved on, and moved on again.

Her B.A. was from the local state university, criminal justice, psychology minor, 3.8 average, her only Bs a couple of painting courses she'd attempted. Some of her college friends were horrified at her career choice. But she wouldn't be anywhere else. In a cheap blue shirt and matching trousers, a uniform shabbier than the ones the inmates got, working impossible hours at insultingly low pay. But none of that mattered. She liked her job. It made a difference in the world, a modest one perhaps, but essential. And the job kept her alert, focused, living close to the bone. And she liked using the camera, being a photographer who never had to tell her subjects to hold still, never got a complaint about unflattering angles.

Alexandra was twenty-nine and had been doing this work for eight years. It still felt new. Every night, every scene, something different, something human and extreme. From eleven till seven, alert for eight hours. Wired. Just after dawn, she'd take her run on the beach, then go home, still pumped from the night before, and make breakfast for Stan and her father. She'd ride that high most of the morning. Just steal a few hours of sleep in the afternoon while Stan was at work and her dad was doing basket weaving at Harbor House, four or five hours at the most; then by eleven the next night, she was ready to go again.

It was a little before midnight, Wednesday, October the seventh. No traffic on Tigertail Avenue. No human noises. Only the jittery fizz of the sulfurous streetlights. She lowered her camera, stepped over the yellow crime-scene tape, walked forward five paces, raised the Minolta again, and took half a dozen medium-distance flash shots of bloodstains on the asphalt parking lot. Several drops gleamed near the rear bumper of a Corvette with dark windows and a BAD BOY logo. She got a shot of the Vette, its license plate. A wide-angle shot of the other four cars parked beside it. Then she knelt down for a few close-ups of the blood. It was dry now but still gleamed in the yellow streetlights.

She got back to her feet and scanned the pavement with her Maglite. She worked between the cars, found more blood near the sidewalk, a bloody footprint. She took one establishing shot of the footprint from five feet out, then placed her ruler down next to the print for accurate perspective and took one shot, then another just to be sure she had something.

Eyes neutral. No personality, no throb of self. The flat, disinterested perspective of an android whose assignment was simply to see and document. No Alexandra, no daughter, no wife, no bundle of dreams and wishes and memories. Nothing but the viewfinder, the square frame, the footprints. Step by step, moving closer to the heart of the crime.

On the sidewalk in front of the apartment, she popped out the used film, marked it, and threaded a new roll into the Minolta. Kodak Plus 200. From the window of the bottom apartment, a cat watched her. It was a gold tabby with a bell on its collar. As she came near, the cat stood up on the inside windowsill and stretched itself, then slid away into the dark apartment as if it had witnessed its quota of misery for one night.

Alexandra took another flash shot at the bottom of the stairway. More speckles of blood and more footprints. She found the bloody outline of a hand on the wood rail and got a medium shot and a five-inch close-up of it. Clear enough to blow up later and use the fluorescent-light enhancement to get a usable print. She took one more shot as she was going up the stairs. The bottom of the bleeder's shoes had deep waffle patterns. The same size ten Nikes he'd worn on the four previous occasions.

The killer had walked down the stairway, dripping blood in front of him, then stepping into the spatters he'd made. His fifth assault in as many months, identical MO as the others. Lots of theories were circulating about why a guy who'd just raped and murdered took such care to leave his bloody prints behind. A taunt, perhaps. A wish to be caught. Or some ritualistic fantasy he was dramatizing. The *Miami Herald* and one of the TV stations had dubbed him "the Bloody Rapist" and theorized that he was trying to show the incompetence of law enforcement. A former cop perhaps thumbing his nose at his old colleagues. Here're my fingerprints all over the place, my DNA, my shoe prints, and you idiots still can't catch me.

But Alex didn't buy the profile. As usual, the media jocks assumed everyone else wanted what they themselves hungered so deeply for: publicity, high ratings. But this guy didn't strike her that way at all. No headline hound. His whole scenario was too intense, too private for that. To Alex, that blood seemed fiercely primal, like the spoor of some fatally wounded animal, a beast too blinded by its hurt to care about the trail it was leaving.

Higher up the wooden railing was another bloody handprint. Alexandra got an establishing shot from five feet away, then two close-in shots. Good clear prints. She moved slowly, warily, eyes roaming in precise concentric circles, five feet out, ten feet, farther. As she'd been trained to look. Second nature now.

Down the hallway, Dan Romano was smoking a cigarette, gazing out at the night sky. Heavy guy with white hair swept back. Thirty years on the force. Homicide lieutenant who was running the Bloody Rapist investigation. Dan was due to retire any day now. Getting philosophical these last few months on the job, bugging everyone with big unanswerable questions. Why is the sky blue? Why does the ivy twine?

"Place is pretty quiet," she said. "You run everybody off, Dan? Your charisma on the fritz again?"

Dan flicked his cigarette out into the night, turned to look at her.

"ME's getting his pants on; everybody else is rolling. Be here momentarily."

"What do we have?"

Dan gave her a wan smile.

"Your guy's been naughty again."

Alexandra shook her head.

"You can drop that crap. It's not funny anymore."

"Hey, I'm not the only one to notice. Folks are starting to talk."

"He's not mine any more than he's yours or anybody else's, so cut the shit."

Alexandra checked the settings on the Minolta.

"Like right now, Alex. How tightened up you are. Stiff-jointed. That thing happening with your eye."

She stared at him.

"Yeah? And what thing is that?"

"That twitch, right there in the corner of your left eye. I'm not the only one to notice it. You got a reaction going on, Alex. This guy's hit a nerve."

"I was winking at you, Dan. Flirting. You couldn't tell?"

He gazed at her for a few seconds and his voice softened.

"I don't think so, Alex. I think this is getting to you. I think you need to talk about this to somebody with some training."

She shook her head, lowered her camera.

"Come on, Dan. All the shit we wade through every day, I guess I'm entitled to a goddamn eye twitch now and then, don't you think?"

He kept staring at her for a moment or two; then he sighed and his eyes drifted off to the horizon. He lit another cigarette, took a hungry pull.

She said, "I'm finished shooting out here. You want to show me around inside? Or just do it on my own?"

Dan blew out a cloud of smoke and didn't move. His eyes were scanning the dark heavens.

"Tell me something, Alex. I been meaning to ask you." His voice with that dreamy edge.

"Oh, brother, here it comes."

He drew in another hit and let the smoke drift out with his words.

"Why do you do this shit? You're a smart, good-looking woman. You got skills, a college diploma; you could do anything. What the hell motivates you?"

He brought his eyes back from the dark and peered at her.

"It was either this or a nunnery." She gave him a light smile, but he didn't notice.

"I'd hate to see you wind up like me. Because you know what I'm starting to think, Alex? I'm starting to think I fucking wasted my life. That's where I am these days. Standing here, on the goddamn threshold of my golden years, I been running these same laps three decades now, and I ask myself what it's all added up to. And the answer keeps coming up the same. Not a hill of shit."

"What do you want, Dan? Want me to try to cheer you up?"

He looked down at the sprinkle of blood near his feet.

"It won't work. I'm inconsolable." He cocked his head and smiled. "I pronounce that right? *Inconsolable?*"

"Sounded right to me."

"I'm working on my vocabulary. One of my new hobbies, getting ready for retirement. Hell, I never needed a fucking vocabulary on this job."

"Well," Alex said. "*Inconsolable* seems like a pretty good place to start."

Dan tilted his head back, stared up at the sky, getting that look again.

Alexandra stepped into the apartment.

The sectional couch was shaped into a U and took up most of the room. It was a green-and-white tropical print. On the glass coffee table was the same bottle of Lucere, a Napa Valley chardonnay that had been at all the other scenes. A high-end grocery store wine, but not rare enough to be helpful.

Sprawled on the beige rug in the center of the U was a pretty woman in her late twenties with short black hair. She was naked and her slender body had been rearranged. The killer had laid her out flat on her back with her arms hugging her belly as if she'd been kicked in the gut and was fighting for air.

"Same as number one," Dan said from the door. "Like maybe he's run out of poses and he's starting the cycle again."

"Maybe."

There was a deep cut at her throat, like the others. She was slender and her eyes were open—dark and disconnected.

"Landlord found her. A week late on her rent. He knocked, walked in. I'm guessing she's been dead more than twenty-four, less than thirty-six."

"Seems about right," Alex said.

The other four women had been naked, as well. All the bodies were laid out in different positions, each one portraying another violent drama. The homicide guys had given each a name. Number one, like this one, was known as "Gasper." Number two was found lying on her side bent at the waist with her hands covering her ears as if she were trying to shut out some gruesome noise. "Hear No Evil" the detectives called her. Number three had given the namers the most trouble. Like two, she'd been placed on her left side with her legs forward, but this one's arms had been extended in front of her, one at chest level, one arm stretching out from beneath her head, a flailing motion as if she were trying to fight off a swarm of bees. They called her "The Swatter." And then about a month ago, they'd found the fourth victim badly decomposed in her Little Havana apartment. Her nude body was lying face up with arms and legs spread as if she were floating tranquilly on the quiet surface of a lake. So "Floater" it was.

The FBI examined the photos and found no matches with any other signature killings around the country in the last ten years. Their profilers theorized the Bloody Rapist was creating particular scenarios from his past, trying to reconstruct moments of abuse he'd witnessed as a child—probably acts of violence against his mother he was helpless to prevent.

But that was far too neat an explanation for Alexandra, too off-the-rack. Just as likely the killer had repositioned the women according to the twisted commandments of some crazed inner voice. But these days everyone wanted a formula, a nifty explanation for guys like this. As if his actions might make a kind of sense, raping women, slashing their throats, repositioning them, then leaving a trail of blood leading away from the scene. Like sure, of course, he must have seen his father beat his mother, then leave her in these exact positions on the living room floor, and he'd walked away bleeding from the scratch marks she'd given him, so now the grown-up boy, that poor, twisted son of a bitch, is compelled to re-enact endlessly those traumatic episodes, laying the dead women out like sacrificial offerings to his past.

Alex hated it, the way the forensic-psychology hotshots had taken over, explaining it all, giving every crime a cute Freudian cause and effect. She hated it because the explanations were always more than explanations. Behind each of their clever scenarios was the same suggestion—that there was logic to evil, a reasonable justification for every fucking horror under the sun.

The media wasn't onto the weird arrangements yet, because so far, everyone working the case had been stonewalling, keeping the reporters beyond the crime-scene tape. If the killer was indeed hungry for newsprint, it wasn't their job to feed him. And, of course, the second the word got out about those eerie poses, there'd be tabloid crews elbowing their way to the front of the pack, making good police work a hundred times harder.

Slowly, she began to work her way around the perimeter of the room, a full 360 degrees. The light was good. Dan had turned everything on, overhead, table lamps, fluorescent kitchen lights. She had to change film again. Marking it, slipping the used film into her waist pouch. Continuing around the edge of the room to get the complete perspective. Then zooming in for the victim. Pretty woman, athletic. That one-inch incision in her throat, a few quarts of her blood spreading into the beige carpet. Alexandra got close-ups of the wound, the stained carpet.

Across from the flowery couch was a leather wing-back chair, a matching ottoman. Something from a lawyer's study. Two cheap oils on the walls, sad-eyed clowns and a pelican nesting on a piling—tourist shop trash. But behind the couch was a large black-and-white photograph, a misty Everglades glen cluttered with ferns and alligators lurking beneath the still waters. A guy's work she'd admired for years. Clyde Butcher.

She'd read about him, how he slogged with his huge camera and a hundred pounds of equipment out into the middle of the soupy Glades. Then he set up his tripod, hefted the camera onto it. Two hours to set up for one shot—all so he could make these huge photographs full of intricate detail. Butcher did magical things with black and white. Made herons and ibises into angels. Put an enchanted sheen on the palm fronds and the saw grass that exposed the sinister grace of that river of grass. Its silence and danger, its holiness.

Nothing at all like the stuff she did—just one color shot after another, stark and standard. Keeping herself out of it. Keeping her mood, her values, her interpretation buried away.

She would snap somewhere around three hundred shots of that particular crime scene alone. Probably over a thousand photos before the night was done. And none of them would be art. That was the skill of the job. Keep it dull. Plain and simple and honest and straight. No spin, no subjectivity. Nothing for defense lawyers to argue about. That was what she did five nights a week. She kept herself out of it. Walked through these rooms with the scrupulous dispassion of a Buddhist priest. Not playing with shadows and perspectives, not stalking, like Clyde Butcher did, that perfect moment when sunlight and shadow and the ripples on the water's surface were in perfect alignment.

Her job was the opposite of art. Pornographic reality. If she had a gift, it was a talent for watchful emptiness. Standing back, seeing, then getting it all down on her negative—the disinterested purity of fact.

"You like that?" Dan said from the doorway. "That photograph?"

"I like it. Sure."

"So take it with you. I'll help you get it down."

She looked over at him.

"Who's going to know, Alex?"

"What're you, cracking up? I'm not taking that thing."

"Why not?"

Alexandra took another look at the photograph and heaved out a breath.

"Well, for one thing, it wouldn't fit in my place," she said. "It's too beautiful. I'd have to take down all the other crap I got on my walls. Or else move to a better house."

Standing in the doorway, he shook his head, stripped a stick of gum.

"You know, Rafferty, I'm developing a new theory about this blood thing he does."

"I don't like the jokes, okay? Not about this guy. Spare me."

"It's not a joke," he said. "What I think is, cutting himself like he does is how the guy gets off. Like a sperm substitute."

"He doesn't have any trouble ejaculating," she said. "There's plenty of seminal fluid."

"Maybe this is like some kind of bigger, better orgasm. He blows his load, kills the woman, then slashes himself. And there's blood flowing and sperm leaking out, and the goddamn freak is flying off into orbit. All the bells ringing, whistles shrieking, lights going full blast, the guy's soaring out there into interplanetary nothingness."

She stared at him.

"Dan, maybe it *is* time for you to retire."

"Pathology boys are saying it's glass he cuts them with, not a blade."

"Glass?"

"Yeah, figure that out. Some kind of special glass."

"Special? How?"

The big man shrugged. "I haven't read the report yet. Just glanced at it on the way over here."

"Let me get this straight. The guy holds a chunk of glass in his bare hand, and when he cuts their throats, he winds up slicing himself in the process. Like either he's totally stupid or for some reason he enjoys the pain."

Romano shrugged again. "Well, I think we can rule out stupid."

"Oh boy, the psychobabblers ought to have fun with that."

She shot the sprinkling of blood on the beige carpet. Got close-ups of the woman's throat. Just like the four others, a gash with a little wrist flick, like the letter *C*. But that was for the ME to figure out, the pathology guys, the blood-spatter techs. Alexandra was just a photographer—cold, neutral eyes.

They'd send the blood and sperm specimens, tissue samples, hair and fiber off to the FBI lab, the FDLE, have them run their blue-ribbon tests. And it would all be futile. This asshole wasn't leaving behind anything he didn't want them to find. They already knew his fingerprints weren't on file in the AFIS database or with the FBI. The DNA was worthless unless they already had the guy in custody.

From the autopsies and blood-spatter patterns, they could tell the guy was highly organized, under strict control. The whole event had the feel of a finely tuned script, a lockstep ritual. Same white wine at every scene. Even the same amount of chardonnay left in the bottle each time.

No witnesses ever remembered seeing him arrive. No one saw him depart. Apparently, the guy was a charmer of lonely hearts. All the women he'd chosen were loners, vulnerable women, recently divorced or separated. Awkward and unsure, back on the market after some wrenching failure. Easy prey.

After two sips of wine, a few hors d'oeuvres, he punched them in the face, slammed them to the floor. He was strong and quick, and once he got started, he was ruthless. Somewhere during the act itself, he reached back for his weapon and plunged it into their throats, stayed mounted until he'd ejaculated, then climbed off their cooling bodies. The ME had come up with that opinion, comparing the temperature of sperm with the temp of the body. Nothing high-tech about it.

Then a few minutes postmortem, most likely after he'd dressed and recovered, the killer arranged his victims into the pose he'd selected, and a minute or two later, he began to dribble that trail of blood away from the scene.

Though the sequence was identical every time, the women were all different. No regularity to body types or hair color or socioeconomic background. Either the killer wasn't that particular or his fantasizing capabilities were so powerful that he could incorporate a lot of different types into his horror show. The only similarity among the women was their ages. They were all in their late twenties.

Based on the very limited evidence he was leaving behind, Alex doubted he'd be caught from police work alone. Probably their best hope was that the killings would someday stop gratifying the guy and his passions would grow so pressurized inside the locked chambers of his heart that the walls would rupture and he'd blow wide open and do something out of character, wild, stupid, clumsy. Or better yet, there was the outside chance he would meet a woman who outmatched him, someone who could block that first punch and answer it with a high-caliber counterpunch—someone with a quick draw and a fast trigger, who'd make him spill his blood in earnest.

Alex only hoped it happened on her shift, so she could take a roll or two of the asshole's corpse.

The apartment was crowded with cops by the time she was leaving. Media trucks in the parking lot, halogen lights blazing, helicopters fanning the moonlight. Alexandra Rafferty got in her van and moved on to a quiet neighborhood in the Grove, a home invasion with a husband and a wife pistol-whipped but alive. After that, she did a convenience-store robbery on Biscayne Boulevard, the clerk shot twice in the face for sixty-three dollars and two six-packs of Colt 45. As the sun was coming up, she did a domestic-abuse case in Little Havana. A Latin man in his sixties who'd stabbed his teenage boyfriend twenty-five times in the genitals. The old man had to be sedated before he would let go of the mutilated body of his lover.

TWO

At the end of their shift, Dan Romano tagged along behind Alex down the overbright corridor to the photo lab. They passed a couple of janitors who were mopping the glaring tile while they exchanged quick bursts of island patois.

"That thing in the apartment." Dan stepped around the mop bucket. "My saying it was okay to steal that photograph off the wall? Hey, I'm sorry, Alex. I don't know what I was thinking about. I was out of line."

"Yeah, you were, Dan. Way out."

"You can forget it happened, can't you?"

"I forgot it the second it occurred."

They rounded the last corner and pushed through the swinging doors. The raw chemical smell poured out of the developing room. Early shift was on already, which meant Junior Shanrahan stood behind the counter, smiling at her. In his early twenties, Junior was an inch or two over six feet, with shoulders so broad, he seemed taller. He was hulking behind the counter, wearing his usual bright blue granny spectacles and a white hair net and smock.

Whenever she showed up, his smile brightened and his eyes seemed to track her every move. Nervous and deferential, like the kid had a crush on her. Junior high stuff. She expected him to pass her a folded-up love note any day now. Invite her to the prom.

"This whole retirement thing's got me fucked up, Alex, facing the void. My whole ethical orientation has gone to shit."

"Understandable, Dan. Perfectly understandable."

Alexandra started unloading her grocery sack of exposed film onto the counter. Each roll in its own envelope, with case information inside.

"Good morning, Ms. Rafferty," Junior said. "How's the Ansel Adams of corpses doing this fine day?"

"Ansel Adams?" Dan was staring at Junior Shanrahan, taking in the hair net, the blue glasses. "Who the hell's that?"

"Famous photographer," Alex said. "It's a compliment."

"More like a joke," said Junior.

"Christ, I'm getting too old for this. Everybody's doing standup, and I'm not getting the gags anymore."

Junior took her rolls of film one by one and logged them on his clipboard, then dropped them into the empty slot. A chute carried them back to the processing lab, where the minideveloper was already churning out new prints. Same kind of machine you'd find in Eckerd Drugs.

"Get anything good last night?" Junior was peering at her through his blue lenses. At his hairline, near the edge of the netting, a small vein pulsed.

"Bloody Rapist again," said Alex.

"Christ, I hate that guy. Turns my stomach looking at those naked girls."

"Oh, come on, Junior. All the bodies you see. All the gore."

"You mean it doesn't bother you? The slit throats? Their bodies twisted up like that? Man, that shit gives me nightmares."

"Nothing wrong with nightmares," Dan said. "Means you still got a conscience. Day you stop having bad dreams, that's when you know your soul's shriveled up. You're on your way to being a psychopath."

Junior dropped another envelope down the chute and looked at Dan with a vague smile. Alex watched him handle the envelopes of film delicately in his large hands. Fingernails nicely trimmed. A well-maintained kid.

"We'd like to get these back by tonight, Junior. Think you can jump them over the ones in line already?"

"Anything for you, Ms. Rafferty."

She couldn't see his eyes behind those glossy blue hexagonals, but she could feel him watching her. A little trick some men performed, a tactile stare.

"So what's our latest thinking on the bodies? Got any idea yet why he repositions them like that?"

"Classified," Dan said.

"Which means," said Alex, "if you come up with any good explanations, Junior, you let us know, okay?"

She turned to go.

"Sure thing, Ms. Rafferty. And hey, maybe if I solve the case, I can get promoted out of this stinking lab. I've inhaled so much chemical soup, I'm starting to glow."

She turned back around to his eager smile.

"You solve this case, Junior, we'll make sure you get a corner office and preferred parking. Hell, we'll even spring for a week at the Delano Hotel."

"Can I have that in writing?"

"I'm afraid you'll have to take my word," Alex said.

She and Dan were almost to the corner when Junior called out, "I'm going to need that offer in writing."

He sounded dead serious.

Alexandra ran the same stretch of beach every morning after work—to get out of her head, back into her body.

Black jogging bra, white shorts, barefoot. Her car parked across at the Seaquarium lot, Alex doing sprints down the empty distances of Crandon Park. Across the bay, the towering limestone pillars of downtown Miami were candied by the rising light, a pink-and-gold coating that gave a sugary, fairy-tale radiance to the city, magic dust sparkling off the chrome and polished glass. From that distance, a mile, maybe two, the city seemed gorgeously serene. None of the grit visible, no stench of gunpowder, nor the haze of tension and danger from the long night before. For half an hour each morning as she did her sprints, the city was washed with a powerful dose of fresh sunlight and the steady breezes of a new day, and for that little while it was almost possible to believe that her hometown might still be saved.

Dash fifty yards, walk ten, dash another fifty. Stay in the soft sand for maximum resistance. In thirty minutes, she could crank her heart rate up to 175, make her skin shine, make every muscle sing. Sweat out the rancid hours of the night before. Go home somewhat cleansed.

She was twenty-five minutes into it, pulse hammering, her left calf on the edge of a cramp, as she slowed to another short walk. Down the beach, headed her way, was an elderly couple; the man leading the way was bald and shirtless, wearing a baggy pale blue bathing suit. Trailing him by a few feet was a woman with her white pants legs rolled up. She had on a loose flowered shirt and her white hair straggled from beneath a blue porkpie hat. She was swinging one of those wands, a metal detector, scrounging for pennies at the edge of the surf.

Alex took a deep breath, rose up on her toes, and began her final sprint.

And nearly ran over him.

It was as if he'd risen from the sand, an apparition in white long-sleeved T-shirt and white shorts.

Dodging to her left, Alexandra stumbled, almost went down. The man lurched after her, but she got her balance and took two quick steps back, out of range.

"Sorry," he said. "I thought you saw me."

"Jesus, Jason."

"My, my, you look particularly luminous this morning."

He smiled, kept coming toward her, and she kept backing. At the surf line, the old couple had stopped and were staring at this strange encounter.

Jason Patterson was a handsome man. Dark hair swept back, black eyes, which she'd only lately learned to read. He had strong cheekbones and his skin was a degree or two lighter than cinnamon, as if perhaps his great-great-grandfather had been an Iroquois warrior. Limber as willow and mongoose-quick, he had only one defect as a fighter—a slight lack of killer instinct, a brief hesitation before he struck the finishing blow.

He was circling left, heading into her weaker side.

"Jason, please. I'm not up to this today."

"Another rough night, huh?" He continued to circle.

"Bloody Rapist again," she said. "I'm worn down. Fatigued."

"Good," he said. "Maybe that'll even things up."

"No, really. Not today."

His smile faded. He halted, his body shifting into *fudo-dachi*, the rooted stance. Four feet away. Surf rolling in behind him. Gulls coasting low. A sandpiper strutted stiffly between them, pecked at the sand. A few miles out on the surface of the blinding water, a crimson sun floated like an abandoned beach ball caught on the outgoing tide, while clouds with the dirty gray translucence of fish scales clustered along the horizon.

A few years younger than Alex, Jason Patterson was six feet tall, around 175 pounds, with a competitive swimmer's cinched waist and deep chest. He was a *Rokudan*, a sixth-degree black belt and assistant instructor at the Shotokan Karate Center in Coral Gables. He worked as a stockbroker and lived at trendy Grove Isle. Beyond that, Alex knew nothing of Jason's personal life.

She knew his body, though, was intimately familiar with his reflexes and the power and quickness of his strikes, the moans he made when he was straining, the tart citrus aroma of his sweat, the tensile strength of his fingers, and the nuances of his customary gestures, like that narrowing of left eye, and the one-inch drop of right shoulder that always announced a roundhouse kick.

For the last six years, Jason Patterson had been Alex's instructor on the mats of the Shotokan dojo. Since the age of eleven, when she'd bullied her parents into letting her, Alexandra had been studying martial arts. First in a run-down strip shopping center near her home, and later in the air-conditioned upscale tranquillity of the Gables dojo. Nearly every week for the last year, it had been Jason Patterson's custom to select Alexandra as his opponent when demonstrating new techniques. It always brought a hush to the other mats, the students gathering to watch her quickness and ingenuity matched against his superior strength and vast technique. She was certainly not his equal as a fighter, only a fourth-degree black, a *Yodan*, so she was flattered that he selected her above the more aggressive and accomplished men in the dojo.

Last July when Alex's dad moved in, something had to go from her schedule, and with considerable reluctance, she'd decided it would be her two evenings of karate. A week after she stopped going, Jason showed up at the beach one morning wearing his white *gi*, standing quietly in her path along the hard-packed sand, waiting in the *shiko-dachi* stance. He said he missed her, that their workouts weren't the same without her.

And that's when he'd proposed this arrangement.

Without giving it a moment's thought, she'd said yes. She liked Jason, and after skipping only a week, she was already feeling logy and stiff.

Their new sessions would be free-form. Unstructured, unpredictable. Anything was legal. To the limit and beyond. No more mat fighting, no more measured and disciplined lessons.

Full contact, all-out fighting until one of them yielded—nine times out of ten, it was Alex. Sometimes the fight was over in a few seconds; some mornings it took fifteen minutes. Two months ago, she'd cracked a bone in his wrist while blocking a punch, and a few weeks back he'd badly bruised two of her ribs. There had been regular welts, abrasions, strained tendons and ligaments. But she was a better fighter now than she'd ever been. More wary, more observant, and once the fight began, she was quicker, meaner, more willing to bring things to a sudden and complete conclusion.

Jason stepped forward, palms raised, shrugging.

She was settled into a relaxed watchfulness. Not tense, not overflexed.

"I mean it, Jason. Today's not good. I'm bushed."

"Okay, okay."

He straightened from the cat stance, shook out his arms like a swimmer loosening up on the starting blocks, half-turned to give the old man a friendly wave, then spun back, lunged, leading with his left foot, a *mae-geri,* the basic front kick.

Day-one stuff. Ten-year-olds just off the street, getting their first lesson, learned a front kick. So Alex discounted it, waited for the punch or roundhouse flying kick that was coming next. But the *mae-geri* was real, his left heel cracking into her solar plexus, taking her down.

And before she could roll, he was on her. Saddling her at the waist, hands at her throat, thumbs digging in. The daylight going yellow, then gray. Two seconds from blackness. And she slung her right leg up, hooked her heel against his throat, levered back.

Then it was his sixty-pound superiority against her wider hips and stronger legs. Her better angle of attack.

It was shootfighting now. A karate spin-off. Submission combat. What happened when you were forced to the ground. A whole new array of techniques, flips, sweeps, suplexes, arm bars, chin locks, chokes. They'd only been training for a year in shootfighting. A tough, bruising, eye-gouging year. This was street stuff, innovative, brutal. A lot of squirming, some elementary wrestling holds, whatever worked.

At that moment, she was losing the leverage battle, her heel slipping against the oily sweat of his neck. Jason grunted and tried to twist the last inch he needed to free his neck and finish choking her into unconsciousness.

"Give," she grunted.

"Me or you?"

"You!" she said. "Surrender."

"Forget it," he said. "Don't make me do it."

She felt a subtle softening in his grip, that familiar hesitation of the prudent teacher trying not to harm his student, and in that split second she locked her knee and straightened, thrust him up and to the left, and broke his hold, sending him sprawling. She scrambled to her feet, and in the instant he was recovering, she knee-dropped to his throat, easing back at contact, blunting the strike so she didn't snap his neck. Then gripping a handful of hair in her right hand, she tipped his head back so his Adam's apple was fully exposed.

"If you so much as flinch, I'll snap your spindly neck."

"I'm thinking clean thoughts," he said.

"Get that smile off your face. I see any teeth, I'll break them."

"Tough broad. Good with the patter."

"Bet your ass I am. I've studied with the best."

"And sexy, too," he said. "Great calves. Ballerina legs."

Abruptly, she released him and stepped back.

"Good work," he said. "Excellent escape and counterstrike."

She let out a long exhalation and flopped down beside him in the sand. Both of them were breathing hard.

After a full minute, he said, "You didn't try to block the front kick."

"It seemed beneath you."

"You missed the obvious, Alex. You can't let your sophistication become a weakness. Just because you're experienced, you can't forget first principles. And you've got to forget it's me. No habits, no expectations. That could've killed you on the street, Alex. You've got to see what's right in front of you. No more, no less."

"Okay," she said. "Okay, okay."

They stared up at the sky and watched the blue seep back into it. The water stirred along the shore, churning up the early-morning fragrances of seaweed and tar and the mild lavender of driftwood warming in the sun.

Then he was up on his elbow, peering down at her. He brushed some sand from her forehead, combed a strand of her black hair into place.

"Don't," she said.

"Don't what?"

She took a quick breath, blew it out. She stared up at the clear blue.

"I can't do this anymore, Jason."

"What?"

Alex swept the hair from her face while Jason propped his head on his hand and looked into her eyes.

"We've got to stop this. These workouts, or whatever you call it."

"What're you talking about? Just because I let you win now and then, you think you don't need me anymore? You're dumping me."

She shook her head and tore away from his stare.

"You're expecting something more, and I can't give it."

"More? More what?"

"You know what I'm saying, Jason. Don't make it harder than it is."

He didn't like what he saw in her face, and he turned back to gaze at the sea.

"Oh, come on. This is exercise, that's all. Skill versus skill. Testing each other, pushing the limits."

"Bullshit. Don't kid yourself."

He shook his head, sighed.

"So what's this about? Stan lay down the law? He want you to give up martial arts, stay home and work on the marital ones?"

"Stan's never said a word. This is my decision."

"This is just a workout, Alex. Staying sharp. Primed, focused."

"It's becoming more than that. We both know it."

"Well, yeah, I wish it were. I'm not going to deny that. But I'd say we've been doing a damn good job of keeping it sex-free so far. Both of us acting responsible, very adult."

He turned back to her, fixed his eyes on hers, then abruptly swung his leg over her waist and saddled her again.

"No," she said. "Get off me, Jason."

But he brought his face close to hers, held it there, vulnerable to anything she wanted to do.

When she didn't move, he tilted down and pressed his lips against hers. Alex kept her mouth rigid, fighting it, but gradually the hard knot in her chest relaxed and began to melt away, and after a moment more she yielded, lips loosening, finding the fit. Softening and opening, a whisper of breath passing between them. His tongue moving in, slipping past her lips. A moan from one of them—she wasn't sure who.

She heard the surf and the raucous laughter of a gull and the insistent shriek of her blood. Then she drew her head away, twisted hard to her right, arched her back and bridged, stepped over his left leg with her right, and pried out of his grasp.

On her feet, breathing hard, she looked down at him. His knees were bent, hands locked behind his head as if he meant to do a few dozen sit-ups.

"Now that," he said. "That wasn't exercise. That was kissing. There's a hell of a difference, Alex. Just so you know."

At the surf line, the shirtless old man and his wife slapped their hands together slowly.

"Bravo," the old man called out. "Encore."

She looked down at Jason Patterson for a long moment, his eyes working on hers, until he seemed to read the depth of her resolve. Then his face changed, going slack, flattening like a time-lapse film of a man falling into profound slumber.

"I'm sorry, Jason. I really am."

"So how are you going to accomplish this, fixing your marriage?"

"I don't think that's any of your business."

"I think I'm entitled to an answer. What're you going to do, go to marriage counseling? Cook him his favorite foods, butter him up?"

"A romantic vacation," she snapped. "Up in Seaside, a pretty little town in North Florida."

"Oh, of course," he said. "A second honeymoon. Yeah, yeah, that should fix it. That should bring old Stan around. Romantic vacations always work."

"Goddamn it, I have to try, Jason. I have to do something."

A few hundred yards offshore, a powerboat raced across the morning chop, the happy voices of fishermen echoing ashore.

"Well, I'll be here," he said quietly. "Every morning, same time, same place. In case you change your mind."

"I won't," she said, and turned and headed up the beach toward her car.

THREE

What she had in mind was two weeks in the Panhandle. Fly up to Panama City, rent a car, drive over to Seaside, rent one of those purple-and-yellow cottages. Then later on, she and Stan could drive around, maybe try to locate that beach house where she and her parents had stayed almost twenty years ago.

The beach, the sunsets. That's what they needed, two weeks in the sun. She and Stan lounging on the white sand, watching the dolphins roll, dining on boiled shrimp and good wine. Both of them on the same schedule, midnight strolls, make love all night, sleep through the morning. Take a shot at rekindling things. A final shot, perhaps. That's how it felt these days, the last embers losing their glow. A puff of breath might just as easily extinguish as revive them. But she wasn't going to let it slip away without a fight. Her folks lasted nearly thirty years, weathering rougher seas than anything she and Stan had known. She was determined, by God, to do as well as they.

She had all the arguments ready. She'd arranged for her dad to stay with her friend Gabriella Hernandez. Both Stan and Alex had lots of furlough time stored. It was off-season up in the Panhandle, prices down from their summer highs, the first cool October nights, a nice break from the Miami heat. She'd even gotten a brochure from a downtown travel agency with great wide-angle shots of Seaside, Florida, the pretty rainbow houses, the immaculate white sand, dunes and sea oats, the gorgeous wrinkled blue of the Gulf.

Stan was finishing his breakfast when Alex set the skillet in the drain and dried her hands, drew out the brochure from the kitchen shelf.

She spoke his name, but he was lost in the sports page. The Dolphins' latest blunder.

"Stan," she said.

He managed a grunt.

"You got a minute to talk about our vacation?"

"Vacation?" He kept on reading.

"You remember. Two weeks off, somewhere exotic. Cuddle late in bed, all that."

He put his finger on the passage and looked up at her.

"Oh, yeah," he said. "Like before you got so goddamn busy."

She held her smile in place, unfolded the brochure, the words gathering in her throat. She'd plead if she had to. Threaten, nag, whatever it took.

"You win the Publishers' Sweepstakes or something?" He looked back down at the newsprint. "What makes you think we can afford a vacation?"

"Stan," she said. "I don't think we can afford *not* to take one."

"Oh, is that a fact?" Stan kept his eyes back on the paper. "And what about the old man? He going along with us? Keep us company?"

"Gabbie's agreed to take him for a couple of weeks."

With a bitter grin, he looked up again.

"You've got to be kidding. That woman's a magnet for disaster. You might as well turn the old man loose, let him wander the goddamn interstate. He'd be safer."

"Gabbie's fine. She's in a secure place now. I wouldn't leave Dad with her if I didn't think he'd be a hundred percent safe."

"Forget it, Alex," he said. "All the money we've been throwing away on that old man, we can't afford a goddamn vacation. What're you thinking about?"

"Look, Stan . . ."

In the hallway, the flinty click of her father's police dress shoes sounded against the tile and Alexandra sighed and turned to watch Lawton Collins march into the kitchen.

He'd shined the black shoes to a high polish and his police tunic was buttoned tightly across his small potbelly. Instead of pants, he was still wearing his pink-and-blue pajama bottoms, shorties that exposed his spindly white legs.

"Christ," Stan said. "Here we go again."

Alexandra refolded the brochure and slid it back into its slot on the shelf.

Her father's mist of white hair was wild, one side mushed flat, the top and other side aswirl with cowlicks. He carried a black suitcase in his right hand, and apparently he'd discovered the drawer where Alexandra had hidden his .38 service revolver. The holstered pistol high on his right hip.

"Dad, what do you think you're doing?"

He set the suitcase down and drew the pistol and aimed it across the breakfast table at Stan.

"Call for backup," her father said. "We have an intruder, Alex. And he looks like trouble."

"Dad, no."

Stan leaned back in his chair and held very still.

"That goddamn thing better not be loaded."

"Dad, give me the pistol right now."

"All right, sonny, don't move a muscle. Put the fork down and stand up and spread your legs. We're just going to give you a quick pat-down for weapons."

"If that gun's loaded, Alex, the old man is out of here today. Sunny Pines, Century Arms, whichever one is cheaper."

"There aren't any bullets in the house, Stan. Just relax and let me handle this."

"You resisting arrest, sonny? That what we have here? A smart aleck?"

Alex rested a hand on her father's shoulder and reached out for the pistol, but he shied away and kept his aim on Stan's chest.

"Dad, please. Put the pistol down."

"I believe I recognize this lawbreaker," he said. "Yes indeed. I put this one away back in the seventies. Armed robbery. Held up a gas station near the airport, wounded the attendant and two patrons. Went by the name of Frank Sinatra. Got a free ride to Raiford, thirty hard ones."

"Frank Sinatra," Stan said. "Jesus."

With his eyes on the pistol, Stan bent forward, scooped up more of his breakfast, and patted his mouth with his napkin.

"Okay, Frank, quit stalling. On your feet, and do it slowly, with your hands in plain view."

"Dad, stop it. This is Stan, my husband. He lives here."

Her father swiveled his head and gave her a careful look.

"You married this ex-con, this goddamn lowlife? Don't tell me that, Alexandra. Don't break an old man's heart."

"Dad, this is Stan Rafferty. He's my husband. You used to watch him play football in high school."

"What? You married a football player?"

"Yes, Dad. You gave me away, remember? St. Jude's. It was July, a hot day. All the bridesmaids in pink. You and Mother were so happy. You remember that. I know you do."

"St. Jude's?"

The pistol began to sag. Alexandra put her hand on his arm and lowered it. Her wedding day was one of the moments he still recalled vividly.

"Pink," he said. "All the bridesmaids. Yeah, and it was hot, and there was some damn bird in the chapel, a laughing gull trapped in there, flying around, squawking. We all thought that was a sign of something. But I never was any good at reading signs."

Alexandra tried to pry the pistol out of his hand, but her father pulled away from her and holstered the weapon and buttoned the safety strap.

Stan shook his head and turned the page of the paper, folded it in half the way he liked, got the creases even, and continued to read.

"You say his name's Stan?"

"That's right, Stan."

Her father narrowed his eyes, trying to catch her in this lie.

"What position did he play?"

"Cornerback at South Miami," she said. "He was all-state."

"Damn right," Stan said. "MVP in the regionals, too."

"Where are my grandchildren? They at school already?"

"There aren't any, Dad. Stan and I don't have any children."

"No children? Nine years married and no children?"

"That's right."

"You got something wrong with you, son? You got a sperm problem, do you?"

Stan looked up from his newspaper. He stared at Alexandra for a few seconds and shook his head again.

"He probably got adopted by one of those weight-lifting monsters at Raiford. Guy wants to have butt-hole sex five times a day. Before you know it, he's banged your prostate to death. No wonder you two don't have any kids."

Stan slapped his paper down.

"Hey, shut the hell up, Lawton. You hear me? Can you understand what I'm saying? Just shut the hell up about my prostate and the rest of that garbage."

"Don't talk to him that way, Stan," she said quietly.

"Yeah, yeah. So tell him to stop saying that trash to me, why don't you?"

"You know better. Just calm down, control yourself."

"Butt-hole sex," Stan said. "Jesus, I have to listen to this shit at breakfast?"

He was about to say something else, but Alex caught his eye.

"Enough," she said. "From both of you."

Stan sighed, smoothed some wrinkles from the paper.

"Hell, what difference does it make? I could call the old fool every goddamn name I ever heard and he wouldn't remember it ten seconds later. There's no water in the well. Drop a brick from ten feet up, there's no splash."

"Well, today's the day," her dad said. He cleared his throat, straightened his shoulders, and his eyes were suddenly bright and clear. "I'm relocating."

He stooped over and picked up his suitcase and started for the door.

"Wait a minute, Dad. Come on, sit down, have something to eat."

"No time to eat. I'm out of here, on my way up the road."

"Dad, Dad. You can't go relocating on an empty stomach, right? Breakfast is the most important meal."

He stopped at the back door and stared at her.

"It's very important," she said. "Keeps you going the rest of the day."

"Well, yes. That's a good point. I suppose I should have something warm in my belly before I start out."

Stan groaned and bent back to his plate, sopping up the runny egg yolks with the last of his toast. He was a big man. Jet-black hair that he wore just long enough for a part. Short arms, brawny from his barbells and morning push-ups, small hands with blunt fingers. He was television-handsome, with a muscular face and light blue eyes. He'd hardly aged in the eleven years she'd known him. One of the two or three most popular boys at South Miami High, co-captain of the football team, senior class treasurer, big-time practical joker. Iguanas and corn snakes set loose in the teachers lounge. Once coaxing half the football team into hoisting the principal's Volkswagen up onto the bed of the vice-principal's pickup.

But it wasn't his status that won her heart, or his looks, or his prowess before thousands of cheering fans. It was the way he treated his sister, Margie. She was a year younger and suffered from an acute case of multiple sclerosis. Stan Rafferty had been fiercely protective of her, leaving his classes five minutes before the bell so he could run to Margie's classroom and help her move down the hall to her next period. They joked and spoke in whispers and Stan seemed to be her one solace and relief from pain. Every game ball he received, he held high above his head and trotted up into the stadium to present it to his smiling sister. The summer after their senior year, Margie died, and Stan sobbed openly. Alexandra was deeply touched. Such a strong, independent boy capable of such mature and sheltering warmth and unguarded displays of emotion.

And for the first few years of living together, sharing Stan's small apartment, and later in the house on Silver Palm, things had been fine. Both of them nineteen, Stan at work for Brinks, helping her parents pay Alexandra's tuition to the local state university. It was a pleasant time. Not blissful, not a swooning romance, but good and sweet. Stan, a tender lover, almost too tender. He seemed skittish and vulnerable. Touching her body with a lightness and caution that seemed childlike and full of wonder, as if her body were made of fine crystal that might break at the slightest miscue. But in some ways, it was exactly what she'd needed. The muscular football jock with the feathery hands, the watchful and delicate strokes. The perfect man to set the record straight.

Over the years, she'd come to find that Stan Rafferty was a mostly decent man, a little childish sometimes perhaps, a streak of self-centeredness. They didn't bicker, rarely snapped at each other. But there were no longer any fond stray touches, either—no foot massages or back rubs, as there had been in the first couple of years, no hand-holding in the dark, no kisses that heated to combustion. Even their regular Sunday-morning lovemaking had become as perfunctory and timed as his calisthenics drills. Not sufficient reason for divorce, but less and less reason to stay married.

Last month, she'd gone to see one of the shrinks who worked for the department. A Latin woman in her mid-forties whom Alex had seen for years around the hallways of Miami PD. They'd had a cordial, nodding relationship, mild water-fountain gossip. The woman welcomed Alexandra into her office and listened to her description of her nine-year marriage. The loss of passion, the growing distance, whole days passing by with fewer than ten words between them. When Alex was finished, Maria Gonzalez stared idly down at the papers on her desk. For a moment, Alex thought she'd dozed off.

"Maria?"

The therapist looked up from her notes.

"This is all?" she said. "He doesn't hit you?"

"No, he doesn't hit. I wouldn't stay a day if he hit."

"No arguments, no screaming, no throwing things. He doesn't berate you, belittle you in any way?"

"No, it's all very quiet. Very low-key."

"And you love him still?"

Alex hesitated a moment.

"Yes," she said. "But it's more like the feeling I'd have for a kid brother."

Maria waved her hand as if such fine distinctions didn't interest her.

"Does he love you?"

"In his way, yes, I suppose he does."

Maria looked at Alexandra for a long time without speaking. It was a look similar to the one she'd gotten over the years from various auto mechanics when she'd brought her car in because she'd heard a creak that she was sure was the telltale complaint of a crucial part about to give way. Inevitably, the mechanics never heard the creak, and they sent her on her way with that same patient but mildly scolding look. They had plenty of customers with real problems, cars that wouldn't run at all.

"Trouble with Miami," Lawton said as he sat down, "it's always summer. I'm sixty-seven years old, and, goddamn it, I'm ready for a real fall. Maybe I'll try Ohio. I've heard that's nice."

"You were raised in Ohio," Stan said, eyes on his plate. "You old fool."

"Stan," she said. "Cut it out."

At the sink, Alexandra watched Mrs. Langstaff across the street. Big woman heaving herself into her van, then pulling out the drive, off to work at her candle shop. A row of neat lawns over there, prim hedges running along the sidewalks. Dogs asleep on porches. Flowers blooming in window boxes. Alexandra's daytime world. Miami Nice. Almost as unreal as her nights.

She walked over to the oven, took out her father's pancakes, carried them to the table, and set them in front of him.

"You like summer, Dad. Yellowtail fishing, dolphin. You used to love that time of year most of all."

"I used to love a lot of things."

He stared into a slant of sunlight, mouth clamped.

"Dad?"

He didn't reply.

"Don't disturb him," Stan said. "He's counting dust motes, picking his lotto number for the day."

Stan stood up, brushed the crumbs off his white uniform shirt.

"You're not funny, Stan."

"Hey, Alex." Stan's blue eyes were hard on hers. "It isn't working. We can't keep living like this. Guns and shit. The old man's got to go. You should just start getting used to the idea."

Alexandra sponged off the counter by the sink, kept her eyes from him.

"After work, I'm going over to the range," Stan said, "hit a few buckets of balls."

"With Delvin."

"That's right, with Delvin."

"The mysterious Delvin."

"He's a guy from work, Alex. He's not mysterious."

"So why have I never met him? Why don't you ever bring him home?"

Alexandra looked over at Lawton, who was pouring more

syrup on his pancakes. There was syrup spilling over the edge of his plate, pooling on the table.

"Look, I'm not having a goddamn affair. I like to hit golf balls, and I like Delvin. Why is it that all of a sudden I can't spend a little free time with a buddy?"

She rubbed hard at a crusty spot on the rim of the sink.

"Just be home before nine, okay? I need to be at work early tonight. There's stuff piled up from the lab."

"The Bloody Rapist strikes again, huh? Guy kills somebody, next day the goddamn overtime starts."

"I don't have a whole lot of choice. It's my job."

"You've got choices, Alex. You're just making the wrong ones."

She turned to face him. She kept her voice under control.

"Is that supposed to be some kind of warning?"

"Take it any way you want. But get one thing straight—I'm not going to keep doing this, baby-sitting your old man. Spending every night listening to his babble. I didn't sign on for that."

Measuring her breath, she leaned her hip against the stove.

"Is that right? And what did you sign on for, Stan? Just the good times?"

Stan wouldn't hold her gaze. He busied himself with his newspaper.

"I've had enough of this. It isn't right. Guns and shit. You said it was going to be temporary, him living here. A couple of weeks and you'd find a place for him. That's what you said, Alex. I remember plain as day. It's the only reason I agreed in the first place."

"Those places are horrible, Stan. I looked at half a dozen and I wouldn't leave a dog in any of them."

"Well, then you're damn well going to have to keep on looking, Alex. Because this isn't working out."

"I can't do that to him, Stan. Stick him in one of those sterile, hopeless places. He's my father."

"No, he's not. Not anymore. He's some five-year-old kid with slobber on his chin."

He was about to say something more when Lawton pushed back his chair.

"Hands in the air, Frank Sinatra. Get 'em up and there won't be any trouble."

He had his pistol out again. Rising slowly to his feet, using his left hand to steady his aim.

"Dad, now stop it. Come on, listen to me."

"Up in the air, where I can see them. And you, young lady, over by the fridge. Hands up, as well."

"Fuck this," Stan said, and started toward the dining room.

"Freeze, you bastard."

Stan kept going and Alexandra's father lifted the pistol and fired a warning shot into the ceiling. A slab of plaster fell to the floor and milky dust clouded the room. He fired again, gouging a hole in the wall above the doorway.

Stan was on his knees in the dining room, hands above his head.

"Jesus Christ! Alex, goddamn it. Do something."

"When I say freeze, I mean freeze, punk."

Alexandra stepped in front of her father. The pistol pointed at her heart.

She took a breath, edged close to him, tried to intercept his eyes. Very quietly, she hummed the first few notes of the wedding march, hearing the shiver in her voice, but going ahead with it. Eyes on her father's eyes, watching them slowly unlock, drift away from the felon he saw beyond her shoulder. His mouth opening as Alexandra stepped closer, singing the notes again, a little louder.

The pistol sagged, came slowly down. Her father took a long breath and looked up at the ceiling as if searching for the laughing gull trapped in the big sanctuary. She slipped the pistol out of his hand and hooked her arm through his and propelled him forward toward the dining room.

Stan was on his feet, fists at his side. His mouth was twisted and his face purple. There were muscles quivering in his cheeks, as if he were chewing on roofing nails.

"Goddamn it, Alex, the bastard could've killed me."

"You're okay, Stan. Everything's fine."

"Where'd he get those goddamn bullets?"

"I don't know."

"Jesus H. Christ. One of the neighbors hears gunshots over here, calls the police . . . I could lose my fucking job."

"All right, all right."

She went back to the wedding march, her arm looped through her father's, leading him down that long aisle of memory.

"I don't need this shit," Stan said. "Not today. Not any day. He's out of here. I'm not arguing about it anymore. When I come home today, that's it. He better be packed. You're going to have to decide, Alex, who you want to live with, your husband or that half-wit."

FOUR

After Stan left, Alex got Lawton into a pair of khakis and a short-sleeved plaid shirt, then settled him in front of a morning news show.

In the bedroom while she straightened the quilt and fluffed the pillows, she listened to the television in the next room, a reporter detailing the background of the latest victim of the Bloody Rapist. A paralegal with a prestigious downtown firm. Recently divorced, the woman had moved to Miami only the month before. Her family back in Baltimore had warned her that Miami was too dangerous, but she'd come anyway. "She believed the travel posters," her brother snarled.

When the TV cut to a commercial, Alex went to her closet, took her fanny pack down, and strapped it on. Stepping into a slash of sunlight, she withdrew the photographs and held them up to the light, four twisted hieroglyphs. Gasper, Hear No Evil, the Swatter, Floater. Studying them carefully one by one, as if in that harsh morning sun she might glimpse the crucial detail she had overlooked before.

It was a violation of department rules, bringing home evidentiary material. But she couldn't help herself. Dan Romano was right, of course: This case was troubling her, disturbing her already-restless sleep. Time after time, she would jerk awake, the answer in her mind, but as she fetched for it, the image faded, staying just beyond her reach, some insistent warning signal that continued to elude her.

Over the last few weeks, she had slipped the photographs one by one into her pouch and now carried them with her everywhere, sneaking them out when she was alone, staring at them, focusing, trying to identify that intangible detail that was prickling silently on the edge of her awareness. The answer was in the photographs—she was certain of it—somewhere in the austere, brightly lit images. Some key, some revelation. At times, she had begun to feel like there was even something larger at stake than solving this particular case, that if only she could see the detail she'd been missing, she would have, as well, the solution to her own unending grief.

These women were not swingers or risk takers. They'd wanted no more or less than anyone else, but in their understandable hunger for love, each of them had opened their doors and admitted the same man into their homes, a man whose savagery must have come clear to them only in the last seconds of their lives.

It was herself Alexandra saw in those photographs. Her naked form repositioned with such hideous care. Eighteen years had passed since she had risen out of her body and hovered high overhead, a loose cloud of energized gas, escaping from the physical self. And even though over those long years she had gradually reoccupied her body, it was never the same again. The fit was wrong. Some inexpressible unease plagued her still. Even the years of martial-arts training—the stretching, the conditioning, the deep awareness of her own body's strengths and limitations—had not enabled her to achieve the wholeness that had once been so natural. She had been driven out of her own body and had never fully returned, and that part of her that still drifted free seemed at times to take up temporary residence in the very victims she photographed.

Staring at their images, Alex could become those women on the unyielding floors of their apartments. As cold and lifeless, as vacant and remote. Those women who had departed now, leaving behind only their latent images, silver-halide crystals in a chemical emulsion adhering to a flat white page.

"Want to look at the book?" Lawton stood stiffly in the doorway.

Alex fumbled the photos back into her fanny pouch, zipped it shut.

Lawton was holding the coffee-table book in his right hand.

"We've got to get you to Harbor House, Dad."

"Hell, if I'm late, what're they going to do, send me to the principal?"

She followed him into the living room and sat beside him on the dark blue velvet couch near the east window, the best natural light in the house.

He opened the heavy book and let it rest half on his lap, half on hers.

Big glossy shots of Seaside, Florida, that carefully arranged clutter of pastel wood houses with tin roofs that had been built along the dunes a half mile from Seagrove, where Alexandra had spent that glorious August. Princess of the Sugary Sands. The Gulf of Mexico spread blue and empty beyond the narrow strip of highway. The same tranquil water stretching away and merging with the sky.

Seaside was only ten years old, but in that decade it had become a famous town. Famous among architects and city planners, who hailed it as a model for the new Florida, a town with the grace and civility of a bygone era. A laboratory for a simpler, more humane community structure, Main Street USA. Famous with travel writers who wanted to take their readers on a one-of-a-kind journey into a colorful fantasy land of the past. The town was a gorgeous blend of modern whimsy and old-fashioned architectural models. Part Charleston, part Key West, part Cape Cod, part sentimental daydream. Narrow redbrick streets, picket fences around every house. Scrub oak and wildflowers and pine-needle mulch for yards. No sod, no lawn mowers.

Brick streets, a town square, fanciful beach pavilions, and all those gorgeous homes, soft purples and sunny yellows with lots of gingerbread and widow's walks and shiny tin roofs. No two architectural plans were permitted to duplicate each other, but all sprung from the same nostalgic vision, a hundred different renderings of the ideal beach cottage. None of the scruffiness, none of the sagging floors and rusty tin that Alex remembered from her time there. As if all those bright young architects had pooled their imaginations to create a past that had never existed. A place more perfect than the perfect place she remembered.

On the couch, her father paged aimlessly through the slick color photographs, mumbling to himself. Weeks ago, he had spotted the book while they were browsing in a bookstore, and he'd refused to leave the store without it. Now he called for it whenever he was anxious or confused. And just a few minutes of looking at those simple wooden houses seemed to tranquilize him.

"Know why I like this book so much?"

"Yes," she said. "Because it's such a pretty place. So serene."

"No," her father said. He pulled the book from her hands and clapped it shut. He frowned at her, his eyes full of reproach, then shifted a few inches away on the couch.

"Well, what is it, Dad? Why do you like the book?"

"Because it reminds me," he said. "It stirs my memory."

"Reminds you of what?"

He turned his face away.

"Never mind. You wouldn't understand. You think I've forgotten everything. You think I'm an idiot child. You'd just mock me."

"I don't mock you, Dad. I never mock you."

"Never mind. I'm sorry I brought it up. Let's go. I'm going to be late for work."

"Okay."

"It's not work. It's that place I go now. What's it called?"

"Harbor House."

"I know that. You think I don't know what the place is called, the place I go every damn day? You think I could forget its name?"

He set the book on the coffee table and stood up.

"What does the book remind you of, Dad? You can tell me."

He looked down at her, rolled his lips inward, and bit down on them, sealing his mouth like a wayward boy refusing to admit his guilt.

"All right, then, don't tell me."

"It reminds me," he said, taking a long breath, "of the last place I was completely happy. Right there, on that beach."

It was a fine October morning; the Miami sky was polished blue porcelain, a steady breeze stirring the palms, the gulls and herons skating across clear heavens.

Going against rush-hour traffic, Alexandra drove her father the four miles to the adult living facility a mile west of Dixie Highway. Half her take-home pay each month went to the fine people at Harbor House who kept her father safe and entertained for six hours a day, five days a week.

Lawton Collins had been a cop in Miami for thirty years. He'd been an excellent police officer, decorated, with steady raises. And he had lots of buddies. A slew of them had gone to his retirement party at Dinner Key Yacht Club, and a year or two later, the same crowd had attended her mother's funeral. Though these days, they'd stopped coming around—two or three visits were all any of them could stand.

At first, her dad knew what was happening to him. He listened carefully to the doctor, understood the diagnosis. He told everybody that he was going to fight this thing. He'd taken on worse shit in his life. Everyone cheered him on.

With piles of books around him, he'd studied what the researchers knew and what his most likely prognosis was. He decided to put himself on a regimen of high protein and lots of exercise. Almost immediately, he was full of energy and seemed to be more alert and focused than ever. Then a few weeks later, he started getting lost on his jogs. Awhile after that, he abandoned the meat and eggs and started focusing on breads and pastries and beer. In six months, he went from a muscular, funny man to this bloated, unpredictable kid strapped beside her in the Toyota Camry. Like the innocent citizens in *Invasion of the Body Snatchers*, he fell asleep one night and the pod grew outside his window, and now this. Still the same face, but his eyes were tuned to a new channel. Static white noise for hours at a time, then suddenly long stretches of perfectly good reception. The father she'd always loved.

These days, he was lucid about half the time. But it was still early in the cycle, the doctors warned. No telling how steep the slide would be or when it would start. "Take pleasure in the time he's still himself," they said. And she tried.

She was at a light near Ludlum when he unfastened his seat belt and reached out for the door latch. But Alexandra had childproofed it a month ago, and Lawton strained at the latch for a moment, then gave up.

"Door's broken."

"Where are you trying to go, Dad?"

"Need to buy some luggage. I'm blowing this town."

"You've got good luggage now. Your initials on it and everything."

She started across the intersection.

"What are my initials, anyway? I forget."

"L.A.C. Lawton Andrew Collins."

"Where are we going? Where you taking me?"

"To Harbor House, Dad."

He tapped on his window and gave a wave to the driver of the car beside them. The young woman frowned and accelerated away. Warmhearted Miami.

Lawton turned back to Alexandra.

"Is Stan a cop?"

She let go of a long breath.

"No, he's not."

"But he dresses like one, that uniform he wears."

"He drives a truck," she said, "an armored truck."

"The ones full of cash? Those big square ones? Steel-reinforced, bulletproof windshield."

She said yes, eyes on the rearview mirror, a tailgating asshole in a black Camaro. Testosterone in the tank, nothing between the ears.

"It's a dangerous job, driving an armored truck. You worry about him?"

"Sometimes."

"Just like your mother used to worry about me. But see, I got through it just fine. Like I tell her. All your worry didn't change a thing."

The tailgating asshole swung around her, burned some rubber, his windows impenetrably dark. He was gone in a blur.

"Dad, what you did this morning, shooting the gun like that, it was wrong. You know that, don't you?"

Lawton reached into the pocket of his red-and-black-plaid shirt and came out with an old scrap of newsprint. He unfolded it, flattened it against the dash, got all the wrinkles out of the paper, then held it out to Alexandra.

"Something from my files."

She took a couple of quick looks but couldn't make out the article. Finally, she got a red light at 124th. She read it quickly. Took a second look at the photograph. And Jesus, it *did* look like Stan!

"Frank Sinatra," he said. "I caught him, sent him up the river. Late seventies, just like I said."

Alexandra had to chuckle.

"What? You thought I was talking about the singer? That Frank Sinatra. Hey, I'm not some loon. I got an excellent memory for names. Names and faces. That's my expertise. Never was any good with directions. Ask your mother. She'll tell you. I never could tell north from south. Hand me a compass, a map, I'm lost in a minute. But names and faces, those I can remember. It's a cop skill. Ask your mother; she'll confirm everything."

"Okay, Dad."

"You know, your mother blames me for getting you involved with police work. She doesn't understand why her little girl would want to do something like that. One awful scene after another. All that grim business. All night, every night. She doesn't understand that."

"But you do, Dad. Don't you? You understand me."

"Sure I do. You're my girl. I know you through and through."

Alexandra glanced over at him. He was smiling sadly.

"But, Alex," he said, staring straight ahead at the windshield, "nobody should have to do penance their whole life."

"What?"

"There's such a thing as time off for good behavior."

"What're you talking about, Dad?"

"You know what I'm talking about, Alex. The thing that happened back a long time ago. The reason you do the kind of work you do."

She slowed for a light, looked over at him.

"And another thing while I'm on a tear," he said. "I know how goddamn annoying I can be, repeating things, going off like I do. I hear myself doing it, but I can't shut up. It's like I'm way down underwater and there's another guy floating up on the surface and I can hear him saying all that nonsense, and I try to yell up at him to shut the hell up, but when I open my mouth, only thing that comes out are bubbles. Bubbles and more bubbles. Because I'm way down there underwater, you know, like a frogman.

"I know it's awful to listen to. And Stan's right. I'm an old fool. But I can't make myself stop yammering to save my life. I'm trying, though. I want you to know that, Alex. I'm down here trying to be good. Hanging on. Trying not to get on your nerves, or

Stan's. But it's hard. It's damn hard. A frogman, down on the bottom. Blowing bubbles. Glub, glub."

He looked over at her. For a moment, his eyes fluttered between the two worlds where he lived. Then they lost their grip on her face and slid away. A foolish smile took possession of his lips.

"We don't see much of your mother anymore, do we?"

Alexandra drew a long breath and pulled into the parking lot of the Harbor House. Some of the other daughters were delivering their mothers and fathers. Twice as many mothers. Even though most of the women were twenty years older, Lawton liked those odds. He had six or seven girlfriends at Harbor House and was always bringing home tins of cookies.

"Your mother died, didn't she?"

"Years ago, Dad. Years ago."

"You shouldn't keep things from me," Lawton said. "I can take difficult news. Believe me, Alexandra, I've dealt with some bad situations in my life. If your mother died, then I should be told."

Alexandra pushed her hair back. It needed cutting. It had been years since she'd had a manicure. Years since she'd bought herself anything frilly or impractical.

"All right, Dad, fine. I won't hide things from you anymore. Everything out in the open."

Most of the time, he didn't bother with the paper. The only reason he bought a *Herald* that morning was because he wanted to see if the reporters had discovered the poses yet.

They hadn't, the idiots. Or else they were cooperating with the police. You never knew for sure anymore. Nowadays, you couldn't trust the stuff in the paper and you couldn't even trust the stuff that wasn't in it.

Taking an early lunch, he sat in a booth at Denny's on Biscayne, with the traffic pouring past, and he read the article slowly and listened to his waitress talking to another waitress about the latest dead woman. His waitress had black dried-out hair and was thick-waisted and tall. She wore her makeup heavy and had bangles on both wrists. The hair on her arm was dark and longer than normal, and he looked at it carefully as she poured him more coffee.

"It's terrible, isn't it? That young woman, with everything to live for."

"What're you talking about?"

"Right there, that article you're reading," the waitress said.

He looked up into her eyes and said nothing. He kept his mouth dead, and in a few seconds she gave a confused little shake of her head and took her pot of coffee and her chirpy bullshit off to another customer.

Rapists and killers in the movies were always flamboyant madmen. They lived in rooms with outlandish insects flying around or with the walls papered with ten thousand creepy newspaper clippings. They were losers who wore polka dots and plaids together and their glasses were thick and greasy. The movie rapists slunk around at night with whores and go-go dancers. But he was none of those things. He was well-informed, well-read, but without intellectual pretensions. He was handsome, but not strikingly so. He could be intense, but he could also laugh. He had good taste in clothes and furnishings, a sense of style that floated between contemporary and classic, and he was bright and had friends, male and female. He made good money. He drove a two-year-old Honda, the most common car on the streets of Miami. He was a good singer, could find the harmony in almost any song he'd ever heard, and he could tell a joke well. He voted in every election and made contributions to environmental causes. He went to church now and then, but he wasn't a zealot. He was polite to people in grocery stores and movie theaters and he was a good driver. He liked to eat and drink but was no glutton. He enjoyed fast food as well as four-star restaurants. He kept himself in excellent shape with weights and running. He played chess and darts in an Irish bar he went to now and then. People knew his name and liked him and called him up sometimes to cry on his shoulder or ask him over to watch a heavyweight fight or a play-off game on the tube. He could go anywhere and not be noticed. He was comfortable and secure in nearly any environment.

He didn't have a creepy bone in his body. Not one.

He watched the traffic go by on Biscayne Boulevard and sipped his coffee. He hated newspapers and he hated television even more. He hated journalists. Their superior, cynical attitude, assuming the worst of everyone. Like they'd seen it all, crime and grime, and nothing surprised them. Calling him "the Bloody Rapist," making a joke out of it.

He shifted around on the bench seat, trying to find a more comfortable position. He was exhausted and his joints ached like he might be coming down with the flu. The bitch probably gave him some germ, all that kissing on the couch, her tongue down his throat like she was starved for something he had inside him and was trying to scoop it out.

He was drained and vaguely depressed. These things took a lot out of him, more all the time. The recovery could take a full week. That long before he even started thinking about it again, looking for another woman, starting to get the prickling in his blood. He wasn't a horny guy by nature—ready to go all the time, like some men his age. He'd never been that way. Slow to rouse, actually.

He hated those television experts with their sound-bite explanations of rape. The so-called authorities claimed rape was about violence, not sex. Saying the act sprang from a man's need to dominate a woman, or his hatred of her, or some other bullshit. But it wasn't like that. If it was about hate and violence, then the guy wouldn't rape the woman; he'd beat the shit out of her, strangle her, and leave her lying on the floor.

No, it was about sex. Sex, sex, sex. It was about the prickle in his blood, that tingle deep in the axons of his cortex. It was about neurons and dopamine and dendrites, all the thousand itchy creatures in his brain. It was about Pavlov and his dog. It was about chemicals that had been stewing for a million years, ever since one of his ancestors, something white and slippery, wriggled ashore and took cover under a rock. Rape was about crinkly folds of skin and the smell of flesh, and it was about hardness and softness, squirming and biting, prying inside the hot, tight sphincter of female tissue, deep inside her blood.

He drank the rest of his coffee and raised his cup high in the air without looking for the waitress. And even after his arm began to hurt, he kept it up in the air until she returned with the pot.

"It's terrible," he said, smiling at her, winning her back. "That young woman. Gruesome and sad."

"Yeah," said the waitress, pouring him another cup. "Myself, I'm getting the heck out of Miami. It's not worth all you have to put up with just for some good weather. I was telling Doris—"

"You're a very good waitress," he said, turning his head to stare out the window. "You're excellent at what you do."

"Thank you," she said.

"I'm happy and privileged to be served by you."

"Well, thanks."

She stood there a few seconds more, then swiveled on her squeaky tennis shoes and marched away.

Rape was about wanting a woman you couldn't have. One woman. An image in your mind that was bright and clear and never wavered or varied. Her face, her body, her voice, the way she swayed and stood. One woman above all others. The craving gnawed at you, a longing, a pang, a slow burn hidden so deep inside your body, there wasn't a name for the place where it resided.

Rape was about having to settle for another woman, a lesser version of the one you truly wanted. Rape was about walking up the steps of that woman's Coconut Grove apartment, a woman smiling in her doorway, her hip cocked, making herself available to you, letting you inside, letting you come into her intimate quarters. It was about walking up those steps, legs weak, the blood leaving them, the twist in the stomach, the heart scudding. Walking up those steps, watching her open the door and stand aside, admitting you to the intimate place that was hers, that dark, small space where she lived, and it was about what happened next, the next hour, those thousand little winks and wiggles and obscene softenings in the voice and flutters of lashes and come-hither gestures and smiles and how she was dressed, her face made up, all of it planned for your benefit, to create the seductive effect, to transmit her sexual willingness. To lure you.

It was about sex. It was about the need to pour yourself out of yourself. It was about the urge to replicate, duplicate, repeat and repeat and repeat until everything got quiet. Until there was relief. Sweet satiation. Everything was still and empty and perfect. The gong in the heart no longer ringing. The shimmer gone. Everything flat and quiet and serene.

That's when he killed them—when the static was silent. He looked down at them and he could see it in their eyes: they hated him because he was stronger and took what he wanted, and that hate was so ferocious that he knew if he didn't kill them, they would kill him. So he did it to save himself, so he could go on. So he could live.

Murdering them wasn't crazy; it wasn't sick or illogical or sociopathic or any of that psychoanalytical bullshit. It was simple baseline self-preservation. It was one animal looking at another animal and seeing that the other animal would kill him if it got the chance, so he did what he had to do. Instinct. Survival of the fittest. Oldest law there was. Buried in the blood a million years. Kill or be killed.

They didn't know shit about rape.

FIVE

By three o'clock, they were carrying somewhere near $4 million. Five sacks of cash, two smaller satchels of coins. A bag of food stamps. Typical day. Savings and Loan, Publix supermarket, NationsBank, a check-cashing joint, another supermarket. Stan driving, Benito riding shotgun. The Winchester in the rack beside him. Following procedure, same shuffle at every stop.

Benito, the courier, wearing his Kevlar vest, carrying a .38, hauled the empty canvas bags from the truck at every stop, brought them back full, while Stan stayed in the truck with the doors locked. Benito got seventy-five cents more an hour for taking that risk. Which brought him up to eight bucks per. Stan could've had the job if he'd wanted it, and, God knows, he needed the money. But he passed. He had something better in mind. Something that required him to stay behind the wheel.

Usually, they made a little chitchat between stops, though today Stan wasn't feeling conversational. His Kevlar vest was tight, lungs unable to expand. Felt like a hot wire was wriggling in his left armpit.

"Your father-in-law driving you crazy again? Talking his bull-shit?"

Stan said no, the old man was fine.

"Then it's your wife," Benito said. "What happened, she find out about your little sugar on the side? Jennifer what's-her-name?"

"Shut up about that."

"Hey, I got no problem with adultery. Just because I'm faithful to my wife, it don't mean I can't appreciate a man chasing pussy. Wife like yours, I understand completely. Pretty, but no interest in sex. Hey, I'll take an ugly one any day. Ugly and horny, those are the best. That's the mistake you made, Stan—you married a pretty one. She looked hot, but she's dry where it counts. Ham and cheese without mayo. Those are the worst. I don't blame you for screwing around, man. Makes perfect sense to me."

"Shut the fuck up, Benito."

"Oh, I got it. I know what it is. This is the fucking day you're leaving, running off with her, your little sugar tit. It is, isn't it? I guessed it."

"Wrong again, asshole. Just another day in paradise. Nothing special whatsoever."

"Don't lie to me, man. I can see it in your face, like something crawled up your ass and died. Looks like maybe it was a porcupine or something. That what it is, man, a porcupine up your ass?"

"Yeah, that's it," Stan said. "A porcupine."

"Hey, you don't want to confide in your partner, okay. We ride together five years, tell each other every sad story, expose ourselves down to the bottoms of our hearts, sure, that's okay. You're hurting about something; your mouth is all twisted up, bones sticking out from your flesh where I can see them. Then you just turn your back on me, shut me out, slam the frigging door in my face. Hey, I can deal with it. I got my own thoughts. I know how to amuse myself."

"So do it."

"Yeah, yeah. I'll just sit here and play back all the women I slept with this past year. Picture their naked bodies. Put them up on the big screen in my head. Remember how they smelled, what they tasted like, all the details. I don't need to talk to you, man. You just drive and be quiet and let me picture my women."

"Fine," Stan said. "Let's see how long you can keep your mouth shut. Maybe you can beat your personal best of eleven seconds."

Benito was quiet for a moment, then said, "You're not thinking of doing something stupid, are you?"

Stan kept his eyes on the back of a red Cadillac in his lane.

"'Cause if you are, you should tell me, so I can get out right here."

"What the hell're you talking about, you nimrod?"

"That look you got, it's the same way my old man looked the night he stuck his freaking pistol in his mouth. I don't want to be riding with no guy has suicide on his mind."

Stan looked over at the little man. Curly black Cuban hair, dark complexion. Might be a mulatto, for all Stan knew. Long eyelashes. Kind of guy you'd see on the street, you'd say he was queer, only Stan knew Benito was married, with four bambinos. Big roly-poly wife, twice Benito's size. There couldn't be any naked women in his head because his wife took up the whole damn movie screen.

"I'm fine," Stan said. "I just got things on my mind is all. Just drop it."

Benito snapped his fingers, then thumped the side of his skull several times.

"Shit, of course. Now I remember. It's the Bloody Rapist. He killed another girl and now your old lady's all wound up, gonna start working all her freaking overtime again. Stomping around, pissed off. And old Stan's gotta catch a bunch of shit for what some other guy did, gotta stay home every night with the shit-for-brains father-in-law, can't get away to suck on his sugar tit. Am I right? Huh? Do I know you through and through, or what?"

Stan shot him another look.

"Eleven seconds, remember? Why don't you see if you can set an all-time record, Benny. Maybe the rest of the fucking day, for instance. That would truly impress me."

Benito pouted for a moment, then pressed his lips together, made a zipper sign across them, then twisted a key for good measure and tossed it away, and sat back in his padded seat.

Stan steered them out onto Biscayne Boulevard. They were way the hell up in Aventura. All the condo commandos out in their Cadillacs and Mercedes, prowling for bargains. He got into the right lane, laid in behind a slow-moving Buick stuffed with blue-haired discount hunters, and worked through the gears from stoplight to stoplight, traveling south toward 151st Street, where they'd pick up Dixie, then 135th, and head west over to I-95. Twenty minutes, fifteen if the traffic was light, and they'd be at the spot. Ground zero. And it would all go down. He was crossing over the line from a normal law-abiding citizen to a major-league felon. That is, if Stan's goddamn nerves held.

You tried to set up a perfect crime, you were doomed to fail. That's how Stan saw it. Crimes got fouled up by little things that came zooming in unexpectedly—some microscopic dust particle that got in the gears and caused them to grind to a halt just at the exact moment you needed to go forward. Or a stray electron misfires and fries the circuitry at the crucial second. No such thing as a perfect crime. Never was, never would be.

Stan knew what he was talking about. He'd read crime books all his life, ever since one afternoon when he was a little kid dumped at the library by his mother while she went off to the bar with one of her soldier boyfriends. Stan snooped around for a while and, what do you know, first book he pulls off the shelf, flips it open, on page one there's a naked woman's body found in a field. Who was she? How'd she get there? Why would anybody kill her? Eight years old, he takes the book over to a corner, sits down, and starts reading, ears getting hot, heart quivering. Trying to picture himself walking through a field, coming upon a naked woman's body. The whole thing grabbing him, not letting him go till his mother showed up an hour or two later and hauled him off. Soon as he could get back, he was in the library, hunting that book down. He found it, read the rest and was still hungry. Finally, working up his nerve, he asked the librarian if she might have anything else like the book he'd just read. "So, you like the crime field, young man?" she said. It felt like a trick question, but finally he said, yeah, he guessed so. "Oh, so do I," she said. "I just adore a good murder mystery." Old woman, could be his grandmother. She wore the same dress every day, dark blue with white flowers, and she's taking him under her wing, steering him around the room, raving about this murder book and that one.

From then on, he was hooked. True crime, crime magazines, crime stories in the paper. All the other kids were watching TV, playing their video games, but Stan's inside reading about the Lenox Avenue Gang, Herman Webster Mudget, murderer, robber, and arsonist, nicest man you'd ever meet, except that he killed over two hundred women. All-time American record holder. Or Dillinger or Frankie Carbo, or Al Spencer, the great bank robber of Oklahoma, the first guy to use souped-up cars for his getaways.

Twenty years later, Stan's head was stuffed with crime facts. Going to school, there hadn't been a teacher who could get him to study or memorize dates or any of it. But here he was, a grown man, and, without even trying, he'd committed to memory a few thousand names and dates, famous mobsters, legendary bank robbers, and a million and one lesser-known people, the ones who got only a paragraph in the *Dictionary of American Crime.* He loved those guys, brash and ballsy, high-wire walkers, guys with passports stamped from every country in the underworld.

Hell, if he'd picked up a Bible that afternoon in the library, the whole thing might be different. Today, he might be studying theology or some shit. Be one of those door-to-door idiots who wanted to talk about Jesus, some weird gobbledygook name for their church.

Stan Rafferty had never even shoplifted a wooden pencil at the dime store, but he knew the mind-set of a big-time robber, a guy with twenty banks under his belt. Some mornings after a night of dreaming about robberies or other mayhem he'd committed, he'd wake up glowing with excitement.

When he finally decided to play around with a plan of his own, first thing he did was make up a list of the natural laws of the criminal universe. He came up with three. Easy to remember, not necessary to write down.

The first law was: The crime itself is less dangerous than what you do with the money later. Most crooks got caught from doing something dumb after the fact. Spending their money in lavish ways. Drawing attention to themselves.

The second one said: Don't give your wife the littlest hint about what you are up to. He couldn't count the number of famous crooks who'd been turned in by their wives after they got jealous or pissed off about some little thing the guy had done entirely unrelated to the crime itself. And with Alex working at Miami PD, it was even more important he didn't let the smallest thing slip. Somehow, it made it all the more exciting, Stan pulling off a major crime while married to a cop.

And yeah, he guessed Benito was right. If it wasn't for Alex, all his plans would've just stayed right there in his head. Alex and her goddamn job. Coming home night after night with the stink of death on her. That sour metallic reek of blood and vomit and gunpowder that didn't wash off. She couldn't hide it with soaps or perfumes. Over and over, Stan had tried to put the smell out of his mind, reach out, touch her skin, stroke her breasts, try to get himself hard and horny, but the best he could do was half-mast. A limber-dicked lover. Getting little flashes of corpses as he touched her, as they kissed, his dick wilting.

And if that wasn't bad enough, then her old man came to live with them. Overnight, the house got crowded. The old man always underfoot. Like having a kid in diapers, only he's 150 pounds and won't shut up. That's why Stan started fooling around, sneaking out, leaving the old man locked in the house while he hung out at a couple of neighborhood bars till he'd met the girl. Cute, young Jennifer, who smelled like flowers and cinnamon, with flesh as soft as fresh-baked rolls. Innocent and clean. Jennifer thought Stan was strong and complicated. That's what she said to him once. Strong and complicated. A father figure, she'd said. Fucking-A.

So that's where he was. Ready to chuck nine years of marriage—make his score; then a month or two from now, when things had cooled down, he'd walk out on Alexandra and just flat disappear.

Rule number three, that was Stan's favorite, his triumph, the one with his own personal stamp on it. It said: When it comes to crime, chaos is a thousand times better than order.

Like the others, it was an idea he'd distilled down from a book. At a bookstore a month ago, totally random, he'd flipped it open and started reading. Though it wasn't about crime, he got hooked immediately.

It was part quantum physics, part philosophy, with some psychology and religious bullshit thrown in. Mainly, it was about chaos. How everything, even the most orderly systems in nature, even the man-made machines that ran the world—computers, internal combustion engines, turbines, generators, radar, all the things we think are operating neatly and efficiently—is actually full of all kinds of chaos.

Fat, expensive book. He started on it that night while Alexandra was off at work. He didn't understand it for shit. You needed a college degree to read the flap copy. But he forged on anyway, feeling himself absorb some of the material, bit by bit, though later on when Alex asked him what it was about, all he could think to say was, "It's about chaos. How everything's chaotic."

"That's it?" she said. "A whole book about that?"

"Yeah, a whole book."

"Seems to me," she said, "you could get that on the first page, then go off to other things."

"It's more complicated than that," he told her. "Stuff you wouldn't understand. I barely understand it myself."

"Oh," she said. "That complicated?" Giving him her smart-ass college smile. Stan with only a year at Dade Junior College, and Alex lording it over him all the time. Very subtle about it, so someone standing right there wouldn't even notice what she was doing, but Stan saw it. Yes sir.

Even though Stan didn't understand but maybe a tenth of what was in that book, the idea he got from it was that chaos was the answer to the perfect crime. You had to throw everything into the blender. Your goal was total disarray, complete and utter confusion. You even took the chance that the whole goddamn thing would get so cockeyed crazy that you couldn't even steal the money at all. There was an excellent chance of that.

But that was the beauty of the plan. If it failed, he could just walk away. Because no one would ever believe there was a plan to steal money in the first place. Nobody would be able to see a plan through all the craziness.

But on the other side of the seesaw from that low-risk potential was the high fuckup possibility. One goes up, the other goes down. If he went ahead with his plan, it was conceivable he could do absolutely everything right and things would get so incredibly fucked up that the money wouldn't wind up where he wanted it to.

That was the trade-off. Low risk, high fuckup potential.

Most bank robbers and heist guys were basically nineteenth-century types. Still back in the Newtonian universe. Gravity, mechanized thinking, gears clanking against gears, all that. Wanting their capers to run with greased efficiency, all the clock-work meshing, all the balls dropping in the right holes, bing, bing, bing.

But Stan Rafferty was going to be the first of his kind, a post-Einstein robber. A totally brand-new thing coming down the pike. So innovative in his thinking, he could even have a chapter dedicated to him in the next set of the *Encyclopedia of Crime*. Except no one was ever going to know his name, since Stan wasn't going to get caught.

Because even though Stan Rafferty could easily walk off with somewhere near $2 million, there was an excellent chance no one was even going to know a crime had been committed.

"Man," Benito said, "you're thinking so hard, it's getting noisy in here."

Stan glanced at his watch.

"You made it exactly three minutes and fourteen seconds, you dumb shit. Now, let's try it again, see if you can break five."

"I don't believe you, man. Everything I confided in you, all the shit I opened up and revealed. My wife, all her medical problems, and when something finally comes along, it bothers you a little, you get lockjaw."

"I got the stopwatch on you, Benito. Tell me when you're ready to start."

"Shit," he said. "And I thought you and me were close. I thought we were friends."

"We are, partner. And this is what friends do. They respect each other's privacy. Get it?"

Benito clamped his mouth and stared straight ahead at the ramp up to 95.

Ten minutes and they'd be there. Ten minutes for Stan to decide if he wanted to start his life over or continue being the gutless loser he'd spent the last twenty-nine years turning into.

SIX

Mrs. Scarlett Rogers, the tour guide for Sunny Pines Assisted Living Facility, was a fifty-year-old woman with a swirl of bright orange hair and a smile that was so rigid, it had to be the result of multiple failed plastic surgeries. Gritting her teeth, the woman looked like someone who'd just stepped off the ledge of a twenty-story building and was still trying to keep her composure. Lawton was crooning to himself while Scarlett Rogers described the excellent amenities package at Sunny Pines. A gym, a sauna, five coed hot tubs, a walking course on their two-acre lawn.

"I want to see these hot tubs," Alexandra said. She had no idea why she said it. As far as she knew, her father had never climbed into a hot tub in his life, and had expressed no interest in doing so. But she didn't like this woman, didn't like the place, and it was the meanest thing she could think of saying.

The woman turned her inflexible smile on Alex, lifted an eyebrow, and scrutinized her for a moment, as if Alexandra might be concealing a miniature video camera. One of those sneaky reporters the TV stations were always sending around.

"Certainly," Mrs. Rogers said. "This way, please."

She led them down the freshly waxed linoleum hallway, past a large recreation room with pool and Ping-Pong tables. Alex noticed the net was down on the Ping-Pong table, no paddles or balls in sight. The corridor was lined with women in housecoats and smocks. They sat on benches or in wheelchairs and several of the women were speaking, but there didn't seem to be any actual conversations going on. An elderly black man was slumped over in his wheelchair near the door at the end of the hall where Mrs. Rogers halted.

She motioned at a heavy gray door.

"The tubs are inside there. I would show them to you, but they might be in use, and we certainly don't want to disturb anyone."

Before the woman could protest, Alexandra pushed the door ajar and peeked inside. There were four large plastic whirlpools arranged in the middle of the room. All were empty. The gray wall-to-wall carpet was soggy and reeked of mildew and chlorine. Except for the tubs, the room was bare.

"This place sucks," her father said. "Like a waiting room at the morgue."

"We have a very well-trained staff," Mrs. Rogers said, shutting the door firmly. "Four full-time RNs and eight state-certified orderlies."

"You're not thinking of locking me up in this hellhole, are you?"

"We're just investigating, Dad. That's all we're doing."

"We have a registered dietician on staff. Our meals are nutritious and low-fat and we offer salt-free and vegetarian specialties."

"Am I here because I shot that gun?"

"Dad, please."

"Send me to Raiford," Lawton said. "Christ, lock me up with the child molesters and rapists. Anyplace but here."

Alexandra took the brochure Mrs. Rogers offered and led her father back out into the afternoon heat.

"Whew," he said as she held open the door to the Camry. "What the hell did those people do to deserve getting locked up in that god-awful place?"

"They got old," Alex said.

"Then I'm staying eighteen years old from here on out. Eighteen's fine."

Alexandra made it back to South Miami by four, just ahead of the rush-hour onslaught. She parked on the street out front and sat there for a moment staring down the row of identical neat white houses, all with two bedrooms and one bath. "Starter houses," they were called these days. The sterile architecture of the early fifties, when those houses served as winter retreats, little more than oversized motel rooms for the yearly crop of snowbirds. Now the neighborhood was a ghetto for university students and widows and newlyweds. No children, only a few pets. Lots of turnover. In the nine years they'd lived on Silver Palm Avenue, seven different families had occupied the house to their east. Nine years married and she and Stan were still starting out. Still exactly where they'd been.

"You forget something?" her dad said.

"I was just thinking."

"Myself, I'm always forgetting things. It's what I do now. It's my full-time employment. I wake up in the morning and I lie there and decide what I want to forget that day. I make a list and scratch things off one by one. Forget my thirty years on the police force. Forget my wife. Forget my teenage years. It's my job now, and I'm getting pretty damn good at it, if I do say so myself."

"Let's go inside, Dad."

"You going to stash me in that place, that nursing home?"

"No. You're staying right here."

"You're going to lose your marriage, Alex. You heard your husband. He gave you a choice. It was him or me—the half-wit."

"He didn't mean it. Stan says things sometimes when he's angry."

"Oh, he meant it all right. I know that husband of yours. We've had ourselves some long talks lately while you were off at work. Heart-to-heart, belly-to-belly."

"Don't worry, Dad, I'm not stashing you anywhere."

"I don't want you to lose your marriage, Alexandra. It doesn't make any difference to me. That nursing home place wasn't so bad."

"I've decided, Dad. Don't argue with me. We're sticking together."

"Even if it means risking your marriage?"

She pulled the keys out of the ignition, took a swallow of air.

"Even if it does, yes."

"Wow," he said. "Guess it just goes to show that blood's thicker than . . ." He turned his head and peered out his side window. With his fingertips, he rubbed several hard circles into his temples. "Blood's thicker than . . ."

"Water," Alex said. "Thicker than water."

"No, that's not it. It's something else. Blood is thicker than . . . I know it. It's there on the edge of my tongue. I've said it a hundred times. Come on, come on. Oh, oh. Yeah, okay, there it is. Blood's thicker than water."

He turned from the window, his smile full of crazy light.

"Blood's thicker than water. See, Alex, I'm doing fine. Yeah, maybe I've got to work a little for it, but I get it eventually. Blood's thicker than . . . thicker than . . ."

He shut his eyes hard, smoothed both hands across his graying hair, mouthing a word that simply wouldn't come.

Stan Rafferty hadn't factored in Benito. That was one problem. He hadn't expected the little guy to play any role at all. Slam his head against the windshield, get knocked unconscious and stay that way until the paramedics came. That's the picture Stan had in his mind, but because he was using chaos theory to guide his thinking, he really wasn't trying for any particular outcome with Benito or any of the rest of it. *X* was as good as *Y*, and *Z* as good as either. The crazier the better.

But still it worried him, Benito studying him so carefully as he drove along I-95, about a mile to the Liberty City exit. Scrutinizing his driving. Stan glanced over at him and asked him what the hell he was staring at.

"I'm trying to figure you out, man. Trying to read what's going on inside that thick head of yours."

Stan was about a mile from the exit, the go/no-go spot, and now with this new development, he'd decided to pull the rip cord, bail, bail, bail. Benito paying way too much attention, the traffic not busy enough. Christ, imagine that. Running along I-95 at almost rush hour through downtown Miami, and the traffic was all of a sudden superlight, nobody darting and cutting.

Just didn't smell right. Not right at all. Bail, bail.

Then he heard his own voice inside his head calling himself a chickenshit. All these years, he'd been thinking about crime, fantasizing about pulling off something like this. Imagining it, getting all hot. Now he had it set up; he'd figured it out, how it would work. He had a theory to support the action. And God knows, he'd need the cash starting his new life with Jennifer. He'd gotten himself rolling, picked his time; then at the last possible second he'd turned chickenshit. Yellow-bellied wimp. But then Stan heard another voice in his head give the other version of things. How another day would be better, a day when Benito wasn't watching him so carefully, when the traffic was heavy, like it usually was, unpredictable, crazy.

Less than thirty seconds from the exit, the voices doing battle inside his head, and Stan gripping the wheel, not sure what his hands were going to do. Looking at the wheel, his fingers getting pink from gripping so tightly.

And then he glanced into the big rearview mirror and there was a car, a red low-slung sports car, must've been doing nearly a hundred, some kid barreling down the middle lane, Stan in the far right.

"Jesus Christ," he said. "Jesus goddamn Christ."

"What?"

Stan pointed at the rearview and Benito peered into his big side mirror, and the voice that had been calling him chickenshit got quiet.

"Don't worry about it, man. He ain't in your lane. Just be cool."

"That dumb fuck," Stan yelled, and swung the armored truck hard to the right, aiming for the downtown exit, cutting off a yellow Chevette over there.

The little car honked and Stan oversteered right, then oversteered left, the big truck doing fifty-five down the exit ramp, careening. A car screeched and there was honking behind them and Benito crying out something in Spanish while Stan made a move with his legs like he was trying to downshift, brake, feet missing the pedals, the truck swerving back and forth, big red stop sign coming up fast, letters obscured with graffiti, heavy concrete beams on either side of the ramp, one sitting off-kilter, as it had been for weeks, its sharp edge hooking out toward the street.

"Jesus, stop this fucking thing!"

Stan guided the truck toward the left side of the off-ramp, toward that sharply angled cement beam. He cut over the shoulder, jounced against the cement, sparks showering from the hard brush, glanced out the rearview, to see cash and coins flying in their wake, and then they were in the cross street, hauling ass through a blank spot in the traffic, Stan hitting the brakes and cursing, wrestling the big wheel as the truck sailed across the avenue, doing an acting job for Benito's benefit. The truck cut across both lanes and jolted over a small sidewalk where the drunks hung out, the homeless, the addicts hunkered in doorways, the muggers scanning the sidewalk, all the poor sad fucks of Liberty City drifting here and there. Stan was counting on them being around, being ready for his arrival as the truck humped over the curb, thirty-five miles an hour, bounced hard, and slammed head-on into the bright yellow fire hydrant.

Money was in the air. Coins tumbling inside a roaring geyser. A great column of water erupting through the floor between their seats and churning against the roof. And bills, a flood of green, swirling with the silver, bubbling out the broken windshield, across the hood, and out the windows into the street. Bright copper and silver, the water, the air, the money, a tumbling whirlwind of cash and water, as if Stan were caught deep inside the tumult of a tidal wave, a thirty-footer curling over him, locking him in its powerful embrace, the white foam, the dazzling silver, bills and coins.

He'd wanted chaos, and Christ, he had it now.

The truck was straddling the broken hydrant. From what he could see, he'd gouged a wide seam down the driver's side of the van and another gash along the driveshaft from the front fire wall to the vault door. Water continued to blast at the ceiling, a torrent all around them. Half-conscious, Benito wriggled inside his safety harness.

Out the windshield, a deranged carnival was under way. A few dozen people out there on the sidewalk and in the muddy vacant lot, downstream of the flow of money. Heavy women, skinny men, children, gang bangers with their ankle-length shorts, old ladies in quilted robes, everyone scrambling for the bills that were pouring out of the truck, pooling up, eddying near the roots of the trees. Yelps of excitement, a little shoving, a scuffle or two. More people coming out of the nearby apartment buildings.

Stan searched the crowd but didn't see the one he was looking for. He twisted in his seat, freed himself of the seat belt, tried to move his legs, and that's when the streak of lightning blasted through his skull. He slammed his head against the headrest and air whistled between his teeth. Behind a thick cloud, the sun dimmed and he felt himself sinking into the cold dusk it left behind.

But he fought it. Blinking, he gritted his teeth against a howl growing in his throat. He clenched the wheel, took several quick breaths, and looked over at Benito again. The little man was waking from his bad dream, the water blasting between them.

This was all Alex's fault. Bitch goddess ice queen. The stench of corpses on her breath. Her and her job. Her and her brainless old man. Without Alex goading him into it, the whole thing would've just stayed in Stan's head, a festering fantasy. No girlfriend on the side, no criminal enterprise. Alex had made him do it. Her and her Bloody Rapist. She'd left him no choice. And now look at the shitstorm he was in, a fucking tornado of tens and fives and twenties.

Stan squinted through the dazzle of pain, ground his teeth, and reached down to explore his legs. Cautiously, he probed his left leg, the damp fabric of his trousers, fingers easing below the knee. He felt faint, a gray swoon. His fingertips touching his left shin, the loose pouch of broken china. Jesus, he'd be in traction for a year. Walk with a limp, if at all.

But he couldn't think about that. Couldn't try to stop the flow of events, redirect things. He had only one thing to do, one small act amid the agony and upheaval. But he couldn't move, couldn't squirm anywhere. His legs were pinned beneath the steering wheel, jangling with pain while a sleepy stupor rose in his head, his mind going gray and mushy.

But this was no time for whining. The window of opportunity was closing; the smallest moment lay before him. Only one choice. As woozy and nauseated as he was, Stan managed to reach over and shake Benito's shoulder. The small man opened his eyes, looked out at the throng of people rushing after all that cash. He swung around to Stan, wiped his mouth, and a snarl twisted his lips.

"You goddamn idiot, what the hell you doing, man! You almost killed our asses."

"It was an accident."

"No fucking way, man. That was no accident. You did that. That was on purpose."

Stan groaned and took a whistling breath. Got the words out in short bursts.

"My leg. I can't move. You gotta unlock the door, reach in there, get those big sacks."

"What?"

"The big sacks. Save from the looters."

Stan motioned at the windshield and Benito looked out at the crowd that had grown to over a hundred now, spilling around them, some of them peering into the rear vault, which had been gashed open by the cement beam. There were sirens in the distance and the water continued to spew through the floor, pummel the ceiling—a fire hose at close range, thousands of pounds of pressure.

"Come on, come on. Get the sacks, Benito. Do your job."

"That's not procedure."

"There's a procedure for this? Get the fucking sacks, Benito. Do it. We got to protect the money."

The man shook his head, wriggled out of his shoulder harness, and took another look out at the people swarming into the muddy lot, on their knees, scrabbling for the cash.

"Hurry up, Benny. Hurry the hell up."

The shadow was coming back again. Something big and dark and cold eclipsing the sun, the mother of all mother ships. Stan held on against the vertigo, watched Benito unlock the door to the rear; then, when it didn't move, Benito put his shoulder against it and heaved it open. Sunlight pouring in back there. A minute later, he was hauling one sack out, then another.

"That's all?"

Benito stood in the doorway, looking back at the vault, the glare of daylight.

"Fucking truck's torn wide open, man. Somebody's already got the rest of it. Or else it's blown away."

There was a knock on Stan's window. Three hard, two soft. Then three hard again.

"Give 'em to me, Benito. The sacks."

"Give you the sacks?"

"That's right. Hand them to me."

Grimacing at another spike of pain, Stan took the bags from Benito and stuffed them through his broken window. A white hand grabbed the first one, then the second.

"Hey!" Benito said. "Who the hell is that?"

Benito sat down on his collapsed air bag and peered around the geyser.

Stan brought his voice down to a gassy whisper.

"It's okay, Benny. *Tranquilo.* What we need to do, we need to talk. I have to tell you something before I pass out."

"You don't have to tell me nothing, man. I already know what the hell you did. You robbed the company. You almost killed the both of us."

Stan motioned for him to come closer. Benito stiffened, drew back.

"That's not how it is, Benny. You got it wrong. Lean over here; my voice is going. I'm passing out. My fucking legs. You need to know what's going on, man, before I faint."

Benny sighed and shook his head in disgust, then bent forward. Stan grabbed Benito's long black hair, levered himself up in his seat, and dragged Benito's head into the jet of water and held it there, facedown. Benny struggled, but even in Stan's weakened condition, even on the edge of unconsciousness, he was too strong for the little guy.

He heard the sirens on the next block, the sound piercing his flesh, packing his blood vessels, sirens in the veins, screaming blood. Holding Benito's face into the powerful spray, arm muscles straining, but doing the job, from all those years of resistance training in high school—"isometrics," they'd called it back then. Football team sitting around the weight room straining against bars that wouldn't move, then back to lifting weights so they could tear more muscle fibers, because that's what it took to make them rebuild larger. Scar tissue. Stan was just one big bundle of scar tissue. All those hours getting his body hard and strong and big so he could go out on a hot Florida night and smash some kid across from him and make the crowd scream. All those hours of grinding pain, torture, and sweat so his sister, Margie, would see him from the stands, be proud of her big brother, proud of him. He still got goose chills remembering it.

When Benito was limp, Stan let him go. A drowned puppy tumbling to the floor. And Stan eased back against the seat and listened to the whoop of the sirens as they arrived, the shouts of the crowd hurrying after the last of the loot, to the wonderful sweet music of chaos whirling around him.

SEVEN

While Lawton stood at the kitchen sink and turned the water off and on, studying the foaming stream, Alex spread his afternoon allotment of taco chips on a paper plate, sprinkled them with grated cheddar and salsa, and put the plate in the microwave for forty seconds. She opened a Budweiser, and when the bell rang, she'd get the nachos out and lead Lawton to the TV room and settle him in his chair so he could watch the afternoon talk shows.

Not too many years before, he'd been merciless with Alexandra's mother about watching those same shows. Mocking her, scoffing at the celebrities who made small talk with the host, or the trailer-park trash shouting at one another about affairs and betrayals. "If you have to watch television," he'd say, "for God sakes at least watch something that's real. This shit's as phony as live studio wrestling." But these days, Lawton refused to miss the TV hour before the evening news began. Sipping his beer while he stared with fascination. Sometimes she'd find him weeping over some guest's particularly horrific predicament.

If Alexandra let it get to her, the television thing could be unbearably sad. But the way she'd decided to look at it was to imagine that her dad was establishing solidarity with his departed wife, some long-delayed rapport that extended beyond this earthly plane.

It was a struggle sometimes to come up with views that coped with her dad's new habits. She'd tried arguing with him, using logic and rational sense when he was being ridiculous. But his illness was stronger than any logic she knew. So these days, what she did was flex. She entered his world, let him set the terms, and then tried to use those terms to quiet him, to comfort him and keep him safe. "Oh, so you're going on a trip? Well then, you'll need a good breakfast first."

Just as the microwave beeped, the kitchen phone rang, and her father spun around and snatched it off the hook.

"Yeah?" he said.

Alexandra took the plate of nachos out and carried them over to the counter.

"Okay," her father said. "I'll ask her."

He set the phone back in its cradle and picked up the plate and started for the living room.

"Dad, who was on the phone?"

"He said his name was Jason."

Alex wiped her hands on the kitchen towel.

"What'd he say, Dad?"

"Wanted to know if you'd changed your mind yet."

Alex smiled.

"Do we know a Jason?"

"It's just a friend from work, Dad. Nothing important."

"Fine," he said. "You got young men calling you at home. I got no problem with that. You're a grown woman. Carpe diem. Make hay while the sun shines. 'Cause it sure as hell won't be shining much longer. Look at me. Let this be a warning to you. Follow your bliss before you forget what bliss is."

He plucked a taco chip from the plate and buried it in his mouth.

Listening to the hoots and laughter from the television, Alex mixed a can of tuna with a can of cream of celery soup. Another tuna casserole.

For the first couple of years of their marriage, she'd tried to introduce Stan to a few exotic recipes that her mom had taught her, but he fought her at every step. Plenty of evenings after he stared grimly at his plate for ten minutes, he got up and made himself a toasted cheese sandwich and ate it silently in the Florida room. Eventually, she'd abandoned her attempts at culinary re-education, and now they had a mindless routine of tuna, hamburger, pot roast, chicken cordon bleu, and burritos, which satisfied him just fine. Though even her father had remarked disdainfully on the unceasing parade of tuna casseroles.

It was 5:30 and she was opening a can of peas for the tuna casserole when her father called out for her to come and see something on the TV.

"Later, Dad. I've got to get dinner started."

"It's Stan," her father called. "He's made a mess. A real big mess."

Alexandra and Lawton were out the front door and across the yard, headed for the hospital at double time, when the big man emerged from the compact car out by the curb. Alex caught her father by the elbow and drew him to a halt as the man slammed his door and headed around the front of his car toward them.

He was well over six feet and was wearing a loose-fitting blue Hawaiian shirt, gray jeans, and silver running shoes. His hair was dark and smoothed back and he had on a pair of tortoiseshell sunglasses.

Coming up the walkway, the man stared down at the pavement and gave a couple of awkward little hops, as if he was trying to avoid the cracks in the cement.

"Can I help you?"

The man looked up from the pavement and his smile dwindled.

"It's me, Junior."

Lawton shrugged out of Alexandra's grasp and stepped up to confront the large man.

"Junior Shanrahan," he said, drawing back from Lawton, raising his hands slowly as if to defend against the old man. "From the photo lab."

"It's okay, Dad. It's a man from work."

For a moment, Lawton studied the bright pineapple slices that decorated Junior's shirt; then he raised his right hand and pointed a finger at the young man's face.

"Well, that may be true. But this boy needs some work on his people skills. In this town, you don't just come stalking up to folks out of the wild blue yonder unless you want to get a bellyful of lead."

Alex stepped up to her father's side.

"It's okay, Dad. He didn't mean anything."

Junior had his hands raised to his shoulders, showing Lawton his empty palms.

"I'm sorry," he said. "I didn't meant to startle you. I guess I should've worn my smock and hair net."

"What're you doing here, Junior?"

"You said you wanted those Bloody Rapist photos in a rush."

He drew a white packet from his jeans and stepped farther out of range of Lawton. Junior held the photos out to Alex.

"I thought you wanted to see them, so I came over."

She waved them away.

"Look, I'm sorry, Junior. It's a bad time. We've got to get somewhere in a hurry. We've got an emergency."

She tugged her dad toward the car.

"I've got a theory about the case, Alexandra. I've been working on it."

Junior was still watching Lawton as if the old man might be about to quick-draw a six-shooter.

"Not now, Junior. We have to go."

"I'd sure as hell like to get out of that lab, do some real police work for once."

"Tomorrow, Junior. Okay?"

"Sure, sure," he said. "Tomorrow's good." And he backed away toward his car, still watching Lawton. "Nice to meet you, sir."

A growl rumbled in Lawton's throat.

Junior walked backward across the grass, stumbled on the sidewalk, then turned and went hustling back to his car. He ducked inside and sped away.

"Was that your boyfriend?" Lawton said. "The one on the phone?"

"No, Dad, it was just a man from work."

"You're married, right? Stan what's-his-name."

"Stan Rafferty."

She opened the car, got in, and reached over and unlocked Lawton's door.

"Call me old-fashioned," he said as he climbed into the Camry. "But I don't think you should be out in your front yard exchanging sweet talk with your paramour in full daylight. A woman's got to be more discreet about these things."

"It was just a work thing, Dad. That's not my boyfriend. I don't have a boyfriend. And I don't want one."

"Well, say what you want, but I know what I saw," Lawton said. "I'm not so old I don't recognize full-blown lechery when I see it."

"I did it," Stan said to the paramedic. "I fucking did it."

"Hang on, bud, you're doing fine."

They were in the fire rescue ambulance, siren blazing, jostling over the potholes and crumbling asphalt between Liberty City and Jackson Memorial Hospital, Stan strapped tightly to the stretcher, his blood on fire.

"I did it," Stan said again to the Cuban man who was kneeling beside him, checking his vital signs. "I fucking crashed the armored truck."

"Yeah, you did, man. You fucking crashed it all right."

The paramedic was grinning.

"Sorry I couldn't stay around and pick up some of the loot."

"No," Stan said. "I did it. I fucking did it."

The Cuban paramedic had probably heard every manner of deranged bullshit on the job—people babbling under the influence of drugs, people crazed from all sorts of violence and mayhem. Stan could probably confess the whole thing to this guy and he'd never give it a second thought. Tell him about chaos, about the plan that wasn't a plan. Tell him about studying crime all his life just so he could reach this ultimate moment. He could probably tell the guy about drowning Benito, how it felt when the man stopped breathing, Stan's hands touching the guy as he went from a wriggling human being to a slab of lifeless flesh. He could probably tell this fat Cuban paramedic the complete and total truth, that Stan Rafferty was now a member of the crème de la crème, the elitist of the elite of criminal wrongdoers.

But he couldn't do it. He couldn't take the chance. It was sad, too. Incredibly sad, now that he thought about it. Stan Rafferty had done it: He'd fucking well pulled off a major, world-class crime, and no one was ever going to know.

"Stan robbed an armored truck," Lawton said. "They'll be shipping him back to Raiford."

"Stan was in an accident, Dad."

"He robbed the armored truck company and now he's going back to Raiford, where he belongs. Back with all the other cons."

It was no use. Alexandra tried to reason with him all the way over to Jackson Memorial, but he wouldn't budge. The idea had taken hold and it might last for hours or days. Stan was a bank robber, a liquor store thief, a car jacker, a kidnapper, and even a rapist. Lawton was replaying some of the crimes still lodged in his memory, assigning each of them to Stan, names, dates, details. And he kept it up, a steady stream of old cases glowing to life, all the way to Jackson Memorial Hospital, Alex fighting rush hour, a headache tightening behind her left eye. And her father continued to list Stan's crimes while they sat in the waiting area of the emergency room, nurses hurrying past, no one telling them anything for the last hour since the young Indian doctor came out to say that Stan was going into surgery for his left leg.

"A messy fracture," the doctor said.

"How messy?"

"Nothing we can't fix," the doctor said. "He should be learning how to use his crutches in a day or two."

She thanked him and he hurried off.

They watched the evening news on an overhead TV. "The Dash for Cash," as one station was calling it, was the number-one story. Hundreds of people had converged on the accident scene to grab some of the spilled loot, drivers piling off the interstate to join in, local residents of Liberty City, kids and grannies, welfare moms and dopers and hardworking citizens. They had a lot of video footage of the scramble, Metro-Dade and Miami PD standing nearby, hands on their hips, unable or unwilling to intervene.

"Finders keepers," one kid said, and held up a fistful of quarters, grinning into the camera.

"Anyone taking money from this truck will be considered a thief," a Metro police spokesman said. "This is not their money. They are stealing."

The young Cuban woman who was reporting the story stood a few yards from the wrecked truck and told her viewers that one of the guards, Benito Rodriguez, had drowned in the deluge set off from a broken fire hydrant. The driver of the truck, she said, was injured, but his wounds were not believed to be life-threatening. Eyewitnesses to the event said the truck had swerved to avoid a speeding vehicle; this vehicle, believed to be a red Mustang, had apparently been involved in a drag race along I-95, and the driver of the armored truck, Mr. Stanley Rafferty, had apparently lost control of his vehicle while trying to avoid a collision. Other unsubstantiated reports described a barrage of gunfire heard in and around the area of the overpass about the time the accident occurred. Perhaps a bungled robbery attempt. No confirmation on either version from the police so far.

At the moment, only a fraction of the money had been recovered. A fire rescue paramedic arriving on the scene had found one bag estimated to contain $300,000. He was being hailed as a hero for handing the money over to the investigating officers. Brinks spokesmen refused to give an exact amount, but informed sources told reporters on the scene that since the accident had occurred late in the afternoon, it was entirely possible that as much as $4 million had been on board the vehicle at the time of the accident.

The second story was about the Bloody Rapist. The victim was identified as Julia Straker, a young law secretary who had recently been divorced. Police spokesmen reported that once again the killer had left a trail of his own blood at the scene. The TV station's psychologist de jour came on for a quickie.

"Informed sources are telling us," the anchor said to the shrink, "that the victims' bodies have been left in gruesome, contorted positions. Does that tell us anything about the profile of the killer?"

"Well, if it's true," the psychologist said, "it would be a very troubling sign. Because it would then suggest we have not only a rapist and murderer on our hands but a man who is on some sort of crusade. Crying out for someone or something very specific. Trying to send a signal."

"Oh, great," Alex said.

"I'm going to relocate," said her dad. "I'm heading north, where I can see the leaves change colors. I miss those damn leaves, even though I get blisters every autumn from all the raking, and then the blisters turn into calluses. Did I ever show you my calluses?"

Lawton held his hands palms up and Alexandra nodded wearily at his smooth flesh.

"That's not an easy job, raking leaves. When you've finished, you've got these big piles, and then you have to burn them. We put the piles in a ditch out by the road; then you light the pile with matches and you stay there and make sure it doesn't spread. That's how you rake leaves in Ohio."

Alexandra sat on the hard bench, the smell of onions still on her hands, still wearing the green-and-black-checked shorts, the white shell, an outfit she'd chosen because it had once earned a rare compliment from Stan. It seemed like a year ago that she had put it on, full of determination to revive their marriage.

Watching the hubbub of the waiting room, Alex listened to the television anchors drone on about the other horrors of the day. Other people's lives splashed onto the TV screen.

"Is someone hurt?" her dad asked her.

"Stan's been in an accident."

"Do we know a Stan?"

"My husband, Dad. My husband was in a traffic accident."

"Oh," he said. "That's too bad."

She watched the sports guy put a microphone in the face of one of the rookie Dolphin players. He was sweaty and his face was bright red.

"Can we go home now?" her father said. "I'd like to eat supper."

"We have to wait until Stan comes out of surgery, know that he's okay. We want to be there when he wakes up."

"I'm hungry."

"I can get you something from the machines. Would you like some cheese crackers to tide you over?"

"When you've got the piles all raked up," he said, "you get a running start; then you dive on your belly, and it doesn't hurt. That's the fun part. Belly flopping into big fluffy piles. And you hide inside the pile. It smells like dust and trees."

Alexandra put her arm around his shoulder.

"I'll get you some crackers, Dad. Maybe something to drink, a Coke, a Sprite?"

The national news was on and they were showing the same footage of people grabbing for coins and fluttering bills. The lead story.

"Why didn't anyone tell me what happened?"

"Tell you what, Dad?"

"That your mother died. Did you think you had to protect me?"

"That was a long time ago, Dad. We've already moved on from there."

"Okay, then," her father said. "How did he drown?"

"What?"

"Stan's partner. How did he drown?"

"The truck hit a fire hydrant, and I suppose the water flooded the cab of the truck. He must have been unconscious."

"Sounds suspicious to me, a man drowning on a city street. Fire hydrant or not, it sounds very dubious. I'd look into that if I were you, Alexandra. I'd give that some serious scrutiny."

EIGHT

Emma Lee Potts tapped four times on the gunmetal gray door, positioned herself in front of the peephole, and let her smile blast.

"Whatta you want?" Norman Franks said through the door.

"It's me, Emma. I saw something you might be interested in."

She pushed a strand of her kinky blond hair off her face and kept her smile at full power.

"You saw something," came the voice.

"Yeah, that armored truck thing. Let me in, Norman. I'll tell you about it. It's good, I promise. It's got a lucrative aspect to it."

Half a minute went by before he started opening his locks. There were five of them and they were damn complicated.

Eight-thirty at night, the hallway was empty. A couple of broken lightbulbs, some gang graffiti spray-painted in red and blue down at the end of the corridor. Still, it was twice as nice as her building across Second Avenue.

Emma was still in her white shirt from work, short cutoff

jeans, showing a good deal of thigh. Bra-less, with the dark buds of her nipples clearly visible through the thin cotton. They weren't huge breasts—on the downside of average really, but they were firm and perky, and not one guy had ever complained.

The shirt was dry now, but from eight in the morning till quitting time every afternoon, it was saturated with sweat and chlorinated water from all the pools she cleaned. Her route was in the southwest part of town, big expensive houses where people paid a couple hundred a month for Emma Lee to scoop the leaves out and dump in the overpriced chemicals. The company supplied her with a yellow pickup, which they let her drive home, and all day she got to work out in the sun and fresh air and stand around in rich people's backyards, so all in all it wasn't a bad job, though it didn't pay but a dollar above minimum wage.

Always in the past when she'd come to Norman Franks's door, she'd made sure she was wearing a bra. Emma didn't like mixing business and sex, especially with a scary guy like Norman. But on this one occasion, she was going to make an exception. Perilous as it might be to get the wild ox excited, this was a situation that called for full deployment of Emma's weapons.

The last chain came undone and the door swung open.

"Hey, Norm. What's happening?"

He didn't blink, didn't move, as if it took all his concentration just to keep that heavy head upright.

"Look, I'm sorry to bother you, but I knew you'd be interested in this."

He'd seen her a hundred times before, but he still looked her up and down as if she were a stranger, starting with her muscular legs, working up the flare of her hips, lingering on the dark raisins puckering against the cotton, then taking in her wide mouth, her hair, which was scorched to bright blond by the sun. She had pale blue eyes that showed up well against her caramel skin. Jamaican mountain coffee with four shots of heavy whipping cream—that was her color. Emma's father had been a red-haired Irishman; her mother, a tall, elegant woman from the barrios of Trinidad.

Emma didn't look much like either of them. Abandoned on the doorstep by some passing gypsy—that's what Emma guessed, though her mother always denied it.

"It's some pretty amazing shit, Norman."

The big man made a face. Maybe he was interested; maybe he wasn't.

"I wouldn't bother you otherwise. Knowing how valuable your time is."

He turned and waved Emma into the apartment; then he shut the door and took a few moments to rebolt it. He wore an undershirt and green trousers. He was only five ten or so, but he was almost as wide as he was tall. Bull-chested. He was more than twice Emma's age, somewhere in his middle forties.

She hesitated a second, then followed as Norman Franks padded barefoot across the one big room to the bath. He picked up a can of shaving cream, shot out a dollop of foam, spread it on his cheeks, and picked up his razor.

He had olive skin and jet-black hair that he wore slicked straight back, and his eyes were so black and fierce, they looked like they belonged in a falcon. He had an extremely heavy beard and mats of hair on his upper back. His shoulders were wide as a doorway and his biceps were huge. Not the shapely muscles of bodybuilder types, but beefy, almost-swollen arms, the kind of mass Emma's daddy once had. Not good for the dexterity sports and not all that attractive to look at, but the kind of muscle you'd want if you needed to lift a freight car.

Though she'd been doing business with Norman for three years, this was the first time she'd been in the guy's apartment. Ordinarily, business was conducted in the hallway. Couple of words, hand over the merchandise, receive your cash, and get the hell out of there.

His place was a musty one-room efficiency with a little bathroom. On the wall at the head of his bed, a Confederate flag was mounted upside down, and on the opposite wall were a bunch of framed photographs and paintings. A big oil painting of Jesus with his hands folded in prayer and, beside it, a black-and-white photograph of Martin Luther King, Jr., another of Elvis, and Liberace and Robert Mitchum, a few other Hollywood types she didn't know. All the faces, including Jesus, had their eyes scissored out and others glued in. Whole wall was filled with photos like that. Four rows of five. Twenty photographs with transplanted eyes.

Next to the bed was a green leather couch, and across from it sat a television on a plastic milk carton. Norman slept on a king-size water bed with a black bedspread and headboard of walnut. Lined up neatly beside the TV, there were about half a dozen cardboard cases of vodka, and beside them was another stack of boxes full of Yamaha amplifiers. Common knowledge around the neighborhood: If it was still in the carton, Norman Franks would pay top dollar. Loose items—jewelry, coin collections, handguns—you might as well deal with the pawnshops. In addition to fencing, word on the street was that Norman did wet work, too. Downsizing with a capital *D*.

Emma's old man, Roy, used to do business with Norman before he died. He'd bring home a few women's shoe boxes or several purses from Burdines, where he worked as a janitor, and he'd go over to Norman's after supper and come home an hour later with a handful of green. Emma's mother was always bitching about how long it took to handle the transaction. Going on and on about Norman Franks like she had some personal vendetta against him.

"I like the guy, Evonne. He's somebody I can talk to," her father used to say.

"You want to talk to somebody, then you should attempt conversation with your wife and child, instead of developing a buddy-boy relationship with that man."

Same scene almost every time.

But that hadn't stopped her father. Norman was the only thing close to a friend her father'd had, only guy in the neighborhood didn't make cracks about a white guy marrying a black island woman. Rest of the neighbors giving him shitty looks every time he passed by.

When the old man died of stomach cancer three years before, Emma took over for him, started bringing Norman the loot she'd plundered from those ritzy neighborhoods where she worked. Bicycles, tools, boom boxes, all kinds of amazing shit those people just left sitting out in their yards or right inside their sliding glass doors. Time after time, he gave her better prices than she found anywhere on the street. But despite all the business she'd done with Norman, their relationship never budded beyond thirty seconds on the landing. Hand over the goods, wait for the cash, and go. Norman kept it brisk and brusque, no matter how Emma tried to charm him.

Norman didn't mingle with the neighbors, didn't shop at the local Quick Mart, or Liberty Liquors, Big Mary's Barbecue, didn't sit out on the stoop in the evening and drink beer like the rest of the men. It wasn't just that he was white. There were a couple of other Caucasians living on the block, and they all hung out with the brothers, more or less accepted in that society of outcasts. But Norman didn't socialize. Wouldn't even return a "yo, Norm" on the street. Just walked around in that lethal trance, people stepping out of his way like he was a freight train rolling mindlessly down the tracks.

Norman stopped shaving for a second and turned those dark eyes on Emma.

"So?"

"So I was coming home from work and I saw the Brinks thing going down and I stopped and watched. You heard about it, right?"

"I heard."

Norman rinsed away the last traces of shaving cream and patted his skin with a thick yellow towel. He looked at her again, a dark twinkle of interest.

"Well, when I was sitting there watching, a person walked up to the side of the armored truck and tapped on the window."

Norman uncapped his deodorant stick and rubbed the white stub against his hairy pits.

"A few seconds later out came two white sacks. And the person who took them lugged them away."

Norman looked at himself in the mirror, recapped his deodorant, and set it down on the lavatory counter. He continued to look at himself for several moments, his chest rising and falling. Then he reached out and ran some more water and scooped up a double handful. He splashed it on his face and rubbed it in, then used the towel to pat himself dry again.

He shook out a couple of shots of Old Spice and rubbed it into his cheeks, then slicked the remains against his thick black hair.

He nodded at his reflection, a strained smile rearranging his face briefly, then disappearing into the gloominess of his normal expression.

Emma moved away from the doorway. The big man was just standing there, his face slack, staring into the mirror.

"No one else saw this?"

"I don't think so, no. Everybody was so busy in all the helter-skelter, going after the money."

"Why're you here?"

"I thought you might be interested. Like in an extracurricular sense."

"What's that mean?"

"Like moonlighting, a second job. There's this money floating around out there. You and me, if we act fast, maybe we could snatch it from the snatchers."

"You tell anyone else?"

"No."

"Male or female?"

"Huh?"

"Person with the money."

"Oh, that. Well, I'm not sure. It could've been a man or a woman. Person was wearing a raincoat, one of those London Fog types, and underneath he had on a hooded sweatshirt, and the hood was up and he had on sunglasses."

Emma took a breath of air heavy with Old Spice.

"Two bags?"

"Two, yes."

"Where'd he go?"

"To a car parked beneath the overpass. A blue Honda Accord. It had rust damage on the rear panel and dark windows."

"You followed?"

"For a little while, but then I lost it in traffic."

"You see the plate?"

"Yeah, I noticed it."

Norman drew his shoulders back a fraction. Still frowning at his features in the mirror, as if thirty years later he still wasn't used to how ugly he was.

"In fact, I remember the plate number. I remember it perfectly. I got it stored away in here." Emma Lee tapped the side of her head.

"Give it to me."

"Whoa, there, Nellie. Not so fast."

Emma stepped away from the doorway. She looked back at the living room, the Confederate flag, the pictures of Jesus and Martin Luther King, Jr., Marlon Brando, the guy who played Archie Bunker on TV, and one of Marilyn Monroe. She noticed a large hunting knife, its shiny blade stuck into the back of the apartment door. His quick-strike defense system.

"We need to talk a little first. Establish a rapport. If we're going to be partners, we should know about each other."

When she turned back, Norman was standing in front of her. His lips were thick, and Emma could see from so close-up that he'd missed a couple of places on his neck, two dark patches of stubble. Below his collar line, there was a neat circle of bushy hair where he stopped shaving, then that thick shadow of beard rising up almost to his eyes. The eyes seemed uninhabited most of the time, like a man who'd had one too many lobotomies.

"Partners?" Norman said.

Emma stepped out of range of the Old Spice.

"Maybe I should leave," she said. "Go down to the police station, report what I saw. That's what a model citizen would do."

Emma pulled a coil of hair off her cheek. She did the thing with her left eye she'd learned to do. Not a wink really—a little flicker that came and went so quickly, nobody could be sure if she'd flirted with them or not. It was something her mother had mastered, a trick of the streets, and for years Emma practiced it in the mirror. So far, she'd tried it out in real life a few dozen times and it worked in every instance. Like throwing bloody meat into the shark tank.

Norman swallowed, his big Adam's apple bobbing, but that was the extent of his reaction.

Emma let a small smile steal across her lips and said, "I was thinking about why there was no mention on the TV news of reward money, and I think it's 'cause people at Brinks don't know they been robbed. They know they had a truck in an accident and they know their money was pilfered by a bunch of poor folks. But they don't know they were the victims of a felonious robbery."

Norman swallowed again and turned back to the mirror.

"I'm listening."

"Why'd you cut the eyes out of those photographs, doctor them up like that? You a weirdo of some kind I should know about?"

Norman swiveled his head slightly and stared at Emma. Then he lifted his eyes and peered over at the photos.

"I don't know."

"Maybe you were thinking they'd be better off if they could see out of each other's eyes. They'd benefit from the multiple viewpoints."

"I was drunk."

"Martin Luther King could have one of Liberace's eyes, one of Marilyn's. Like that, all of them getting to see a part of the world they never would otherwise."

He didn't reply, just kept staring at his handiwork.

Emma took a half step to her right and looked back across the bedroom.

"You got a spooky side to you, Norman. You got eerie dimensions."

"What's the plate number?"

"I love it," Emma said, "A money truck breaks open; all our good neighbors are scrambling and grabbing and celebrating. A pot of gold fell out of the sky and, by God, they're going to get what they can. They stand right up and look in the TV cameras and they grin and say what luck it is that truck busted open.

"Because if that same goddamn thing happened out in the suburbs where I clean swimming pools, well, those fine people would never in a million years think of getting down on their hands and knees to scrape up dollar bills and nickels. No sir, they'd call up their lawyers, have them do it for them."

Norman's lip twitched, like he was trying to remember how to smile.

"You don't talk very much, do you, Norman? I mean, I've noticed that about you. You're very laconic and terse."

Norman just looked at her, face blank.

"I take it that you're one of those less-is-more kind of guys. Max out at four, five words. Never uttered a compound sentence in your life, never used a subordinate clause or a participial phrase. Like with that Hemingway guy in school, those fucking hard-assed stories of his. All his people talk like you, Norman. Three, four words are all they can manage at one time, like every goddamn syllable is a kidney stone they're trying to pass.

"Well, hey, that's fine. That's okay. I talk enough for two people anyway. So don't worry—that's not going to annoy me or anything. I can deal with it just fine. Maybe I should try that sometime, an experiment, ration myself to three, four words a sentence, see if I could get by for a day or two."

Norman was silent, looking at her as if she were making him sleepy.

"Know what has eighteen knees and white blood?"

"White blood?"

"Yeah, eighteen knees and white blood. It's a riddle."

"I don't know."

"You just going to give up? Not even hazard a guess? Oh, come on, Norman. Think. Imagine. Sounds like some kind of space creature, doesn't it? Eighteen knees and white blood."

"Space creature?"

"Wrong," she said. "Not a space creature. One of these."

She raised the flap on her shirt pocket and fished the cockroach out by the green thread she'd glued to its carapace, one end knotted to the top button of her shirt—its leash.

"Norman Franks, I'd like you to meet Amy. I call her that. It's how my name would sound if you spelled it backward. Not that I couldn't have come up with another name. I mean, I'm plenty creative enough to invent a better name than that, but it just seemed appropriate. Emma the human, Amy the roach."

While it waved its long antennae, Emma lowered it by the thread to the black spread covering Norman's water bed and let it roam over the folds. Right away, Amy zipped into a crevice beneath the pillow and Emma had to reel her out before she burrowed in too deep.

"You got any problem with roaches, Norman?"

He looked at her for a moment, his eyes so vacant that he might be made of wax.

"Lots of people have biases against them. But that's just because they're uneducated about the finer points of cockroaches. The more you know about them, Norman, more you respect them. Blattida, that's their taxonomic classification; genus and species *Periplaneta americana*. American cockroach. They've been thriving on earth around four hundred million years and they'll probably be here four hundred million years after we're gone.

"The entomologists call them 'subsocial,' which means they're loners. Not like termites or ants or bees with all their caste systems, workers and drones and soldiers and all that. Subsocial is supposed to be bad, like it's some kind of lower evolutionary form. But we know better than that, Norman, don't we?

"'Cause you and me, we're subsocial omnivorous scavengers

ourselves. We're loners; we eat what we have to so we can survive. Doesn't matter what it is. We're the bug people, living in dark cracks. We'll eat the paint if we have to, chew the paste on the wallpaper. We're out of sight, only come out at night. People look at us and go '*Ugh*' and try to crush us underfoot, but we're too quick for them. We scurry off, carry off our crumbs with us. We know about that, don't we, Norman? We're the baddest fucking cockroaches in all of Miami."

She dangled Amy over her open pocket and lowered her back inside, then buttoned the flap.

Norman Franks stared at her, then let his gaze drop to her breasts. Saliva crackled as he opened his mouth to breathe. When he spoke, his voice was full of the hot sludge of his agitation.

"How big were they?"

"How big were what?"

"The money bags?"

"What? You don't have any response to my cockroach speech? I thought I was pretty eloquent. You're just going to ignore that? Subsocial. Omnivorous scavengers. The metaphorical connections I was making. Jesus."

"How big were they?"

"Okay, okay," Emma said. "The bags were big. Very big. Huge. Stuffed tight. This big."

Emma spread her arms out wide enough to embrace a potato sack.

"Good," said Norman. "Big is good."

Emma had to laugh.

"Yeah," she said. "Big is very good. In this case, I think it's safe to say, big is fucking great.

NINE

From the one working pay phone in the emergency room, Alexandra called in to work and got Sylvia Rigali, one of the senior administrators. They'd seen the news and had called somebody to take Alexandra's shift that night. Everybody was worried about how Stan was doing.

Alex told her Stan was going to be fine and thanked her for being concerned.

"Something else, Sylvia."

"Yeah?"

"Anybody we know work that scene?"

"Matter of fact, your buddy Dan Romano was driving past, coming into work. He was one of the first ones who called it in."

"He say anything about it?"

"Like what?"

"Anything strange. About the accident, how it happened."

Sylvia paused a moment, then said, "The whole thing was strange, Alex. Start to finish. Money everywhere. People going nuts. A riot."

"Yeah, I saw that part on TV. But I mean the technicals. The crash itself, skid marks, how fast the truck was going. Those things."

"It was pretty straightforward. Dan didn't say anything looked strange. Why? You got something we should know about?"

"No," she said. "I'm just in shock. Letting my imagination race. Forget I mentioned it."

"Forgotten," Sylvia said. There was a voice in the background and Sylvia told Alex to hold on. When she came back, she said, "That was Shonberger. He said to take the rest of the week off if you need it. We'll get by. You got a ton of vacation time stored up."

"Tell him thanks, Sylvia. I appreciate it. I'll check in tomorrow, let you know how it's going with Stan. I don't think I'll need the whole week, but maybe a day or two till things settle down."

Next, she called Gabriella's cell phone. Her oldest and dearest friend.

Their high school friendship had deepened when they found themselves in several of the same courses at the local state university. Even in high school, Gabbie had known she wanted to be the first woman governor of Florida. And she'd worked tirelessly in that direction for the last fifteen years. But Alex knew two Gabriellas, the one who showed up in front of the TV cameras, the tough, outspoken politician, defender of the disenfranchised, a woman willing to take on unpopular crusades even if they hurt her at the polls, and the other Gabbie, a vulnerable, sensitive woman driven by a desolate childhood, an alcoholic father, a mother crippled by depression.

"I knew you'd see it on TV and be worried," Alexandra said.

"How bad is it? Will he walk again?"

"Oh, it's not that bad. Broken leg," Alex told her. "Supposed to be up and around before the end of the week. Crutches, that's all."

There was a roar in the background on Gabriella's end. It lasted twenty or thirty seconds.

"What the hell is that?"

"This new place," Gabriella said. "I'm in the flight path of Miami International. It's like that all day, every few minutes. It was the only house I could find on such short notice."

They waited till another jet roared away.

"How about Lawton? You want me to pick him up, bring him over here for a few days? I can kick Hugo and Felix out of their room."

She said, "No, but thanks."

A young black man in jeans and a torn T-shirt came over to the pay phone and stared at Alex and jingled some coins in his fist.

"Is everything okay with you, Gabbie? You sound terrible."

While another jet took off over Gabriella's house, Alexandra looked past the black man. Her dad was immersed in one of the Hollywood tabloid shows, a handsome young actor smiling, jabbering on about his new movie. A security guard stood nearby, and the two of them seemed to be sharing jokes.

"I hear it in your voice, Gabbie. Something's wrong. Are you safe?"

Alex heard her draw a long breath.

"Damn it, Alex. A car's been driving up and down the street all day, dark windows, going very slowly. I think they found me again."

Until early last month, Gabriella Hernandez had been running fifteen percentage points ahead of the other candidate for Miami mayor. Then a photograph of her surfaced, a snapshot taken a year earlier on a trade mission to Cuba. The photo caught her in the act of giving the island dictator a kiss on the cheek. The *Herald* put the photograph on the front page, and all the TV stations led with it, too. Gabriella claimed it was just a diplomatic air kiss of greeting. But on the evening news, one of the TV stations used computer-enhanced graphics to show that Gabriella Hernandez's lips indeed had come into actual contact with the tyrant's bushy beard. Cuban exile leaders were enraged, calling the kiss an act of treason and demanding her immediate withdrawal from public life. Later that night, despite a police car parked down the block from her house, bullets blasted out Gabriella's front windows.

After her campaign headquarters were firebombed and she endured a week of death threats, she withdrew from the election. But the fanatics kept hounding her, and in the next month she changed residences twice more, and now she was in hiding. Not even her ex-husband knew where she was.

"I gotta make a fucking call."

The young man was leaning in close. He had a bandage across his right cheek and a halo of marijuana clung to his clothes.

"When I'm finished." Alex turned her back on him.

"I could go down there right now," Gabriella said. "Bring your dad back here. Say the word."

The surgeon Alexandra had spoken with earlier was standing out in the middle of the waiting room, scanning the area.

Alex sighed and waved over at the doctor, catching his eye.

"Look, Gabbie, I've got to run. I'll call you later tonight."

"If you need the name of an attorney, Alex, I know a few excellent ones."

"Why would I need an attorney?"

"To sue Stan's company, of course. Good God, Alex, the TV people are saying the tires on the truck were bald. It wasn't Stan's fault there was an accident."

Alex felt the sudden dampness on her leg and swung around. The tall man had his penis out and was pissing on her jeans.

"Gabbie, I'll call you later."

She clapped the phone down and, swiveling quickly, shot out her right hand, seized the black man's left wrist, gripped his thumb, bent it hard against the joint, and twisted. As the man gasped, she lowered her shoulder into his chest and slammed him up against the wall, got her left forearm against his throat.

Through watery eyes, the man stared at his paralyzed hand.

"Now reach down with your free hand and put your pathetic dick back in your pants."

The man gasped.

"You're fucking killing me. I can't breathe."

"Do it. Put that thing away before I tear it off."

She backed off the pressure slightly. He took a raspy breath and managed to snake his hand down to his zipper and put himself right.

"Okay, okay, you can let go."

From across the lobby, the security guard came jogging over. Alexandra wrenched the young man away from the wall. Something in his wrist popped and he yelped.

Stepping in, the security guard got a hammerlock on the man's free arm. Alex let go and moved away.

"You want me to call one of the cops outside, lady?"

Alex looked down at the spreading darkness on her jeans.

"It's okay," she said. "I'll survive."

"She broke my fucking thumb, man. Arrest that bitch."

Alexandra summoned a pleasant smile, turned it on the man.

"You're free to use the phone now, sir."

The man leaned against the wall and rolled his eyes up to the ceiling. Apparently, he'd lost his urge to communicate.

When she got back to her father, Dr. Satawana was sitting in the chair beside him, the doctor mopping his face with a handkerchief. He was in his blue scrubs. He couldn't have been more than thirty, but there was a lot of gray in his hair.

"Stan's been hurt," Lawton said. "I saw it on the television."

"He's going to be fine, Mrs. Rafferty," the doctor said. "He's a very strong man. Very fit. And that helped a great deal."

"Stan plays football," her dad said. "Defensive end. He was MVP for Ohio State. Or maybe it was Florida. I'm not sure."

"Can I seem him now?" Alex asked.

"They're moving him to the west wing, room three twelve. Give him an hour to wake up. He'll still be groggy, though."

The doctor smiled, and as he was about to say something else, his name boomed from the overhead speakers. Wanted immediately in ICU. He rose, patted Alex on the shoulder, gave her an exhausted smile, and left.

While Lawton dozed, Alexandra settled back in the red plastic chair and watched as the ambulances arrived every few minutes, causing a momentary stir as the next victim and the family members swarmed into the room. Several children were playing tag, running around the perimeter of the room, squealing. There was a teenage girl alone on a seat two rows away, cradling her pregnant belly and singing a lullaby. Up and down the rows, a young black man in a white uniform swished his mop, rapping aloud to the music in his headset.

Alex nudged her father and Lawton jerked awake and looked around at the room.

"Was I snoring?"

"No, Dad. We need to go."

"You used to wake me when I snored, put a hand on me until I woke, and then I'd lie there and try to stay awake until you went back to sleep, so I wouldn't bother you again. But sometimes I couldn't do it and I'd go right back to snoring and you'd have to wake me again."

"That was Mother, not me."

"Mother?"

"Yes, your wife. Grace."

"Has Grace been hurt? Is she in the hospital?" He was staring around at the noisy waiting room.

"No, it was Stan. Stan was in an accident."

"Stan, yeah, sure. I saw him on television. He robbed an armored truck."

"It was an accident, Dad. His truck ran off the highway and Stan was injured. Now we're going up to his room, duck in and see if he's awake; then we're going home."

"Good," her father said, standing up. "I need my beauty rest."

Outside in the emergency driveway, the full moon rustled behind the fronds of a royal palm. In the grass beneath the flagpole, a half dozen egrets poked listlessly for beetles. The October air was balmy and rich, carrying the aroma of fermented fruits and the sugary vapors of jasmine, that alluring musk of sexual promise.

It was a night in this same season eleven years before that Stan Rafferty had bestowed his first fumbling kiss on her eager lips. And every October since, catching that same tropical scent in the air, Alexandra found herself replaying those awkward hours with the muscular football star, the swoon, the aching desperation she'd felt. He was the first and only man she'd allowed to touch her body. A man she'd once believed was as strong and protective as her father.

Out in the hospital parking lot, it took her a moment to get her bearings, but finally she spotted the west wing, and Alex led Lawton over to the building, marched past the nurses' station, and took an elevator to the third floor.

"You're not going to lock me away in this place, are you? I don't want to stay here. Their cheese crackers are stale. And it stinks around here. Smells as bad as a hospital."

Alex was counting down the rooms to 312 when a young blond woman backed out a nearby doorway, kissed her fingertips, and blew the kiss into the room. As she turned to leave, she caught sight of Alex, swung around, and rushed off down the hall in the opposite direction. She had a schoolgirl freshness, late teens, early twenties, with the elastic walk of a woman who'd had considerable practice being watched. Alex felt a low, hollow space open inside her. A cold clamor in her heart.

Two steps more and she could see that the door the young woman had exited was 312.

For a moment, she hesitated outside the room, staring after the retreating figure; then she budged the door open and peered inside. It was a single room. Stan was propped up against pillows, his eyes closed.

Alex eased the door shut.

"Where now?"

She took a long breath and blew it out, then led her father by the arm down the hallway to the gray doors that were still rocking from the young woman's passage. There was an elevator beyond them and the illuminated numbers were counting down, until they stopped at the basement level.

"Come on, Dad, we need to hurry."

They took the stairs and, mercifully, her father didn't lag, didn't question. He seemed thrilled to be leaving the building so quickly. Alex chided herself for such impulsive behavior. Racing after some young woman she'd barely glimpsed coming out of her husband's room. It was lunacy. The woman had probably stepped into the room mistakenly and no doubt had ducked away in embarrassment, the little finger kiss only a gesture of apology.

At the bottom of the steps, she paused, debating the silliness of this.

"You forget where you parked the car?"

"No, I remember where it is."

"Well, what're you waiting for? Let's go. I'm so hungry, I could eat a house. Or a horse. Which is it? House or horse?"

"Horse."

"Doesn't make sense. If you were hungry, you'd rather have the biggest thing around. A house is much bigger than a horse. Am I right?"

"You're right."

"But then, I guess it would be hard to eat a whole house, no matter how hungry you were. Unless you were a termite."

As Alex pushed open the basement door, she heard a nearby car engine turn over and race to life. Spotting the exit arrows pointing to her left, she looped her arm into her father's and headed that way.

While Lawton continued to brood over the difficulty of eating a house, Alex heard the car approaching behind them. With the barest turn of her head, she saw it was a blue Honda Accord, half a dozen years old, with a rusted circle missing from the left-rear panel. The windows were tinted dark, and in the weak light of the parking garage, Alex couldn't tell who was driving.

Tugging her father's arm, she angled to the right and timed their pace so she and her dad passed by a dozen feet away as the Honda halted at the cashier's booth. The driver's window lowered and, yes, it was the same young blond woman. Alexandra turned away and steered her father behind the car and read its plate. ALP 290.

"Are we lost?"

"No," she said. "We're not lost."

"Stan's a thief," her father said. "A killer, too. You're lucky he's hurt, because now you can run away while he's laid up. It's a damn convenient circumstance, if you ask me."

"We're going home now, Dad. We'll see Stan in the morning."

"I missed my supper entirely," he said as they climbed the steps back up to the street level. I'm about to die of hunger. In which case, I could eat a hearse."

She stopped and peered at him. His face was blank, and she was about to turn back to the stairs, when a smile surfaced.

"It's a joke," he said. "Play on words. Horse, house, hearse. About to die of hunger. Die, hearse."

She shook her head, frowned.

"Now you're mad at me," he said. "You're going to blow a casket."

She chuckled.

"You can be really funny sometimes. Your know that, Dad?"

"I know. I've always been funny. I was born funny."

It was nearly midnight. The one bulb he allowed her glowed dimly in the hallway. He was reclining on the plaid couch with the 16-gauge needle stuck deep in the *ante cubital fossa*, and into the large artery in his left arm. Tubing ran down to the pouch that lay on the bare floor. Around 300 ccs had already dripped into the clear plastic bag. Another three or four minutes and it would be full.

She stood in the doorway, gripping the fresh quart of vodka by the throat, a couple of good swallows gone already. When she inched closer, he could see the woozy sway in her step.

"You killed another girl, didn't you?"

"That's right. You want to hear about it? The gory details."

"No."

"This one was very sad."

"Stop it. I don't want to hear."

"When I entered her, she started weeping like a child. Poor little girl, bawling there on the floor of her nice rented apartment. Pretending to be upset, to be scared, but the truth was in her eyes. They try to fool you with their tears, with their pleading, but I can see through the surface. Behind the sobbing, I saw her rage. I saw her hatred, her murderous desire."

"No more."

"Oh, come on. You love it, Mother. Your know you do. I'm your window on the world. I'm your personal soap opera."

She blinked at him, trying to bring her eyes into focus.

"That blood you're taking, it's the blood you leave behind."

"Yes, yes. That's good. Very good, Mom. I leave it behind at the crime scene. Why do I do that, Mom? Do you remember what I told you?"

"You're the Bloody Rapist. You've killed five girls."

"Oh, good for you. A regular Miss Marple. You're not as dotty as you pretend."

"You're going to burn for eternity. You're going straight to hell."

"Well, it'll be a short trip, then, won't it? Practically around the corner from this place."

There were bars on the window of his mother's living room, bars on every window in the tiny house. Those steel rods cost more than he'd paid for the whole place. Not exactly prime Miami real estate, with a tumbling-down crack house on one side, scabby men and women coming every hour of the day and night. It was over there that he'd learned the needle techniques. Standing around in that foul-smelling house with the IV drug users and the crack smokers, he'd studied their crude tourniquets, the way they thumped the vein to make it rise. The careful insertion of sharpened steel into the fragile vein.

On the other side of his mother's house was an abandoned gray warehouse. A rat factory. Hundreds of them scrambling in and out of the broken windows. Her wood cottage was in the middle of the city, yet as isolated as if it were on the moon. It had oak floors and thick plaster walls and had been a pioneer house, the last of its kind along the Miami River. He could probably apply to the Historical League, request a brass plaque for the front door. Give the house a fancy name of some kind. Alma Mater.

"Have another swig, Mom. It's so comforting, so warm in your gut."

She trembled in the doorway, a passing shiver on this warm Miami evening. She was wearing her ragged housedress. It was blue, with yellow cornflowers, and in the last few months it had turned to shreds around her knees.

He allowed her to keep that one piece of clothing only because he didn't want to see her naked bones whenever he came for a visit. Her hair was a yellowed white, and in the last few months it had clumped into greasy dreadlocks around her face. She hadn't bathed in months. Each week, he brought her a case of Alpo lamb and rice in the can, and he opened the dog food himself and took the lids away. Couldn't have her slashing her wrist with the ragged edge.

As far as he could manage, the house was suicide-proof. One mattress, no sheets. No electrical cords. Of course, she could always drown herself in the toilet. Or break out a pane of glass and slit her own throat. But she was in such an alcoholic fog these days, he doubted she could hold a single thought long enough to execute any kind of plan.

"Why do you do these things?"

"Do what things, Mom?"

Her tongue slid between her lips and dabbed at the corners of her mouth.

"Kill these girls. Keep me prisoner. Why do you do it?"

"Oh, you're not a prisoner, sweetie. You're free to go at any time. Just say the word and I'll unlock the front door and you can waltz off to whatever glorious destination you choose. Wander the neighborhood, be a bag lady under the interstate, take a jet to Tahiti, anything my mother wants. Nothing's too good for you, kind lady."

With a quiet moan, she closed her eyes, hefted the bottle up to her lips, and bubbled down a hit. She gasped, then turned and wandered back into the dark house. Probably headed to the west window to stare out at the drug house. Her scenic vista.

When the blood bag was filled, he inched the needle free, then swabbed his arm with the alcohol-soaked cotton ball and dropped it on the dirty floor. He pinched the end of the tubing and clamped it with a metal grommet. Then he carried the plastic pouch to the padlocked storeroom at the rear of the house. He unlocked the door, picked his way across the dark room and swung open the small Frigidaire, and slipped the pouch onto the top shelf beside the others.

For a moment in the weak refrigerator light, he stared at the bladders of blood. His own vital fluid, loaded with the dark and secret messages of his ancestors, notes dashed off centuries ago, placed in bottles and set adrift in a sea of plasma, to ride the currents for generations, until finally they washed ashore at his feet. And one by one, he uncorked them, read their telegraphic sentences, the sum total of their ancient wisdom, their faint and futile calls for help, their mad directives, their gibberish. It was his inheritance, his only legacy, this rich and viscous fluid.

He stared at the four glowing sacks of blood.

Five down. Four to go.

TEN

"She's looking for a license number, Suzie. She's my daughter and she wants to find the address of the person driving this vehicle."

Her dad passed a slip of paper across the counter to the stout woman. Lawton Collins, bless his heart, was having a good day. As if he were picking up Alexandra's wobbling vibes and had determined that he must compensate, hold himself together, sensing at some animal level that if one of them didn't stay somewhat sane, both of them might soon be swirling down the drain together. Some natural law of symbiotic dysfunction—a craziness of lesser intensity temporarily yielding to the greater one.

Alexandra could have pulled the name and address of the plate owner from one of the computers upstairs in her own office, but she didn't want to risk having one of her snoopy friends lean over her shoulder, start asking questions. And anyway, her dad had assured her that Suzie Cuevas owed him sufficient favors to make this a simple and quick operation.

Suzie looked up from her computer and drew on her unfiltered cigarette. A large red sign on the wall behind her claimed CLEAN AIR BUILDING, but there was an ashtray spilling over with butts on the desk beside her.

Suzie was a failed redhead. Maybe it had been her natural shade a half century earlier, but now, apparently, so many of her proteins had leached away that her hair had a hard metallic tint. She was peering up at them through heavy black horn-rimmed glasses that looked like they'd been plucked off a dime-store rack about twenty years ago, $1.99, with glass thick enough to deflect bullets.

"You're retired, I believe, Lieutenant Collins. No longer enjoy the privileges and rights to departmental services and facilities."

"Thirty years, Suzie. Thirty long years on the streets."

"I seem to recall I attended your retirement banquet. Cheez Doodles and onion dip. Worst party food I've ever seen—even for cops it was terrible. Rap music on the stereo. Disgusting."

"I'm a man of humble tastes, Suzie."

"I heard you've been sick."

"Had a few problems," Lawton said. "Nothing a license-plate check won't cure."

"I can't do it. Not legal. Got to do a ton of paperwork on any Motor Vehicles request."

"Well, we wouldn't want you to participate in anything you'd feel guilty about later. You should certainly let your heart guide your decision."

Alexandra watched the woman stare at her father. She'd seen him work on people before, noodle the truth out of them, nudge them ever so slightly this way and that until he had them where it suited him. Her mother had called him "a master manipulator, a psychological strategist." Lawton claimed not to know what the hell she was talking about. He just presented his case as well as he could, put it up against the reasoning of his adversary. May the best case win.

Suzie tapped her eraser against her desktop.

The hallway behind them bustled with police officers and secretaries and the sloppily dressed prosecuting attorneys. Alex kept her face turned away from the stream of people. More than half she knew by first name.

"What do you want it for? Somebody cut you off in traffic, so you going to show up at their front door, slap them silly?"

"No, not a traffic beef," Lawton said. "We wouldn't waste your time, Suzie, with anything so trivial."

"Marital dispute? Trying to track down the other woman?"

"All right, goddamn it," Alex said. "Yes, that's it. The other woman. I need to talk to her, find out what's going on. Now, are you going to do it, Suzie, or should we go?"

As she peered up at Alexandra, she sucked in her cheeks, working on her cigarette like it was a straw stuck into the thickest chocolate shake ever concocted. She drew the smoke deep, then let it out with raspy delight. Blue gas filled the air between them.

"Pretty woman like you. Why would your husband cheat?"

Lawton settled his elbows on Suzie's countertop and leaned forward, smiling with beatific charm.

"We've seen it happen, Suze, haven't we?" Lawton said. "Around these very halls, you and me, seen this same sad drama played out countless times. Pretty wife, sweet and kind and hard-working, a hundred percent supportive, excellent cook. Husband gets a twitch in his loins, and next thing you know, he's wallowing in the trough of adultery. There's just no accounting for it. And no easing its pain for the wife. The only cure for a woman so rudely mistreated is to have all the information she can before tearing off the nuts of her offender."

As she eyed Lawton, Suzie's lips twitched on the edge of a smile. A woman who'd been sweet-talked so much, she would accept nothing less than a colossal dose of indulgence before performing even the most perfunctory aspects of her job.

"You're an old rogue, Lawton Collins. One crafty, silver-tongued coot. But I really shouldn't, your being retired and all."

Alex edged in front of her father. She lifted her right hand above the counter and smacked it down hard. Suzie's eyes enlarged behind the thick lenses.

"Goddamn it, Suzie. Type in the number and give us the name. No more bullshit."

Suzie Cuevas licked her red lips and measured Alexandra for a long moment. Then her puckered mouth relaxed into a sweet smile, as if Alex's tantrum was exactly what she'd been trying to evoke all along.

She used the eraser of her pencil to poke the six keys and hit the enter button. Alex glanced over at her father. His eyes were crawling up the far wall in what had become a familiar gesture of disengagement, losing his grip on the moment. He'd worn himself out on her behalf and now was slipping off again into the confusion of his endless daydream.

Suzie Cuevas's cough was a phlegmy rattle in her throat. When she'd recovered sufficient breath, she pointed at the screen, ran her finger along the lines of data, and spoke without looking up.

"Name is Jennifer McDougal, lives at two seven oh nine Leafy Way in Coconut Grove. Glitzy part of town. Maybe that's what's going on—a classy dame, money's the attraction."

"When I used to burn leaves," Lawton said, "they smelled so good, I could barely stand it. Gold and red and orange, crackling. Sugar maple and oak and birch. It's the sweetest odor there is."

Alex put her arm around her father's shoulders.

"Burning leaves?" Suzie said.

"You shouldn't ever hide in the piles. I tried it a few times, but Mother comes along with a sharp stick, pokes it hard. And I always get those little particles of leaves in my shirt, my underwear. Itches like crazy later on."

"Is he okay? Suzie said.

"He's fine," said Alex. "Just fine. Thank you, Suzie. Thanks very much for your help."

Alexandra took Bayshore Drive to the Grove, the back way,

slower, a circuitous and shady route. She wanted time to think, to build a picture in her head, what she was going to do at 2709 Leafy Way. Middle of the day. Sunny and clear. Temperature in the eighties. She should be at Jackson Memorial, holding Stan's hand. Comforting him, fulfilling her wifely duties. She hadn't even been to see him yet, her injured husband.

Maybe at Leafy Way she'd knock on the door, stand there with Lawton at her side, and the three of them could discuss the odor of burning leaves in Ohio earlier in the century. Or maybe she should simply sucker punch the blond girl, then say something cruel: "I'm the wife, you slut."

Her face was hot. Brain waves dancing, a hard swelling in her throat, like a fist had tightened around her air passages. The windshield with a red tinge, as if it were filmed with blood. She and Stan had been drifting away from the shores of their marriage for so many years now, it surprised her to feel the blood roaring in her ears at the possibility of his unfaithfulness.

"I told you," her father said. "I told you about Stan, what he was up to. But you wouldn't listen to me."

Alex slowed for a light across from Mercy Hospital.

"I should've shot him when I had the chance," Lawton said. "Aren't we going to Harbor House today? I'm supposed to get a box of chocolate chip cookies. Elaine Dillashaw is baking them for me. My favorite. Chocolate chips with coconut and raisins. She throws the whole kit and caboodle in there, maybe even macadamia nuts if I've been good. I should go over there now to Harbor House and get my cookies. Where are we going?"

"We're going to see someone. A friend of Stan's."

"His girlfriend?"

"It looks that way."

"But he's married. Stan's married. I know. He tied the knot with my daughter at St. Jude's. There was a seagull in the church that day. It meant something. We knew at the time, but we forgot. What does a seagull mean when it comes into a church, flies around the ceiling? It can't be a sign of anything good, that's for sure."

Doped up on his morning ration of Tylenol and codeine, Stan stared at the blank wall across from him and waited for sleep to pull the covers over his head. In his narcotic stupor, he was imagining the life of Edward W. Green, born in 1833, the first bank robber in America. Thirty years old, Eddie Green was the postmaster of his little town just down the pike from Boston. Crippled as a youth, Eddie grew into a dark and twisted man, who began to drink heavily, then got himself into serious debt.

A couple of weeks before Christmas in 1863, Eddie walked into the local bank and saw that only the seventeen-year-old son of the bank president was on duty. A shitstorm broke out in Eddie's head. He trotted home, got a handgun, and trotted back to the bank. He rushed in, shot the kid twice in the face, grabbed up five thousand dollars in cash, and bolted. A couple of days went by before the dumb shit ran afoul of Stan Rafferty's first principle. He began spending cash extravagantly, somehow thinking no one would notice in that tiny village.

But police came to his door, questioned him. Eddie promptly confessed, and he was executed a month later. Swift, swift, swift.

Something about that case had always clung to Stan's memory. The spontaneity of it. A quick, brutal act. Down and dirty, no plan, no blueprint. Bam, bam, run home and count the cash. Of course, nothing about the aftermath was appealing. The police nab him, ask him some questions; he breaks down. Bing, bing, bing. A simple world back then, one-dimensional. The early Newtonian universe of crime. Comfy, cozy. Nothing like the way it was now. Video cameras, DNA testing, space-age satellite imaging. Some CIA wonk with access to film showing every single goddamn thing happening out on the face of the earth. They could run back the film, see which lane that red Mustang was in, calculate how fast it was going, the exact careening path the

Brinks truck took as it veered down the off-ramp. That is, if they cared to do all that, were willing to spend the money.

Big Brother up there, eye in the sky, everyone armed with video cameras, looking to be the next one-night hero, catch the cops thrashing another poor dumb speeder, spark another go-round of riots. These days, the world was a thousand times more challenging for crooks than it had been for Eddie Green.

Poor twisted, stupid, impulsive Eddie, first bank robber in America, the first rash fuckup. Now that Stan himself was a criminal, he could put himself there with Eddie—doing the crime, no plan, just flat-out panic and drunken urge, stumbling in, shooting, grabbing up the greenbacks, then home, waiting a day, sweating, drinking up every drop of liquor in the house, maybe another day, sobering up, finally going out to the store, picking out the most expensive sour mash, flashing some bills, some gold coins, on purpose maybe, flaunting a little. Feeling big and free for the first time in his life.

In the last century, Eddie Green's criminal career had lasted a week, but it wouldn't last a millisecond these days. Big Brother watching, seeing him trot home, trot back, seeing him walk inside, come hauling ass back out a few minutes later. All there on nice clear tape.

Stan looked over at the blank wall, the dead TV screen. Thinking of Eddie, the first bank robber in American history, feeling the codeine grapple with his brain, his blood warm and sluggish, as if rice pudding were clogging his veins. The pillow cool against his head. Thinking of Eddie Green. Poor dumb, unlucky bastard, at least he got half of it right—the chaos part. Rush in, kill, grab, go. It was the aftermath that got Eddie. The aftermath, which was the trickiest, most dangerous part of any crime.

And then it struck him, a thought he hadn't considered till that moment as he slid away into the gray broth of his nap: Now that Stan Rafferty had committed his crime, he was going to be stuck in that one place the rest of his goddamn life—the aftermath.

ELEVEN

Jennifer McDougal's small white cottage at 2709 Leafy Way was wedged between two Coconut Grove mansions. To the west was a massive high-tech structure with severe angles, skylights, buttresses, heavy concrete archways, and dozens of columns holding up a grape trellis. A neon flamingo was lit up beside the massive front doors and neon numerals flickered beneath it. On the east side of the cottage was a monstrous Mediterranean standard issue with a porte cochere that was as big as the Raffertys' entire house. The roof was a red barrel tile, the walls white stucco, and several third-floor balconies looked down on the oaks and banyans and the rusty roof of the humble pioneer house next door.

"I used to live in that place," Lawton said, staring at the white frame bungalow.

"No, you didn't, Dad."

"One just like it. We spent August there. You don't remember?"

"Yes," she said. "I remember. But it was bigger and it was yellow and it was a long way from here."

"Yellow, yeah. 'Mellow yellow,' we called it. We had fun that summer, didn't we? We had a grand time."

"Yes," she said. "Yes, we did."

Slowing the car to a crawl, Alexandra stared across at the small white house. The broken asphalt pad that took up most of the front yard was empty, but she continued on, driving to the end of the cul-de-sac. The rest of the houses on the short street were hidden behind dense jungles of palms and bougainvillea and the viny native vegetation that was allowed to flourish in neighborhoods like this one because they had enough armed security floating around for the residents not to worry about their houses being out of sight. The neighborhood was profoundly quiet, as if frivolous activity of any kind had been banned on this tiny street. She saw no cars, no pedestrians, not a dog, not even a bird fluttering on a limb, only a single vehicle parked on the edge of the street half a block down from the white cottage, a yellow pool-service truck.

In the turnaround, she circled back to the house, then pulled onto the asphalt pad and switched off the ignition, got out and zipped her keys into the waist pouch. Mumbling to himself, Lawton extricated himself from his seat belt and began to hammer on his window until Alexandra came around and unlocked the door and helped him out.

"Ohio's the ticket," he said. "It's too damn hot here. I mean, for Christ sakes, it's October already, time for autumn."

Alexandra drifted up the walkway to Jennifer McDougal's front door. This morning, she'd dressed her father in a light blue jumpsuit and tennis shoes. She'd chosen navy walking shorts and a beige knit top, along with a pair of white Nike running shoes and a woven leather belt. No jewelry, except the wedding ring.

The deep wraparound porch was cluttered with an assortment of secondhand furniture, old couches, a wooden swing, a rattan throne chair. Upside-down milk crates were wedged between the seats, used as side tables, and littering them were empty beer bottles and magazines and a couple of plastic toys, an orange dump truck, and a red-haired rag doll with a moon face and freckles.

Alexandra drew open the screen door and stood for a moment staring out at the street, a light wind stirring the fronds around the telephone poles. Not much air today, humidity crowding in again. Lawton picked up the rag doll and studied its face, saying nothing, lost in his soundless trance.

Alex turned back to the pitted pine of the door, as torn up as an old dartboard. As if perhaps a long string of outraged wives had stood on this porch and tried to claw their way inside.

She knocked three times on the door and the sound seemed to wake her from the electric drone of her anger. She was standing on a stranger's porch with the scantiest evidence of her husband's infidelity. She had no phrase on her lips, no image of how she would proceed.

She straightened her shoulders, lifted her fist, and rapped hard on the door again, but something about the hollow echo of her knocks made her certain the house was deserted.

Willing herself back into motion, she closed the screen door, went down the steps, and marched around the west side of the house, peeking in the windows, trying to read the personality of the place from its decor, the furniture, some stray piece of art. Maybe catch a glimpse of some article of Stan's.

Staring through the window, the image framed itself like a photograph. The rectangular tableau, silent and dead. She held herself very still, snapped it in her mind, freezing that moment that lay before her, distancing herself from it. No corpse this time. Just Jennifer McDougal's furniture, the kind of mindless foam-filled stuff that was bought and delivered on the same day. Drab green couch, matching chairs, a coffee table swarming with saucers and tipped-over beer bottles. A bullfighting poster hung above the fireplace and below it on the mantel was a collection of wine bottles with wax drippings running down the throats. Near the window, a mobile of clear plastic dolphins stirred in the breeze of an overhead fan. A black cat was coiled tightly on top of the television.

It could be the house of a college student or a nurse or a grocery story clerk or the crash pad of a comic who played local Holiday Inns. There was nothing distinctive about anything she saw, nothing flavored with an identity, certainly nothing that would suggest how the resident of this narrow and shabby place could have won Stan Rafferty's love.

She moved to the next window, but the venetian blinds were tilted shut. She circled behind the house through a dusty backyard. A redwood hot tub sat starkly in the center of the tiny yard, the plastic pipes running overland, a hasty and improper setup that violated any number of building codes. Just like something Stan would sling together in his usual half-assed hurry.

Alex continued her journey around the house, halting at the first of two windows on the east side. Several thick vines of bougainvillea meandered around the frame of the window—this one with an unobstructed view of the bedroom, an unmade king-sized bed, no headboard, no bedside table. A Spartan love nest for the oblivious sweethearts. As she was pressing her nose flat to the blurry pane, trying to decipher the photograph hanging on the wall to the left of the bed, someone entered the room.

Alex ducked away, a knot tightening in her chest. On Main Highway, a siren passed by, heading north. The down on her arms bristled and she felt a thorn from the bougainvillea stab through the yoke of her blouse, holding her in place.

Out of view of the bedroom, she reached back and freed herself from the vine, then swallowed a long, deliberate breath and inched her head forward till she could peek her left eye around the frame.

On the edge of the unmade bed, Lawton Collins was bouncing hard, as though he was testing the springiness of the mattress. The black cat wound in and out between his legs as Lawton sang loudly and unconcerned, the words of a song without a name or consequence or history. A tuneless ditty that seemed to be piped up directly from the tattered remains of his reason.

"A termite queen lays thirty thousand eggs a day. She lives for years, and that's all she does, lay eggs. What kind of life is that, Norman? I ask you."

The ox just kept staring down Leafy Way at the white house.

"The way I see it, termites and ants and bees, they're what the bosses want us all to be. Play our roles, do our jobs, round and round we go, shoulder to the wheel. Every day exactly like the day before it and the day coming up. Thirty thousand eggs a day, Norman, think about that. Is that any kind of life? And that's the fucking queen, the head lady. Think about the workers, the soldiers.

"Man, I'll take the cockroach any day. A freelancer, independent agent. On its own, surviving any way it can. You know a cockroach can live for a week without its head? Did you know that, Norman? It only dies because, without a mouth, it can't drink water and withers up from thirst. I know 'cause I snipped off one of their heads as an experiment. That's when I was younger. I'd never do something like that these days. I respect them too much. They're my friends. Pets, really. Very affectionate. I know it's hard to believe, but they are. You just have to know the signs, be able to read the telltale body language to see how affectionate they are. They way they wave their antennae, mainly."

His face came around, eyes sleepy, looking at her.

"Do you ever stop?"

She smiled.

"What? Do I ever stop talking? Well, no, the answer is no. I talk to relieve the pressure building up inside my head. It's my way of letting out the gases. And believe me, at this particular moment, I have a lot of pressure building. About as much as I ever remember. You wouldn't want me to shut up, would you, Norman, have my skull explode all over you?"

He shook his head hopelessly and his eyes wandered back out the windshield.

"I'm a language person," she said. "That's because of my mother, how she was. You knew my mother, right?"

"I knew her." He turned his head slightly to look out his side window.

"You know she wrote poetry?"

He nodded.

"In French, in English, Spanish. The woman was a genius with words. She could've been the poet laureate of the Southern fucking Hemisphere if she hadn't fallen for my old man, got stuck living in the goddamn ghetto."

"Your mother was nice."

"Damn right she was. And smart, too, and cultured. That's where I get my facility with words. That's why I talk so much. It's all that genetic shit circulating in my blood. And from all those books she had me reading. Woman thought books were the answer. With Daddy, it was guns; Mother thought it was books. Read enough, get smart enough, you could be anybody you wanted. You could go off, travel through exotic kingdoms, fight wars, dance with princes and dukes, all that romantic fairy-tale horseshit.

"She had me doing it, too, reading books. I was gobbling down five, six, sometimes eight books a week, and it was okay for a while, but then I started to notice that every time I looked up from the page, I was still living in the same fucking ghetto. Same bad shit going on all around me. And it hit me, if I was going to change my luck, I was going to have to put down the goddamn books and start figuring out how to deal with the real shit."

Norman turned his eyes back to the white cottage.

"So what do we do, Norm? Go in there, or what? What's the plan, a full-scale frontal assault perhaps?"

He stared straight ahead down the narrow street and said nothing.

Maybe the big man was stupid. Emma was starting to consider

that as a possibility. Or maybe his body's motor was so taxed from growing massive quantities of hair, he had no horsepower left for thought.

"I say we go in."

"And do what?"

"Whatever's necessary."

"They're not thieves."

"Well, this is the house, isn't it? This is two seven oh nine Leafy Way. Unless your cop friend gave you the wrong address."

"They're not the ones."

"That old man and the woman, they could be part of the gang, the masterminds behind the caper. I say we go in there, throw them up against the wall, shoot them full of lead till they talk."

"Shoot them, huh?"

Emma had convinced him to use her pool truck as cover. Drive over to the house, do reconnaissance, get the lay of the land before they proceeded further. A good idea, as it was turning out. Two seconds after they'd parked, a white Camry came driving up the street, going slow like a neighborhood crime watch or something; then it turned around at the end of the street and came back and parked in front of 2709.

It was a wonder nobody'd called the cops on them yet. Norman sure as hell didn't look like he belonged in the front seat of a pool-service truck. Wearing a shiny gray shirt with geometric designs and a long collar spread wide over his canary yellow sports coat, no belt holding up his sky blue pants, and white socks with white loafers. Crash-test dummies had better taste.

"You bring your gun?"

He drew it out, a Glock 9, then slid it back inside his coat.

"I'm carrying, too. They're under the tarp in back. Two Mac-tens, an Uzi, the Heckler & Koch carbine."

"You're shitting me."

"No, no. They were my dad's. My inheritance. You knew my dad, the gun nut, a true-blue paranoid. He was sure our apartment was going to be stormed any second, by the police, by the neighbors, by Martians, who knows. So all that money he got from you for stolen goods over the years, every nickel of it went for guns. Guns and guns and more guns. We couldn't afford a goddamn TV. We ate off paper plates. Beans and cabbage. But the apartment was jam-packed with guns. Is that ironic or what? He's got all those guns, and what is he protecting? Just more guns. That dumb shit."

Emma dug a finger through the frayed hole in the thigh of her cutoffs. White T-shirt today, tennis shoes, hair back in a ponytail, just one curly strand loose and hanging down beside her left eye, giving her that sultry look.

"Money's the only thing that really protects a person. Not guns, not smarts, not muscle. None of that. Only thing that works is cash. Money, money, money. You get enough dollar bills together in one pile, nobody can touch you. That's not what they want you to believe, the teachers, preachers, the goddamn politicians. Root of all evil, my ass. The guy that said that never lived in our neighborhood. You want to see the root of all evil, drive down Second Avenue at three in the morning.

"Uh-huh. If money's the root of all evil, then why's that collection plate going up and down every pew piled up with cash dollars? Yeah, right. The holier-than-thous are driving around in air-conditioned cars, cold air blowing in their faces all day, and what do I get? I get a broken-down truck with a crank window, sweating all day, nothing I can do about it."

She leaned back in her seat and looked out at the pretty street. The green trees waving, the sharp, pure sunlight. The day was going on without her. It didn't matter if she was there or not. That same wind would stir those same trees. The shadows would move along the asphalt. Birds would sing the same tunes with or without Emma. Stepping outside of herself for a few seconds, leaving the husk of Emma Lee Potts on the front seat of her employer's Nissan pickup. That same feeling had been coming over her a lot lately. Like all at once she was there and not there at the same time.

It wasn't a bad feeling really, not scary. A kind of pleasant release, like she was practicing being dead.

"While we're waiting out here, nothing to do, you feel like a hand job, Norman? I mean, just to pass the time."

"No."

"Way I look at it, if we're going to be partners in crime, hanging out together for long hours on stakeouts and shit, we should get to know each other on a more intimate basis, work on a few secret handshakes. Get our chakras humming the same tune, our harmonic clocks synchronized."

"I said no."

"What? I don't turn you on? Not the least little bit. You don't look at me and get any kind of tingle at all? Little hot gnawing feelings in your belly."

When he turned his head this time, there was dark fire in his eyes. His mouth moved as if he were chewing on his words before speaking them. He drew the air through his nose and blew it out his mouth.

"Not interested," he said.

"What're you gay, a homosexual or something?"

He turned back to the view out the window.

"Or maybe you're an out-and-out abstainer. Now there's a seriously kinky approach to life. There's a man marching to a totally radical drummer. A monk. A high priest of apathy." Emma reached out and jingled the keys hanging from the ignition. "Okay, fine, you've decided you want to abstain, withdraw from the human race, the animal kingdom in general, hey, fine and dandy. I can handle that. No problem whatsoever."

She tinkled the car keys, tapped her foot.

"So what makes you tick, Norman? It's not sex; we've established that. So what is it?"

Norman was quiet. A fly buzzed around his face, circled his nose, then landed on his lower lip, took a couple of steps, then flew off again. The whole time, Norman never twitched or tried to wave it away.

"Come on, Norman. Talk to me, big guy. What makes you tick?"

"I don't tick."

"Sure you do. Everybody ticks. Something winds your clock and you tick. It's that simple. Otherwise, you wouldn't be able to get up in the morning, get out of bed, put one foot in front of the other. No tick, no life. So what is it, Norman? Down there at the center of your massive physical self, what's the engine that drives the beast?"

He shook his head.

"Open up, Norman. Let the sun shine in. There's something there burning inside. I know there is. Some itch you're trying to scratch. It's the thing that put your ass in the seat beside me right now. Come on, Norm. I told you mine. I opened up, laid it all on the table. Money's what I'm after. Pure, sweet, simple money. Now it's your turn. What makes you tick?"

Norman looked over at her with that drowsy stare, then turned his gaze back to the house.

"Okay, okay. Jesus, you want to be an enigma, fine, you're a big fucking enigma. Great. A cipher, a conundrum. Terrific."

Emma looked up as the tall dark-haired woman hurried around the side of the house and climbed up onto the front porch again.

"Something's going down."

Emma looked over at the big man. He turned his head slowly and settled his dark eyes on hers.

"So, Mr. Enigma, you think you could focus on this project for a little while? Getting that money, making it ours? You think you could do that?"

She waited for him to reply, but it was useless. He'd said his quota of words for the day.

TWELVE

Alexandra Rafferty pulled out the lock pick that was wedged into the slot of the keyhole; then she nudged the scarred door open and stepped across the threshold into the house.

Her father's singing guided her through the dreary living area and into a bedroom bathed in sun. He was cradling the cat in his arms, still bouncing on the edge of the mattress.

"What have you done, Dad?" Her voice was an aching whisper.

He looked over at her, and the cat dropped its head back and stared at her upside down. It was a fluffy, thick-necked creature and seemed quite content with the jostling ride. Lawton's lullaby dwindled to a discordant hum.

"You wanted to come in here, didn't you?"

"I wanted to talk to the woman, not break into her house."

"Well, we're here now. Might as well look around, check out the competition."

"Get up, Dad. Right now."

"Don't you want to see this place, where Stan and Delvin come after work. Hit buckets of balls."

"No, I don't. This is wrong. We have to leave."

"The front door was ajar; we walked in. No crime in that."

"You picked the lock, Dad. You *broke* in."

She held up the lock pick.

"I did?"

"Yes, you did."

"Well, good for me. I haven't lost my touch."

"Come on, Dad. Get up. Let's go. Now."

"It's okay. I'm a cop. I can break into people's houses. I have the full weight of the law behind me. As long as there's probable cause, and in the present case, I think there certainly is."

"You're not a cop anymore, Dad. You retired."

"Don't contradict me, Alexandra. I guess I know what profession I'm in. Good grief, I'm not that far gone. Now, you look around, and when you've made a thorough examination of the premises, we'll leave."

She went over to the bed, took him by the arm, and tried to tug him to his feet, but he made himself heavy and wouldn't budge. He smiled at her as he continued to pet the large black cat.

When he fell into these mulish moods, there was no wrenching him back. She could see in his eyes, lightless and opaque, that he was so mired in the bog of his delusion, not even the wedding march would stir him now.

Alex stooped down beside him and made a show of lifting the dust ruffles and peering under the bed.

"Well, nothing there," she announced.

Then she hustled into the small bath, opened the cabinet, gave the crowded shelves a perfunctory look, and shut the door quickly. Her heart knotted and went cold. From a quick glance, Alexandra knew with perfect clarity the woman who lived in this place. Jennifer McDougal, with her collection of froufrou perfumes and trendy hues of lipstick and nail polish, was the kind of girl who religiously pored over the monthly tips on man-catching from those slick and empty single-girl magazines, a girl with sufficient time and expendable income to indulge herself in every costly ointment and elixir that might help her spin her magic web.

With eyes blurred, Alexandra marched back into the bedroom.

"All right, Dad, I've seen enough. Now let's go."

As he scratched the cat's neck, her father squinted at her and shook his head.

"Is that the way they taught you to investigate a crime scene, Alexandra? That kind of cursory effort? Department standards must have slipped."

"Dad, come on, damn it. I'm serious. Get on your feet."

"I want you to turn around and go back in there and peek and peer, dig under the cushions on the couch. Open every door, sniff and poke until there's not a square inch you haven't touched. There must be a thousand hidey-holes around a place like this, crevices you haven't even considered."

Alexandra stamped her running shoe on the hardwood floor.

"Dad!" she shouted, loudly enough to wake a sleeper from the death throes of a nightmare. But Lawton just smiled at the air.

"Now go on, young lady, do a decent job this time. And be thorough, or you're going to have to do it all over again."

Her pulse was misfiring, stealing blood from the muscles of her legs. Lawton Collins bounced lightly on the bed, the cat riding with him like an old friend who'd been down this bumpy road before, bright sunlight straining through the dirty windows, and somewhere nearby the combative libretto of a mockingbird staking out the perimeters of his territory, while in the living room the dolphin mobile clattered in the moving air.

In a nervous daze, she made a circuit of the house and stared at every item, knowing that without intending it, she was storing everything she saw in these long-term banks of memory she'd never be able to expunge. The sink was cluttered with dishes, crusted with half a dozen dinners, and high atop the sugar canister a roach waved its antennae, sensing Alex's shadow sweeping across the counter. There was the funky scent of garbage left too long beneath the sink, onions rotting in some drawer, a sinuous trail of sugar ants that made four S curves across the stove to a lake of Alfredo sauce.

Clearly, Jennifer McDougal was no hausfrau. A girl who didn't sully her hand with dishrag or Brillo pad. Whose skin was baby soft, lightly scented, a delicate girl who had spun out her fine coquettish net of perfumes and body oils and blushes and lip gloss and had trapped a helter-skelter, buzzing husband.

Alex wanted to break everything she saw, then pick up the fragments and break them into smaller pieces.

She turned from the sink and wrenched open the door of the Kenmore and peered into its frosty depths. Tecate beer, Stan's favorite, a packet of hot dogs, jar of mustard, a Tupperware container full of white rice, a skim milk carton, and a box of Frosted Flakes that she must have kept there to save it from the bugs. Every item on those shelves was so squarely in the mainstream of Stan's diet that they alone could indict him in Alexandra's court of law. But it was the cheese that rocked her back. A wedge of Brie stripped of its cellophane, left to harden on the egg shelf, its pointy end bitten off, the grooves of a man's teeth marking the blunt edge of the soft white cheese. It was one of Stan's crude habits, which had once seemed a charming, boyish idiosyncrasy. But now as she stared at the cannibalized wedge, it was as damning as bloody footprints tracked across a murder scene.

She could stand no more and slammed the door and headed back to the bedroom.

The black cat had taken command of one of the pillows, but her father was gone. As she whirled back to the living room, she heard the voices of men somewhere outside. Halting, she hissed her father's name, but there was no reply. With her heart knotted, Alexandra marched to the bamboo screen that covered the double front windows and peered through the slats.

In the middle of Leafy Way, a buffalo of a man in pale blue pants, yellow sports coat, and a gray shirt was talking to Lawton Collins. Watching from a few feet away, a blond girl with a mocha complexion leaned over the tailgate of a yellow pickup truck and was digging around under a blue tarp.

Stiffly, her father stood a yard in front of the man, and in her father's hand was a brown leather duffel. From forty feet away, Alex could clearly make out the image printed on the side of the bag—a white cobra outlined in orange, rising up from its coiled base. It was the dreadful mascot of South Miami High, with its logo: GO COBRAS, GO. And when her father shifted the bag in his hand, the sunlight lit up the solitary white scuff mark that several months ago, unsuccessfully, Stan Rafferty had tried to stain back to its original brown.

The room was suddenly as cool and transparent as an aquarium, and as Alexandra swept to the door and walked onto the porch and down the steps, it was as though she were streaming through the bright unreal obstacles of some glassed-in undersea world.

Without a glance at the big man standing in front of her father, she strode around the rear of the car, took Lawton by the crook of the arm, pulled him toward the passenger door of her Toyota, settled him in his seat. Then, with a quick nod at the large man and a glance at the girl, who was hurrying over, some kind of shotgun in her hands, Alex raced to her door, jerked it open, got in, and turned the key.

The girl yelled out, "Hey!" then again, "Hey!" And the big man tried to block their path, but he was ponderously slow. Alex burned the tires, veered hard to the left, then swung the car straight, and the man pranced out of the way like a frightened horse.

Lawton Collins, with Stan's duffel on his lap, gave a courteous wave to the huge man and the girl, but they couldn't see him, for they were scrambling back toward the yellow pool truck.

She turned onto Main Highway, lurched in front of a UPS van, switched lanes at the last second, and ran the light, going straight onto Douglas, north, then a quick left at Crawford, another left over to Poinciana, right and left again, then continuing south through the serpentine streets of the west Grove, running stop signs at a full tilt, putting as much crazy distance as she could between them and the yellow pool truck, them and Leafy Way. At Cocoplum Circle, she cruised around twice before deciding which exit to take. Out Sunset Drive, down the shady tunnel of banyans, heart racing, eyes on the rearview mirror, then swinging right through a maze of Gables streets, straying vaguely north toward US 1, where she might lose herself in the endless flood of cars.

"What'd he say, Dad? That man, what'd he say to you?"

"Not much," her father said. "He asked about the duffel."

"The duffel."

"Yeah, he wanted to know what was in it. I told him it was none of his goddamn business."

Alexandra was on Alhambra, waiting for the light, or a break in the traffic, so she could turn right onto Dixie Highway.

"While you were poking around in the kitchen, I searched the bedroom closet, and that's where I found it." He patted the brown duffel. "If I'm not mistaken, this belongs to your husband. Mr. MVP in the football regionals."

Alex looked over at him.

"By the way," he said, "the girl Stan's shacked up with, she's a size six. Little thing. I looked at her dresses, her shoes. She likes to go out dancing. She has a lot of those kinds of dresses. Shiny, low-cut, red or black, a couple of them made out of vinyl. Red appears to be her favorite color. And she wears very high heels—spikes. I looked for a riding crop, but I didn't find one. A little vixen, that's who Stan's mixed up with."

"Stop it, Dad. That's enough."

The light changed to green and Alex floored the Toyota, lurching north toward the city.

"Well, now we know," Lawton said, shifting the duffel. "Now we know the story behind the headlines."

"What?"

"The story you won't find anywhere else. Late-breaking news, exclusive footage at eleven."

"What're you talking about, Dad?"

"This," he said. And he reached inside the duffel's main compartment and drew out a green brick of cash. "A mess of cash is what I'm talking about."

THIRTEEN

At Jackson Memorial Hospital, Alexandra parked the car in the underground lot, not far from where she'd seen Jennifer McDougal pull out the night before. She sat for a moment, the car idling, while her father worried over a loose thread he'd found on the sleeve of his jumpsuit.

Then she switched off the engine and sat listening to the concrete echoes of the parking garage. Her body felt emptier than seemed possible for someone still alive. She sat for several moments listening to the hollow thunk of her pulse.

The morning's rage had burned itself out and left nothing but char where her heart had been. Her exhaustion was compounded by a sleepless night, lying in their dark bedroom at that unaccustomed hour, listening to the saw and flutter of her father's snore through the wall.

"We going to sit here all day or what? Not that I mind. One place is as good as another."

She heaved the door open and plodded around the car to free her dad.

"What about this?" He patted the duffel.

"Leave it."

"Leave it in a parked car in a public parking lot in Miami? A million buckaroos?"

"Somebody steals it, fine. More power to them."

"Are you mad at me?"

"I'm not mad at you, Dad. No."

"Have I done something I should be ashamed of? I mean, yes, I know there was the breaking-and-entering incident. And I suppose I've tampered with evidence now. Removed items from a crime scene. Some smart young lawyer could make something of that."

"It's okay, Dad. You've been good. You're not in any danger."

"I don't know about those leaves, either. Leaving them in piles like that. Some kid could come along, little tyke who doesn't know better, and hide inside one of those piles, and who knows what could happen? I could be liable."

"It's going to be fine," she said. "We've got it under control, Dad."

"I told you, didn't I? The minute I saw it on the news, I knew it was Stan's work. I've got a nose for crime."

"Yes, you do."

In his attack of fidgetiness, Lawton had unzipped his jumpsuit down to the brim of his small potbelly, leaving the coarse white hair on his chest exposed. She helped him zip it up and then led him over to the elevator and they rode silently to Stan's floor.

Her fingers felt numb, the prickly insensate feeling of frostbite. Her toes were going, too. Everything below her neck seemed to be sliding into shutdown.

But her mind was sharp, every synapse clicking clean and hot. This man whose sophomoric pranks had once been the talk of the high school hallways had graduated to the national news. This man with sea blue eyes and a bullish determination to prolong his boyhood as long as possible. This was her husband, adulterer, thief, and perhaps even a killer.

"Should I wait here?" her father asked just outside Stan's room.

"No, come in. We need to stay together."

When she eased open the door, Stan was dialing the last two digits of someone's phone number. Then he leaned back against his pillows, his chin tucked down, eyes intent on the noise in his ear. His expression was smooth, joyless, flattened by the drug perhaps, robbed of its coarse vitality. She had a moment to study him in this unguarded repose, to witness the bland and bestial muscularity of his face. With a grim objectivity she'd never exercised, she noted how his forehead broadened near the hairline as if he had battered his head once too often against a skull more unyielding than his own. And she saw the piggishly narrow set of his eyes, their implacable flatness. His neck was too short, too wide. His ears tilted out a few obscene degrees too many, as if he were perpetually eavesdropping on the secret affairs of his neighbors. This was the man who had hauled her out of high school obscurity, crowned her with his spurious status, promoted her to the upper ranks of adolescent aristocracy. It had meant nothing then and now it meant even less. That the lingering love she'd felt for this man could have ended so abruptly and completely did not shock her as much as the idea that she had ever loved him at all.

When he looked up and saw them standing in the doorway, his wooden composure barely altered. Without a word, he reached out and set the phone aside.

"Pretty clever, aren't you?" her father said, jabbing a finger at Stan as if he were a delinquent Lawton had nabbed. "Had it all figured out. Cause a big ruckus, get yourself injured, and no one would ever suspect. Pretty damn clever. Except you didn't put us in the picture, Mr. Smart Guy. Me and Alex here. That was your mistake."

"Get that old fool out of here."

"He stays."

Stan shifted against his pillow. His IV bag wobbled on its stand.

"Where've you been? Why haven't you come to see me until now?"

She stepped up to the foot rail of his bed.

"Who were you calling, Stan?"

"I was calling you."

"Bullshit."

"What's going on, Alex? What the hell's with you?"

"Tell me, Stan; I think I deserve to know. Why did you do it? It wasn't for us, was it? We didn't need the money. We were doing all right. Not rich, but all right."

He was shaking his head, eyes straying to the wall.

"Did she put you up to it, your size-six Jennifer? Was this your nest egg? You were going to run off and start over with her?"

He clicked his eyes to hers and his lips turned ugly.

"I don't know what the fuck you're talking about." But his voice was no longer into the lie.

"Don't bother, Stan. We've been over at the driving range. The Leafy Way Golf and Country Club."

Lawton chuckled.

Stan's eyes were working, little flicks of thought happening back there. A cornered weasel trying to remember his escape routes.

Alexandra brushed a strand of hair from her eyes. She caught a glimpse of herself in the bathroom mirror. A tall woman with smooth white skin. None of it showing in her face, the bombs that for the last few hours had been detonating in her gut.

"You know, Stan," she said, holding his slippery gaze, "what fooled me was Margie. How caring you were. You loved her so much, it radiated all around you. You were there to protect her, catch her if she started to fall. It was incredible to see. A high school kid with that much love for his sister. That's the man I fell in love with. That's the man I thought you were. But I was wrong, wasn't I? You used it all up on Margie, didn't you? You just had a little bit inside you and you spent it all on her; then it was gone."

"You fucking bitch. You have no right to talk about her. No right at all."

Alexandra stepped back from the bed, a dizzy elation taking her.

"We have your duffel down in the car, Stan. It's all over, your little caper."

Stan opened his mouth to speak, but there was wild static in his eyes, everything crossing out everything else.

"Don't tax yourself, Stan. There's nothing to say. Nothing at all."

"Give him hell, Alex."

"I'll turn you over to the police, you whore," said Stan.

"What?"

"I'll give them you and the old man."

"Are you crazy, Stan? You can't dump this off on me. You're a son of a bitch, and you're going to jail for a long, long time."

"No, Alex. No, I'm not."

With a lazy snort of scorn, Stan turned his eyes away from her, drank in the bare wall for a moment, then turned his gaze back. A triumphant light burned in his eyes.

"Take the money home, Alex. That's what you're going to do."

"You're confused, Stan. You're not calling the shots."

"Listen to me. Jennifer will come by and pick up the money later on this afternoon. She'll ask you for the duffel, you'll hand it over to her. That's how it'll work. Then everything'll be okay. When I get out of the hospital, we'll stay married for a while, keep up appearances; then when the time is right, I'll divorce you and go away."

"Bullshit, Stan. Wake up! You're deluded. You're not going anywhere but jail."

She reached out for Lawton and took him by the arm. He was humming a song to himself, worrying over a thread on his sleeve.

"I know about Darnel Flint," Stan said.

Her mouth went dry. She dropped Lawton's arm.

Stan said, "I know about all of it. All the gory details. You're a murderer, Alex. If I take a fall, you do, too. And the old man goes down with us."

There was a tightening in her inner ear, a pang of pressure, as if she were on an elevator whose cables had snapped, the floor dropping beneath her.

"Lawton told me the whole thing a couple of weeks ago. Didn't you, you old fool? Babbling away, he told me how the kid molested you, killed your dog, so you walked next door and shot him in the face. He told me about the cover-up, the drugs on the floor. He even saved the gun you used on the kid. The murder weapon, Alex. He showed it to me, and I took it away from him. I got it put away nice and safe. The pistol you used to murder that kid. I hid it, in case I might need it someday. A day just like this.

"As you know, Alex, they keep the ballistics reports on open murder cases. It's all still there in the records. I think your friends at Miami PD would be real interested to learn what their father-daughter team was up to back then. Get out their microscopes and look at the slug that killed Darnel Flint and match it to the pistol your old man used for thirty years on the force. Yes, sir, I think they'd be quite interested in that."

"I told him," Lawton said. "I didn't mean to. It just came out."

She draped her arm around her father's shoulder, drew him to her.

"So you go to prison, Alex, and the old man goes to the nuthouse, where he belongs. Maybe I can bargain my way down to a year or two. Worth a try, don't you think?"

"It'll never work."

"Oh, it'll work. Sure it will. A woman with the Miami PD accused as a child killer. Oh, that'll be a pretty headline. That'll knock the Bloody Rapist out of top billing. You bet your ass. No statute of limitations on murder, sweetheart. The papers will eat it up. State's attorney gets the Brinks money back, and in the bargain he solves an eighteen-year-old homicide. Probably be able to run for governor."

"You fucking bastard."

He resettled himself against his pillow, smile widening, glancing around the room as if he were basking in the cheers of a dozen of his closest buddies.

"You getting raped by this Flint kid, that explains a lot," he said, eyes coming back to hers. "Your bedroom behavior, for one thing. Right from the first, me doing all the work while you lay there like you were suffering through it, eyes closed. Like you were afraid of sex or hated it.

"I think you had maybe two orgasms in all the years we've been together, Alex. And you were probably faking those. Two. That's supposed to keep your man interested? But now I see what made you such a cold fish. This Darnel Flint thing. Christ, you should've told me up front what happened to you, that you were damaged goods. Full disclosure and all that, you know."

He looked at Lawton and snorted in disgust.

"Only reason I did this Brinks thing at all was because of you, what a cold, dead fucking fish you are. It never would've happened if we'd had a halfway decent sex life, Alex. And then, like things weren't bad enough already, you gotta bring that old bastard home. He's babbling at the door while I'm lying there trying to get my dick hard. Christ, that's all we needed, him in the next room, pawing on the wall, whimpering. It's your fucking fault, Alex, the shit we're in here. All of it. Every little bit."

Standing near the doorway, she felt the air move in and out of her. She looked at the gray light pouring in the window, heard the bells and voices of the hospital as another shift of healthy folks stepped forward to take charge of the endless onslaught of injured and diseased.

"It's simple, Alex. You do what I tell you, or you go to jail.

They slam the old man away with the criminally insane. You want that, then go ahead, pick up the phone, turn me in."

Alexandra glanced at her father, then shifted her eyes back to Stan. He was lying back easily against his pillows, like a gambler relishing a well-played hand.

She stepped forward and ran her fingers along the cold white foot rail of his bed. Lawton hummed and shuffled on the linoleum beside her, doing the box step, a tight square without his partner.

"I'm already in jail," she said. "I've been in jail as long as I can remember. You can't do anything to me, Stan, that I haven't already done to myself."

He sat forward an inch or two. His smile lost half of its glow, forehead tensing.

"So go on, do it, make the call, Alex. Watch them cart that old man's withered ass off where you'll never see him again."

She felt the heat gather in her face, bands of steel tightening around her chest. She kept her eyes on his, drew a breath.

"You're good, Stan. You've found a very cute way to turn this all around, make yourself the victim. You rob your employer and kill your partner and this is all my fault and Dad's. You're simply doing what we made you do. That's great. Real slick. It must be wonderful to have such a handy scapegoat for anything you want to do.

"Well, let me tell you something, Stan. When the state's attorney finds out what you've done, they're not going to plea-bargain. You can forget that. I'm no lawyer, but I watch those people work every day. If you're determined to take me down with you, then fine, go for it. I'm sure they'll be happy to oblige. But don't kid yourself. You're going to spend the rest of your goddamn life on the other side. Get used to the idea."

She held his eyes for a moment more, then turned to Lawton and took him by the elbow.

"Come on, Dad. Let's get the hell out of here. We have things to do."

Lawton jerked free of her grasp.

"MVP, my ass," Lawton said, facing off with Stan. "I never bought that story for a second. We're sending you right back to Raiford, young man, where you belong. And this time, there's no returning to civilized society for you. No, sir."

FOURTEEN

In the hospital lobby, Alex called Gabriella, got her new address, a neighborhood just west of the airport. She took the Dolphin Expressway, keeping to the far-right lane. Holding to the speed limit, she was at Gabriella's new neighborhood in fifteen minutes. Once or twice, she thought she spotted the yellow pool truck lurking several cars back in the traffic, but she decided it was only an attack of anxiety.

"Where are we?" her father asked as she pulled into her friend's narrow concrete driveway. "I don't recognize this."

"We need to talk to Gabbie Hernandez. You remember her. We were cheerleaders together back in high school; she ran for mayor last month."

"The one they caught smooching with the dictator."

"That's right."

"Why you want to see her?"

"She knows people, Dad, lawyers, politicians. She's very well connected. I think she can help us pick the right attorney."

"We should make a run for it, Alex. Take the money and go."

"No, Dad. I've got to face it once and for all. We're not going to let Stan hold us hostage. But first, we have to find someplace to put you out of harm's way. Just until it's over, till it's settled between Stan and me. I'm not going to risk having them ship you off somewhere."

"Hell, a lunatic asylum? No problem. Play checkers all day with a bunch of droolers, how bad is that?"

It was two in the afternoon; a stupefying blaze of sunlight filled the street. No cars in the driveways of that working-class neighborhood. Most of the tiny houses had barred windows and elaborate religious statuary planted safely behind high chain-link fences. Rottweilers, Dobies, and German shepherds patrolled the treeless front yards or lay in the shade of Mary, Joseph, or Christ himself.

Gabriella met them at the door and ushered them quickly inside. She gave a glance up and down the street, then bolted the door, wedged a steel brace into a fitting in the floor, and locked it tight against the back of the door.

Alexandra set Stan's duffel on the dining room table, unzipped it, and drew it open for Gabriella to see.

"Good God, Alex."

Gabriella wore baggy jeans and a man's white dress shirt, the tails knotted at her waist. She was a fragile woman, flat-chested, with the narrow hips of a twelve-year-old. Without makeup, her face showed each dreary sleepless hour, every torment from the last month of her public humiliations. There were long-suffering pouches beneath her eyes, puffy and dark, and a tight puckering in the corners of her mouth, as if she were constantly on the verge of whistling for her attack dog. Her coarse black hair was pulled back severely into a bun. And when Gabbie held up two banded wedges of hundred-dollar bills, Alex could see she'd been gnawing her nails to the quick.

Gabriella waited till a passing jet had rumbled away.

"We have to call the police."

"No," Alexandra said. "What I need is a lawyer."

"A lawyer?"

"That's why I came over here, Gabbie. All I know is the courthouse crowd, public defenders, but I need somebody good."

"A defense attorney? What? For Stan?"

"No, for me. And for Dad."

"Alex, what're you saying?"

"There's more to it now. More than just the money. Let me catch my breath, and then I'll tell you the whole story."

"This may call for a glass of wine."

"His name was Darnel Flint," her father said. "That's where this all began."

Gabbie looked across at Lawton, who had sunk into the flowered couch beside the front window. He was thumbing through a copy of an old *National Geographic*, a song burbling on his lips.

The house vibrated as another jet lifted off above them, china rattling in the hutch, the overhead fan going temporarily out of balance.

"The Realtor said I'd get used to it," Gabriella shouted through the whistling scream. She looked up at the ceiling as if expecting the plaster to give way. "I guess I'm going to need more time."

When it was quiet again, Gabriella asked her if she wanted red wine or white, and Lawton called out that he'd like both. Alex followed her into the kitchen and Gabbie turned, gave Alex a comforting smile, and opened her arms. Alex stepped forward into the embrace.

"Tell me, Alex. What is it? What's happened?"

Alex drew out of the hug and they sat at the dinette table, Gabriella holding Alex's hand in both of hers. Alex told her the story. Darnel Flint. The long-ago rape, the cover-up. Stan's threat to expose it all. When she was finished, Gabbie sat back in her chair and patted her shirt pocket as if searching for the cigarettes she hadn't smoked in years. She stared up at the ceiling, blew out a breath.

"Wow."

"Pretty grim, huh?"

"Grim, yeah. But at least I understand now."

"Understand what?"

"How you could have made such a mistake marrying Stan. It's because you were traumatized as a child. You were severely wounded and you never healed, and it distorted your judgment about men."

"I'll say it did."

"All these years, I never said anything. Friends can't come right out and say things like that. What good would it have done anyway? As much as we care about each other, I don't think our friendship would have survived that. But it was clear from the beginning, Alex, that man was missing a crucial part. He's got the emotional development of a fifteen-year-old."

"You're being generous."

"Twelve, then."

They laughed. But it died out quickly.

Gabriella rose from the table and went to the refrigerator.

"You have to get your father somewhere safe."

"I know. That's priority number one."

"I'd take him in, of course. But this would be the first place Stan would look. He'd find me. You know he would."

"I know, Gabbie. Not here. I've got to get Dad out of town, a long way off, make sure he's safe; then I'm turning right around and coming back with both barrels blazing. I'm going to take care of this thing with Stan. And Darnel Flint and all of it. It's time to face this whole damn mess. Long overdue."

"You have an idea where you'll go?"

"I think so."

"I suppose you shouldn't tell me. If I'm questioned later, I don't want to have to lie. You can call when you get there, let me know you're safe."

"Is this ever going to end, Gabbie? It just keeps going on and on and on."

Gabriella swallowed and squeezed out a smile that she meant to be encouraging.

"I ask the same question a lot."

"It doesn't end, does it? Once something this bad happens, it never stops; it changes everything. You can't go back, rewind the tape, start over, all innocent and fresh."

"No, but you can survive a lot more than you think, Alex. I've learned that much. You can find happiness, a few seconds here, a few seconds there. But it's still happiness. It's like when you're grieving over someone's death. You never think you'll get over it, but you do. You still hurt, but you learn to breathe again, breath by breath. You have to."

"When Dad first got sick," Alex said, "I read some of the same books he was reading. About memory and his illness, you know. There was one story about a man who'd had an operation to cure his epilepsy, a patient named Mr. M. It became a landmark medical case, because his doctor, some kind of hotshot who was experimenting with radical lobotomies on mental patients, tried a totally unheard-of procedure on this Mr. M. He wanted to see what happened when he removed a large portion of the brain. So he drilled a hole in Mr. M.'s skull, with a hardware store hand drill, then stuck a silver straw into Mr. M.'s brain and vacuumed out a fist-sized piece of it. His hippocampus."

"Jesus."

"When Mr. M. woke up, he had no memory. None at all. He knew how to speak, but that was all. He was wiped clean. From that moment on, he couldn't remember anything. You could speak to him one minute and walk away, then turn right around and come back, and he wouldn't know you'd ever been there before. He was blank. Totally, completely empty. He could hold nothing. Somehow, he still had a sense of humor, still enjoyed going places, seeing people. But he remembered nothing later. Absolutely nothing."

"And you wanted to be like him."

"That's right. It sounded blissful. It sounded perfect."

"Well, I've got a drill around here somewhere."

Alex smiled.

"You'd do it, wouldn't you? If I asked you, you'd suck my brain right out."

"I don't much like blood, but if that's what you wanted, Alex."

As the throb of another jet began to build, Lawton sang out from the living room, "You got a swimming pool at this house?"

"No, Lawton," Gabriella called back. "No pool. Sorry."

"Well, these guys must be confused, then."

Alex pushed away from the table and hustled into the living room. Lawton was sitting forward on the couch, peering out the picture window at something out of Alex's line of sight.

"It's that big guy again and his weird little girlfriend. Looks like they mean business this time. Armed to the teeth. You gals better stay down. Flat on the floor."

"Dad!"

Inches from Alexandra's shoulder, the door molding exploded and a plug of wood thumped her in the neck. Lawton was still leaning forward on the couch, staring out through the bright maze of shattered glass.

"Those are some heavy damn weapons they're playing with," he said as the jet's thunder died. "Using the noise of the planes to cover their salvos."

"Dad, get down! Get away from the window."

Alex pressed her back to the wall and began to inch around the perimeter of the room.

"Telephone's not connected," Gabriella screamed from the kitchen. "Cell phone's on the coffee table. I'll get it, Alex. You stay there."

"Forget the phone," she said. "We need guns, Gabbie."

"There aren't any guns. I hate guns."

As the next jet passed above them, more glass erupted from the window. On the dining room table, a blue vase shattered; the roses it had been holding sprayed across the room. Gabriella dropped to her hands and knees and wriggled ahead close to the floor.

Lawton brushed chips of glass from his lap and leaned back against the couch with a leisurely sigh.

"Some neighborhood you got here. Is it always this noisy?"

Gabriella reached out for the cell phone. The jet's clamor was rising.

Lawton dug his fingers in his ears.

A foot from the couch, Alexandra pressed her back hard to the wall. She saw nothing out the window except the silent houses across the street, no signs of the shooters. But as the jet's racket reached its height, the last shards of glass blasted from the window frame, and bullets sprayed the far wall, tearing into the hutch, the china ballerinas Gabriella collected, ivory girls raised up on pointy toes, pirouettes of glass, gravity-defying leaps. The bullets continued to pump into the back wall several seconds after the jet's noise ended, as if the shooters were becoming bolder. Figuring they had softened up their target, gotten no return fire, and now were about to make the final assault.

Gabriella had the phone at her ear. She was hunched forward on the floor. Frozen there with three red ruptures in the back of her white shirt, bloody blossoms opening. Alex stared at the wounds, framing them, holding, snapping her pictures, the same practiced detachment she employed every night.

Lawton stood up and turned his back to the window.

"I thought I heard something about wine," he said.

Another plane rose above the roof and slugs peppered the far wall, dinged the aluminum window frame, blasted the white batting from an easy chair. With the crazy grace of an idiot child, her father stood unharmed through the first of the barrage. Alexandra leapt across the coffee table, shoved him backward until he was flat against the far wall, and held him there as more slugs chewed through the plaster and cheap drywall behind them.

"Hey! Easy now! What the hell!"

Through the next volley, she kept him jammed against the wall. Gabriella was slumped forward on the Oriental rug. The phone had spilled from her hand, and her head was twisted to the left, dark eyes sightless and remote.

When the rumble of the jet passed, Alexandra seized her father's hand and hauled him toward the kitchen. On their way, the old man snagged the duffel and lugged it along. At the back door, Alex came to a sudden halt and cursed. There were half a dozen locks and dead bolts up and down the door. She spun around, searched the room for another exit. But there was none. Out in the front yard, a man shouted and Alex heard the metallic ratchet of heavy weapons being loaded.

In a fury, she fumbled with the locks, working her way from top to bottom. Someone began to batter the front door as she slid back the last of the bolts, kicked the steel brace aside, threw the door open, and blundered out into the narrow, shrubless backyard.

Dogs barked wildly on either side of them, a shepherd tearing back and forth along the fence line of the house directly behind. Alex headed that way and helped her father over the chain-link fence and then hurdled it herself. The shepherd squared off before them, snarling, but Alexandra was having none of it, and she shrieked at the animal, a banshee curse that startled the big dog to silence and sent him backing away toward the safety of his doghouse.

With Lawton floundering at her side, Alex sprinted for the cover of a row of hedges, then scrambled over another fence, cut through two more backyards, and crossed an adjacent street. No cars anymore, no sight of human life, as if that bomb had detonated, the one that kills the people and leaves the structures standing. No one anywhere, a ghostly emptiness along street after street.

Until five minutes later when she and the old man, both panting, reached a bright, busy thoroughfare. A safe haven of hamburger and fried-chicken joints and used-furniture stores. Traffic humming.

"I can't remember the last time I had so much fun," Lawton said, his face bright with sweat.

"Stop it, Dad. Goddamn it. This isn't funny."

"It's not? Okay, okay. But there's no need to snap at me."

Alexandra cut across a lot crowded with used cars and a young man with a fresh haircut marched down the adjacent aisle and intercepted them beside the door of a ten-year-old Ford pickup, black with red trim.

"In the market for a good truck?" the young man said.

"You bet we are," Lawton said. "We're relocating. Blowing this town, once and for all."

"Great," the guy said, turning his vacuous smile on Alexandra. "We're a full-service company. Got financing available on the premises. Just sign on the dotted line and drive away."

"We'll be paying cash," Lawton said. "Won't we, dear?"

Alex looked into her father's helpless eyes.

"Where's your phone?"

"Inside the office. Help yourself."

While Lawton took a seat in the pickup and turned the wheel left and right, Alex dialed 911. The operator answered the phone midlaugh, a joke with a colleague.

"There's been a shooting," she said. "One woman dead."

The operator was still chuckling.

"Listen to me, goddamn it. Pay attention."

"Calm down, honey. I'm here."

She gave the operator a thorough description of the yellow pool truck, the large man and short blond woman who'd killed Gabriella.

"I didn't get the license, but I'm almost certain the truck was from South Miami Pools. Probably stolen."

The operator asked for her name.

"Don't worry about that," she said. "I was there. An eyewitness. Get this out on the radio right away. APB. Do you hear me? Right now, before they have a chance to dump that yellow truck."

"I need your name and your location, please."

Alex hung up. She walked back down the row of cars. Lawton was standing beside the black pickup, kicking its right-front tire.

"I got us a good deal, sweetheart. Got Rafael to knock off two hundred dollars. Didn't I, boy?"

"Yes, ma'am. Your dad's a hard bargainer."

Down the row of cars, someone slammed a door, and Lawton whirled around and clawed at his right hip but found neither holster nor revolver. Alex snaked an arm around his waist, drew him near, and spoke his name, then repeated it over and over until he quieted.

The young car salesman was grinning nervously, not sure where to look.

"Are they after us again, those people?" Lawton whispered. "Are we going to be killed, Alex? Are we going to die?"

She tugged him closer.

"No, Dad. Not if I have anything to say about it."

FIFTEEN

Fifteen minutes after Alexandra and the old man walked out of Stan's room, the cops walked in.

Stan was on the phone with Jennifer, five words past hello when the two of them marched into the room and took up positions at the end of his bed, standing there unsmiling till he told her good-bye and put the phone down.

They were Miami PD, both guys Stan had met at parties over the years. Romano, a puffy old guy with white hair and a boozy face, and Danny Jenkins, a tall man about fifty with the sharp eyes, the tan and limber look of a professional golfer. Romano in a white short-sleeve shirt and dark pants, Jenkins in a black polo shirt and khakis. Bad cop, badder cop.

Stan tried not to swallow or let the sweat start on his face. Conjuring up a memory of stoicism—those Friday nights back in high school, before the game started, guys slapping him on the back, trying to pump him up, trying to get him mean and excited. But getting pumped up wasn't how Stan got to be MVP in the regionals. He did it by staying cool. By putting his mind down around his navel, feeling the calm glow, the warmth radiating through his body. And that's what he did with the cops standing looking at him. He turned off all the lights inside, relaxed his fists, and nodded hello to the two men.

"Sorry to bother you, Stan," Romano said. "You in any pain?"

"I'm dealing with it."

"Just wanted to ask you a couple of questions, that's all. Cover one or two items about the accident. Ten minutes tops."

"Fine," Stan said. "I got all the time in the world."

And the questions came. Slow softballs thrown underhanded. They needed a description of the speeding Mustang. Wanted to know if he'd recognized any of the looters. How fast was he going when he exited the interstate? Was Benito buckled up?

Romano jotting down his answers, the other guy, Jenkins, delivering the questions. After half a dozen questions, all fluff, Stan felt his gut relax. It was clear Alexandra hadn't spoken to them. Stan's threats holding her in check so far.

Romano with his eyes on his pad, scribbling away, an occasional glance up at Stan, but nothing suspicious in his eyes. Jenkins was bored, going through the exercise. Until the last question, which caught Stan off guard, coming in the same deadpan voice.

"You attempt to rescue your partner? Pull his head out of the water, anything like that?"

Stan swallowed, tried to keep his eyes clear of worry.

"I was passed out," Stan said. "I woke up, the paramedics were there, and Benito was gone already. It's terrible. Him and me were very close. How's his wife taking it?"

Jenkins looked over at Romano.

"How would you say, Dan? How's the guy's wife taking it?"

"First thing she wanted to know," Romano said, "could the Brinks people give her an advance on his life-insurance check."

"Yeah," Jenkins said. "Wanted the money so she could buy the top-of-the-line casket. Preferably something metal she could have welded shut so the guy couldn't ever bother her again."

"So, all in all, I'd say she's taking it pretty well." Romano flipped his notebook closed. "Hey, thanks for your time, Stan. Tell your pretty wife hello for us, would you?"

"You bet," Stan said.

And a minute after they'd left, Stan was back on the phone. "Get the hell over here, Jennifer. Bring my sweat clothes and a pair of crutches." Before she had a chance to say a word, he slammed the phone down.

Knowing Alexandra like he did, he figured he had maybe another hour or two before she got her shit together, stashed her father somewhere, and came back full throttle to bring Stan Rafferty down. He was pretty sure if he stayed put, next time the cops walked through the door, they'd have their holsters unsnapped.

He was taking Friday afternoon off from work to scout for women. Not in a hurry, no pressure, but a quiet prickle heating his loins. An urge to browse, to mingle, to dangle his bait in the clear waters and see what nibbled.

It was early afternoon and he was at the mall, Dadeland out in Kendall, with all the yummy mummies and their strollers and their cell phones and manicures and Ann Taylor outfits. He sat near a play area in the main thoroughfare and watched them talking on their tiny phones and to one another while they supervised their kids with an occasional Spanish bark. Ninety-nine percent Cuban in this mall, all of them wearing loud perfume and louder jewelry. A few with nannies in white uniforms, Guatemalans or Mexicans who considered themselves lucky to wipe the asses of bratty Cuban-Americans.

He was smiling. He was watching a couple of four-year-olds chase each other around the carpeted play pit. He tried laughing at their antics. It was a good laugh, hearty with rich contralto sincerity. It caught the attention of one of the Cuban yummy mummies sitting nearby in a red blouse and stiff white shorts. He turned his eyes her way and she smiled coolly at him. He nodded back.

"Are they yours?" he called over.

"Mine, yes."

"Brother and sister?"

"That's right."

"Very cute."

"Thank you."

She was ten feet away, perched on the second step. Her legs were shiny, just shaved and moisturized. She had long brown hair that she was wearing loose. Coming to the mall not to shop but to put herself on display. To luxuriate in that fluorescent aura of overripe perfumes and gaudy goods. Teaching her children about America, its bounty, its vacuity.

The children had noticed him now, noticed that he was watching them and that he was talking to their mother, which made them increase the heat of their activity. The boy chasing the girl while she toddled along squealing with that blend of horror and delight that seemed obscenely sexual.

He stood up, stretched, then angled a few feet in her direction.

"I always wanted kids," he said.

She looked at him for a moment.

"They are wonderful," she said. "They fill your life with riches."

"Your husband must be very proud. You *do* have a husband?"

Her eyes drifted away to the storefronts.

"I'm sorry," he said. "I'm being forward. Excuse me, please."

"It's all right," she said. She turned her glance back to him and forced a smile.

"No, no, you're right to be on guard. A beautiful woman can't be too careful today. Paranoia is the number-one survival skill in this town. With things the way they are, you have to assume everyone is a killer, that any man who strikes up a conversation in a public place might just turn out to be the Bloody Rapist looking for his next victim. Trying to seduce you, get you alone, have his way with you, his violent, degenerate fun."

She looked at him for a long moment. He bore it for a while, although he could feel her eyes crawling around inside his head like she was profiling him, a psychologist analyzing the structure of his personality, probing the soft folds of his cerebellum, searching for some telltale coil of cells, some twist in the DNA that would confirm his depraved condition.

So he shut his eyes. Blocked her out. Kept them shut moment after moment while he listened to her gathering her children, while she shushed them and hurried them away. Standing stiffly on the stairs to the play pit, he kept them shut as the other yummy mummies nearby followed her lead, lowering their loud Cuban voices, moving off. He kept his eyes shut for five minutes, maybe ten, inhaling the machine-made air, the artificial mall scents, until a security guard tapped him on the shoulder and said, "You having some kind of problem, mister?"

He opened his eyes, looked squarely at the guard.

"No. Are you?"

He was a black man in his thirties who looked like an ex-tackle for some half-assed football team. A radio on his belt, a nightstick on the other side.

"I was meditating," he said. "That's a crime now?"

"Well, maybe you should just go meditate back at your own place," the guard said. "You're spooking the kids. And their mothers."

"Sure," he said. "Sure, Officer. Certainly don't want to spook anybody. No, no, we positively can't have that, can we? Bad for business. Suppresses the shopping instinct, doesn't it? A spooked customer is a hurried customer."

"All right, sir. Why don't you just move along, take your bullshit somewhere else where they might appreciate it."

"Yes, Mr. Rent-a-Cop, whatever you say, sir. Happy to oblige.

I have no problem with authority figures. Oh, no, not me. Always eager to comply with the universal laws of good manners and social rectitude."

Twenty minutes after the assault, Emma still felt the vibrations of the Heckler & Koch, eight hundred rounds a minute, her arm muscles quivering. She'd probably be sore tomorrow, her triceps anyway. That's what usually hurt when you hadn't fired your weapon in awhile and took an hour's practice at the range.

Twenty minutes since they'd gone into that house and found the skinny Hispanic woman dead in the living room. They'd scoured the place, run out the back. All the dogs barking, but the money and the old man and the woman had vanished. Twenty minutes later and Norman still hadn't said a word. Just sat there in the passenger seat of the pool truck, the knees of his sky blue pants wedged against the glove compartment, staring straight ahead.

Emma just drove around aimlessly for a while until she found herself drifting south toward the neighborhood where most of her pools were. She got to a back street, pulled off under a banyan tree across from a pink Spanish-style mansion, and put the truck in neutral.

"They can run three miles an hour," she said. "It's not Olympic class, but hey, for an insect, that isn't bad. They can hold their breath for forty minutes, squeeze through a crack the size of a dime, and it takes forty-eight hours for soft food to move through a cockroach's gut."

Emma looked over at him. Norman Franks's face had muscled up into a scowl.

"I talk too much," said Emma. "I know I do. I get wound up and I just go on and on. I get excited and that's the way I ventilate. Some people find it annoying, I realize that, but there's a lot of people who find it stimulating. But the thing is, I'm just being me. A talkaholic.

"I guess I'm a little wired about killing that lady. Not that she was the first person I've killed. No, the first one was a girl. Tawana Bartley. You remember three or four years ago, that body they found in the Dumpster over on Sixth Avenue, all razor-slashed? It was on the news for a couple of days. Well, that was me who did it. Tawana and I had a financial dispute and I settled it. And killing her didn't bother me any more than killing that woman today bothered me. So you can quit your analyzing."

"You're a killer, are you?"

"Damn right I am. A killer of color."

She unbuttoned the flap on her shirt and reeled Amy out of her pocket. The roach seemed dazed or sleepy. Emma dangled it over the black dashboard and lowered it till it was standing on the hundred perforations where the radio speakers were. Amy waved her feelers around a little to see where she was, but she didn't try to make a run for the air vents like she usually did. Probably still a little stunned from the concussions of the Heckler & Koch.

"Largest roach in the world lives down in South America. It's six inches long and has a wingspan of one foot. It hisses when it's angry. The mother ship of all roaches. You get out the bug spray, turn it on that roach, and it'll spin around and fly in your face, grab you by the collar, pick you up, carry you off to its goddamn roach nest. Yes, sir. I want to be there the day that roach sneaks into the USA. Oh, boy. Turn on the light in your kitchen in the middle of the night and there's five or six of those, one-foot wingspan, buzzing around the cookie crumbs, oh, yes, that'll be an exciting day. Beginning of the fucking revolution."

Norman dusted a thread off the lapel of his canary yellow sports coat. He reached up to his throat and felt the stubble. His eyes squinted out into that expensive sunshine blazing on that expensive street.

"So what's next, Norm? What's the plan? Got any ideas, big fella?"

"The hospital," he said. "Jackson Memorial."

"What?"

"Guy broke his leg."

"What guy? What're you talking about, Norman?"

"Guy driving the armored truck."

She peered at Norman Franks for a minute. The big man stared patiently out the windshield.

"Oh," Emma said. "The hospital. Yeah, of course. The hospital."

SIXTEEN

Stan and Jennifer were in the third-floor corridor of Jackson Memorial. Stan gimping along on the pair of aluminum crutches Jennifer had smuggled into his room. His left leg in a cast that went almost to his knee. Ten pounds of plaster. He was wearing his blue Adidas track suit, razored up the seam of his left leg so the cast would fit.

While Stan hobbled on the crutches, Jennifer rested her hand on his shoulder like that would've helped catch him if he lost his balance. As they approached the nurses' station, some kind of argument was going on between two black women, everyone else listening in. Stan kept his eyes on the floor, moving steadily but not too quick. Passing by without a word from any of them.

Then they were in the elevator, grinding down to the basement, where she'd parked the car. Jennifer stood beside him.

She said, "Whew. That was tense."

Stan waited till they were between the first and second floors and then reached out and smacked the red stop button.

Jennifer looked up at the numbers and waited. She had on a low-cut red dress that showed freckles on her shoulders. For the last three months, every chance he'd had, Stan had been trying to lick those freckles off. She wore dark leather sling-back sandals and earrings made from feathers and beads, more of the Navaho crap she was so fond of.

From all the supercharged sex they'd had, Stan had stored up a lot of goodwill for Jennifer McDougal. Which was how he was managing at the moment to keep from punching her in the teeth.

"So, tell me, Jen. You left maybe a couple of million dollars sitting in your closet. That was your idea of hiding it?"

She kept her eyes on the lighted numbers.

"It wasn't my closet. It was the guest room closet."

"Oh, the guest room closet. Well, yeah, that should've thrown them off. How in the world did they ever figure it out, do you think?"

"Look, I feel bad about it, Stan. I do. I'm sorry. But these things happen. And anyway, you and I don't need all that money. We're happy like we are. Aren't we, Stan?"

"These things happen," he said. "We don't need the money. Just like that, blow it off. Are you crazy, Jennifer? Are you fucking out of your mind? Of course we need that money. I risked my goddamn life for that money. Without that money, I got nothing."

"You got me, Stan."

With a jerk of her head, Jennifer tossed her hair back over her shoulders, like a horse flicking its tail at the flies. Only there were no flies in the elevator. No reason for her to be flipping her goddamn hair every three seconds. Maybe she'd done it all along and he'd never noticed it before. Maybe it was one of ten thousand annoying habits he was just now starting to become aware of, because Stan wasn't horny for her at the moment, clear-eyed, seeing her for what she was, a girl whose mind hadn't caught up to her body yet, probably never would.

She was waiting for him to say the right thing back to her.

You got me, Stan.

Yeah, baby, that's enough for me. I don't need no million dollars.

But Stan wasn't playing that game, and Jennifer gave up waiting.

"You told me to hide it, so I hid it." Her voice getting pouty. "I don't know what the big deal is."

He crabbed over to the left side of the elevator, as far from her as he could get, and leaned against the wall.

"In the guest room closet. That's what you call hiding it?"

"I put some sweaters and stuff in front of the duffel."

"Oh, good. Some sweaters."

"I don't like it when you're sarcastic, Stan. I don't like that. It's a total turnoff."

Stan could feel the blood ballooning his face.

"You don't like it when I'm sarcastic? Well, Jen, hey, guess what? I don't like it when you're so fucking stupid. Which, as far as I can see, is most of the fucking time."

She was staring at her blurry reflection in the steel doors—her slightly bony face, a thin, straight nose, blond eyebrows, narrow lips. She said she wanted to be a model, but she'd never tried out for anything. Just kept plugging along at her job as receptionist at Kendall Toyota, calling out the names of Cuban salesmen all day long over the PA system.

"I know you don't mean it, Stan. I know you're only testy from the drugs they've been giving you. And the shock of losing so much money. So that's why I'm ignoring how mean you're being."

She flipped her hair again, got it back over her shoulders.

"And stop doing that."

"Doing what?"

"That fucking thing with your hair."

She cocked her head to the side like she was trying to catch the echo of what he'd said.

"I don't know what you're talking about."

"That horse thing with your hair. Flipping it at the flies."

Jennifer McDougal turned and clasped her hands behind her back and leaned against the opposite wall. She tucked her chin down and looked at him with a sulky frown. She'd chosen a red knit dress to wear this morning. Scooped so low at the neck, the fabric missed the rosy edge of her nipples by about a hundredth of a millimeter. The kind of dress that made it hard to be missed walking down the hospital hallways full of starched white nurses.

"You just left it, a million, two million dollars. You went out with it just sitting there. I'm trying to understand this. I'm trying to picture how your fucking mind works, Jennifer."

"Jeez," she said. "I just left the house for half an hour to get my hair cut. If we're going on a trip, I wanted to let Sheri do my split ends one more time before we took off. But then I was sitting there and thinking how everything was going to be different now, you and me together finally, starting over somewhere else, and I said to Sheri, what the hell, go on, give me a whole new look, layer the sides like that TV girl we like. That's what I said, and she asked me was I sure, and I said yeah, I was very sure, so she just snipped it right off. And then I walked in here, and all you can talk about is the money, going on and on, without even saying a word about my haircut. I didn't think you were like that, Stan. I thought you were more sensitive. Not so money, money, money all the time."

She was chewing gum. Stan could smell it across the elevator, Juicy Fruit. He didn't know why he hated the smell so much. It reminded him of those little blue disks they put in urinal stalls to keep the smell down.

"Could you spit out the gum, please? Stick it in the ashtray there."

"The gum? Why?"

She looked up at him. She was moping. Taking her licks because she'd lost the money and maybe felt a little guilty about it and didn't really know how mad Stan was, what he was likely to do to her, so she was accepting her whipping. Stan didn't know what he was likely to do, either. He'd just have to wait and see.

"Why?" he said. "'Cause I fucking asked you politely to spit the gum out. Because I'm about to vomit from the smell of it. The combined smell of that and all that other shit you're wearing."

"If you're going to keep being mean to me, I'll just leave you here. I have my pride, Stan Rafferty. I'm not one of those bimbos you can take it out on when things aren't going your way. Some punching bag. I'm not like that."

She made an exasperated noise, tugged on the hem of her dress.

"You're not going to say anything about my hair at all, are you?"

"Fuck your hair, Jennifer. Sheri could shave you bald, okay? I don't give a pig's butt hole about your hair. The money's gone; Alexandra's got it."

"Alexandra! That's who was in my house?"

"She has the money and she knows the whole thing. She could put me in the electric chair, Jen. She could have my ass toasted."

"Can we go on down to the car now, Stan? It's getting claustrophobic in here. All right?"

"Get rid of the gum, damn it. Before I puke."

She hesitated a moment more. Then she moved the gum around in her mouth and made a show of swallowing it; a gulping noise came from her throat. Giving him a proud look like, see what I'll do for you, Stan. See what lengths I'll go to. Same look she'd given him that first night, gulping down his cum. The moment he knew he was hooked.

"Okay, good."

He watched the quick clip of it in his head, that first night, how hot it was with her. Leaping and screaming, wrestling, both of them sweaty as hell. Licking, biting, scratching. Nothing like Alex—so cool, so dead.

"Okay," Stan said. "Let me give you an illustration, Jen. An example of what's expected of you, this new life you're a part of from now on."

"Is this more stories about criminals? 'Cause if it is, I should tell you, Stan, I'm getting bored hearing about criminals all the time. Like that's all we ever talk about."

"Just listen to me. Okay! Shut the hell up and listen for about two seconds."

She mashed her lips tight, giving him her prissy, hurt look.

"So you've heard of Meyer Lansky, right?"

She frowned.

"Of course. I'm not stupid. He was some kind of crook over on Miami Beach. Back in the Civil War or something."

"Not the fucking Civil War. Jesus. He was a modern-day Mafia guy. A kingpin. Boss of bosses. One of the biggest crooks this century. And Meyer Lansky had a wife. Her name was Thelma, but they called her 'Teddy.' And Teddy, although she was married to this big-time gangster, she still behaved like a lady. She had class, wore nice clothes, good makeup, great hair, all the shit you like, Jennifer. Crystal and good china. You and her have that much in common, anyway. Expensive tastes."

"Well, thank you, Stan. Thank you for recognizing that."

Stan rubbed a knuckle across the bristles on his chin. His shinbone was aching inside the cast, and the crutches were too short, making him slump forward, putting another pain in his back.

"The thing is, see, the reason I'm telling you this, Jennifer, is because of the way Teddy acted when Meyer was in trouble, if he was sick, or needed an alibi."

"Yeah, okay."

"Teddy was always a thousand percent supportive. Even if it meant perjuring herself, risking prison. There was one famous time when she told the court her husband couldn't possibly have made a payment for a gangland hit that one of his rat-fink cronies testified he did, 'cause, according to Thelma, Meyer Lansky was in a Boston hotel at the time recovering from a hernia operation, with her being his nurse. The jury believed her and Meyer got off. That's 'cause she had class. Nobody believed a classy woman like her would tell lies.

"She was smart. And totally, completely loyal. She could stand up to the best cross-examination there was. Because she knew if she fucked up anywhere along the line, it would be the same as cutting her own throat. That's what she knew, and it kept her operating at a very high level of efficiency."

"But they were married," Jennifer said. "Married's different."

"Married, not married, it's all the same, Jennifer. You gotta be there for your man."

"I'm here, aren't I? What's your point?"

Stan settled his armpits against the crutch pads. His lungs felt as if they were filled with sand. He tried to say something, but all that came out was a grumble.

"So if I'm Teddy, that makes you Meyer Lansky. Is that what you're trying to say, Stan? One robbery and you're a kingpin and I'm a gun moll. I don't know. It seems a little quick, like you're getting ahead of yourself. Way ahead. Especially since you don't even have the money anymore. Are you still considered a kingpin if the money you steal gets stolen from you?"

She gave him a cute smile.

"See? I can be sarcastic, too."

"Never mind," he said. "Never fucking mind. This is hopeless."

Jennifer stepped forward, gathered some hair with her right hand and lifted it off her neck, then dropped it and did her horsetail flick again.

"You know what, Stan? I think you're still in love with your wife. That's what I think. A wife is a wife is a wife. And I'm just the girlfriend. You don't truly and completely appreciate me. Because obviously you don't know, Stan, you don't know how hard it was to do what I did yesterday.

"I had to dress up in that ugly hot raincoat and hooded sweatshirt and go out there and take those two heavy bags and drive away. That was so scary, driving down into a dangerous part of town like that, all those black people around, the looters and drug addicts.

"And then a couple hours later, there it is on the news. The whole world looking at what we did, on all the talk shows, the radio, everywhere. And next thing I know, I go out to make myself pretty for you, and when I come home, the house is ransacked and people have been into my things, lying on my bed, touching my stuff. And you never told me anything about that. You didn't say anything about people breaking into my house, or me being in danger or anything.

"I go to all this trouble and put myself at risk and now all of a sudden you don't like my clothes or my chewing gum or my hair or anything. You don't thank me for doing my part in this. Instead, you're giving me lectures about some Mafia guy's wife. Hey, Stan. It's not my fault the money is gone. If you'd wanted me to put it in a safe place, you should've told me. You should've said, 'Jennifer, hide it under the floorboards, honey, or in the hot tub or somewhere creative like that. Because people may come looking for that money.' But since you didn't tell me any of that, I put it where I thought it was out of the way. I don't have a lot of storage room in that house, you know. It's not easy to hide things there. It's very cramped. I just got those two little closets."

Stan closed his eyes, rubbed the creases at his temple, tight circles of hurt.

"Good, Jennifer, fine. Whatever you say. Your house is cramped. It's all my fault." Eyes still shut. Maybe while they were closed, she'd grow a brain.

"So, what about my hair? You don't like it, do you? You think it's ugly."

"It's fine. It's beautiful," he said, opening his eyes. "You're a beautiful, sexy girl. I'm a lucky man to have you."

Saying the words he knew she wanted. What the hell. This was the ticket he'd bought. Jennifer McDougal with her tight twenty-one-year-old body. Like it or not, he was going to have to ride these rails a little longer.

Stan leaned forward, smacked the red button, and the car

lurched into motion. As the doors rolled open onto the basement garage, a big man in a yellow sports coat and blue pants blocked the door. Ugly man about five feet wide, with a head shaped like a cement block. Beside him was a blond girl with mocha skin and eyes a creepy bleached-out shade of blue.

When the big man didn't get out of the way, Stan said, "Hey, fella, you mind?"

"Mind what?"

"It's customary in our country to step back and let people get off the fucking elevator before you try to get on. You know what I'm saying? That's the way we do things here. In case your fucking raft just washed ashore."

"What raft is that?" the man said.

"Come on, Stan. Let's go." Jennifer had him by the biceps and was trying to pull him away. "We got important things to do, remember?"

Stan was staring at the girl, eighteen maybe, twenty at the most. A large brown roach was crawling up the front of her shirt, a green thread trailing along behind it.

"Jesus," Stan said. "This fucking town."

He hobbled forward into the parking garage, into a cloud of carbon monoxide. Glancing back once, seeing the big guy and the girl step into the elevator, both of them eyeing Stan as the door swished closed.

"I need to go home, finish packing," Jennifer said. "Then we can head on out to Taos like we planned. I can get a job out there, nurse you till you're back on your feet."

"No," Stan said. "First thing we're going to do is get that money back."

"Oh, Stan, give it up. I'll find a dealership out in Taos. I know how to do phones. I have the voice for it. I'll be fine. Just you and me and those cool desert nights."

Jennifer led him down a row of cars till they got to the Honda. She opened the rear door, helped Stan into the backseat, got him laid out, and then shut the door. She went around and got in the front seat and started the car.

"First thing I've got to do is kill her," Stan said. "Kill her, get the money; then we'll go out west. Enough of this chaos bullshit. I'm using a goddamn plan this time. Logical, orderly. Seek and destroy. Fuck chaos."

Jennifer put her right arm on the back of the seat and swiveled around to look at Stan. The skin on her face was drawn tight. A lump moved in her throat, as if the gum hadn't made it all the way down. She started to say something, then stopped and shook her head.

"What is it, Jen? Go on, say it."

"You like my hair or not? Just tell me."

"I love your hair, Jen. It's beautiful. An incredibly great cut. Makes you look cuter than ever. Beautiful hair. Gorgeous fucking hair, Jennifer. Okay? Is that enough? Is that fucking sufficient?"

She turned back around, pulled out of the parking space, wound around to the cashier, and handed in the ticket. As the old man was counting out her change, Jennifer caught Stan's eye in the rearview mirror.

"Thank you, Stan. Thank you very much."

SEVENTEEN

Parked out on Silver Palm Avenue, closing in on eleven o'clock Friday night, Stan stared at his darkened house, then up and down the street. No sign of cops, no sign of anybody. He'd had Jennifer drive around till it got dark, till the adrenaline and codeine were filtered out of his blood. Stopped at McDonald's for supper, then at a 7-Eleven to pee and call the house. No one home. No one answering anyway. They parked out at the airport, watched the jets take off and land for a couple of hours. Then he couldn't stand it any longer and he had Jennifer drive by the house three times, looking for stakeouts. And finally at eleven, he told her to park out front.

"If you can come here to your house, why can't I go to mine, just to pick up a few things? Why is that? That doesn't seem fair to me."

"Because I need to go inside. Because if I don't, this whole goddamn thing falls apart."

"Oh, come on, Stan, you can't expect me to go to some motel and hole up with you for who knows how long without any of my bathroom stuff, or clothes or anything. What am I supposed to do, use the little bar of soap in the paper wrapper, get by on that? Wash my hair with hand soap?"

"All right, goddamn it," Stan said. "Go to a drugstore, buy whatever you want. But don't go home. Forget your clothes. We'll pick you up a new wardrobe on the road somewhere. Alex knows where you live, so the cops could have it staked out by now. Okay? Is that clear?"

"And what about Pooh Bear? I'm just supposed to leave him?"

"Your fucking cat can fend for himself, Jennifer. All right, got it? Mice, birds, shit like that. Don't worry about the goddamn cat. It's too fucking dangerous to go back over there."

"You never liked Pooh Bear. You said you did, but I knew you didn't, not really."

"Look, Jennifer, you had one freebie. But you fucked up and lost the money. Now you're in the penalty. Every screwup from here on is going to cost you. Go to Eckerd's, buy your shampoo and shit, and get back over here quick."

"All right, all right," she said. "I'll show you. I can be faster than Meyer Lansky's wife."

She gave her hair a flip and smiled.

"You're lucky you're so damn cute," he said.

"You think this comes easy, Stan? Looking this way? You think I was born like this?"

She leaned over and kissed him on the lips, let her hand brush his crotch. He cringed away.

"Later," he said. "Not now. There's no time."

"You still love your peach fuzz, don't you? You haven't changed your mind, have you?"

"I haven't changed my mind. Just go, Jennifer. Just go and get back."

"Aren't you horny for me, or anything?"

"I got a fucking broken leg, Jennifer. My fucking wife's going to try to put me in the electric chair. All in all, I'm not feeling real sexual at the moment. You see what I'm saying?"

"I bet Meyer Lansky didn't push his wife away when times got tense."

"Go, goddamn it. Hurry up."

"You sure it's safe going into your house?"

"Hell, no, I'm not sure it's safe. But I don't have any choice. My 'Get out of jail free' card is in there. So go. And hurry up. Longer you take, more dangerous it gets."

Stan hauled his broken ass out of the car and Jennifer started the engine and rolled off down the street.

His white Ford was sitting in the driveway, thanks to one of his buddies at work dropping it off. The house was totally dark. Stan hobbled up the walk, got the door key from under a rock out front, and let himself in. He stood there a minute in the dark, listening. He watched the shadows move on the living room floor.

With his pulse thudding, he went from room to room, but she wasn't there. The old man's smell was heavy in the guest room, but he wasn't around, either. Stan checked the closets. Everything still where it was supposed to be, luggage, clothes.

On his crutches, he hauled himself out to the Florida room and eased down onto the tiles beside his green La-Z-Boy; he reached up under the front dust ruffle, peeled the electrical tape away from the .38 Smith & Wesson, and pulled it out. For twenty years, Lawton Collins had kept that pistol cleaned and oiled and loaded, and that's how it still was.

Stan got his crutches back under him, then humped out to the kitchen and dragged a Tecate out of the six-pack. He took it back to the Florida room and sat down. A cold beer and a loaded gun, the only companionship any real man needed.

He didn't turn on any lights. He didn't turn on the TV. He rocked back in the La-Z-Boy and listened to the night birds out in the backyard and drank his beer. He listened to an occasional car pass by on Silver Palm. The pistol lay on his lap, heavy but comfortable.

As far as Stan knew, Alex only had one friend—Gabriella Hernandez. But Gabbie was being pursued by those Cuban exile wackos. Not exactly a safe haven for Alex, a woman on the run herself. Then there were people at work or at her karate class she might call on, but Stan doubted it. She'd never mentioned any of them, never got calls at home from them. Alexandra, the loner.

No, she probably took the old man and drove off somewhere. Could've gone to Clewiston or Fort Myers or Palm Beach or down to the Keys. She could be anywhere. A motel, a rented room. Sleeping in her car. Five hours away, two hours. Or she could've caught a plane and gone any goddamn place in the world.

Stan Rafferty watched the shadows on the floor flutter and sway from the breeze through the palms next door. He sat and rocked and let his mind work on the problem. But he got nowhere.

It was his stomach that did it finally. Eleven-thirty, he had a rumble in his belly. Stan pushed himself to his feet and hobbled into the kitchen, going to make himself a toasted cheese sandwich, get another beer. That's when he saw the plaster dust on the floor. The gouge in the ceiling where the old man had shot his gun during breakfast. All of that happening yesterday, right after Alex had been talking about a vacation. Going off somewhere. She'd even had a brochure.

Stan switched on the kitchen light. He limped over to the shelves above the stove, seeing the shiny folded-up pamphlet. His heart waking up, starting to bump. Feeling that old heat come back into his muscles, that urge to hit somebody, get his body moving full speed and collide with another guy just as big, coming just as fast. Only the other guy never liked it as much as Stan did. That was the difference between winners and losers in football, and in a lot of other things. You had to like to hit and get hit; you had to love the pain.

A minute or two later, he was at the kitchen table, just finishing his Tecate, hunched over the pamphlet that showed the white beaches and colorful houses of Seaside, Florida, when the phone rang.

He looked at it but didn't get up. Five rings, six. He let it get up to twelve; then he reached over and snapped it off the wall and listened to half a minute of silence at the other end. Then finally a voice.

"Stan?" It was Jennifer. She sounded stiff, out of breath.

"Hey, where the hell are you? It's almost midnight, for Christ sakes. I told you to hurry."

"It's taking longer than I thought."

"Well, guess what? I know where Alex is. I figured it out."

"Good, Stan. I'm happy for you."

"She's up in the fucking Panhandle. Place called Seaside. Some little resort town near Panama City. We leave right away, we could be there tomorrow noonish."

"Stan," she said. "You told me not to go back to my house. But I went anyway. I disobeyed you. I'm here now. I'm at my house."

"Jesus Christ, Jennifer. Get out of there. They could be watching the place. Get over here, and make sure you're not followed."

"No, you've got to come over here. Something's happened."

"Something's happened?"

"Do me this favor, Stan. Please. Come on over here. Can you do that for me, honey?"

A car passed by on the street and Stan pulled back the drapes and watched it cruise past.

"What the fuck's going on, Jennifer? You in trouble? Is there somebody there?"

"I'm trying to be Mrs. Lansky, Stan. I'm trying. But you got to come over here. You got to come right away. You'll come, won't you, Stan? Won't you?"

■

"That was good, Jennifer," Emma said. "She's a bright girl, don't you think, Norman?" Emma put down the other phone she'd been listening on. "Cute little figure, too. She might've gone a long way in this world, except she got mixed up with a bunch of losers."

Jennifer was duct-taped to a swivel chair.

"Where's Seaside?" Norman was sitting on the green couch. Sinking deep into the foam rubber.

"Jennifer's heartthrob said it was up in the Panhandle. You got a map, Jennifer? A map of the state of Florida?"

"Oh, come on. I did what you asked. Now let me out of this chair, okay? I have to use the bathroom."

Emma walked into the kitchen, started opening drawers and cabinets, searching for a map.

"You whining, Jennifer? Is that the sound I heard in your voice? It sounded like a whine to me. Is that what you heard, Norman?"

"Yeah, a whine."

"You think your boyfriend's going to come and save you, Jennifer? You think he heard some signal in your voice, and now he's on his white horse riding over here?"

Jennifer made a face and didn't reply. Emma came back into the living room, carrying something in her hand.

"What's this thing, Jen? What's it for? Some kind of medical instrument?"

"It's to open wine bottles," the girl said, a wretched look on her face as she stared at the device.

It was a plastic air pump with a long syringe on one end.

"How's it work, Jen? Could you explain that to me?"

"You stick the needle through the cork, pump the bottle full of air, and the cork pops out."

"You ever see one of these gadgets, Norman? A wine-bottle opener."

"On TV," he said.

"What's wrong with a regular corkscrew, Jen? Not Yuppie enough for you?"

Emma gave the pump a couple of strokes, touched a finger to the sharp tip of the needle.

"Let's see if it works, Norman? You feel like a little wine?"

"No."

"How about you, Jennifer? Care for a sip?"

Emma touched the needle tip to Jennifer's cheek, scratched a red line in her flesh.

"Don't," Jennifer said.

"I wonder what would happen," Emma said. "Stick this needle in a whiny girl. Maybe go in through her eardrum, pump her skull full of air, see what pops out. What do you think, Norman? You think I should pump whiny Jennifer full of air, see if she blows a cork?"

"You're sick," Jennifer said. "You're disgusting. Both of you. Perverts."

"Or maybe the cat. Pump up the cat, see if any mice blow out."

"Leave Pooh Bear alone. If you're going to torture somebody, let it be me."

"Don't worry," Emma said. "I'm not going to hurt you, not at this particular moment. We're just getting to know each other, that's all. I'm testing your reflexes, see how you respond, so we can be all ready for when lover boy Stan gets here. He'll come, won't he? He'll do anything to save his Jennifer, his pretty little whiny girlfriend. Won't he, Jen? Won't he?"

She touched the point of the wine pump to Jennifer's temple.

"He'll come," Jennifer said. "And you'll be sorry."

"Oh, I hope he comes. For your sake, I hope he does. It would make things a lot neater."

"He'll come." But she didn't sound certain about it. And Emma, despite how good-looking the girl was, despite how whiny, felt a little pang of pity for Jennifer.

Emma set the gadget on the coffee table and sat down on the foam couch next to Norman.

"Hey, Jen. You know what has white blood and eighteen knees?"

Jennifer gave her a long appraisal.

"Well, do you?"

Jennifer flipped her hair and said, "A space creature?"

EIGHTEEN

Stan was roaring north on Main Highway, pedal to the floor, two blocks from Leafy Way, when he saw a yellow pool truck roll through the stop sign at the end of Jennifer's street, turn north, and head up the highway right in front of him. Three people crammed in the front seat. He caught them in his headlights for only a second. A big guy driving, a curly-headed blonde riding shotgun, and squeezed between them was another blonde, this one with straight hair. He set his hands on the wheel, about to swerve into Leafy Way, when he saw the blonde in the middle give her hair a flip.

"Jesus Christ, what the hell?"

He jerked the wheel back straight and fell in behind the truck, staying a couple of car lengths back.

He followed them north across Dixie Highway, then west out Bird Road to the Palmetto, up the ramp, onto the expressway. Fifteen minutes, twenty. Keeping them in sight through the late-night traffic, weaving drunks, racing teenagers. The pool truck was working its way north, slowest damn car on the road, north and north till the signs for I-75 started showing up. Alligator Alley, that dead, dark highway across the width of the state to Naples and Fort Myers. And the pool truck eased into the exit lane and followed the signs, leaving behind the lights of Miami, the throb of the traffic, leading Stan across the high, sweeping ramps west into the dark chaos of the Everglades.

That's when the thought flashed into his head, and his stomach twisted. That fucking brochure. Seaside, those pretty houses, the white beach. In his mad stumble out to his car, Stan had left the goddamn pamphlet sitting on the kitchen table, right out in the open, for anyone to see.

He was in a cowboy bar near the university, watching a new one.

It was closing in on midnight, Friday turning into Saturday.

This one had curly red hair and wore cowboy boots and tight jeans and a leather vest over her red-and-white-checked shirt. She wasn't tall enough. She was too heavy. But if she was the right age, he was going to use her anyway. He had a new idea, a master stroke of genius.

The cowgirl knew he was watching her. She was sneaking looks back at him in her peripheral vision. That's what they did, women. They didn't look squarely at you. It was too bold, too overt. But they did look. They always looked. He'd never had trouble with that. He had the bone structure they liked. He had good lines.

The cowgirl didn't have a girlfriend to consult with. No one to warn her to be careful. She was sitting at a booth in the corner, sipping a long-neck Bud. The other eight people in the bar were paired off, leaning close or dancing. The jukebox was playing Waylon Jennings. He hated cowboy music and cowboy bars and girls who dressed up like cowgirls, like their horses might be tied up out front in the Miami night. He didn't like liars, impostors, or pretenders of any kind. He wasn't one himself. If someone had come up to him at that moment and asked him if he was the

Bloody Rapist, he would have told them, "Yes. I don't particularly like the name they gave me, but yes, I am." And if they asked him why he did it, he would reply, "I do it out of self-defense. A preemptive strike. Do them before they do me. And yes, I feel something. I'm not dead inside, emotionally numb, or anything easy like that. I feel like anyone else. I feel sadness and anger, and I'm always deeply disappointed that these women put me in the position so that I have no choice but to do the things I do."

He always told the truth and he always dressed the way he felt and gave them his real name, no aliases, and where he lived, his job, everything they wanted to know.

Liars were the true evil in the world. Hypocrites, posers, deceivers. People who felt one way and acted another. People with an outside that didn't match their inside, who mouthed morals they didn't observe. Those who wrote laws they broke in secret. College girls who dressed like Annie Oakley on a Saturday night so they could pretend to be brave and rugged and exploratory, when in fact they were more than likely cowardly and frail and boring.

He was attracted to this one despite her extra twenty pounds. Despite her shortness. Despite her cowboy gear. He was aroused by her, though it had been no more than a few days since his last one. He had rekindled his drive in record time. Bounced back. Necessity was the mother of perversion. This one would do just fine. He would leave her out in the open, the canvas exposed to the heavens. A clear, pure message.

He ordered another Budweiser, and when it came, he paid for it, then picked it up and carried it across the empty dance floor through the harsh blue lights of the jukebox to the corner of the room where the cowgirl sat. She could no longer pretend she wasn't looking at him.

She lifted her eyes from her beer, from the rings of condensation on the table, looking up at him as he halted beside her booth and set the Budweiser down in front of her, an offering.

"I've been watching you," she said. "I didn't think you'd come over."

He smiled at her. She smiled back. Pitch, catch. Tit, tat.

"I'm slow to rouse," he said.

"Oh, really? Well, you're the first one of those I've met."

"I'm a dying breed."

She liked that. Her eyes glittered.

"You're not thirty yet, are you?"

"A woman's age is her own business."

"I'd guess twenty-eight."

"Off by a year," she said, her eyes hardening, looking away.

"The reason I ask," he said, "I have a soft spot for twenty-nine-year-olds."

"Do you now?"

"If I'm being rude, I'm sorry."

Her eyes drifted back to him. She looked him over, making her choice.

"You're in luck. I'm twenty-nine."

"Wonderful."

"You going to stand there all night? Or sit down and try to sweet-talk me?"

"I'm slow to rouse," he said. "But when I get going, I'm unstoppable."

She had a sip of her beer, eyeing him the whole while.

"I'm no one-night girl," she said. "If that's what you thought."

"I'm more interested in eternity," he said. "The long forever."

Her smile lost its edge, eyes taking a quick anxious detour toward the bartender.

"Are you a student around here?"

"A student of some things," he said. "And you?"

Her eyes came back. She looked up at him, serious.

"Anthropology. Take my doctoral exams in January. U of M."

He was standing so close beside her, she could have reached out and stabbed him in the belly, sliced him open, torn out his small intestines. If she'd known who he was, what he wanted from her, she surely would have done it.

"So you're a young Margaret Mead," he said. "Is that why you're here? Studying the natives?"

Her eyes crinkled and the light rose behind her smile.

"That's right," she said. "The bizarre dating rituals of the North American redneck."

"That's what you think? I'm a redneck?"

"Well, you don't talk much like a redneck."

"And you speak very uncowgirl-like yourself."

Her smile deepened.

"I just put this on to fit in. You know how it is."

"Yes, the native dress."

"That's right."

"And you feel comfortable in that getup?"

"Not really."

"Well, then you should take it off. Or have someone take it off for you."

She looked down and smiled to herself, had another sip of her beer, and set it aside.

"Picking up women in a bar, it's so trite. A bright guy like you, it doesn't seem to fit."

"Well, it's my first time."

"Oh, is that right? Where do you usually troll for women?"

"The grocery store."

"That's original."

"Frozen-food aisle. Arrive at about six, six-fifteen, stand there like I'm mulling over my choice for the night."

"But you're actually scouting the women."

"That's right. Someone dressed from work, panty hose, a suit, picking out her frozen dinner for the evening. A single dinner, so I know she's not married or living with anyone."

"And you hit on her."

"I don't hit," he said. "I say hello. I say the beef bourguignonne is good. Weight Watcher's Mexican is fair. Like the two of us have this in common, this sad, pathetic, lonely existence."

"That works?"

"It has."

"Single working woman, in a rush. Easy prey," the cowgirl said.

"Exactly," he said. "You're quick."

"Not all that quick," she said. "Actually, I'm a little slow to rouse myself."

"And do you do that, rouse yourself?"

She hesitated, then said quietly, "If I have to."

Pitch, catch, tit, tat.

"I know somewhere better than this," he said. "A more honest place."

"Yeah, I bet you do. Where, your apartment?"

"No. I call it my Edenic garden. Quiet and beautiful, sand, water. Moonlight and stars and jasmine."

"I know karate," she said. "I'm a second-degree brown belt."

"Good," he said. "You can protect us from the moonlight."

She touched the hair that curled near her cheek. She drew out a strand. A gesture he'd noticed quite often, when women were being coy, feeling pretty, in control of the chase. Touched their hair. Played with it.

"All right, I'll go with you, but just for a little while," she said. "Just to see this Edenic garden."

"Whenever you want the night to end, it will end," he said. "I promise."

And she slid out of the booth. Stood up beside him. Taller than he'd thought. Eye-to-eye. She'd do fine.

"So. Will you put me in your research paper, Ms. Mead?"

"Maybe," she said. "It depends."

"And on what does it depend?"

"Whether you can teach me something I don't already know."

NINETEEN

Fingers clenched to the shimmying wheel, Alexandra steered the Ford pickup through the night. Ahead, the highway signs and headlights flared up from the dark like spring-loaded targets in a shooting gallery. Every few seconds, she peered into the rearview mirror, and whenever a pair of headlights began to gain on them, her chest clenched, lungs shut down, until finally the chasing car moved safely past and she could breathe freely again.

Lawton slept through the night, head bumping against his window. He woke twice and replied with scorn to some bothersome character in his dream, then fell immediately back into his black slumber.

Three times, she stopped for gas and to use rest rooms. They were working their way along the corridor of I-75, heading north up the skinny, interminable state of Florida. The same four restaurants at every brightly lit plaza, same hot breeze stirring the same thousand insects that hovered around sputtering fluorescent lights. She was numb and wired, her mind chattering with voices, snatches of conversations recycled from the last forty-eight hours. Stan's threats, Gabbie's entreaties, the blather of TV reporters, her dad's aimless rant, Scarlett Rogers touting her assisted-care facility. Stray fragments firing off in her head as though she were twirling the radio dial up and down the frequencies of memory.

And throbbing in the background was his name. A hateful chant.

Darnel Flint. Darnel Flint.

His name on Stan's lips was a curse, pulsing with foul black magic, full of the bile of Stan Rafferty's hatred. The man she'd married had become the man who haunted her dreams—the seventeen-year-old boy who lowered his weight onto her flesh again and again whenever she felt herself drifting into sleep.

It was as if nothing else had happened in her youth. That one morning looming so high and wide that every other event of childhood was lost in its shadow. No birthdays or Christmases, no bright red bicycles, no Easter dress, no doll, no happy afternoon baking cookies with her mother. Not a single movie or television show, no teacher's name, no happy mornings waking full of the raw power of adolescence, no fragrant summer evening dancing with fireflies, no ball games in the yard, no fishing trips with her father, nothing escaped the shadow of Darnel Flint.

The memories were there, surely they were. But each of them was contaminated, dulled to oblivion by a larger, darker recollection. Like some ravenous tumor that swelled and stretched until no corner of her brain was safe from its tentacles.

Darnel Flint had made her learn karate, the art of deflecting human touch. Darnel had chosen Stan Rafferty as her husband, a man bitterly incapable of providing the affection she needed most. And he'd selected Gabriella as her friend, a woman, like Alex, whose childhood wounds had never healed. Darnel had even selected a career for her, a job that required that night after night she sight through her viewfinder and contemplate his bloody remains.

Eighteen years ago, Darnel Flint had sent her running for her life, and goddamn if she wasn't running still.

At dawn as the trees and hills began to emerge from the gloom, she pulled off the interstate and into a 7-Eleven and stood in line with speechless construction workers holding Styrofoam cups and packages of Twinkies. Hangovers in the air. Lawton used the bathroom while she paid for a *Tallahassee Democrat* and two large black coffees.

Back in the truck, with her dad slurping his coffee, she found the small item in the state roundup section.

> Well-known Miami political figure Gabriella Hernandez was killed Friday afternoon as her quiet neighborhood erupted in gunfire. Discovered by one of her two sons as he returned home from school, Ms. Hernandez's bullet-riddled body was sprawled on her living room floor. When asked if he believed Ms. Hernandez's death was related to her recent controversial encounter with the Cuban dictator, Harry Antrim, spokesman for the Miami Police Department replied, "In this city, your life can be in serious danger if you happen to have the wrong foreign policy." Deepening the mystery of Ms. Hernandez's murder was the Toyota Camry found in her driveway. The Camry is registered to Alexandra Rafferty, an ID technician for the Miami Police Department. "Damn right we're worried," Antrim said. "Ms. Rafferty didn't report for work Friday night and she didn't call in. Yes, we're all quite concerned."

Alexandra set her coffee aside. She stared at the pale brick wall of the 7-Eleven and held very still. She tried to breathe evenly, to keep it settled. But a moment later, she felt it rising inside her, the constriction in her throat, the hot rush behind her eyes.

She bent forward, pressed her forehead to the steering wheel, hugged her chest, and wept. A mourning she had not allowed herself in years. The tears burned—stored so long and deep, they had turned to acid. Covering her mouth with her hand, she sobbed quietly until she was breathless and her stomach began to cramp. Until Lawton reached out and touched her arm.

She wiped her eyes clear, settled back in the seat, and looked over at him.

"Are we in the newspaper? Our names?"

She shook her head.

"No, Dad."

"I used to get my name in the paper a lot. Did I ever show you my clippings? I was quite the media darling."

"I've seen them, yes."

Alexandra found a Kleenex in her fanny pouch, blew her nose, wiped her eyes. She braced herself against the back of her seat until she found the natural rhythm of her breath. Then she folded the newspaper and wedged it between the seats.

She started the engine and wheeled the cumbersome truck out of the lot and back up the ramp onto I-10, heading west now. The Ford labored up to cruising speed, smoothly and without complaint.

"Well," her dad said. "Nothing like a fresh start."

"I killed her, Dad. I killed my best friend."

"You did?"

"I led those murderous bastards to her."

"Who were those guys anyway?"

"I don't know. Some of Stan's friends, I suppose. His accomplices."

"You sure they weren't there to clean the pool?"

"No, Dad. They were killers."

"Well," he said. "Then they're the ones who'll burn in hell, not you. You didn't know they were out there. You can't feel guilty for everything, Alex. There's a name for that. Some term—I forget what. People thinking they're to blame for the world's problems. You can't live like that. Christ, nobody would get anything done if they were always feeling guilty about every damn thing that happened. Where we going anyway? Are we going to Ohio, Alex?"

"No, Dad."

A moment later, he said, "Are we out of Florida yet?"

"Almost."

"*Martyrs*, that's the word. Martyrs, like Joan of Arc. Who, by the way, they burned at the stake for believing such nonsense."

She held the wheel steady along the wide and empty stretch of highway while overhead the clouds slid by low and fast, dark silver corrugations. Here and there, bright shafts splintered through, beaming down like searchlights from a dozen police helicopters.

"Did we steal that money? Are we on the lam?"

She looked over at him, then back at the unfurling road.

"No, we didn't steal it, Dad. We're just carrying it with us until I decide what to do next."

"It sounds obscene," he said. "Being on the lam. Like a bad farm joke."

He chuckled to himself and opened the glove compartment, then slapped it shut it again.

"I've been wanting to relocate," he said. "Miami's gotten too damn dangerous lately. You can't go anywhere these days without running into stray gunfire. That's not how it was when I first took your mother there to start a family. No, sir, it was safe and secure. Everyone in town got along, spoke the same language, 'cause back then everybody was from Ohio or Indiana. Now you meet somebody on the street, they might just as likely be from Tibet. It's gotten crazy. Have you noticed that, Alex?"

"I've noticed, yes."

"That's a lot of money we're carrying. It's mostly hundreds. I could count it if you want."

"I don't want to know how much it is."

"You don't? Why?"

"Because it's not ours."

Lawton leaned forward and Alex looked over at the old man's crooked smile.

"Sure it's ours."

"We're going to give it back, Dad."

"Why would we do that?"

"Because it's somebody else's money."

"Not now it isn't. We got it in our possession. That's nine-tenths of the law, remember?"

"It's not ours, Dad."

"I think we earned it, all we've been through."

She sighed. Having to teach him ethics like he'd once taught her.

"Just because someone's suffered an injustice doesn't mean they can throw away the rules. You know better than that."

"God, I smell terrible," he said, plucking the armpit of his jumpsuit and pulling it close to his nose. "I need a bath. I need two baths. Maybe three."

She looked over at him to see if he was joking again, but he was staring at her, his forehead tensed with worry.

"You sure we aren't on the lam?"

"No, Dad, we're not." She reached over and patted him on the leg. "We're making a strategic retreat, that's all. Just stepping back, taking a breather, a little time to plan our next move."

Alexandra watched the hawks slice through the rippling clouds. She took a long look in the mirror, watching a big red and chrome semi roaring up the outside lane.

"You know it's dangerous," Lawton said, "always watching the rearview mirror. That's no way to drive a car. You can't see where you're going."

"I know, Dad."

"It's not smart," he said, "heading one direction, looking in another. You can go for a while like that, but eventually, sooner or later, you're bound to crash into something that's right there in front of you."

She glanced over at him as the wake of the big truck rocked them.

He drummed his fingers on the dash, rubbed at a smudge on his window.

"I know about rearview mirrors. Oh, yes, I do. I know that condition all too well."

"I'm a careful driver. You know that, Dad."

"Oh, it's bothered me every day of my life. I should've been there to safeguard you. And I should've been the kind of father you could have confided in, instead of you feeling like you had to go over there and face that kid alone. I thought about it so much, it was like I was stuck right there, caught in that same groove in the record, going round and round, hearing the same few moments play over and over, like I was never going to move forward. So I know, Alex. I know how rearview mirrors work.

"But lately, this thing that's been happening to me, losing my memory like I am, it's almost a relief, everything disappearing. A little more every day. Not that it's the most pleasant thing in the world, getting so confused. But at least I've been spending more time in the here and now, and that's not bad. I highly recommend it."

Alexandra stiffened her arms and pushed her spine flat against the seat. Her eyes were misting, but she blinked that away, fixed her gaze on a white car way out ahead of them.

"Don't pay any attention to me," Lawton said. "What the hell do I know? An old man, brain in meltdown. Who the hell am I, giving advice to someone as smart as you?"

"I listen to you, Dad. I always listen."

"We're running for our lives," he said. "With nothing but the shirts on our backs, and a sack of cash. Whooee, what fun."

She kept the truck at the speed limit through the rolling hills of gnarled scrub, palmetto, piney woods. Traffic was light, only an occasional big truck booming past. Her father zipped and unzipped his jumpsuit, humming a song from a long time ago, before everything got so complicated.

Several times, she had to pull off the highway to check the map, but finally she worked the truck south through a maze of narrow county roads until they were on 30A, the beach highway. And suddenly, the air smelled richer, full of the thick, juicy scent of the sea. The sunlight was clean and sharp, the blue of the sky a deeper, more perfect shade than it had been a mile earlier.

They passed the sprawling bayous of Grayton Beach State Park and crossed a low concrete span, then rounded a sweeping bend and emerged on a straightaway that shot along the edges of the dunes. And then there it was.

Springing up from the brown scrub and low pines, it looked like a whimsical cake-frosting village, a frothy confection of pastel purples and yellows and pinks and ultramarine. Dozens and dozens of peaked and gabled Victorian dollhouses with tin roofs and white porches and balconies, picket fences and gingerbread scrollwork and filigree. A startling fairyland, dreamy and absurd.

"What the hell is this place?" Lawton was leaning forward against his seat belt, peering at the town.

"It's Seaside. Seaside, Florida."

"Well, I'll be damned. What is it, an amusement park?"

"It's a town, Dad. From the book you like so much."

"A town?" he said. "What book?"

"They built it right next to where we stayed that summer. You remember? Seagrove."

"I remember that, sure. But why the hell did we come back? Did we forget something?"

"I thought maybe we could work on that sand castle again. You remember that, Dad? That gigantic castle we built together?"

"They got any rides here? Tilt-A-Whirl, merry-go-round. I like Tilt-A-Whirl best. Yes, sir. And goofy golf. I was pretty good at that once."

She stared over at the pleasant jumble of beach houses with their tasteful colors and stately designs, rising out of that drab scrubland of palmetto and slash pine and oak thicket like some storybook kingdom, beautiful and ludicrous.

"This is where we're going to stay for a while, Dad. We should be safe here until I can make some arrangements."

Leaning forward, he studied the bright town as they rolled forward into its midst.

"Well, it's not Ohio," he said. "But hell, I guess it'll do for now."

He watched from a parking space across the street as the morning shift began to arrive. In his blue Honda Accord with its dark windows, he was anonymous and invisible, his car positioned so he could survey the events through the windshield, a full panoramic view.

The cowgirl had believed he was sincere and kindhearted. She'd warmed to him in the ride from the cowboy bar to downtown Miami. He entertained her with stories from his past, the same stories he'd used before, and they never failed to charm. Women liked anecdotes about mothers and sisters. They trusted men who had good relationships with females, men who were observers and appreciators of women. The cowgirl was so touched by one of his stories about his mother that she reached out and lay a hand on his shoulder as he finished it, and she kept her hand there until he parked in the sandy lot.

"Do you feel safe here?" he said when the engine was quiet.

She looked over at the tall building.

"This is your Edenic spot, next to the Miami Police Department? God, you're some kind of weird."

"That I am," he said. "That I most surely am."

Now he sat in his car with a copy of the *Herald* and looked up every now and then from the national news to watch the late-arriving secretaries and detectives pull into the four-story parking garage for the police department. The Saturday shift.

There was a lull about nine o'clock, just as he finished the national section. Floods and riots and political disgraces and criminal outrages in distant cities. He set the section aside and picked up the local pages and read a paragraph or two from the *Herald*'s star columnist—a middle-aged guy who'd discovered sarcasm in the fifth grade and had never gotten over it.

Today, he was being snide about a new real estate development out on the edge of his precious Everglades. A scathing attack on some businessman who had the gall to want to build some houses where the columnist used to fish with his cane pole as a kid. Because the guy had grown up in Miami and remembered it when it was a drowsy backwater tourist town, he thought he was the goddamn pope of alligators. Everybody was supposed to squirm up to him, kiss his ring, and let him decide what got built, what didn't. Fucking journalists.

When he looked up from the newspaper again, the business day was finally under way. A few good citizens with law-enforcement business, unable to find street parking, started to pull into the sandy lot beside the garage where a dozen palm trees were planted.

It was a young man getting out of his white pickup truck who spotted the cowgirl. The young man stood for several moments staring down at her naked body; then he backed away slowly and screamed for help. A uniformed attendant in the parking garage stepped out of his booth as the young man shouted the news, and the parking attendant got on his phone.

Five minutes later, there were three dozen police officers in the lot and yellow crime tape stretched among several palm trees. There were TV crews and a helicopter hovered high overhead.

But he wasn't paying attention to the scene before him, because his eyes had fallen on the major local story of the day. A three-column piece about Gabriella Hernandez, well-known county activist, whose bullet-riddled body had been discovered late Friday afternoon by one of her two sons.

That's not what had his attention, though. He didn't give a shit about political activists. What he was reading over and over to himself were the next few sentences.

> Found at the scene of the murder was a late-model Toyota Camry registered to Alexandra Rafferty, an employee of the Miami Police Department.
>
> Spokesman for the Miami PD, Harry Antrim, re-

> sponded with concern late Friday night. "I have no idea as to the whereabouts of Ms. Rafferty. And now her husband has disappeared, as well. Damn right I'm worried." Mr. Antrim was referring to Stanley Rafferty, who turned up missing from his hospital room at Jackson Memorial, where he had been recovering from injuries suffered earlier in the week during the widely reported Brinks armored truck mishap.

When he finished the article, he carefully refolded the paper and set it on the passenger seat. He stared out at the policemen doing their work. The bright neutral sunshine of another day. Valves were opening inside him, bright stimulants trickling into his bloodstream. The hair on his arms was fully erect.

"Fuck," he said beneath his breath. "Fuck, fuck, fuck."

TWENTY

They had breakfast at a sausage and grits diner down the beach from Seaside, and when the rental office finally opened at nine, she and Lawton were standing at the door.

From the snazzy color brochure, Alex chose a two-bedroom cottage on East Ruskin Street, a Frisbee toss from the beach. It was called the Chattaway, and it was the cheapest rental in Seaside, owned by Chad and Molly Chatwick, a couple from New Orleans, who used it for only a month in the summer. Alex took it for a week.

She counted out fifteen one-hundred-dollar bills and the lady at the rental desk stiffened sharply at the sight of so much cash.

"We're from Miami," Alex said, as if that explained all types of ill-mannered behavior.

"Oh," said the woman. "I see."

Lawton was mercifully quiet through the whole transaction, in a deepening fog of bewilderment from the long sleep-disturbing drive, this unfathomable journey.

A young man in a golf cart directed them to the house, a one-story green-and-salmon bungalow with a white picket fence out front and a tin roof. There was a narrow drive along one side, where she parked the pickup. And the front yard was no larger than her Miami kitchen. A ten-by-fifteen plot with scrub oak and flowering goldenrod and beauty berry, the ground layered deep with pine mulch. From Lawton's coffee-table book, Alex knew that sod was not allowed in Seaside, or lawn mowers or edgers. A controlled scruffiness required by code.

A screened-in porch covered the front of the house, and inside the glass front door, the living room was airy and cheerful with its white gauzy curtains, polished oak floors, and walls painted a safe ivory. The couch and chairs were covered in lavender denim and were littered with bright pillows. Several wicker chairs and tables had been painted an array of primary blues and yellows and reds, which gave the room the jittery energy of a kindergarten. The furnishings and the house itself were less than five years old, but all of it had been contrived to echo an older and more graceful era, while somehow staying insistently modern.

On the oak dining table sat a plastic-wrapped gift basket, compliments of the rental agency. Coffee beans, croissants, fresh fruit, and a small bottle of chardonnay, a Yuppie starter kit. A white high chair with hand-painted blue flowers was wedged into a corner near the pass-through to the kitchen. Everything struck Alex as unerringly tasteful, nothing like the ragtag feel of that long-ago beach house. No layer of sand on the floor, no cobwebs or rusty sinks or the tenacious scent of mildew.

Alex chose the front bedroom for herself. Close to the street, a better vantage point to monitor her father and any traffic that might pass by. While Lawton showered, she took off her running shoes and fanny pack, then began to search for a nook to stash the duffel of money. She settled finally on a floppy woven basket that was perched on a cabinet high above the kitchen sink. She dumped the banded bricks of cash into the straw basket one by one until they reached the brim; then she hoisted the basket back to its place. She stacked the half a dozen remaining bricks next to the ice-cube trays in the freezer.

"This isn't the same place we stayed before," Lawton said. He was standing naked in the living room, dripping onto one of the colorful rag rugs.

"That's right, Dad. But this will do fine, don't you think? The beach is the same. Anyway, we don't need to stay in exactly the same house."

"We don't?"

"No, that's not important. Don't you like this place? It's so clean and sunny."

"I'm tired," he said. "I need to lie down and sleep. I'm getting very old."

"That's fine. You can sleep all you want. Later on, we'll walk on the beach and watch the sunset. We'll explore the area, see what's changed."

"Everything's changed," he said. "Everything's different from how it was."

"Some of it's different, sure. But you like Seaside, don't you? This place we're staying."

"I should be at Harbor House. I'm going to get an unexcused absence."

"I'll write you a note, Dad. They'll understand. They can get along without you for a few days. We're here now. Let's enjoy our vacation."

"Is this a hideout?"

"We're on vacation, Dad. We're having a holiday."

"Elaine Dillashaw is baking chocolate chip macadamia cookies. If I'm not there to get them, she'll give them to that goddamn George Murphy instead."

"We need to find you a towel, Dad. You're getting the floor wet."

"Look at me." He reached down and lifted his flaccid penis, then let it drop. "Look at this old worthless flap of flesh."

"Come on, Dad. You need to rest. We both do."

"I wasn't always this way. I was a virile young man once. You remember?"

"Yes," she said. "You were very dashing. All the women thought so."

"They did, didn't they? I could have had any of them. But I chose you."

"You chose Grace, Dad. My mother, Grace."

"Grace?"

"Let's put you to bed. Come on now. Enough talk."

She got him into the clean sheets, turned on the ceiling fan, lowered the blinds. It was nearly ten o'clock, the temperature outside not more than seventy. At least fifteen degrees cooler and with a lot more oxygen in every breath than that subtropical broth six hundred miles to the south. The sound of the surf was a distant drone; a freshening breeze from the north seemed to be spiced with the crisp hint of evergreen, pure mountain lakes and glaciers. It would be at least another month before that autumn air penetrated all the way down the peninsula to Miami. A day's drive, a different season. A different America.

She sat on the edge of Lawton's bed and he smiled at her, a mischievous light in his grin.

"It's nice here," he said. "Just like the book."

"Yes," she said. "Just like the book."

She returned his smile, stroked the dry, loose skin on the back of his hand. After a minute or two, she watched his eyes sag and finally fall shut. When his breath deepened and began to flutter through his nose, she rose and quietly shut his door.

She found a spool of string in the kitchen pantry, and then picked out a heavy serving ladle from the silverware drawer. She lashed one end of the string to Lawton's doorknob and played out the line as she walked into her own bedroom. Pulling the cord taut, she tied the other end to the ladle and positioned it on the edge of her own bedside table. As good an alarm as she could rig on such short notice.

Her eyes strayed to the bedside table and she stared for several moments at her leather fanny pouch lying there. Finally, she sighed and picked up the pack and unzipped it. She withdrew the four photos and spread them on the wicker side table, then took out the small half globe of glass she carried in a protective felt pouch, a magnifier the size of a lime cut in half.

She placed the glass on the Gasper and rubbed her eyes clear. Then she began to inch the glass from right to left, ever so slowly, rising up the woman's body from her curled toes, past her thin ankles, the small scythe-shaped scar on her right shin, a drop of blood near her knee.

It was a process she'd re-enacted dozens of times, but in that carefree room, in that sharp and uncorrupted light, the photograph was more obscene than it had ever been before, more grimly distinct.

Alex continued to slide the magnifier up the young woman's slightly spread legs to her shaved pubic patch, her narrow waist and tiny navel. The breasts were flattened, the nipples dark and small, like her own. And finally, she came to the gash at the woman's throat, a ragged C, a quick twist of the killer's hand. The wound was virtually identical to the other three.

She kept the glass still on the woman's face. This one a brunette with shoulder-length straight hair, bangs. Her eyes open, a depthless blue. Dark eyebrows, long lashes. And the bruise on her left cheek where he'd struck her right-handed. Alexandra held on the bruise, squinted. She rotated the photograph so the intense ocean light was focused cleanly on it. She leaned in close.

The bruise was smaller than she'd noticed before, smaller than an average fist. Not more than two knuckles wide.

She pushed the photo aside and laid the Floater in its place. She waited till a cloud had moved past the sun, then held the glass to the woman's pale skin and found the same bruise in the same location, the same miniature size. Two knuckles wide. She checked out the other two and they were the same. Bruises she'd seen before, another case or another context entirely. She couldn't recall.

She stood up and paced the room. If she were back at work, she would go down to storage, prowl through her old files, take as much time as she needed to search the stacks of photos until she found the one she was trying to remember.

She couldn't think, couldn't concentrate. Her thoughts were foggy and scattered from the sleepless drive. She'd have to store the bruise away for now, something to let her unconscious gnaw on, another reason she needed to call Dan Romano.

Alex showered and shampooed her hair, wrapped herself in a towel. She gathered her shorts and blouse and underwear and her father's jumpsuit and carried them out to the tiny washer she'd seen in the kitchen. When she got it chugging, she went back to her room, lay down on her sheets.

She listened to the scrape of branches against a windowpane and a mockingbird running through its borrowed repertoire in the narrow yard between their house and the cottage next door. She drew in a long breath of that rich North Florida air.

It was as if a cathedral bell were tolling deep inside her. This place was getting to her already, as though every breath were laden with soul-stirring pheromones, those potent chemicals secreted by the trees and the rolling surf, seeping up from the pores of the earth until the air was irresistible, resonating with memories. All of it coming back with such force and vividness—her last golden month of childhood, those indulgent hours with her parents, the world a safe and generous place, beach and sea, the rolling scrubby hills, lagoons, pelicans and gulls coasting on the breeze, that sweet, healthy aroma of pine-planked cottages baking in the sun.

Alex lay back against the pillows, looked over at the drawing of a hundred pink flamingos gathered around an Everglades lagoon. It was an Audubon lithograph she'd seen dozens of times before, composed and hand-painted by the great naturalist in the previous century, when flamingos in Florida were as abundant as buffalo on the plains. It took her a moment to realize what was so unsettling about the print. It was the flamingos. They were not pink at all, but had been colorized a vivid blue, only the tips of their wings left unaltered. Some clever decorator's visual joke, a reminder of art's contrivance, that the past and present were forever intermingled, forever modifying each other. A principle that Seaside itself was founded on, the nostalgic shell game it was playing.

Alex closed her eyes, felt the pressure subsiding from her veins. She began to measure her breaths, following each inhalation all the way down to her lungs and all the way back out again. The yoga discipline she'd practiced for years at the beginning and conclusion of every karate class, usually better than a double jolt of café cubano for clearing the mind. Though today it was just deepening her drowsiness.

She needed to think, needed to formulate a plan, decide exactly how much she would confide in Dan Romano. But at that moment, she was far too weary. Too tired for remorse or worry or for plottng her counterstrike. Too exhausted to do anything but drop away into a dark and bottomless river of sleep.

"Are you going somewhere?"

His mother stood in the doorway of the storage room. The belt of her housecoat was undone and the robe had fallen open, exposing her gray moth-eaten pubes and the loose folds of skin where once her breasts had been.

"I'm taking a little vacation," he said. "Going upstate for a few days."

He slid the third and final plastic pouch of blood into the cooler, settled it deeper into the ice.

"I hate to be a bother, but I'm thirsty. I'm out of liquor again."

"Don't whine," he said. "I brought it."

She wet her lips and staggered forward, gave him a wretched smile.

"You're a good son," she said, reaching out a nervous hand. "You've always been good to me. Looking out for my welfare. You're the one I could always count on. The only one."

Brushing her hand away, he jostled past her and carried the cooler into the living room and set it by the front door.

"Here it is," he said. He squatted down, opened the cooler, and drew out the quart of Smirnoff. "But don't try to con me with this 'good son' shit. It's too late for that, old woman."

"But it's true," she said. "You're my youngest, my darling sweet-faced baby."

"Fuck that."

She moved toward him in her stiff-jointed gait. Arthritis or gout, he wasn't sure. She hadn't been to a doctor in years. Hadn't been out of this house.

"You were the favorite of all my children. You were."

"You worthless old liar, you ignored me from the second I was born. Went off with your booze and your gloom, and you only looked up long enough to scowl."

"No, no. I loved you, I did. You were my baby, my sweet, gentle baby boy."

"It won't work," he said. "Give it up. There's not a goddamn thing you can say now, no apologies. I was five years old, crying out for you, standing right in front of you, and you never noticed. You were too busy cracking more ice out of the tray, making yourself another whiskey sour. You can't go back and fix it now. It's done. It's history. You fucked me up, and now you're suffering the consequences. That's how it works. Karma kickback."

"I had some rough times, too," she said. "My life hasn't been easy."

Her gaze wandered the desolate room. Tears gathered in her eyes.

"Spare me the weepy bullshit."

"You wouldn't do this if your father were still alive."

That stopped him for a moment.

"Your father would get out his strop and he'd—"

"He'd what, Mother? He'd beat the shit out of me? He'd whip my bottom till it bled, till I couldn't cry anymore? Is that what you were thinking about?"

"Why am I here, son? Why are you doing this to me, my sweet boy?"

"It's called vengeance, Mom. Also known as justice."

"But you're so good. So sweet. This isn't right, son. And what you're doing with these women, that's wrong, too. Very wrong. You know that, don't you?"

Stretching out a hand, she started toward him, but he dodged her and headed to the front room, where her mattress lay in the middle of the bare floor. The air stank of urine and rotting dog food. In the bathroom, the toilet seat was gone, the porcelain stained orange and black. Roaches roamed the walls. He stood before the toilet and stared down into the bowl, at the few inches of brown water.

The family Bible sat on the lid of the porcelain tank like a fat, heavy brick. Its black leather cover was curled back from years of humidity. Its flimsy pages were the only toilet paper he allowed her.

He twisted the cap off the vodka, held the bottle above the toilet.

"No!" she screamed, and lunged for him, but he shoved her frail body aside and she collapsed to the floor. She sat up, studied him from deep inside her hazy eyes.

He tipped the bottle, let it splash into the bowl.

"You're cruel," she said without emotion. "A cruel, cruel boy."

"It's not my fault. I'm just carrying on family tradition."

"Your father was an unhappy man. But you're better than that, son. Much better. You're a good boy."

"Sure I am." He grinned at her. "I'm a fucking saint."

"You are. You've always been good. Such a bright, sensitive child. I always knew you'd make something of yourself. Be somebody important."

"Oh, I'm important all right. I'm front-page news."

He set the bottle on the edge of the sink. She stared at it, her mouth quivering. An inch of the clear liquor remained.

He felt himself grinning. There was a dazzle in the air. A feast of energy in his veins. The floodgates of adrenaline were thrown open and he was gaining altitude with every passing second.

"Got to run, Mommie, dearest. Got a plane to catch. Anything comes up and you need to reach me, I'll be at the beach consorting with all the pretty people in their pretty houses. On the fine and sandy shores of Seaside, Florida."

TWENTY-ONE

A car alarm woke her, its siren blaring for several seconds, then abruptly clicking off with a double chirp.

Alexandra sat upright, blinked her eyes, tried to place the white walls, the lithograph of flamingos. It took several moments for the events of the last few days to emerge from the fog, seep back into her mind, arrange themselves in an orderly narration. The Brinks crash, the grim scene in Stan's hospital room, Gabriella's riddled body, the numb and endless drive from Miami to North Florida.

She squinted at the bedside clock. Five-forty-eight. A seven-hour nap that had given her no rest. Her muscles were sore, a leaden tonnage filled her limbs. It was as though she'd spent the long afternoon trying to claw herself out of the dark vaults of dream.

She yawned and stretched, then swiveled her legs over the side of the bed, her toes nudging something on the floor, cold and metallic. She bent forward, looked down, and saw it. The silver serving ladle.

Bolting to her feet, she rushed into the living room. She was naked and still half-muddled from sleep, but waking fast now.

Lawton wasn't in the kitchen or his bedroom. He wasn't in the bathroom.

She called his name three times before she saw the front door standing ajar, the street beyond glowing amber with late-afternoon sunlight.

Her shorts and blouse were in the washer, soaked and wrinkled. She struggled into them, slipped on her running shoes, and marched out the front door. Surrendering to panic wasn't going to help. She needed to focus, stay calm, do a precise reconnaissance of the area. With probably less than an hour of daylight left, she couldn't afford to make wild miscalculations.

But surely he couldn't have gone far. From what she could tell, there was really nowhere to go in that small insulated community, three hundred houses backed by impenetrable scrubland on one side, the Gulf on the other.

For a moment, she halted on the red bricks of East Ruskin and looked out to the narrow highway and back into the depths of the town. She chose the beach. It's where *she* would have headed first. Maybe some of the same memories were calling Lawton down to the sugary sands. Perhaps the old man was remembering those long walks that he and Grace had taken together, leaving Alexandra to labor unmolested on her sand castle.

Her shorts and blouse flapped cold against her skin, clammy and ponderous. On the stairway down to the beach, she passed a troop of sunburned tourists clomping up, the men in gaudy golf clothes with their tinkling old-fashioned glasses, the women wearing long dresses and too much jewelry and carrying goblets of wine. As Alex hurried down, their laughter and conversation abruptly ended, the entire group stepping aside in unison, as if making way for an untouchable.

When she hit the deep shifting sand of the beach, her Nikes squeaked like boots in new snow. Up and down the beach, the last of the sun worshipers were shaking out their towels, folding up beach chairs, heading up the stairways.

To the east along the high dunes were dozens of sprawling bungalows anchored uneasily to the sand, and a mile or two beyond them began the dreary condos and motels. Off in the other direction was the two- or three-mile stretch of Seaside's beach and the high grassy dunes that eighteen years ago had served as shelter for her sand castle.

She headed that way, striding fast down the hard-packed path near the water. She passed a couple of bikinied high school girls ankle-deep in the surf, skimming a Frisbee back and forth above the shallow waves.

Beyond them, a band of eight-year-olds played twilight tag, flopping and diving into the silvery Gulf. Up on the beach, some older folks were propped up in their lounge chairs, occupied with their magazines or icy drinks.

It took her almost half an hour to reach the last few hundred yards of beach. By then, the sunbathers had dwindled to zero, and the sands ahead of her were deserted, only a young couple jogging toward her with their black Lab loping at their side. The last of the daylight was fading—red ridges and golden welts ripened against the sheer blue canvas to the west.

Alex turned and started back.

Dread was radiating through her gut, a fidgety beat in her pulse. She fought it, tried to convince herself of a dozen harmless explanations. That he'd simply wandered into the picturesque town itself, perhaps for a shopping spree at the local market, or he was sitting at the outdoor bar sipping a beer and chatting with some local raconteur. Or she'd find him sitting in the living room at the Chattaway when she returned, watching television and ready for his happy-hour beer.

She broke into an easy trot on the return trip, staying on the damp sand, glancing out at the oily sunset sheen that coated the water. Her clothes were nearly dry, but she was shivering more now than a half hour ago. She pushed faster through the gathering dark and was almost back to the stairs when she saw the large misshapen silhouette stumbling out of the surf fifty yards ahead.

She blinked, wiped her eyes, jogged faster till the man came into view.

And she stopped abruptly, panting.

"Dad?"

She stepped forward and through the dusky light saw her father cradled in the arms of a tall young man. Lawton Collins's hair was wet and straggling, head sagging back against the man's slick chest. Lawton wore a pair of red boxer shorts that were drenched and pulled up high over his small potbelly. His eyes were open; a confused smile played on his lips.

"He's okay," the man said. "He just swam out a little too far. Got tired."

"My God," Alex said. "Dad, are you sure you're all right?"

Sheepishly, Lawton nodded that he was, and he spit a shot of water into the sand. Then he turned his head, stared up at the man cradling him.

"Do I know you, kid?"

Alex stepped closer and looked at her father's savior. His khaki shorts and white T-shirt were soaked. His dark eyes glittered with diamond light and a familiar smile spread across his lips. Her heart skipped and a giddy swirl of air filled her lungs. For a long moment, she couldn't put a name to his face. So out of context, so many miles from the world they shared.

"Jason?" she said. "Jason Patterson."

"In the flesh."

"What the hell!"

He shook his head and smiled awkwardly, as if this wasn't working out as neatly as he'd planned.

"I decided I needed a vacation," he said. "You spoke so highly of this place, I thought I'd check it out."

"Bullshit."

"It's pretty," he said. "A little synthetic, but pleasant to the eye."

"Jason, what the hell are you doing here?"

"Well, I was walking the beach and I saw him flailing around offshore. I didn't know he was your father. It was just a coincidence. A lucky accident."

"Stan robbed an armored truck," Lawton said. "That's why we came to this place. And because of Darnel Flint."

"Darnel Flint?"

"We got the armored truck money back at the cottage. You want to look at it?"

"Money?" Jason said, peering at her. "Alex, what's going on?"

She stared out at the opaque waters flickering with the last seconds of daylight.

"It's a long story," she said. "Too long."

"I have time," Jason said as he set Lawton back on his feet. "All the time in the world."

Jason was smiling absently. The breeze tossed his dark black hair. He raised a hand to settle it back in place. And Alexandra knew she was staring at him, at his arms and the coppery flesh visible at his throat. More aware of his physical presence than she'd been before. Those Iroquois cheekbones, eyes as dark and glittery as fossilized coal, his languid smile.

"You two know each other, do you?"

"Oh, yes," Jason said. "We've been sparring for years."

He turned his eyes to hers and his smile deepened.

"I'm hungry," Lawton said. "Is it time for supper yet?"

Alex pulled her gaze away from Jason, looked at her father. Then she sighed and looped her arm through his.

"You're always hungry, Dad."

"I could eat a hearse," Lawton said. "Hell, I could wolf down two hearses. How about you, son? You hungry? Care to join us?"

Jason bent down and pried his tennis shoes off and poured out a trickle of sandy water.

"I'm famished," he said, smiling up at Alex. "Faint with hunger."

She shook her head.

"Come on, Dad. Let's dry you off."

"How about me? Or do I have to stay wet?"

Twenty feet behind him, a gull dropped from the dusky sky and splashed into the Gulf, violet ripples spreading toward shore.

"Sure, Jason, you come, too. I want to hear your story. And this better be good."

TWENTY-TWO

"Amy likes you," Emma said. "She's crazy about you, Jen."

"How can you tell?"

With her chin tucked against her throat, Jennifer watched the roach climb up the front of her white silk blouse.

"If you'd stop cringing, she'd like you even better. She can sense when someone's afraid of her."

Norman said, "We need gas."

"So pull off and get it," said Emma. "You have to ask my permission every goddamn time? Good grief, Norman, be bold, take an exit ramp without clearing it with me for once, would you?"

Emma gave Jennifer an exasperated frown.

"Men," she said.

"Men," Jennifer replied.

Emma was riding shotgun, with Jennifer wedged in the middle, straddling the transmission hump of the pool-service truck. It was dusk. Sparse traffic on I-10, two hours west of Tallahassee, maybe half an hour, forty-five minutes from their destination, Seaside, Florida.

Six hundred miles should've taken them twelve hours max, but it was turning into half again that much. Somewhere outside of Fort Myers, the goddamn pool truck had developed a carburetor problem, the engine sputtering whenever Norman tried to push it past fifty. They'd had to decide whether to stop and try to have it fixed or forge on. They forged.

No air-conditioning, hot as hell, even with the windows wide open. Emma was soaked with sweat. Driving since midnight the night before, all through the day Saturday, six hundred miles at no more than forty-eight miles an hour. Eighteen hours after they'd left Miami, they were still in Florida.

"We should've flown," Norman said.

"Oh, yeah," said Emma. "I could picture us trying to check the Heckler & Koch, the Mac-ten on a commercial flight. We'd be on our way to Leavenworth right now."

"Or stolen a car."

"Right, and get stopped by the Highway Patrol ten miles down the road."

"Could you put the roach away, please, Emma?"

Jennifer moaned and wriggled in her seat

"Stop cringing, goddamn it. You'll scare her."

Amy stepped across from Jennifer's collar to her long, skinny neck. Emma held on to her green thread leash. Overhead, the interior light was on so that she could keep track of the roach. Soon as the sun went down, you had to be on full alert with roaches, since that was their normal time to roam. Feeding and mating.

"It's just so yucky," Jennifer said.

"Yucky is a state of mind," said Emma. "Think of it as a tickle. Your boyfriend blowing on your neck, whispering his fingertips across your skin. Your boyfriend does that, doesn't he? Tickles you, caresses your tender places?"

"Not really. He's kind of rough."

"Rough and quick?"

"Yeah," Jennifer said. "Rough, quick, plus he snores."

"Men," Emma said.

"Yeah, men."

"Women are from Venus," Emma said. "Men are from Penis."

Jennifer laughed.

A minute went by, everyone listening to the rumble of the truck. Until Emma said, "We need another road game."

"I'm sick of road games," said Jennifer.

"How about Dream Job?"

"Oh, all right," said Jennifer. "What are the rules this time?"

"No rules. Everybody comes up with their dream job. You know, like a fantasy thing. You describe what it is, how it would be to have it, what you'd do all day. Like that."

"Let me think," Jennifer said.

Emma said, "I know what Norman's dream job is. Norman would be one of those guards outside Buckingham Palace. One of those guys with the chin straps who never moves, never says anything. You can jump around, spit right in his face, he just holds still and stares out into space. That's Norman's dream job. Never has to think for himself. Takes orders about everything. Like a drone. A soldier ant. He's just there to serve the queen."

"I know mine," Jennifer said. "I'd run the phones and the PA announcements for the biggest Lexus dealer in the world out in Dallas, Texas. All those good-looking salesmen walking around on the lot, waiting for me to call their names. My voice would carry for miles. And all the oilmen and wealthy ranchers who come shopping every day, they'd hear my voice booming out of the sky like God's. A sexy female God."

Norman looked over, then back at the road.

"That's a dream job?" Emma said. "Hell, Jen, that's just the same job you got now, only more so."

Jennifer pouted for a second, then said, "Well, okay, I didn't want to say it because I know you'll make fun, but my real dream job would be to have kids and a husband and live in a big house with lots of windows for all the sunshine and have a maid to clean every day, and my kids would be beautiful and smart and never get on my nerves and my husband would want to have sex every night and he'd be devoted to me and proud of what a good mother I was and what a good wife. I'd drive them to soccer and go grocery shopping, fix these great dinners, and we'd take vacations to the mountains or the lake. And I'd have a garden with flowers and cucumbers."

"Jesus," Emma said.

"I knew you'd make fun."

"That's your dream? You could have anything in the whole world and you choose to be a housewife? Fuck, Jennifer. That's dull. Cucumbers, for Christ sakes. Did you hear that, Norman? The girl wants to raise cucumbers."

"I heard."

"Well, you don't like any of my dream jobs, then let's hear yours, Emma. Go on, tell me, so I can pooh-pooh your dream, too."

"A roach wrangler," Emma said.

"A what?"

"For the movies—they're always looking for people who know how to handle roaches."

"They are?"

"Sure they are. Haven't you ever seen it? In some scary movie, a roach comes crawling out of the wall and walks up the side of the bed and up the sheets and covers, and the camera's following it very carefully as it climbs the blanket and starts walking up the hand of someone in the bed, and then up the wrist and the arm, higher and higher, until the roach is right there at the girl's face and we don't know what we're going to see—maybe the girl is sleeping; maybe they're making love or watching the roach coming closer and closer—until finally, bang, the camera tilts, and we see a knife sticking out of the girl's forehead."

"Gross."

"Sure it's gross. That's Hollywood, Jennifer. And they pay very big bucks for somebody who can make that roach go in exactly the right places, make that long trip up the person's arm. Very large salaries are out there waiting for people with my abilities. I'd take that money, and I'd buy a big mansion in Bel Air or Beverly Hills, one of those places where all the stars live. And I'd take my Great Dane out for a walk every morning."

Norman slowed for a cluster of gas stations coming up on the right.

"Exxon or Shell?" he asked.

"Norman," Emma said, "why don't you dip into your vast reservoir of testosterone and make your own determination about what kind of gas to buy. You think you're up to that?"

"I'll try," he said.

"Men are from Penis," Jennifer said, and chuckled.

"Norman's an enigma. He's from a planet all his own. You know what an enigma is, Jen?"

"I think so."

"It's like the Sphinx," Emma said. "It's big and it's ugly and it just sits there and doesn't do anything."

"Like Norman."

"That's right, just like Norman."

The roach prowled through the peach fuzz on Jennifer's cheek and she closed her eyes and leaned her head against the back of the seat.

"Is she tickling you, Jennifer? Is Amy stroking your sensitive skin?"

"Yes," Jennifer said. "Yes, she is."

"Good. Now you're starting to see one of the many fine qualities of *Periplaneta americana.* So just relax. Relax and enjoy."

"I don't believe it," Jennifer said. "Even a damn cockroach is better than Stan Rafferty."

"He wasn't any good, was he? He was a lousy lover."

Norman looked over at her and shook his head.

With her eyes closed, Jennifer said, "He made me do things. Things I didn't like."

"What things, Jen?"

"Hey," Norman said. "Cut it out."

Emma gave Norman a cold stare. Leave us girls alone.

"What things, Jen?"

"He tied me up some times, you know, lashed me to the bed frame and used objects on me."

"Objects?"

"Fruit mainly. He was big on bananas, and he tried pears once or twice. Even grapes."

"The asshole."

"Yeah," Jennifer said. "He did that, too."

Emma chuckled.

"Cut it out," said Norman.

"And there was this guy, too. A guy from work named Delvin."

"Stan made you do a threesome?"

"No, he just watched. He sat there beside the bed and watched Delvin and me screwing. It was weird and sick, I guess. I just did it because he asked me to, because I was trying to make Stan happy. But I didn't like it. And the more I think about it, the madder it makes me."

"He just sat there and watched? What, like he was naked? Jerking off?"

"No, just there in his street clothes, watching."

"Man, oh, man."

"Stan has problems. Sexual dysfunctions."

"Sure as hell sounds like it."

"He can't always get his thing hard. He could at first, but then it started wilting a lot. More and more as time went on."

"Enough," Norman said. "Both of you."

"Stan's a very bad man," Jennifer said. "He studies crime day and night. He knows all about famous robberies and shoot-outs and court cases and all about the private lives of criminals. He's very bad."

"Book learning is what that sounds like," Emma said. "That's bullshit, Jennifer. Books aren't real life. Not even close. Until the guy's wallowed around in muddy trenches with bullets whizzing over his head, he doesn't know what the fuck he's talking about.

Till he's pulled the trigger on another human being, seen the bullet blast away flesh and marrow, he's just jerking himself off."

"Stan knows things. He's immersed himself in all kinds of evil shit."

"But he didn't come over to your house and try to rescue you, did he? We waited and he didn't come. All that study, all that reading about crime, it didn't give him the intestinal guts to come and save you even after you pled with him to come. He could hear your quivering voice on the phone, all frightened like you were, and he didn't ride to your aid."

"But he's still bad," Jennifer said. "He's a very dangerous man."

"Well, don't you worry, pussy boots. Don't worry about Stan. Me and Norman are badder. Much badder."

The roach was on her right eyelid, antennae probing her long eyelashes.

"Emma?" Jennifer let go of a long sigh.

"Yes?"

"Thanks for not killing me."

Emma gave the roach more slack as it climbed up the bridge of Jennifer's nose and onto her forehead.

"You're welcome, Jennifer. You're very welcome."

"Why'd you do it anyway? Why didn't you just shoot me and walk away? You don't need me. I'm just a burden."

"I brought you along because you're cute, Jen. 'Cause I like your smile."

"No, I mean it. Why?"

"And because I needed somebody to talk to," Emma said. "This guy, Norman Franks, in case you haven't noticed, he doesn't say much. He's verbally constipated. Aren't you, Norman? Plugged up, obstructed."

Norman kept his eyes on his driving.

"A girl like me can manage only so long carrying on a one-sided conversation. And the fact is, Jen, you're growing on me. These last eighteen hours, you've gotten cuter and cuter. I'm beginning to think you might be just the kind of special friend I need in this period of trepidation and disquietude."

Jennifer considered that for a minute, the roach tracking up the part of her blond hair.

Then she reached over and found Emma's hand and picked it up and gave it a warm squeeze.

"I really appreciate your not killing me. I'd do anything to thank you."

Emma shot her a little wink.

"We don't need men anyway. What've men ever done for us but cause us trouble? Am I right, Jen?"

"Trouble and more trouble," Jen said. "Men are from Penis."

"The hell with them," Emma said. "Do we need their hairy, muscular help? No, we don't. Do we need them watching over us, protecting us? Hell no. They could all turn into monks for all we care, huh, Jennifer?"

"Absolutely."

Jennifer gave Emma's hand another sly squeeze.

"I'm finished with them forever," Jen said. "I feel better already."

Norman pulled up to the gas pump and turned to Emma.

"Somebody's following us."

"What?"

"Over there, the Ford."

A five-year-old Galaxy was at the pumps of a gas station across the road.

"Jesus Christ," Jennifer said. "It's him. That's Stan."

Norman opened the door and got out. He bent down to the open window. His head filled the whole space.

"Regular or high-test?"

TWENTY-THREE

Stan Rafferty pulled up to the full-service pumps at the Shell station across the road from the brightly lit Exxon plaza where the yellow pool truck was gassing up.

He tapped on his horn, but nobody came out of the office. Red-and-green plastic flags rattled in the breeze. In the grass beside the building, there were half a dozen chickens pecking at the dirt where someone had sprinkled corn or seed or some shit. Probably a litter of pigs living in the rest room and a cow grazing back in the weedy shadows.

That's the way it was in Florida. You got a mile outside of Miami, you might as well be in Fart Blossom, Georgia, or some little Alabama shithole. Every radio station for the last eighteen hours had been playing twangy you-done-me-wrong songs, or else some idiot preacher was throwing his thunderbolts out into the sinful darkness of radio land.

Stan backed the car up and ran over the air hose again, chiming the bell somewhere nearby. It took two more taps on his horn before a pale, red-haired three-hundred-pounder threw open the door of the fluorescent office and came lumbering over to Stan's open window. Every step a seismic event.

The guy's left cheek was bulging and a brown dribble showed in the corner of his mouth. Probably been inside the station all night gawking at the pinups in the new issue of *Barnyard Monthly*, Stan thought.

Stan took the last sip out of the quart of Colt 45 and dropped the bottle on the passenger floor. He'd drunk three quarts, had four more getting warm in the backseat. He'd bought them at the last gas stop. Painkillers for the damn ache in his leg. They were only halfway working.

The big redneck came up to Stan's window, bent down to look him over, then said, "Don't do no full service after seven P.M. Gotta pump it yourself."

Stan looked at the dashboard digital clock.

"It's only six-fifty."

"'At's not what my watch says. And my watch is what we go by around here."

The big man was wearing a railroad cap and overalls and an orange T-shirt that was giving Stan an instant headache.

"Jesus Christ, man, I've got a broken leg," Stan said, tapping on the white plaster. "I'm in a goddamn cast. Cut me a little slack, why don't you?"

The big man stepped away from the window.

"Don't be cussing me, mister. Rules is rules."

The man started back to his office.

"Hey!" Stan yelled. "Hey, you porker. Look at me. Turn around, doofus, and look me in the fucking eye."

With his back to Stan, the man halted, shot a thick dollop of tobacco juice into the weeds beside the pumps, and turned slowly. His mouth was set in a snarl, but when he saw the .38 pointing at him out the window, his face went slack.

"You know who I am, pig man?"

"Don't reckon I do."

"I'm Machine Gun Kelly is who I am. I'm Richard Loeb and Alfred Packer and Lee Harvey Oswald all rolled up in one. I'm Charles Starkweather and Frank Nitti and Joseph Michael Valachi."

"You're all those people, are you?"

"You bet your sweet ass I am. Them and more."

"If you say so.

"So fill it up, fat boy," Stan said. "Regular unleaded."

While the guy pumped the gas, Stan kept one eye on him in the rearview mirror and the other eye on the yellow pool truck across the highway. Jennifer and the dark girl had gotten out and gone off to the john together while the water buffalo who'd been driving the truck was filling the tank. Stan just got a glimpse of the two women together, but he didn't like what he saw. Reading their body language, it didn't look like Jennifer was a hostage at all. Way too friendly. A couple of girls out for a Sunday ride, kidding around, playful.

For close to six hundred miles now, Stan had been following them. Never saw anyone drive so slowly. A hundred times, he'd considered passing them by, speeding on ahead, getting to Seaside a few hours before they did. But things could go wrong with that. He could have car trouble. They could pass him, get there first. This way, at least he could keep them in sight, and maybe, if the opportunity arose, ambush them somewhere along the way.

He'd always hated that white Galaxy, but now he'd begun to appreciate the car because it was so damn bland, it was practically invisible. Even with no traffic to speak of for the last few hours, the three of them didn't have a clue he was back there. Just another boxy white car.

"You're full up," the porker called.

Stan looked over at the pump, then pulled out his wallet and counted out seventeen dollars and held them out to the man, but the big guy eyed the money suspiciously and backed away.

"Take it," Stan said. "This isn't a fucking holdup."

"It's not?"

"No, you idiot. I just wanted full service. That's all."

"We don't do no full service after seven P.M.," the porker said.

"Yeah, so I heard."

Stan waggled the money at the man until he leaned over and snatched it out of Stan's grasp.

By then, the pool-service truck was pulling out of the Exxon plaza and cranking back up the highway.

"Before I go," Stan said, and showed him the gun again, "I want you to swallow that plug."

"Say what?"

"That chewing tobacco, swallow it." Stan sighted on the man's broad, smooth forehead. "The whole damn mess, gulp it right on down."

Stan thumbed the hammer back.

"Shit," the man said. "It's too got-damn big to swallow."

"No cussing. Just swallow it down, you oinker. The whole thing. Hurry up. I gotta go. Do it or I'll shoot your measly pecker off."

With his eyes on the gun, the porker craned his neck and took a quick breath, then choked down the wad.

"That stuff'll kill you, boy, if you aren't careful. Give you mouth cancer and kill you deader than a bullet through the heart."

Stan uncocked the pistol, put the car in gear, and rolled onto the highway.

When he looked back, the porker was bent over the grass, vomiting, and a couple of the chickens were scurrying over to feed.

Stan kept the pickup's taillights in sight as they cut north through the dark Florida night. Mile after mile spooling out in front of him. He left the radio off for a while. Went inside his head, snuffling around, looking for something to amuse himself with for the next few miles.

Long ago, he'd used up the five women he'd had sex with. Having trouble falling asleep or sitting in the dentist's office, sick of reading magazines, a thousand times he'd gone over and over every single moment he could recall with those five females, every act, every part of their bodies he could still remember. Size and shape of their nipples, the coarseness of their pubic hair. Their smell, tightness. Everything.

Of course, it wasn't much of a list. Subtract Jennifer and Alexandra, there were only those two cheerleaders back in the eleventh grade who'd given him a few blow jobs and spread their legs for a couple of listless fucks on the backseat of his yellow Dodge Dart.

And then there was his sister, Margie.

Just that once with her, and only because she'd wanted him to do it, so she'd know what it was like, to have the experience before she died. She was definitely going to die, everybody knew that. The doctors, their parents, everyone knew. And Margie told Stan she didn't want to curl up in her grave without ever knowing the pleasures of a man inside her flesh.

Despite all Stan's attempts at interesting his football buddies in Margie, none of them showed the least willingness. So finally, he agreed to it.

One night when their parents were at a party, he'd gone into her bedroom, switched off the lights, and slipped in beside her. He touched her small pink nipples; he sucked on them for a while, then showed her how to touch him. She'd been very eager to try everything he knew, which wasn't a hell of a lot. But when he rolled off her and lay on the sheets beside her, she began to weep. She sobbed and sobbed and wouldn't stop no matter what he said or did.

He dressed and left the room, made himself a sandwich and ate it, had some milk, watched a few minutes of TV, and when he went back, she was still crying. So he hit her. Not hard. A slap on the face to wake her. 'Cause he'd seen it in a movie, a man breaking through the hysteria of his girlfriend. Just a slap.

It worked. Margie stopped bawling and looked at Stan.

"I'm sorry," he said. "I'm sorry, I'm sorry. We shouldn't have done it. It's unnatural."

"That's not why I'm crying, Stan."

"It's not?"

"You really don't know, do you?"

"Is it because you're going to die and you're not going to be able to enjoy sex anymore?"

"That's not it, either," she said.

"No?"

"I'm crying because my first and only sexual experience was with someone so incredibly clumsy."

Stan just stood there and looked at his sister. He stared at her withered legs, her frail naked body on the sheets. All these years later, he could still picture the moment perfectly, remember exactly how he felt. The room turned to white fire. He heard pops behind his eyes, little crackling explosions, as if his brain were disintegrating.

Stan wanted to murder her right then, right there. He wanted to put his hands around her throat and break everything his fingers could find. All the little bones, vessels, and veins. He wanted to squeeze the breath from her, watch her eyes roll back.

That was the moment he first knew he had an evil heart. When he understood that reading about crime was more than a hobby. He'd been drawn to it because he was inherently corrupt. Crime was his true religion. It was what he had instead of praying to God and singing hymns. Reading about all those twisted perverts from the past, the gunslingers and bootleggers and kidnappers, was for Stan as inspirational as a normal person reading about saints and holy men.

That night, staring down at his sneering sister, he'd realized with sudden and absolute knowledge that there was no crime, no sin under the sun he wasn't willing to commit.

"He still back there?" Emma asked.

"Yeah," said Norman. "Still there."

"Has he been back there the whole time?"

"Yeah."

"Ever since Miami? Eighteen hours he's been back there?"

"That's right."

"Jesus, Norman, and you just now got around to mentioning it."

Emma stared out her window at the dark, boring landscape. Pine forests and scrubland.

"Well, hell, Jennifer, I guess your boyfriend must like you after all. At least he likes you enough to tag along for six hundred miles anyway. Or maybe he wants to kill you. Keep you from turning him in, testifying against him. Maybe it's not love at all."

"Why don't you try to shake him, Emma? It wouldn't be that hard."

"What kind of car is that he's driving?"

"A Ford."

"Does it have air conditioning?"

Jennifer said yes, it had air.

"Well, goddamn. You mean to tell me while we've been suffering up here in the heat, eighteen goddamn hours, and he's back there with cold air blowing in his face? Doesn't that make you mad, Jennifer? The selfishness of it. The stark injustice."

"I guess so."

"Well, it should. It makes me mad. And I'm sure it makes Norman mad. Doesn't it, Norman? You're angry at how selfish old lover boy is being, aren't you?"

"Whatever you say, Emma."

Jennifer was quiet for a mile or two; then she reached over in the dark and found Emma's hand and gave it another secret squeeze.

"You like my hair, Emma? The cut, I mean. It's new. I did it special for Stan. We were going to Santa Fe or Taos, one of those places, and buy an adobe hut, live close to the land, in harmony with nature and the universal cycles. So I told Sheri, my hairdresser, what the hell, she should just cut off a whole bunch, give me a fresh look for our new start in life. And then Stan, he looked at me and didn't even notice. He didn't say a kind word about it or anything."

"Men," Emma said.

"Yeah," said Jennifer. "If they didn't have penises, they wouldn't know their fronts from their backs."

Emma chuckled.

"Hey, Norman. This girl's funny. And smart, too. Don't you think?"

Norman stared out at the dark highway and said nothing.

"Pull over, Norman. Right here, pull onto the shoulder and turn off your lights. Let's see what lover boy does."

Norman slowed the truck and wheeled them onto the shoulder.

Emma swiveled around and stared back into the dark. The white Ford was fifty yards back, parked along the shoulder with its lights off.

"Come on, Jennifer. Get out."

"What?"

"We're going back and say hi to lover boy. See how tough he really is."

Stan didn't see them coming till they appeared out of the gloom ten feet in front of the Galaxy.

"Holy shit!"

He switched on the headlights, punched the brights, but they didn't even flinch, just kept walking. A small blond woman with whitish eyes and Jennifer, walking with that sexy sway she had. Both of them carrying automatic weapons.

Stan lunged for Lawton's .38 on the passenger seat, but he knocked the fucking thing on the floorboard and had to unlock himself from his seat belt before he could squirm over and get it.

When he was upright again, a cold barrel jabbed into his neck.

"Put the gun on the seat," the woman said.

"Jennifer?"

"Yes, Stan. I'm here."

She was at the passenger window, aiming an assault rifle at

him. Thing was so big and heavy, she was stooped over from cradling it.

"Put your dinky gun down on the seat," the other woman said. "I don't want to have to shoot you and mess up the upholstery with a lot of gore and gristle."

Stan dropped the pistol on the passenger seat and Jennifer reached in and picked it up.

"That's good. Now turn the headlights off and get out of the car. And don't even think of trying to make a run for it."

A car came whizzing out of the dark, lighting them up, then roaring away in the same direction they were headed. But if anybody saw the assault rifle, they didn't slow down.

"I got a fucking broken leg," Stan said. "I'm not running anywhere."

"So get out of the fucking car, macho man."

Stan did as he was told, dragging his heavy plaster cast out the door. And the girl ordered him to turn around and walk to the other side of the car, over toward a ditch.

"Jesus Christ, Jennifer, are you going to let this woman shoot me?"

"You know what I found out, Stan? You know what I learned these last few hundred miles? I discovered a common household cockroach is a better lover than you are. That's what I discovered."

"A roach?"

"That's right. A common household pest."

"Jesus, have you been drinking? They slip you some drugs or what?"

"I've come to my senses, Stan. I see which side my bread is buttered on. It took me awhile, but I finally realized it. You're a man, and you've spent your whole life learning how to be something that's very sick and twisted. And even if you started right now, you're never going to get over it."

"Give him hell, Jen."

"I'm sorry, Stan. It isn't going to work out between us. I'm involved with someone else."

"You are? Since when?"

"Enough of this shit," Emma said. "Stand back out of the way, Jen. You don't want to mess up that nice silk blouse."

Stan said, "Wait a minute. Let's talk about this. You can't just walk up to a man and kill him on the side of the road without any provocation whatsoever. It isn't done. That's not how it works."

"Oh, no?"

There was a loud crack, and Stan felt a jolt in his back. He went sprawling forward like somebody had blindsided him with an illegal block. One of those cheap shots that started bench-clearing brawls. People pouring down from the stands to get in a few licks, coaches running onto the field, trying to separate everyone. That's what it felt like. A wallop to his spine, numbing and hard, and it made him mad.

But he couldn't do anything with that anger because his face was in the dewy grass and he was numb. And he knew they'd have to bring out the stretcher for him on this one. The golf cart and the stretcher and take him off to the hospital and lay him down on the clean sheets, where he'd wake hours later not remembering any of it, amnesiac, and there would be a couple of his teammates, all showered and dressed, and their girlfriends, and there'd be some of the cheerleaders, too, with expectant smiles.

"Hey, he's waking up. He's waking. Can you hear us, Stan?"

And he'd smile because there was that one cheerleader. Alexandra Collins. The best-looking damn girl in school. And smart, too, and funny, but with a sad side. Like Stan had. A sad and quiet part of her that was the thing that drove Stan crazy about her. He wanted a girl he could confess to. A girl he could tell about Margie, what they'd done together, and his feelings of inadequacy, a girl who'd share her own secrets, and they'd be close because of that. So close they could say anything at all to each other.

His face was in the dewy grass, and she was there at his bedside when he woke. Alexandra Collins.

"Is he dead?"

"No, he's still breathing."

"Then you do the honors, Jen."

"Oh, Christ, Emma. No, I can't."

"You have to, Jen. You don't have a choice."

"Emma, please."

"Come on, sweetheart. We're all in this together now. It's a joint venture."

Stan heard Jennifer whine; then a long while went by, Stan breathing in the scent of the wet grass.

Then he felt another jolt in his back. No pain, though. None at all, just a golden radiance expanding in his head. A silence deeper and more pure than any he'd ever known.

Gathered around his bed in the hospital were his other high school buddies. His teammates. All those guys. What were their names? He couldn't remember. He couldn't remember their girlfriends, either. He couldn't even remember his own sweetheart's name. Jesus, his best friends in the whole world and he couldn't remember their fucking names. Not even his own girlfriend, the girl he wanted to marry. Man, what the hell was wrong with him, he couldn't remember that wonderful girl's name?

And then Stan couldn't remember anything.

There was just the dew.

TWENTY-FOUR

They were in a high-backed booth at Bud and Alley's, a waterfront restaurant on the dunes across from Seaside. Lawton and Jason on one side, Alex on the other. Her father was wearing his jumpsuit, clean and dry. Hair combed, face with color again, but acting subdued, staring around the room as if he were trying to reconstruct the chain of events that had brought him to this place. Missing a few links.

Jason had gotten his suitcase out of his rental car, taken it into Lawton's bedroom, and changed into tan jeans and a dark blue shirt printed with golden palm trees. First time she'd seen him in street clothes. She'd been trying not to look at him too often, but her eyes kept straying.

Bud and Alley's was an L-shaped building with crank windows that opened out on the cool Gulf breezes. Modeled on beachfront joints from the same era as the homes across the highway, the restaurant seemed less make-believe than the town it served. It was both spare and elegant with its polished oak floors, a small homey bar, and basic cherry chairs and tables. Decorating the walls were black-and-white photos that showed the barren dunes and rolling hills as they'd been in the last century, before the Redneck Riviera became a chic getaway for Atlanta dentists and Tuscaloosa plastic surgeons. At least that's what they looked like, the raucous, boozy folks in the adjacent booths in their swanky sports clothes and hundred-dollar haircuts.

The dinner at Bud and Alley's was superb. Best meal she'd had in years. Flaky yellowtail, delicious roasted potatoes, a crisp wine Jason had selected. Everything fresh, homemade, subtly seasoned—the sauces, the savory vegetables, the warm, grainy bread. Even the service was executed with easy efficiency. A crew of keen young people in shorts and T-shirts who were neither jaded nor too eager. There seemed to be a golden hue in the air, a firelight glow that radiated from the walls and wrapped the dining room in its protective halo, as if they were sipping sherry before the hearth in some wintry English country inn. At any other moment in Alexandra's life, the evening would have seemed flawless.

"Walk me through this one more time, Alex. You stumble onto this house in the Grove and find a bag of loot just sitting there?" Jason topped off her glass with chardonnay and wedged the bottle back into the ice. "Like right out in the open. I mean, come on, that's pretty wild."

"It wasn't out in the open; it was on a shelf," Lawton said. "And don't forget, son, she was accompanied by a trained investigator. Me."

"And," Alex said, "we're not exactly dealing with master criminals here."

"These people who chased you, they were the same ones who murdered Gabriella Hernandez? You're sure about that?"

"In a yellow pool truck," she said. "Same people, absolutely. Either they're working with Stan or they've homed in on the cash from some other direction."

"Okay, so why'd you run? Why haven't you just called one of your buddies at Miami PD, told them the whole story, turned the money over? You trying to cut a deal, or protect Stan or something?"

"I like this young man," Lawton said, beaming at Jason. "I like how he thinks. He's got a head on his shoulders. Not like so many young folks you run into these days. Take that Frank Sinatra character, for instance. Now there's a born loser."

Alexandra wiped her lips and set her napkin beside her plate.

"I'm not protecting Stan. The bastard's going to jail. He's a thief and murderer."

"And he's having an affair, too," Lawton said. "Little bitty girl, size six. Disco bunny is how I picture her."

Jason gave her father a vague smile, still not sure what to make of him.

"I don't see the problem, Alex. Just pick up the phone, turn him in. Or were you thinking of holding on to the money?"

Her mouth tightened.

"There's more to it than the robbery," she said.

Lawton said, "Yeah, Stan knows about Darnel Flint. He's threatened to expose the whole sordid mess."

Jason glanced around the dining room as if checking for eavesdroppers, then steered his eyes back to Alexandra, his voice dropping a few decibels.

"And who is this Darnel Flint?"

"He's a boy," Lawton said. "A long time ago, he took a bullet in the face."

"Dad, please. I don't want to talk about this."

"I guess not," he said. "It makes for pretty unpleasant dinner conversation."

Jason straightened his shoulders. His face was flushed and he was staring hard at Alexandra, as if he were trying to see past her eyes, read her thoughts. She flinched and turned away.

"A bullet in the face? What the hell's this about, Alex?"

She looked back at him, kept her face as empty as she could manage.

"Let's just say my husband and I are having a standoff. He's made threats, and I take them very seriously. Leave it at that, okay?"

He filled his lungs and released the breath carefully. He stared down at his empty plate.

"Fine. Whatever you want."

Lawton busied himself with the last of his angel-hair pasta, rolling a clump onto his fork, aiming it unsteadily toward his mouth.

"Now it's your turn, Jason. I want to hear the story. What are you doing up here?"

He looked at her, pushed a dark strand of hair away from his eyes, and finger-combed it back into place. He feigned a smile.

"So," he said, "do we want dessert? Coffee?"

"No dessert for me," Lawton said. "Got to watch my waistline. Don't want to turn out like that goddamn George Murphy, balloon up to three hundred pounds. The girls wouldn't take a second look at me then. No, sir."

Jason raised his hand, got the waiter's attention, and did an air scribble for the check. He swung his smile back at Alex and had a sip of wine.

"I thought we'd walk on the beach, look at the stars. Bathe in the moonlight."

"No thanks," her father said. "I believe I've bathed enough for one day."

"It's not a coincidence, is it, Jason? Your being here."

He watched a young family rise from their booth and head toward the exit.

"Like I said. I was looking for you."

"And you came here? Out of the blue you picked Seaside?"

"You mentioned it on the beach Thursday, remember? Your romantic getaway. It's all I could think of, so I took a shot."

"But why, Jason? Why did you come at all?"

"You were in the *Herald* this morning, Alex, the story about Gabriella Hernandez's murder. Your car was found in her driveway. I saw that and I've been scrambling ever since."

"You got on a plane and came all this way, on the off chance I might be here."

"It's a trek all right," he said. "Had to fly to Atlanta, change planes, turn around, take a puddle jumper back to Panama City, rent a car; then it's still an hour's drive on top of that. A real odyssey." He finished the last of his wine and pushed the glass aside.

"I want to hear *why*, Jason."

"Because I was worried," he said. "Stan's involved in a violent wreck. Money's flying all over the street, a national news story. Then the very next day your car's found at a murder scene. And as if that's not enough, the two of you disappear."

Alex bent forward, her voice a strained whisper.

"Stan's out of the hospital?"

"Apparently, he walked out last evening," Jason said. "Police checked your house. You weren't there; he wasn't, either. TV people are speculating that the same Cuban extremists who hit the Hernandez woman had something to do with you and Stan. That the two of you were innocent bystanders, dragged into the line of fire by associating with that woman."

"*That woman*," Alex said, "was my friend. My closest friend in the world."

He was quiet for a moment, studying his empty plate.

"I'm sorry," he said. "I sounded callous. I'm very sorry, Alex."

She tried once more to swallow away the hot mass that had been bunching in her throat for the last few hours, but it wouldn't budge. She stared out the window at the sea oats that blazed in the restaurant lights like a field of platinum wheat bowing to the evening breeze.

"Anyway," Jason said. "I listened to the TV coverage, read the paper, and somehow the Cuban angle didn't wash."

"And what did you assume? That Stan and I ran off together? That you'd find him here, too?"

He shrugged.

"You thought we were accomplices, that my disappearing was related to the Brinks money."

"It crossed my mind."

"And you decided to play bounty hunter."

"Like I said, I was worried about you, Alex. Concerned. It didn't sound like something you'd do. Unless you were coerced."

"Coerced. You thought Stan coerced me into being his accomplice?"

"I don't think anyone could coerce you into anything, not Stan, not anybody."

Lawton turned to Jason, tapped on his arm.

"Know what's thicker than water?" He sucked the last inch of a string of pasta into his lips. "The answer is blood. Blood's thicker than water. A lot thicker." He smiled at Alex. "See. I can remember things. I just have to concentrate, that's all. Bear down."

Alex reached over and patted his hand.

"Dad's been having some memory lapses for the last few months. But he's been working hard on it, as you can see."

"Yes. He's very sharp," said Jason. "I'm impressed."

Their waiter, a young blond man with a ponytail, set the bill next to Jason's hand.

Jason set a credit card atop the bill and the waiter scooted away.

"I'm ready for bed," Lawton said. "I think I'm coming down with jet lag."

Alex gave Jason an apologetic smile.

"We'll have to take a rain check on the moonlight walk."

"Sure," he said. "Tomorrow night perhaps. Or the next."

Outside, they ambled through the promenade of outdoor shops, tasteful T-shirts on display, high-end bric-a-brac. Down the boardwalk, Lawton paused at the window of a small and charming bookshop.

"What the hell's it doing in there? That's my goddamn book." He thumped his finger against the windowpane, pointing at a coffee-table book of Seaside. "Somebody stole it."

"It's okay, Dad. The store's closed now. We'll come by tomorrow and get it back."

"Probably that goddamn Frank Sinatra again. I wouldn't be a bit surprised to find that thief's been dogging our every move."

"Everything's fine, Dad. Feel that cool breeze. Isn't it wonderful?"

"Goddamn Sinatra. I should have filled him full of buckshot when I had the chance."

There was a pleasant chill in the air as they meandered silently through the winding streets and sandy footpaths back to East Ruskin. Most of the houses dark, only a few stragglers moseying down the lanes. At the front gate of the Chattaway, the three of them stood for a minute and looked up at the sky. It was cluttered with stars, more than she'd seen in the decades since her last visit there.

"Do you have a place to stay, Jason?"

"I saw a motel down the road when I drove in this afternoon."

"Stay with us," Lawton said. "We could use the company. In case we want to play some hearts or gin rummy. Three's better than two. We always play a lot of card games when we come up here. Especially if it rains."

"Thanks, but no, the motel's fine. I'll see you all in the morning."

"We have a couch," Alex heard herself say. "It looks fairly comfortable."

"No, really. I couldn't."

"You could sleep with my daughter," Lawton said. "I think she'd like that. She's been giving you a dreamy look all evening. I'm not so old I don't recognize a dreamy look when I see one."

"Dad! Stop it. You're being impolite."

"Well, maybe the couch," Jason said, chuckling. "Just for tonight."

Alex looked off at the sky for a moment more, glimpsed something flittering overhead, perhaps a bat doing its erratic dance, or just a lifeless scrap of paper bumped along by the wind. She felt both of them looking at her, the eyes of the two men standing in the dark, the silent touch of their gaze.

The bat circled overhead, dipped and flashed like a frantic angel. As if some departing soul were taking one last flyby, one final sip of the earthly atmosphere before it sailed forever beyond the limits of the planet.

"I remember this place," Lawton said. "It's all coming back to me now."

"What do you remember?" said Jason.

"This place. Seaside. We were happy here. Walking on the beach, playing gin rummy. 'Mellow Yellow,' that's what we called the house where we stayed. We enjoyed ourselves. It was only for a month, thirty short days, but I remember every one of them like it had all just happened. Like it's still happening right now."

"Come on, Dad. We need to get you into bed. It's late."

"Same stars, the same moon, same surf. None of the important stuff has changed." Lawton opened the gate and started down the path. "That's one bit of good news for you young folks. The important stuff doesn't change. It isn't allowed."

"Too expensive," Norman said.

"Come on, Norman, live a little. Let's splurge."

The woman at the check-in counter had been staring at Norman Franks since they'd walked into the room. Polished wood floors, screen doors, a vase of daisies on a shelf behind the counter. Bright white paint on the walls and exposed rafters of the ceiling. A lazy paddle fan. Looked like a summer-camp cabin. Summer camp for well-heeled adults.

"I don't care how expensive it is," Jennifer said. "I want to stay here."

"Come on, Norman, we're loaded. We're swimming in loot. What's the problem?"

The check-in lady had curly white hair and was wearing pleated khaki pants with sharp creases and a blue polo shirt with SEASIDE printed above her left boob. She looked like a recent widow who was doing this job so she could save up for a face-lift.

"Too expensive," Norman said.

"Our friend thinks you're asking too much." Emma smiled at the woman, but she didn't smile back. "Think maybe we could cut a deal? Negotiate a more reasonable rate? Maybe we could slip you a little hard currency for your kind assistance. The old payola palm rub."

"Perhaps you'd be happier down the road at the Marriott," the woman said. "Their rooms are considerably cheaper."

"I want to stay here," Jennifer said. "It's so pretty. After what I had to do tonight, I think I've earned it."

"Jenny wants to stay here," Emma told the check-in lady. "And look out, if she doesn't get her way, she's going to start whining. And believe me, you don't want that. The woman is a very annoying whiner."

"The Marriott," Norman said.

The face-lift lady looked at him again. She'd never seen anyone so big. So big and so ugly and with such a heavy beard. Nobody had ever come into this room wearing sky blue pants and a canary yellow sports coat and a silver shirt with geometric designs. The check-in lady's eyes slipped to the telephone below the counter. Like she was considering a quick 911 call to the fashion police. Hey, come quick. There's a guy here with shiny hexagonals on his shirt. A few parallelograms, too.

"What do you call this place, anyway?" Emma smiled at the lady, trying for a sincere effect.

"Seaside," the woman said dryly.

Norman was looking at the wall behind the lady, his eyes fixed on the daisies as if any second he was going to hop the counter, go over there, and sniff them. Godzilla meets Bambi.

"We *know* it's Seaside," Emma said. "That's why we're here. We want to stay at Seaside. But what the hell is it, a motel?"

"It's a town," the woman said, pronouncing it with two syllables.

"Well, it's not like any goddamn town I ever saw. I mean, we drove around a little already and we didn't see anybody walking the streets. If it's a town, where is everybody?"

"This is off-season. The owners don't live here year-round."

"They don't, huh? Nobody lives here at all?"

"We have six full-time residents."

"Oh," Emma said. "Six people, and you call that a town. I don't call six people a town. That's not even enough to play a good volleyball game. I think what you got here is a motel and you don't want to call it that because that doesn't sound classy enough, so you call it a town so people think it's something special, some cute little village. But hey, as far as I can see, it's still a goddamn motel."

"Please watch your speech. I'm offended by your cursing."

"Oh, my. Forgive me all to hell."

"Will that be all?" The woman was giving Emma the schoolteacher's stare. Get back in your seat. One more problem from you, young lady, and it's another day of detention.

"You allow pets?"

"No pets."

"How about roaches? Or aren't they welcome, either?"

"I think the Marriott is what you want, not Seaside."

Emma smiled brightly.

"Okay, I've decided. We're going to take the nicest place you have. Big attractive house, three bedrooms, four, whatever's the best in town. Wraparound porch. A fireplace, widow's walk, tower, the whole ball of wax."

"Thank you, Emma," Jennifer said, and took her by the arm. "Thank you very much."

The woman cut her eyes to the ceiling as if to summon all her good breeding. The shit she had to put up with for tightened skin.

"I'll need to see a credit card," she said.

"You got one of those, Norman?"

"Sure."

"Well, give it to the fine lady, so we can stay in her town."

While the woman was running his card, Emma said, "Oh, by the way, we were supposed to meet some friends of ours here."

The woman gave Emma the schoolteacher's thousand-watt stare.

"There're two of them," Emma said. "An old man and a young woman with long black hair. Rafferty is her name."

Emma gave Jennifer a questioning look.

"Alexandra Rafferty," Jennifer said.

"That's right. Alexandra Rafferty. Know which house she's staying in?"

"The Chattaway," the woman said. "On East Ruskin."

"Whew, now that's a relief," Emma said. "After driving all this way, we'd sure as hell hate to miss her."

"So let's get a house near hers," Jennifer said. "Within shooting distance."

Emma stepped back and grinned at Jennifer.

"Hey, Norman. I'm really starting to like this girl."

"Yeah," he said. "She's something else."

Emma turned to the schoolteacher and dredged up her best smile.

"The nicest house you have that's close to Miss Rafferty's. But it's got to be within shooting distance."

TWENTY-FIVE

Alexandra lay in the dark and listened to the wind heave against the house. There was a storm out over the Gulf, the lightning, muffled by massive clouds, was illuminating entire quadrants of the sky. Cool, sugary air seeped beneath the cracked window. She could see the lightning from her bed and hear the creaks of the house and a crackling sound that at first she thought was fire but soon realized was only beach sand peppering the windowpanes.

She'd been lying awake for over an hour, listening to the house and the wind and for any signs of Jason stirring in the living room. Wanting to get up, go out there, put a hand on his shoulder. Wake him, talk. But more than that, too. More than she'd allowed herself to consider. His kiss from the other morning still glowed on her lips like the tingle of the sun that abides in the flesh for days.

It struck her then that she was more familiar with Jason's body than she was with her own husband's. Its strengths, its tendencies, its quickness and restraint. She knew his scent at rest and after long exertion. The taste of his breath when straining and when calm. From dozens of clinches over the last few years, without ever intending it, Alexandra had made a study of his muscles and sinews, his fingers and nails and the dark hairs at his wrist.

In some ways, she knew his body better than her own. So many times she'd watched it blur toward her, demanding her quickest and smartest response. She'd learned to read it, to anticipate his mood, his disposition, the likelihood of his going left or right or down the middle. She knew him like a figure skater knows her longtime partner.

She stretched her legs, pointed her toes. She yawned without conviction, resettled on her side, and stared out the window at the erratic pulses of light. The wind was lowing between the houses like a lost animal. There was an itch in the air. A prickling aroma. Something off, some dissonant note. A hungering silence that filled the house.

She pushed herself up and got out of bed. She was wearing a T-shirt of Jason's she'd borrowed. Lifting her right arm, she pressed her nose to the cotton sleeve. Buried beneath the scent of detergent, she detected a hint of his bay rum aftershave, the sharp whiff of his accumulated musk.

She stood at the window a moment. Watched three quick strobes in the south. But no thunder and no rain. No release of the tension brewing in the sky.

Suddenly, for a few vivid seconds in the flashing light, she became again that girl at the cottage window long ago, and in another flash of light she was the woman she had become, teetering between those twin states. As she had her entire life, coexisting, never completely the one and never completely the other. Not then, not now. A lifetime of unease, an imperfect fit in her own body, in her own heart.

She turned from the window, took a long, strengthening breath, and stepped quickly to the threshold, and without a thought of what she would do or say, she drew open the door.

And he was there, standing a foot before her, eyes agleam from the distant lightning, a half smile on his lips, immobile—as rooted to the hardwood floor as if he had been planted there for years, waiting for Alex to finally summon her courage.

"Jason?"

"Who were you expecting?"

"How long have you been there?"

"Years."

She stepped forward and he opened his arms and absorbed her into his heat. They held each other in the dark and the distant rumble of thunder out over the Gulf mingled with the throb of her pulse. On the street nearby, something clanged, metal ringing against metal like a halyard in the breeze.

The wind was flowing off the water, sweet with the fragrance of rain. From the beach came a howl like the eerie lament of a whale passing dangerously close to shore.

She was not ready for this, this slow dance backward toward the bed. She was too disoriented, too fragile, too bewildered, too angry. But she didn't resist as they swayed to the soundless tune, Alexandra fitting her body to his, feeling his strength rippling an inch below the easeful surface. His warmth, the relaxed embrace.

"I'm scared," she said.

"Of me?"

"Of this."

"I know," he said. "It's scary."

"Maybe we should stop right now. While we can."

"Do you want to?"

"Of course not."

She stepped away and looked at him in the flickering light. Then her arms began to rise as if she were spreading her wings, and Jason reached out and drew the T-shirt over her head and in one fluid motion stepped out of his boxer shorts.

In the yellow glow of the streetlights, Alex stood naked before him. She made a soft fist and aimed a slow-motion strike at his chin. He smiled and blocked it just as languidly, caught her by the wrist, and swiveled her so she was facing away, a karate minuet.

And he pressed himself flat against her backside and slid his right forearm beneath her chin, his wrist bone pressing lightly against her throat, a standard chokehold. He kissed her ear, then her other ear. She let him hold her for a moment more, his cock rising along the crease of her buttocks; then she gripped the thumb on his choking hand and twisted delicately against the joint, peeling out of the hold as she turned to face him.

"It's not like we're strangers. We've got a history. We've seen this coming for a long time."

"Shut up, Jason."

She stepped forward and kissed him on the lips and drew him closer into the lazy sway of the embrace. And then they were on the bed, inside the sheets, the cool cotton, bright white and pulsing from the strokes of lightning. Jason's fingers whispered across her flesh, learning her body, reading the textures, tickling through the fine dust of hair on her arms and cheeks and belly—as if he was trying his best to memorize her angles and slopes and the exact grain of her skin.

And then it was her doing the same. The breathless tingle of discovery, massaging, molding, fingertips tracing this fresh terrain, the grooves of his ribs, the taut pucker of his nipples, the wedges of muscle, the trickle of hair that ran from navel to his groin, this man who was opening himself to her, who was lying back luxuriating in her touch, vulnerable, safe.

When the storm finally came ashore, its winds lashed the house for only a moment or two; then the rain swelled around them. Its sudden drumming resounded on the tin roof as if dimes were dropping from the stratosphere. Louder and louder, until there was no other sound but the rich clamor of rain.

They rode the surge of noise, burrowing deep inside its sheltering static. Alexandra felt herself letting go of the dense gathering of dread, releasing breath after breath that had been stored away too long, left moldering inside her. Loosening the steel cords that gripped her chest and kept her lungs pinched and shallow.

She was on top of Jason, controlling the moment; she was on her side and her back and he was inside her and she was opening herself to him, peeling back, drawing him in deeper and deeper until the two of them fused and there was only a wordless heat, a resonance. A thawing of that hard knot in her chest. Swallowed by the tumult of the rain, melting into the racket. And then it was over, as quickly as it had come; the storm moved inland. But by then, they no longer needed its reassurance, its concealment. They were on their own in its trickling aftermath. The *pings* and *splats* of gutters overrunning. A few xylophone plonks and the last drizzling patters.

They had blundered into these deep waters and now were thrashing to stay afloat in the sheets, a crawl, the breaststroke and butterfly, diving and rising, sleek forms in the airless sea. An hour, maybe two, impossible to tell. He chasing her, she chasing him, the two of them slithering away and slithering back. The touch, the groan. The gasping aftermath. Pulling up the pillows from the floor, propping them against the backboard.

"Are you sore?"

"Not yet. Are you?"

"I can't tell. Is numb the same as sore?"

"Oh, no. Did I make you numb?"

"I'll let you know when I'm so numb I can't go on."

And she was pleasing herself and pleasing him and pleasing something beyond either. It was flesh and nerve endings. It was the rocking loss of breath and sailing off freely into the atmosphere. It was sleep that was an hour long and ten miles deep, a waking that was tender and aching. It was dawn showing at the curtains, blue light, perfect air, a stretching yawn, Alex filled beyond the brim with something so new, so inexpressible that she had to struggle for several minutes before she could remember who she was and where.

Emma let the roach meander along the peach-colored railing of the porch. She gave her lots of slack on the green thread. The roach's antennae were waving wildly, as if she were nervous. Too exposed. Out in the full sun.

"What're we waiting for?"

Norman wore a pair of black boxer shorts he'd bought that morning in one of the shops across the highway. A yellow Seaside T-shirt, triple extralarge. He was standing at the porch railing on the third floor of the Ooh-La-La, their seven-hundred-dollar-a-night cottage. Four stories tall, with two enormous bedrooms, a tower, and two porches that ran the length of the second and third stories. With the appliances and paintings she could steal from that one house alone, Emma could live for a year.

Across the street and two doors closer to the beach was the Chattaway. Cute little bungalow where the two million dollars was stashed. Emma's Heckler & Koch with its glinting barrel lay at her feet; the Mac-10 was perched on a bright green Adirondack chair. With the ammo she'd brought along, they could hold off the Montana militia for a month. Or put so many rounds in the house across the street, its walls would disintegrate.

"What's your hurry, Norman? You got a sudden urge to get back to Miami? Miss the grit and grime, do you? Miss the dead dogs rotting in the alley, the Dumpsters overflowing with newborn babies? Or maybe it's your apartment. The garbage smell in the hallway, police sirens day and night. Tell us, Norman. We'd like to hear, wouldn't we, Jennifer? We'd like to know why the hell anyone would be in a hurry to leave this place and get back to fucking Miami."

"Yeah, Norman, why?"

A cool breeze was coming off the Gulf, tossing Jennifer's thick mass of golden hair.

"Forget it," Norman said.

Jennifer was wearing one of the outfits she'd bought, too, an ankle-length paisley dress with a scooped neckline, turquoise earrings, sandals, and a baseball hat with SEASIDE embroidered on it. She looked good in clothes. She was smiling, relaxed. Emma caught her eye and winked at her, and Jennifer winked back.

Emma had on a pair of tan sweatpants and a matching sweatshirt with the Seaside logo on it. Nothing fancy, but still it made her feel good, a new outfit, a new start. An unexpected direction to her life. Taking some deep breaths, the all-new-and-improved Emma Lee Potts about to be unleashed on the world.

She and Jennifer had shared a king-sized bed last night. First time either of them had been with a woman. There was a little clumsiness at first, Emma reaching out, touching Jennifer on the hipbone, Jennifer yipping in fright, both of them fumbling around, apologizing, drawing back, then lying there in awkward silence for a long time.

But finally Emma said what the hell, rolled over, started with a big mouth kiss, giving her some tongue, then worked her way down Jennifer's lean, smooth body, kissing and tweaking, until she found herself all the way down in Jennifer's soft, damp, sugary folds, and suddenly she was doing to Jennifer all the things she'd always wanted someone to do to her. And it drove Jennifer so wild, she began to wail quietly like a wolf having a dream. The two of them writhing and bouncing so hard and so long that Norman came barging into the room to see what was the matter.

"Nothing's wrong," Emma said, looking up from her work. "We're just getting to know each other, that's all. We're bonding."

"You're okay?"

"Better than okay," Jennifer said in her drowsy voice. "About ten miles past okay."

Sunday morning, they woke early and did it again, slower and quieter, trying a couple of new kinks, nibbling and giggling and then getting deadly serious. It surprised Emma to find that Jennifer had things to teach her.

"Are we dykes?" Jennifer had asked as they were showering off.

"We're not dykes. We're just a couple of women who've successfully transcended men."

They giggled at that. They'd been giggling most of the morning. Their secret, these new, surprising feelings.

"I like this place," Jennifer said, getting serious. "It suits me."

She leaned out over the railing, surveyed the view to the south. The Gulf, the colorful town with its narrow brick streets and white gazebos and park benches.

"I want to live here forever, Emma. Never leave. It's like some perfect quaint little village in New England. Only warmer. And with a beach. And palm trees."

"That's because it's Florida, not New England," Emma said.

Jennifer giggled again.

"This place might be too good to be true," Emma said. "I haven't decided yet."

"Oh, Emma. Be nice. I like it here."

"It reminds me of one of those movie towns where Jimmy Stewart owns the hardware store and everybody knows everybody else's business. They all go on hayrides together and attend the same church and at night they sit around on park benches out under the stars and tell each other sweet, stupid stories."

"Don't spoil it, Emma. Don't make fun of it. I could be happy in this place. Really, I could."

"Hell, if the membership committee ran background checks on us, Jen, we'd be blackballed in a minute. I don't think they have a lot of career criminals in Seaside."

"Don't be so sure," Norman said.

"Well, even if they don't, we'll just have to be the first. Goddamn it, I like this place."

"Does that mean you don't want a husband and kids anymore? You giving up that fantasy all of a sudden?"

"It was a dumb fantasy. That was before I knew how it could be . . . You know, how it could be . . ."

"Without a penis," Emma said.

And they giggled again. Emma couldn't remember ever giggling before. Not even when she was young. Especially not then.

Below them on the brick street, a mother and her two red-haired daughters were riding clunky bicycles. The two girls noticed Emma and waved and called out hello.

Emma waved back.

"This is fucked," said Norman.

"Norman, give it a rest, would you? We're going to get the goddamn money. That's our number-one priority. But the Rafferty woman is right there, fifty feet away. She doesn't know we're here. Let's just take our time. Find the right moment to strike. So we can do it quiet and without any fuss. Because if me and Jennifer decide we want to stay here afterward, we don't want to start off on the wrong foot, getting busted for murder. Okay? Can you deal with that?"

"Sure," he said. "Whatever."

"Good attitude, Norm," Jennifer said. "Very laid-back. Very Seaside."

Emma smiled at Jennifer and she smiled back.

"I think I'm hungry," Emma said. "I know I just ate, but there it is, I'm hungry again. It must be this cool weather, or the smell of the ocean or something. But I'm hungry as hell. How about you, Jennifer? You hungry?"

Jennifer raked the hair away from her eyes.

"Oh, yes. I'm starving. I can't remember ever being this hungry."

"Great," Norman said. "So go eat."

"Yeah," Jennifer said. "Let's."

TWENTY-SIX

Sunday morning, Jason slipped out of bed and snuck off, and in twenty minutes he was back with warm cinnamon buns and Jamaican coffee. Alex roused her father and the three of them ate their breakfast in the front porch rockers.

Lacy strands of fog twisted between the houses. In the pine-needle mulch in their front yard, sparrows pecked for beetles. A couple of kids on creaky bicycles rode down the quiet street, carrying their floats under their arms. A shaggy black dog waddled after them.

"Norman Rockwell," Jason said. "Painted by the numbers."

Alex smiled.

At nine, when the shops opened, Alex and Lawton crossed the beach road and spent an hour exploring the shops. Each of them bought a couple of new outfits. Lawton chose some garish tropical gear. And Alex found a green-and-red-plaid flannel shirt, a pair of white jeans, and some cotton mock turtlenecks. They dropped the shopping bags off at the house; then the three of them took a prowl around the town, peeking in each of the cafés, galleries, gourmet shops, and boutiques. Strolling up and down every residential street and every sandy lane.

They chuckled at the cutesy house names. Each dwelling with its hand-lettered plaque on the front gate, another detail legislated by the building code. Dreamweaver, EcstaSea, Margaritaville, Sundaze, Narnia, Pleasure Principle, Ooh-La-La.

All the buildings were gorgeous reproductions. Greek Revival, Victorian, Plantation, and Florida Cracker. Crayola colors, splashy creations of purple and teal, salmon and hunter green. Each house was a quirky blend of traditional and contemporary. In every detail, every cornice and garden and window-frame molding, there was a witty and self-conscious ingenuity. One beautiful trick after another. Towers and widow's walks and spacious balconies and tin roofs and outside staircases and cupolas everywhere. It was like walking through a dreamy watercolor. For Alex, the place was irritating and beguiling. She felt bullied by so much cleverness and good taste, a little weary and inadequate.

"Disney World without the rides," said Jason.

"Trickier than that," she said. "It's so close to being real, you're almost tempted to believe it is. The kind of place, if you lived here long enough, you'd start dreaming in pastel. I feel guilty for not liking it."

It was sunny, with the temperature hovering in the low fifties. Chilly gusts from the north that seemed to give Alexandra's energy a boost. Her appetite, as well.

They had lunch at Bud and Alley's, another fine meal of catfish fingers and grilled vegetables, a creamy risotto, a wonderful apple pie. And afterward when Alexandra proposed a nap, no one complained.

With sunlight streaming through the transom windows, she and Jason made love again. And this time as he explored her body, he whispered questions and she murmured her replies, guiding him to her favored rhythms and stresses. But Jason did not stop there. With slow and careful strokes, he found some new surprising half tones hidden inside the larger, more familiar melodies. Shades of touch, fine trills and counterpoints she had not even guessed at.

His tongue and fingers, his lips and the lean muscularity of his torso.

She stretched herself, flexed and twisted, finding fits of flesh with this new man that came and went so quickly, she could not begin to imagine how they could ever reproduce them.

It was not her release or his they worked together to achieve, but holding off their own final pleasure, they moved toward some state she'd never heard mentioned by friends or magazine experts. A place so distant from that room and time, so removed from the limitations of flesh and the noisy sludge of conscious thought, that when they arrived there, a golden hush came over her. Still joined, they did not move or speak or even breathe. A plucked string chirred somewhere near, but that was all. Otherwise, a perfect emptiness. A shedding of the weight of her life so clean and quick, it was as if the bed had been launched beyond the pull of gravity.

And then they were back.

Lawton Collins was rapping on the door. Wanting to go down to the beach, soak up some rays.

"I love this shit," Emma said. "People going off, leaving their doors unlocked, middle of the day. Renews your faith in humanity. I think I could live in a town like this."

They entered the Chattaway through the back door. Emma nosing the barrel of the Heckler & Koch around the doorjamb. Jennifer right behind her with the .38 they'd taken off of Stan Rafferty, and Norman with the Mac-10 bringing up the rear.

Three in the afternoon, sunny day, walking into the bright white kitchen of that small beach house while the good folks were sunning on the beach.

"I've never done a home invasion before," said Jennifer.

"You still haven't," Emma said. "Owner has to be present for it to qualify. You got to tie them up, pistol-whip them. This is just simple breaking and entering."

"Cut the shit," said Norman.

He shut the back door and stalked over to the refrigerator.

"What're you? Hungry?"

He clinked some bottles and shuffled some things around on the racks, then shut the door and popped open the freezer.

"Here's some of it." Norman drew out two handfuls of frosty cash.

"Jesus, Norman. You're quick. You must've done this kind of thing a couple of times before."

Emma slipped the cash into the white plastic garbage bag she'd brought along.

"But this can't be all of it. Christ, this isn't but thirty, forty thousand."

Jennifer came out of the back bedroom carrying the brown duffel with a South Miami High logo on its side. She turned it upside down and shook it.

"It's empty," she said. "You don't think they spent it already, do you?"

"On what? Suntan oil?"

"It's around here," Norman said.

He lifted the edge of the couch, peered under it, then let it crash back down.

"Easy, Norman. We don't want to set off somebody's fucking seismograph."

Emma went to the front bedroom, set the carbine on a chest of drawers, and searched the closet, under the bed, under the mattress, in the bathroom vanity, in each of the drawers.

"Bingo," Norman called from the kitchen.

Emma picked up the assault rifle, and as she was coming through the bedroom door, she bumped into the old man.

Sixty, seventy years old, with a sunken chest and gray hair, wearing baggy yellow surfer's shorts and a pair of aviator sunglasses.

"Hi," he said. "You think I look sporty in my new duds?"

Emma pointed the carbine at him and backed slowly away.

The old man shut the front door and turned the dead bolt. Then he cocked up a leg and brushed off the bottom of his bare left foot.

"Goddamn sand," he said. "It gets in your sheets, you can barely sleep."

He cocked up the other foot and brushed it off, then glided past Emma into the kitchen.

Norman was climbing down off the stove with a floppy straw basket in his hand. Emma could tell from the way he was holding it that it was heavy. In the doorway of the other bedroom, Jennifer stood with the .38 at her side. Her mouth was sagging open.

"Freeze, motherfucker," Emma said. But the old man seemed not to hear.

He marched into the kitchen and halted to examine the Mac-10 that Norman had left lying on the counter. He took off his sunglasses and set them down next to the Mac.

"Nice weapon," he said. "Yours?"

Norman nodded. Then he looked over at Emma to see what he was supposed to do.

"Freeze, goddamn it," she said. "This is your last warning."

The old man stepped over to Norman and put a hand on the lip of the straw basket, tipped it forward, and peered inside.

"Wow," he said. "Now there's a pile of greenbacks."

He turned and opened the refrigerator door and drew out a pitcher of lemonade. He raised the pitcher to his lips, tilted it, and drank. When he was done, he looked around at the three of them, wiped his mouth, and said, "Where are my manners? Any of you care for a drink?"

"Not me," Jennifer said.

Norman shook his head.

"You, young lady?" He swung the pitcher around and offered it to Emma.

"Is that it, Norman? Is that all the money?"

"Appears to be."

"Then let's go."

"What about him?"

Holding the straw basket with one hand, Norman reached around the old man and picked up his Mac-10.

"We can't just leave him," Emma said.

"You hit the jackpot this time," the old man said. "Happy for you. I truly am. We just came into some cash ourselves. Rolling in dough at the moment. Apparently grows on trees around here. Can't wait for autumn. Rake up the piles, go running, jump right in. Yes, sir. That's going to be some fun. Money to burn."

"He's nuts," Jennifer said.

"Old," said Norman. "Not nuts."

"Dump the cash in the garbage bag, Norman. Put the basket back up where you got it. I like to leave a neat campsite."

When he was finished, Emma edged up to the old man and pressed the barrel against his spine.

"Don't, Emma," Jennifer said. "He's harmless."

"He can fucking well identify us."

"No, he can't. Look at him; he's a pathetic old man. His brain has come loose inside his skull. He's not going to testify against anybody."

The old man stepped over to Jennifer and reached out for the .38.

"I've been looking all over for that pistol. Where the hell has it been?"

"Go on, Norman, lug the money on out of here."

Norman looked at the old man, looked at Emma, then turned and went out the back door.

"What're you going to do, Emma?" Jennifer was letting the old man examine the pistol without letting go of it. He was peering at the flat butt.

"That's mine all right," he said. "Same serial number, that little scratch on the grip. Yes, sir. That thirty-eight and I go way back. Way, way back."

Jennifer tried to pull the gun from his grasp, but he wouldn't let go.

And now there were voices in the street. Emma spun around, peered out the front window. It was Alexandra Rafferty and some guy, their arms full of beach towels, hurrying through the front gate.

"Come on," Emma said. "Get the hell out of here."

Jennifer tried once more to wrench the gun from the old man's hand, but he held on.

"Jesus Christ, Jennifer, come on. Let him have it. Let him have the damn gun."

"You gave us a scare, Dad, wandering off like that."

"I was thirsty," he said. "I wanted some lemonade."

Through the wall, she could hear Jason humming in the shower. Her father lay on his bed, staring up at the ceiling. Alex stood in the doorway.

"We turned around and you weren't there, and it was very upsetting, Dad. Do you understand why?"

"You thought I was lost."

"That's right. We were worried. You can't just wander off like that, okay?"

"Okay."

"And why did you lock the front door, Dad? Why was that?"

"I always lock the doors. It's for safety. Keeping my family protected."

Alexandra took a deep breath.

"Do we have a lot of money?" He looked over at her, then back at the ceiling.

"What do you mean, Dad?"

"I mean money. Cash, greenbacks. Hard currency. Do we have a lot of that kind of stuff?"

"We've got some, yes. Not a lot."

"It grows on trees around here. Did you know that?"

"What're you saying, Dad?"

"Nothing. Nothing at all. Absolutely nothing."

She went over and stared down at him.

"I think I got too much sun," he said. "I think my brain's come loose inside my skull."

She stooped down and felt his forehead. It was cool and dry.

"Is this Ohio?"

"No, Dad. It's Seaside."

"Where's that? In Florida?"

"Right. Seaside, Florida. In the Panhandle."

"I'm going to take Grace to Florida. Start a family. I hear it's nice down there."

"I've heard the same thing," Alex said. "Orange trees as far as the eye can see."

"Well, you should talk to Grace, then. She's awfully stubborn. Says Florida's just for old people. But I don't think that's true. I think there're all kinds of people there. Young, old, in between. I've heard it's a great place to start a family."

"I've heard the same thing," Alex said.

"Well, talk to her, then. Would you? Talk to her. She's so damn stubborn."

"I will," Alex said. "I'll talk to her."

TWENTY-SEVEN

It was five in the afternoon. Jason had gone to shop for dinner at the local gourmet market. Her father was on the front porch, giving one of the rockers a workout. Sitting on the beige couch, she gazed out at her dad and dialed Dan Romano's home number.

Sunday, Dan's day off—this late in the afternoon, he'd still be sleeping. But that was okay. She needed to do this while the house was quiet and her mind clear.

Dan snapped up the phone on the first ring, but he fumbled it, and for a moment she thought he'd dropped it on the floor and fallen back to sleep. But then his voice, thick with phlegm and roughened by cigars and rum, demanded to know who the hell it was bothering him in the middle of the goddamn night.

"It's almost sunset, Count Dracula. Time to rise and shine."

"Who the fuck is this?"

"It's Alex."

There was a pause. A groan, the shifting of sheets, and another sleepy voice, a woman's. Dan had been divorced for years.

But he knew the first names of more hookers than any pimp in Miami.

"Alexandra Rafferty? Former employee of Miami PD?"

"That's right."

"Where the hell have you been, girl?"

"I can't tell you that right now."

"You okay? In any danger?"

"I'm fine. Everything's fine."

"That's what I thought. That's what I've been telling people. You'd surface and be okay. The papers were playing it up, but I knew you'd land on your feet. Care to talk about it?"

"Not right now."

"Okay," he said. "But hey, you're missing all the fun. I guess you saw your boy's been bad again."

"I haven't read any papers."

"Well, he killed another one, dropped her body Friday night in the goddamn vacant lot outside Miami PD. You know that sandy place beside the parking garage. Dribbled his blood right up the front steps of the department. Big spectacle. The press loved this one to death. Had helicopters circling, satellite trucks blocking both ends of the street. You gotta get back to work, Alex; your guy's about to blow wide open. That's what it looks like.

"And oh, yeah, the pathology boys determined that he does them with a piece of glass, a little shard of mirror he uses as a blade. That's the latest. The ME found traces of the silver backing they use on mirrors in a couple of the wounds. An old mirror, he says, though how he determined that is beyond me. And there're paint particles in the wounds, too, little specks of black oil-based paint."

"Paint?"

"Hey, it's getting weirder and weirder, Alex. If you don't hurry, this thing'll get solved without you. You won't get any of the fucking glory."

"That's fine by me."

"Where'd you say you were staying?"

"I'm out of town."

"Where out of town?"

"I can't tell you, Dan."

"You can't tell me. Why's that?"

"What about the bruises?"

"The bruises?"

"On the victims' faces. The ME have anything on them?"

"Nothing in his report. Not that I recall. They're just bruises. Why?"

She watched as Lawton rose from his rocker and said hello to a white-haired lady walking down the center of the street. She returned his greeting cheerfully and came over to the porch.

"Look, Dan, I called to tell you I was safe and to see if you'd caught Gabriella Hernandez's killers."

"Nothing to go on yet. No eyewitnesses, nothing. Just a bunch of Mac-ten slugs."

"I called it in, Dan. Friday, I called nine one one and gave a description of the killers and their truck."

"You did?"

"I did, yes."

"Well, it never made it to my desk. Or anybody else's I know about."

"Goddamn it."

"So you saw them, did you? What, you were there at the time?"

She told Dan about the young woman and the man and the yellow pool truck. She described them, their clothes, the girl's weird eyes, the huge guy.

"Were they Cubans?"

"I don't think so. It wasn't about Gabriella. This isn't political."

"How do you know that?"

"Look, Dan. Are you awake now? Can you make sense of this if I tell you the whole thing?"

"I haven't been to bed yet. Oh, I been to bed, but I haven't been to sleep, if you catch my drift."

The hooker giggled.

Lawton and the white-haired woman were chatting through the screen. She was laughing at something he'd said.

"So listen, Dan. Just listen to me, okay? Don't interrupt. I don't think I can do this if you trip me up."

She told him about Stan, the armored-truck robbery. She told him she'd wound up with the money from the heist, and that the people who killed Gabriella were most likely after that.

As she spoke, Lawton wandered into the house and stood for a moment gazing up at the circling ceiling fan.

"That was Grace," Lawton said. "That was my wife."

He looked at her, smiled, and drifted into Alex's bedroom, humming to himself.

"You still there?"

"I'm here," Dan said. Cop voice. Hard-edged. Wide fucking awake.

"I guess you want to know why I have the money."

"That would be a good place to start."

"It kind of fell in our laps. Then a little while later, we were at Gabriella's, and the bullets started flying. I was out of it, Dan, totally panicked. My husband is a thief and killer, my best friend murdered right in front of me."

"So that's it? That's your defense? You panicked? Drove off somewhere with two million dollars."

"Look, Dan, you're going to have to trust me. The money's coming back. I just had to get out of harm's way for a day or two. I couldn't leave the cash behind, could I? Let the shooters have it?"

"So you ran. So you're hiding out somewhere."

"I ran, yes. But I'm coming back. Tomorrow, the next day, as soon as I get something settled here."

"Oh, good. I'll call the Brinks people, let them know. One of our ID techs has your two million, but don't worry, she's coming back sometime soon. Trust me."

Lawton called out to Alex from the bedroom.

"I've got to get a situation worked out first; then I'm coming back."

"What situation? What the hell're you talking about?"

"Something happened to me a long time ago, Dan. There was a crime involved, something bad. It got covered up, but now it's got to come out in the open, and when it does, I'm going to need your help in a big way. This could get very ugly. Stan's going to try to incriminate me, bargain down his charges. He's going to be saying some nasty stuff."

"Wait a minute, wait a minute. You're losing me, Alex. I'm not following this."

"I'm trying to tell you, Dan. It's hard to get out, that's all. Bear with me, all right? Cut me some slack here."

Lawton shouted her name. His voice with a rising edge.

"Hold on, Dan, just a second, okay?"

"I have a choice?"

She went into the bedroom and Lawton was standing at the foot of her bed, looking down at the four crime-scene photographs. Her fanny pouch was lying on the floor at his feet. Lawton had arranged the snapshots in correct chronological order and placed them side by side.

"Dad! What have you been doing in my purse?"

"Alex," he said.

"I'm here, Dad."

"No, Alex. A-L-E-X. The name."

She stepped to his side and stared down at the photos.

"*A*," he said, counting them off. "*L*, *E*, *X*."

She looked at the four dead women.

They seemed very far away. The photographs, the bed. She felt the blood drain from her legs. Her cheeks were so stiff and numb, they felt frostbitten. A yellow glaze pressed on the edges of her vision.

"Alex," Lawton said. "So do you know this guy or what?"

She turned from the bed, drifted back to the living room,

picked up the phone. The air was thin, the light excruciating. Her eyes wouldn't focus. Parched, she felt the breath burning her throat, as if she had been wandering the desert for weeks. Her voice was reedy when she spoke.

"Dan?"

"Hey, I hate it when somebody calls me, then fucking puts me on hold. That's pretty goddamn discourteous, wouldn't you say?"

"Dan."

"Still here, sweetheart. Hanging by a thread."

"The body you found, the new girl."

"One in the parking lot?"

"Yeah. Was she twisted up like the others?"

"Whole new position. One we haven't seen before. Haven't even given her a name yet. Kicking around a few ideas, but nothing's stuck."

"Don't tell me," she said. "Let me describe it, the position she was in."

"Yeah? And how you going to do that? You been taking clairvoyant lessons?"

"She was placed on her side, with her knees cocked up, arms flat against her side. Like the letter *N*."

Dan was silent for a moment. The hooker squawked behind him, a burst of impatience. Alexandra heard him breathing into the mouthpiece.

"Okay, yeah. I guess you could describe it that way. It's like an *N*. What? You talk to somebody in the office?"

"I haven't talked to anyone but you."

"Okay, I'll bite. How'd you know?"

Her voice surprised her when she spoke. How empty it was, how far off.

"He's spelling my name, Dan."

Lawton came out into the living room. He'd unzipped his blue jumpsuit to his waist and was trying to get the zipper back up, but it was caught on the fabric.

"Spelling your name? What's that supposed to mean?"

"Think about it. He's twisted the victims into letters."

"Letters?" He paused for a moment, then said, "Aw shit."

"*A*, Gasper. *L*, Hear No Evil. *E*, The Swatter. *X*, Floater. And then *A* again. And now *N*. It was looking us in the face the whole time."

Dan said, "Where are you, Alex?"

"I can't tell you."

"Where, goddamn it?"

"I'm going to hang up now, Dan. I'll call you later."

"Is it at least safe there?"

"It is, yes. It's famous for its safety."

"Then stay there. Stay put."

"Okay."

"What's this about, Alex? Why's this fuckhead spelling your name?"

"Maybe it's not me. Maybe it's some other Alexandra."

He gave that a few seconds' consideration.

"No, you're right," he said gloomily. "That must be why he left the last one at the police station, a trail of his blood up the front steps. We weren't getting it. We were being too stupid. So he lays one right under our noses and we still don't get it. What the hell's this about, Alex? What the fuck is going on here?"

"I don't know, Dan."

Frustrated with his zipper, Lawton began to whimper.

"I'll call you back tonight, okay? Give us both a chance to think this over, see what it might mean."

"You got a weapon, some way to defend yourself?"

"He doesn't know where I am. Don't worry about me, Dan. Let's just think this through. We'll talk tonight."

"Goddamn psychologists, that's who's to blame here. Fuckers get paid for being so damn smart; well, they're too fucking smart for their own good. Best police work is stupid and simple. Look at the obvious, see what's right in front of you. But no, the shrinks got us going off into some never-never land, all this childhood re-enactment bullshit."

"Tonight, Dan," she said, and hung up.

The beach was empty.

Alex walked along the water's edge.

Head buzzing with shock, she couldn't remember the day of the week, the month, the season. She had no idea of the year, the century, which planet, which galaxy. She couldn't recall her name or the date of her birth or why she was even there at all. Filled with hot white noise, she was as blank and vacant as Mr. M., as though her own hippocampus had been vacuumed away through a silver straw. A slate as clean as the white sands that stretched before her, as pure as the cloudless sky, as barren as the air. She could remember nothing. It was as if she had breathed too deeply of that transparent air and it had somehow permeated her blood, dissolved every worrisome thought, the dreary weight of her past, the accumulated residues of a lifetime.

She kicked off her shoes, carried them along as she continued her walk down that empty beach, letting her feet sink into the crystalline sand, feeling the grit, its pleasant burn between her toes. She looked out to sea, the water still today, and bluer than it had ever been before. As blue as it would ever be. And the sky was bluer still and even calmer than the sea.

Along her way, she saw three sand castles rubbed smooth by the wind, the ceaseless breeze eroding them back to shapeless humps of sand. She saw a couple of molded human forms, primitive sand sculptures, featureless beings with arms and legs sprawled out like pale sunbathers. She saw a discarded towel and a candy wrapper tumbling past her feet and a twisted aluminum chair half-buried in a drift of white sugar.

She walked and walked until the beach ran out of sand. Until the daylight began to drain away and the prism of the sky was spraying the full spectrum of light into the western horizon, bright bands of gold and red and green and yellow.

She turned and walked back down the beach, but she was without destination. There was nowhere to go. No appointments, no responsibilities. Absolved of every moment but this one. Unfettered by the noise of memory, the whispering spirits of long ago, the great choirs that sang their hymns of lost days.

Twilight in the air, twilight in her head. With the sea to her right and the land to her left and the sky far away overhead. She could look and see. She could breathe. She could move. But there were no memories.

If only for that little while, she had no past. If only for that hour, that exhilarating emptiness, that buoyancy. The thrilling release.

A mile, two miles, Alexandra marched back down the beach and with every step she felt gravity's return. Twenty-nine years old. October, the twentieth century, the earth with all its buried treasures, its ancient artifacts, its archives, its scriptures. The past, the past, growing heavy in her blood.

Alexandra Rafferty had captured the fascination of a killer. Six women had died on her behalf. Murdered so a goddamn maniac could conjure her, spell her out, so she would know that he existed, feel his presence, experience the depth of his tortured love. Some bullshit like that.

Alex marched back to the dunes of Seaside and with every step the hot white static of shock dwindled.

A killer had made love to six women and while looking into their helpless eyes, he had sliced their throats. Driven by his mad craving, he lay these twisted offerings before Alex, as if it were a private performance, his idea of seduction, his tease, his purgation. Then the freak drizzled out his trail of blood so that Alex might bear witness to his yearning, so she might tremble at the intensity of his agonizing love.

So she might hear his cry:

Who am I and why am I doing this?

What do I have in store for you?

Alexandra climbed one of the graceful Seaside stairways that swept up the steep dunes like the sculptured crest of a wave. It was dark now, cool and breezy. She'd left her father alone for hours. She'd lost her mind and gotten it back.

Some bastard had murdered six young women simply to spell out her name.

TWENTY-EIGHT

"I went out for a walk, that's all. You weren't here. Your boyfriend wasn't here, so I took a stroll and I met Grace. She lives two blocks from here. I wish you wouldn't yell at me all the time."

Alex squared her shoulders, took a breath. She looked at Jason rinsing dishes. He was keeping his head down, amused but trying not to show it. She looked at her father. She wanted to hit something. To drive her fist through the walls of the house. Again and again, till she'd mangled her hand, turned it to pulp.

"Her name is Grace," Lawton said. "I met her through the screen this afternoon; then I went over to see her. Two streets over, that's where she lives, and she remembers us from when we were here before. Mellow Yellow, that house we rented. She remembers that. She remembers your sand castle, too. She loaned me this camera to use while we're here. To document our once-in-a-lifetime vacation."

Lawton craned his neck and peered down into the pop-up lens

of the Brownie Reflex, aimed it at Jason. He was putting the last of the plates in the dishwasher. He'd made lasagna from scratch, and a Caesar salad, French bread. A store-bought Key lime pie for dessert. Alex tried to eat but couldn't. She apologized, didn't try to explain.

"Go on, Alexandra, go over and stand next to your boyfriend. Yeah, yeah, I know how you hate having your picture taken, but you always love looking at the photos later on. You just have to realize, sweetheart, you can't have the looking without the posing. Now come on, shake a leg."

Alex closed her eyes and opened them. Nothing had changed. Jason was watching her, keeping the smile off his lips, but it still lurked in his eyes. She walked over and stood next to Jason. He put his arm across her shoulder.

"Okay, good. Now come on, you two, I want you to say *cheese.* Don't pout, give Daddy a smile you'll be proud of later on. Let's see those pearly whites."

Her father snapped the picture, then rolled the knob on the bottom of the camera to advance the film.

"Memories to last a lifetime."

"Dad, where'd you get the camera?" She pulled away from Jason.

"I told you. Her name is Grace. She's an herbalist. Two streets over. Got a pantry full of pills. Never saw so many vitamins in all my life. Must work, though, 'cause she says she's seventy-two, but I'd swear she isn't a day over thirty. Claims she knows just the thing I need for sharpening up my memory. Combination of five, six pills, roots and bark and flower stalks. That kind of thing. I think she's part witch, got her little stew pot bubbling away. But she's a good witch. Says her name is Grace. Which rings a bell with me."

"I told you just this afternoon—I don't want you going off on your own, Dad. Is that clear? Can you remember that simple thing?"

"He met somebody," Jason said. "What's wrong with that?"

Jason slipped the leftovers into the fridge, recorked the cabernet.

"I don't want him wandering around. Especially not now."

"Why? What's happened?"

She turned and looked at the dark window.

"Nothing's happened. It's just not safe."

"Hey, Alex, we're a long way from Miami. This place is Mayberry, USA. They don't lock their doors; they keep their windows wide open. Hell, they don't even have a Barney Fife."

"There's no sheriff in Seaside? No law enforcement?"

"That's right."

"How do you know that?"

"What's wrong with you, Alex? Why're you snapping at me?"

"I'm not snapping. How do you know there's no sheriff?"

Jason rinsed off his hands, wiped them with the dish towel, and hung it back on the rack. He gave her a hurt look.

"Because I asked at the front desk. The nearest police are in Panama City. Maybe forty-five minutes to an hour away. They cruise by now and then, but there's no one posted here."

"Why'd you ask, Jason?"

"I wanted to know. That's all. I mean, come on, Alex, this place is as safe as it gets. What's the harm if Lawton walks around a little, enjoys himself?"

"Well, for one thing, he almost drowned yesterday. Have you forgotten?"

"I think he's learned his lesson about swimming in the ocean. Didn't you, Lawton? Didn't you learn not to swim out beyond the surf?"

Lawton stepped over to the couch and regarded her a moment, then held out the camera to Alex.

"This is for you, sweetheart. It's a present. So you'll have some lasting impressions you can look back on someday. Memories to last a lifetime. I know how much you've been wanting a camera. And this one is very good and very simple at the same time. All you do is look in the lens and you see the picture, full-size, brilliantly clear, while you're making it. It's the latest thing. Uses Kodak one twenty-seven film. What starts as a hobby can sometimes grow into a career."

She took the camera from him.

"Thank you, Dad."

"I even got the yellow box it came in and the instruction pamphlet and everything. Did I tell you about the herbalist I met? Two blocks over. Tupelo Street. She's a peach. Says her name is Grace, but she might be lying about that. She doesn't look like any Grace I ever knew. But then, you never know about women. Women can fool you sometimes."

She got Lawton into the new pajamas he'd picked out. Blue and yellow with a Hawaiian motif—parrots and surfers and fire-spitting volcanoes.

He climbed into bed and tugged the bedspread up to his chin. Alex perched on the edge of the mattress.

"Have I been bad?"

"No, Dad. You haven't been bad."

"Why am I being sent to bed early?"

"It's ten o'clock already. That's your bedtime, isn't it?"

"I guess so."

"You aren't sleepy?"

"I suppose I'm a little tired. It's been a big day. Lots of new things. I met a very nice woman today. I'm warning you right now—I may just marry that woman."

Alexandra shifted on the bed, leaning toward him. She lowered her voice.

"Listen, Dad, something's happened. I'm going to have to go back to Miami to take care of it."

"You don't like it here?"

"It's fine here, but I've got to go back."

"Well, I'm not leaving. No, sir, I like it here a whole lot. I mean, it's not Ohio, but then, what is? Tomorrow, I'm going to start taking herbs so I can get my memory back. That's what Grace said. She's an herbalist who lives on Tupelo Street."

Alex sighed. She looked back at the closed door, bent forward to see if Jason's shoes were visible at the crack. They weren't.

She turned back to Lawton and spoke in a hush.

"We'll get somebody to stay with you while I'm gone. I'll just be away for a few days."

"So go. Who's stopping you? I'm a big boy. I don't need a guardian."

She looked back at the door again. Kept her voice low.

"I need to ask you something, Dad."

"Fire away."

"Yesterday, when you went swimming . . ."

"Was it yesterday? Yes, yes, that's right, yesterday."

"Did you swim out too far? Is that what happened? And Jason came along and saw you and swam out and saved you. Is that how it went?"

"If you say so."

"But I want to know. Is that what happened?"

"Damn it, Alex. You're always testing me."

He shut his eyes and pressed his lips together in a silent pout.

"I'm sorry, Dad. But I need to know this. I need to know what you remember. If the story Jason told about what happened is the truth."

He opened his eyes again and smiled slyly.

"You don't trust that boy?"

"I want to. God, I do."

"He's seems all right to me. And, oh, by the way, I heard you two in there last night and again this afternoon, going at it pretty good. You might want to try to be a little quieter from now on. These walls are pretty thin. Not that I minded or anything. It was all very pleasant really. But it's just not exactly proper for a father to eavesdrop on his daughter's lovemaking. Even if it *is* unintentional."

She shook her head, and a smile escaped her.

"Okay, we'll be quieter. I promise." She bent forward and kissed him on the cheek.

"Her name is Grace. After I married her, I took her to Miami to raise a family. We've come up here on vacation. Going to stay the whole month of August. Can't really afford it, but what the hell, you only go around once."

Alexandra took a long breath, let it out slowly.

"Okay, Dad, listen. Just try for a second to remember what happened yesterday. Can you do that for me?"

"Sure. How hard could that be?"

"You were swimming. You were in the water. What happened then? Did you go out too far? Did Jason see you and swim out?"

"Hell, how am I supposed to remember every little thing? If you say that's what happened, fine. Who am I to dispute it? Even if it does sound damn suspicious."

"Why is it suspicious?"

"How would I know? It's your version of things. But why the hell would an old man swim out so far? Unless he wanted to drown himself, stop being such a burden to his loved ones."

Alex stared into his milky eyes for a moment, then bent forward and lay her ear against his chest and wrapped her arms around him.

"You're no burden, Dad. You're no burden at all. I love you. I'd do anything to make your life better. Don't feel that way, please. I love having you around, spending time with you. I wouldn't have it any other way."

He moved his hand to her head like he'd done when she was fevered as a child. Cupping his palm around her forehead as if to draw the heat from her skull.

"Grace is an herbalist now. I never knew she had such an interest. But I'm glad she's developed it, because herbs just might be the ticket to cure these damn forgetful spells I've been having."

Her father's hand was cool against her forehead.

"That would be wonderful, Dad. I'd like to meet her."

"Sure. I'll introduce you. She's a schoolteacher, you know. Teaches tenth grade back in Miami. And we've got a daughter, too. Alexandra. Pretty little girl with a wonderful imagination. She's out there in the sand every day playing, building her castle, and there're about a hundred people who live inside it, and Alex knows every one of them by name. Can tell you a story about each one. She's amazing, the imagination she has. A hundred people. Blacksmiths and soldiers and handmaidens and plowboys. She's got a first and last name for every one and a complete history. Jill McGowan, the minstrel. Bart Raymond, the evil count."

With her head against his chest, Alex said, "I'd forgotten that."

"Forgotten what?"

"About the people in the castle."

"Oh, yeah, there're lots of people. It takes a ton of folks to run your average castle."

"I'd totally forgotten."

"Yes, yes, don't I know how easy it is to forget things. All too easy. Believe me, I'm an expert on the human memory. I made quite a study of the subject a few years ago. Read books and articles. Yes, sir, I'm a regular expert on memory. All kinds of trivial info.

"Take the Greeks, for instance. They're the ones with Lethe, that river of forgetfulness. Fall into that river and you were a goner. Stick a toe into it and you could wipe out your whole damn childhood. And they had a goddess, too, Mnemosyne. Mother of all the muses. She and Zeus created them together—the poets, the musicians, the painters. They reported directly to the goddess of memory, and they were under orders to make up stories and songs so human beings wouldn't forget the important things, so it all would be passed on from one generation to the next. That was the goddess's job—to supervise all the renegade artists, make sure they kept the heroes alive, the heroes and the legends."

Alex sat up slowly and peered into her father's eyes. They were barely open. He was drifting away, vision blurring, but the words still came in steady succession, growing faint and slow like the last few rotations of a Victrola record.

"My daughter, Alexandra, I don't know how she does it, remembering everybody in that castle. From the king right down to the toilet scrubber. She has a history for every one. She's something else, just amazing. I'm awful proud of that girl."

TWENTY-NINE

On the front porch, Alex settled into the rocker next to Jason's. The street was shadowy and all the houses she could see were dark. A breeze was coming from the northwest, a flood of more cool Canadian air. Geese honking just beyond the range of hearing. All the seasonal migrations about to begin again.

"You're very tense, Alex. Very far away."

"I am," she said. "About as tense and far away as I've ever been."

"What's going on? What is it?"

"I've been thinking about things. Who I am, what I've been doing."

Jason was quiet.

"I've been running all my life," she said. "Retreating, avoiding. That's the pattern. I learned it early and I kept at it. I'm a pro now. A full-time dodger."

"Running away from what?"

She looked at him. There was a buzz in his voice, an undercurrent of impatience or irritation.

"I'm whining," she said. "I'm coming down with a bad case of self-pity."

"Running away from what?" His voice still showed that strain.

"Running away from everything."

Jason gazed out at the street, where a dog was sniffing the shadows.

"You take pictures of crime scenes, for God sakes. That doesn't strike me as avoiding anything. That's looking right into the eyes of some pretty bad shit."

"I look, I see, but I don't cause anything to happen. I photograph the crimes, that's all. I'm just a looker, a watcher. A goddamn voyeur. I've done it all my life, and if I'm not careful, it's the way I'll always be."

"So? What's so bad about that?"

"It's passive. It's dead. It's letting other people decide my fate. It's abdicating, Jason. That's what's so bad."

"What're you supposed to do, buy a cape and a sword and go questing for justice?"

She was silent.

"You want to swap lives for a week?" he said. "Try answering the phone all day, taking stock orders. Buy, sell. Sell, buy. That's guaranteed to boost your sense of self-worth in a hurry. A lackey. A grunt. A nothing.

"Hell, Alex, for my money, the whole thing with controlling your destiny is overrated. Whatever happened to the Zen of letting go. Like what we do on the mat. Using your opponent's momentum, turning his strength and aggression against him. It's the same idea."

"That's apples and oranges, Jason. Fighting isn't the same as living. What applies on the mat doesn't apply out here."

"Sure it does. You're either a victim or you're not. There's no middle ground."

She studied him for a moment, wanting to tell him, knowing she couldn't.

She turned her eyes back to the empty street. The dog had snuffled away.

"I'm tired of waiting to be attacked, Jason. Always on the defensive. Looking over my shoulder, listening for footsteps, weighing every situation for its danger potential. That's no way to live."

"Well, I admit, when you put it that way, it sounds pretty bleak."

She lay a hand on his arm.

"Something happened to me when I was a girl. Something bad."

Jason stared down at the moonlit planks of the porch.

"It involved this kid, Darnel Flint?" Jason turned his head, looking off toward the beach. The moonlight seemed to be gathering there, a white glow beyond the dunes.

"That's right. Darnel Flint. He was a neighbor boy. He was older."

"And he molested you."

Alexandra sat back in the rocker. She heard the crunch of sand beneath the blades of Jason's chair like small bones fracturing.

"Look," she said. "I'm sorry, Jason. But I think I need to be alone for a while. Do you mind?"

"Hey, I'm sorry," he said. "I was rushing you, finishing your sentences. Don't stop. Please. I'm sorry."

"It's okay, Jason. I'm just not ready to talk about this yet."

"You don't trust me."

"I don't trust myself," she said, and looked at him, but in the frail light, his eyes were unreadable.

"Look, Alex. I didn't mean to bully you. I'm sorry."

"It's all right. Really, you were fine. I just don't feel like going into it right now. I need some privacy for a while. That's all."

He was quiet for a moment. Then said, "You want me to go to a motel?"

"No, no. Just for an hour or so. Maybe you could take a walk on the beach, go have a drink or two at Bud and Alley's. I need to make a phone call, that's all. A business thing."

"You're sure? You're sure you don't want to finish talking about this? I'll just sit here and listen. No interruptions this time, I promise."

He turned to her, reached out and rubbed his thumb lightly down the line of her jaw, but she stiffened at his touch, and he drew his hand away.

"Thanks," she said. "But no, not yet. I'm not ready."

His mouth twitched as if he was fighting off a rash response. He kept his eyes on hers as he rose to his feet.

"I guess I'll prowl the beach, then. An hour? Is that enough?"

"An hour's fine."

"Okay, then." He gave her an anxious smile. "I'll count the stars, give you the latest tally. What's fallen, what's still there."

She rose and kissed him on the cheek, and when he was gone, she went back inside and sat on the couch, staring at her ghostly reflection in the glass door.

After a short while, she lifted the phone, dialed Dan's number. When he answered, she took a quick breath and said hello.

"Where are you, Alex? Tell me where you are."

"Dan, don't make me hang up."

"You know," he said, "I could've traced this call. Gotten a court order, just based on what you told me this afternoon."

"I know that, Dan. But you didn't, did you? You didn't do that. Because you trust me."

He paused a moment, then in an exasperated voice said, "I had a sit-down with the goddamn shrinks again. Called them in from their golf games."

"You told them about the son of a bitch spelling my name."

"I told them. They didn't buy it at first. Fought like hell. Said it was just a bizarre coincidence, the bodies laid out like letters. They said we were reaching, fabricating, imposing our own bullshit on these dead women. But that didn't last long. They didn't like it one goddamn bit, but they came around eventually. Now they want to talk to you, ask you some questions."

"I bet they do."

"So, come on, Alex, spit it out. I want to know what you've been thinking. Who this fuckhead might be, what this is all about."

"I've been thinking, yeah."

"Cut the coy shit, Alex. I'm running out of patience."

"I'd like you to do me a favor."

"Oh, would you now?"

"Look something up for me, Dan. Run a couple of names. See if you can find current addresses, employment, that sort of thing."

"A couple of names. And who would they be?"

"Darnel Flint, Sr., approximate age, sixty. Last known employer, Coca-Cola. His wife, too, if they're still married. Even if they're not, I want her maiden name, her whereabouts. And the daughters, too, Molly and Millie, and a son, J.D. The boy would be twenty-four, twenty-five years old; the girls would be twenty-nine. They attended Norland Elementary about eighteen years ago. That's all I know. You got that?"

"Not the family dog?"

"You can do it, Dan. I know you'll do this for me. You want all that again?"

"I got it, I got it. I don't know what the fuck it's about, but I got it."

"It may be nothing. But I need to know anything you can find out. Employment records, current addresses. Anything at all."

Dan was fuming silently.

"So tell me about the psychologists," Alex said brightly. "When they finally came around, did they have any insights?"

"One or two."

"I'm listening."

"Based on the crime scenes so far, they're saying this guy is compulsive to the tenth fucking power. A goddamn nut for detail.

He's got to do it all just exactly the same way, caught in a loop, a ritual or whatever."

"We knew that already."

"The point is, with that makeup, it's more than likely he's going to try to finish the cycle."

"Spell my name all the way out."

"That's right. Three more. *D-R-A.* The fucker's locked onto his own personal monorail, can't get off, no matter what. According to the shrinks, that is. But I'm not so sure. I'm thinking if he knows we're onto him, if he knows you've finally gotten the message, maybe that'll change things. Maybe that's his goal. Just to get your attention, spook you. That might cool him off."

"I wish it were true, Dan. But no. I think he's warmed up now. He's having a good time. He's damn well going to try to finish the thing he started."

"Fuck it. I knew you'd say that."

"Anything about Stan?"

"Not yet. But we'll find him, don't worry. Faxed his picture all over the state. The FBI's in on it; the TV's going with his photograph on the evening news. It's all out there on the airwaves. Brinks is offering a hundred thousand for his capture. That should get things percolating. But he hasn't cropped up yet."

"You didn't tell anyone I had the cash?"

"Like I said, Alex. Based on the evidence I've provided from your statement, Stan Rafferty is the prime suspect in the robbery. Find him, find the money. That's how we're proceeding, and that's why Brinks is offering a hundred thou for his capture."

"Thanks, Dan."

"Now, you owe me one, Alex. I need to know where you are."

She watched a blue car cruise slowly up East Ruskin Street.

"I can't do that, Dan. Not yet."

"Christ, Alex. Stop being such a goddamn hardhead."

"I bet I can guess the shrinks' other insight."

"Talk to me, Alex. Give me a location."

"After he's done two more, *D* and *R*, and his appetite is in high gear, that's when he comes for me. I'm the last *A*, the grand finale. Is that what they said?"

She heard Dan sigh.

"That's what they said."

THIRTY

She was so near, he could taste her. Within breathing distance. Sharing these same molecules with her, drawing them deep inside, letting them out. He could smell her on his tongue, an iridescent scent. A cold burn with bright edges. She had tried to flee from him, but she could not. She could not hide her distinctive fragrance by crossing streams or jumping precipices, or running six hundred miles away. He was tuned to her smell. An infallible homing device. One particle was all he needed, one fleck of sloughed-off skin, one invisible dot of her evaporated sweat. She was in his nose. He was inhaling her, taking her into his body, directly along the neural pathways. Flakes of her physical self were chafing his brain stem. He was alive with her. Tingling in the dark. "Tiger! Tiger! burning bright/In the forests of the night . . ." His invisible flames, orange and red and yellow, leaping up to the sky. He was on fire, a transparent wraith. Incandescent and unseen.

Standing perfectly still in a sandy lane across East Ruskin

Street, white picket fences to his left and right, fifty feet away from her, he peered through her flimsy curtains. Fifty feet of sheer darkness, only that diaphanous veil of sweet nighttime air between them. In seconds, he could cross the street, be up the stairs and through her door. Hit her, take her, enter her body, watch the hatred surface in her eyes, the murderous loathing. Then he would have to slice her throat to save himself. His final salvation. So effortless, so exquisite in its symmetry.

But for now, he stayed put, watched her speaking on the phone, watched her rise, pace in front of the couch. Watched her stare ahead, her eyes meeting his through the dark, though she did not know he was there, for he was profoundly shrouded. A shadow within a shadow. Darkness shielded by darkness. A swimmer in the black sea of midnight.

He was in no hurry. On the contrary. Over these last few months, as he had made her name take shape on the bloody floors of Miami apartments, he felt an increasing serenity, a warmth, a crystal focus. The relaxed readiness of a man poised before a hissing rattler. Looking for his moment. Waiting with every nerve fiber twinkling, each muscle cocked, waiting for the perfect instant.

No reason to hurry, for this was the final chapter. When it ended, there was nothing for him afterward. Nothing. For years, he had immersed himself in her life. Following her on her ceaseless rounds, even at times following her husband, Stan. He had given over his life to watching her, and he was fully aware of the void that awaited, but it did not disturb him in the least. That endless stretch of empty time without Alexandra in the world would be his fulfillment, his time for contemplation and reflection.

Maybe he would simply become another. Sink away beneath the surface of the personality he had already created. Assume that identity. Marry, have children. Go about his job, his daily rounds of exercise and eating and companionship. Disappear into that shell of a man that the world saw. So benign, so trustworthy, so interchangeable with any other man. Maybe that was his future, his job done, his quest complete, a quiet death of personality, the wolf softening into the lamb.

He was watching her, watching her move, watching her talk into the mouthpiece of her phone, watching her breathe, when from the edge of his vision he noticed movement.

He drew back and peered up into the dark.

Three doors away on the dark balcony he saw the glimmer of faces, the flit and flicker of two women, both blond, one short, one tall. And a man, large and unmoving. All of them stood at the railing as they stared down at Alexandra Rafferty's rented beach house. He heard the clink of their glasses, their soft laughter.

He would have thought nothing of it. He would have looked away, gone back to his own watching were it not for that inexpressible movement of the tall one's head, some tic with her hair, a flip perhaps, that made him catch his breath. Pushed him even farther into the shadows.

It was body language he had seen before. A gesture so precise, so exactly duplicated that there was no doubt. He had seen this woman earlier. Watched her from afar. Several moments passed before he could remember where or when or who. But then it came with sudden clarity, with the intense brilliance of revelation.

In watching Stan, he had encountered this one, apparently his mistress. The name on her mailbox was Jennifer McDougal. From what he could tell, she was a woman filled with fluff. Stan's diddle-headed lover. A feather to any wind.

Seeing her there at Seaside, watching her look down at Alexandra's rented house, he felt the bowstrings draw taut within him. Jennifer McDougal. For months he had watched Stan Rafferty coming and going from her house. He had watched them kiss good-bye on her front porch. Seen that same hitching toss of her hair, a gesture no doubt meant to be sultry and alluring but repeated so often and so mindlessly, it meant nothing, a dead echo, a parody.

Jennifer McDougal and her two friends. He didn't know why she was there, didn't need to know. He watched them watching. He watched them glimmer in the dark, listened to their laughter, the tinkling of their glasses. Three doors down, two floors up. Perfect. Absolutely perfect.

The Red Barn was a rock-and-roll bar in Grayton Beach, two miles from Seaside, beyond the halo of the town's lights, beyond the gravitational pull of its charm. The Red Barn was a loud and smoky honky-tonk with a thousand beer cans decorating the shelves. A stale taste in the air of a deep-fat fryer that hadn't been shut off in years. Guys in dirty T-shirts, jeans, and construction boots mingling with retirees in pink shirts and green trousers and college kids with their baseball hats on backward. An occasional amateur staggering up to the stage to play his harmonica or banjo with the raucous, kick-ass band for a song or two, a lot of hooting, a couple of serious pool games going on in the back room.

Nice loud cover for whatever he wanted to do.

Jennifer McDougal and her two friends had been there for half an hour. They were wearing low-cut cotton dresses, Jennifer in burgundy, the dark girl in a paisley print. Something about the way the dress fit the shorter girl, or the way she wore it, suggested that she had never worn a dress before.

Six guys had approached their table and were sent packing, the girls howling with laughter as the rejects marched away. In their quiet moments, the girls gazed at each other, held hands below the table.

A minute earlier, he had followed one of the cast-off suitors out into the parking lot and with only minor physical pressure, had secured from him the password to these girls' affection.

Now he called up his best smile, pushed himself away from the wall, and ambled over to their table. He stepped close, blocking their view of the stage, his green knapsack slung casually over his shoulder.

"You girls out for a night on the town with your daddy?"

"This is Norman," the small blond one said. "He's nobody's daddy. He's a sphinx. An enigma."

"He's from the planet Penis," said Jennifer McDougal.

"I see."

"How about you? You from Penis, too?"

"Of course I am," he said. "Aren't all men?"

"If you want to sit down with us, you've got to answer a question first. That's the rule," the short one said. "A riddle. Get it wrong, you gotta fuck off."

"All right," he said. "That's fair."

"But we have to warn you. Nobody's gotten it right. Five flameouts so far."

"Six," he said. "I counted six."

"Ohhh," Jennifer said. "He's been watching. He's been plotting. I think we have a naughty boy here, Emma."

"Yeah," she said. "He looks naughty all right."

"What's in the knapsack, good-looking? A gross of condoms?"

"Blood," he said.

"Blood?" Jennifer lifted a theatrical hand to her mouth. "Oh, boy, we got a live one this time."

"What do you mean, blood?" said Emma.

"I mean two plastic pouches of blood. Five hundred ccs per pouch."

Emma frowned.

"You're lying."

"I don't lie," he said. "It's the one thing I will not do."

"Get out of here, you weirdo."

"Emma is asshole-intolerant," Jennifer said. "I guess you'll have to go."

"What about the riddle? Don't I get a shot?"

Jennifer took a deep sip of her margarita and backhanded the foam off her lips.

"Okay, all right. We'll give you two chances. That's what we've been giving the others. That's fair, isn't it, Emma? Two chances for the naughty boy?"

"All right," said Emma, not meeting his eyes. "So here it is, lover boy. What has eighteen knees and white blood?"

"The President of the United States?"

Jennifer laughed. Emma stared at her friend, unsmiling.

"One more guess," said Jennifer. "Eighteen knees and white blood."

"A cockroach," he said. "A common brown roach."

Jennifer squealed and clapped her hands. Emma turned her head away and stared at one of the red exit signs.

"Can you believe it, Emma? He got it right."

"How'd you know that, penishead?" She refused to look at him. He liked her better every minute.

"I know a lot of things. I'm a man with considerable arcane knowledge."

"Okay, Mr. Arcane, sit your butt on down." Jennifer patted the chair next to her.

"I believe your friend would rather I shove off. I don't think she wants to share."

"Oh, she's just being cranky. Go on, sit down. Join us. You got the riddle right, so you win the right to buy us a drink."

"How about the enigma—does he mind?"

"Hey, Norm. You give a shit if this good-looking guy sits down and pays for the rest of our drinks?"

"No."

"Okay, then, pretty boy. I'm Jennifer and this is Emma. Snag us a waitress, why don't you? Make yourself useful."

When the waitress had left with their orders, he turned back to the young women and said, "You seem to be celebrating tonight. What's the occasion?"

"We won the lottery," Emma said coldly.

"Wonderful. And how do you intend to spend your loot?"

"Emma and I are going to become home owners in Seaside. Going to join the leisure class." Jennifer was beaming.

"And you, Norman?"

"I don't know."

Jennifer laughed and said, "Norman's one of those guys you read about in the newspaper, this hermit who's got only one shirt and one pair of raggedy underwear, lives like he's penniless, saves string and has jars full of buttons that he's been squirreling away for forty years, but then when he dies, it turns out he leaves about two hundred gazillion dollars to his goddamn parakeet. That's Norman."

Emma's frown defrosted and she turned a faint smile to Jennifer.

"Wow, Jen. That was good. That was a good one."

"I'm sky-high," Jennifer said. "I guess being rich must agree with me."

A half hour later on the moonlit beach, he and Norman followed fifty yards behind the girls. He was carrying a bottle of wine, Lucere, a crisp and spicy California chardonnay that had been chilling in the ice chest in his car. Just the thing for a beach party.

The girls were skipping along at water's edge, hand in hand like sprites, dancing like dryads along some ancient Grecian shore. Even from a mile away, the Red Barn's booming bass still shook the air.

It was perfect, perfect, perfect. An exquisite night, one to remember, when all things became congruent, when the neat round pegs of the past fit into the neat round holes of the present. When one hand pressed against the opposite hand, a flawless fit. Ying merged with yang, pit answered pat.

"So what's your story, Norman?"

The big man trudged beside him as they moved deeper into the dark.

"I don't have one."

The earth seemed to cringe beneath his tread. Small quakes at each footfall. The man must have weighed three hundred pounds. Hard fat, a lumbering mind.

"Why're you with these girls? An older man like you hanging

out with children. Why is that? And why do you let them pick on you? Mock you? Twist your nose, ridicule you. Why, Norman? There must be some good reason you subject yourself to that. Do you have low self-esteem? Are you slow-witted, a moron of some kind?"

"No."

"What you remind me of is an indulgent parent, unable to discipline his unruly teenage girls. Is that what you are, Norman?"

The big man halted and turned to face him.

"Oh, I've struck a chord, have I?"

Norman filled his lungs with night air and blew it out.

"Yes, yes. I thought I saw something twitch in your eyes when I first came to the table and asked if you were their daddy. You are, aren't you?"

"No."

"You're a bad liar, Norman. I like that in a person. Truth is important, don't you think? The most important of the virtues."

Norman walked on in silence.

"But of course. The dark one, the mouthy one, Emma, she's your daughter. Not the other one, lovely Jennifer. Yes, of course. I see the family resemblance. Emma's broad face, her heavy Slavic cheekbones. Yes, of course."

Norman halted again and stared into his eyes.

"Who are you, asshole?"

"I'm the man inside your head, Norman. I'm the one who can sense each and every secret circulating in your blood. Emma is your daughter, but you'd rather no one knows. You'd rather pretend to be just a friend, their peer. Why is that? Is it because you sleep with her? Have you spread her legs, Norman, and forced yourself inside her? Is this why she's become a lesbian, because her daddy screwed her?"

"Hell no."

"How sad it is. How terribly poignant. What's the world coming to when a child can speak so harshly, with such malice to her own father? What a sad, twisted world we live in."

"She doesn't know."

His large face went dull and he turned his eyes to the shadows.

"What? You're telling me Emma doesn't know she's your daughter?"

"You can't let her know."

"You've been associating with your daughter and hiding your identity? Well, how fascinating. How utterly strange. What happened? Did you have an affair with Emma's mother long ago and now you're embarrassed to reveal the truth? You're unsure of Emma's response if she was to find out. Perhaps she'd be outraged. Perhaps she'd exile you from her kingdom. So you've chosen to suffer her derision rather than risk having her know the truth."

"I'll kill you if you tell."

Norman turned away and plodded after the girls in silence.

"Oh, my," he said, as he hurried after Norman. "Now death has reared its ugly head."

Norman tramped through the dark.

"Do you ponder death a great deal, Norman? Drawing your last breath. Are you death-obsessed?"

He didn't respond.

"You don't care, do you? I sense that. You're one of those who don't see a huge difference between this life and the afterlife. It's no big fucking deal. Is that you, Norman? Do I have you pegged?"

"Maybe."

He shifted the backpack on his shoulder, felt the cold blood wobble.

Thirty yards ahead, the girls were ankle-deep in the surf, Jennifer splashing water playfully at Emma. The throaty barks of their laughter.

"And that's because of your childhood. Something happened, didn't it?"

Norman halted and looked at him.

"Who are you?"

"Oh, I'm just another tortured soul. A lot like you, I dare say. I suspect we carry the same passport, members of the same club. Of course, I've only just met you, but I'm quick to read a fellow sufferer's vibrations. I'm certain we have a lot in common. A loveless childhood, a traumatic event. Scarred souls, aberrant pathologies. That's us, isn't it? I'm not being too impertinent, am I? You're a lost soul, a man without conscience or remorse. A man so cold and empty, you sometimes frighten yourself."

Norman resumed his stride. The girls were squealing somewhere ahead in the dark.

"Would you mind if I killed you, Norman? Would that bother you a great deal?"

"Try it, asshole."

"Oh, Norman. You're so contemptuous. Why? You don't think I can kill you? Because you're so large and ruthless and I'm just an average-size man? Is that what you think? You're a believer in appearances, are you?"

The big man continued to plod toward the girls.

Out beyond the surf, a trawler was moving through the dark. Its lights winking, a stray piece of country-western music escaped across the waters.

"You see, Norman, I know exactly how you think. I can get inside your brain and read your shapeless thoughts. I'm in there now. It's a skill I have. I can be inside your head, feel your mind at work. I can experience you from the inside out. It's a thing I can do, an ability, a gift. Do you believe that, Norman? Do you believe I'm inside your mind right now, sensing the world as you sense it? Do you think I have that genius?"

"If you say so."

"Oh, yes. I say so. I most assuredly say so. And what I know from being inside your large and spacious skull is that you had the same terrible childhood that I had. You had a mother who was not a mother and a father who was no one's father, and there were men who beat you and women who preyed on you and teachers and policemen and neighbor children who tormented you and drove you to the horrible cave where you dwell now. I think you stood too near the bonfire of your misery, Norman, and it incinerated your soul. Am I wrong? Or do I speak your thoughts, Norman? Do I give words to the song of your horror?"

"Fuck you, Jack."

"Oh, yes, fuck me. Yes, yes. That sad refrain. I would expect no less from you. Your last pathetic words. Profane, hackneyed. So predictable. So lamentable. Not your fault, really, but sad nonetheless."

From his rear pocket he drew out the glass blade, its grip tightly wrapped with white adhesive tape. He angled swiftly in front of Norman, and with a practiced backhanded swipe, he slashed the big man's throat. And then to be sure, he reset his feet, and staring into Norman's flabbergasted eyes, he made a second quick incision.

For a moment, Norman gargled on his own blood. He staggered forward a half step as if he'd stumbled across the trip wire of his pain. Then the big man lifted his hands and patted his throat and stared with confusion at his glistening fingers.

Norman mumbled something, and he reached out slowly as if to take the mirror blade away and toss it out to sea, where it would harm no one else. A last valiant act. A final gesture of nobility and honor.

Dodging out of range of the big man's lurching jabs, he watched as Norman's legs gave way and the large, sad, lumbering man went down to his knees in the sand.

And then he began to talk.

A gushing jabber of words. A hoarse, attenuated sentence flooding out of him, blood-garbled and uninspired, it came, a last soliloquy, as if in cutting the big man's throat, he had also severed Norman's restraints, his embarrassment and confusion. Released him to speak his mind, speak and speak and speak the interminable sentence of his grief. Words and words and more words, disgorging like hunks of undigested meat. The crude eloquence of death.

He waited till the big man's speech dwindled to a few final indecipherable words and Norman sank facedown into the sand; then he turned back to the frolicking girls.

"Hey, ladies," he called out. "Emma, Jennifer, wait up. Wait for me. I've got an idea. I've got a fabulous idea."

"What is it?" Jennifer called back. "A threesome?"

She tittered.

"Close," he said quietly as he marched in their direction. "Very close."

The girls were slopping around in the knee-high surf, dousing each other with slaps of water and giggling hilariously.

"Where's Norman?" Emma said.

"He's back there a way. Lying in the sand."

"What happened?"

"He's just relaxing. Gazing up at the stars. Contemplating."

"Norman, contemplating? I gotta see this."

Emma and Jennifer started back along the shallow surf. Jennifer kicked a spray of water at Emma and both girls squealed.

"Norman is your daddy. Did you realize that, Emma?"

"What?"

"He just confessed it to me. He's your father. How does that make you feel?"

She spun around and staggered through the knee-deep water toward him, her dress saturated and glistening with moonlight.

"Norman was the love of your mother's life. You mean you didn't know?"

"What the fuck're you talking about?"

"Go ask him. See what he says."

"What're you, crazy?"

"That's why he's been so patient and long-suffering with you, Emma. He's your flesh and blood. And you're his. You're inextricably linked, the same galactic materials, the same crystalline web of biology."

Emma stared at him for a long moment, then swung around and headed down the beach at a trot. Jennifer started after her, but he grabbed her shoulder and halted her.

"I think they need to be alone at a time like this, don't you?"

"Hey," Jennifer said, trying to shrug free of his grasp. "You're hurting me."

He smiled at her, let the wine bottle fall to the soft sand; then he snapped out his right hand and stunned her with a blow to her cheek. Jennifer's knees sagged, but he got an arm around her back and caught her before she dropped to the sand.

He took hold of Jennifer McDougal's jaw and turned her narrow face to the available light. He needed to see her eyes. He needed to watch the fear turn to anger. To rage. He needed to see that.

Jennifer swallowed hard and tried to say something, but he was holding her jaw too tightly for her to speak, lifting her up on her toes, peering into the shallow girl's shallow eyes.

And there it was. The terror subsiding, the rage flowing in. Hatred, repulsion. Just enough moonlight to see her eyes, to see the flicker of pure murderous loathing. She flashed her nails at his face, but he ducked away. And then he let her see her eyes. Their reflection in the slender blade of mirror. He let her look for the briefest second—the last vision of this world she would ever have.

"Jennifer!" It was Emma's wail coming through the dark. "Run, Jennifer. Run away. That guy's a killer. Run, Jennifer. Norman's dead."

But by then, of course, her warning cries were useless.

He let Jennifer's body sag from his hands, crumple into the surf, and he turned and waited peacefully for the small dark girl with the pale eyes to come hurtling out of the dark. This poor girl who had discovered her birthright a few seconds too late.

THIRTY-ONE

In her white jeans and hunter green turtleneck, Alex sat on the front porch and waited for Jason to return. She rocked and rocked, listening to the grains of sand she was grinding against the pine planks. Eyes unfocused as she gazed through the aluminum screen at the hazy, darkened houses across the way.

A long-ago fragrance stirred on the breeze, the sweet green scent of pine needles mingled with the hearty musk of the sea. One stray breath and she was again that sun-browned girl rocking on the porch of the Mellow Yellow. Unformed, full of naïve hope and confidence. Still there, trapped in the innocent past. As if she'd been left behind, forgotten as her parents drove home to Miami without her. Alex chasing after their retreating car with the dark-haired girl sitting in the backseat, that little girl looking over her shoulder, staring numbly out the rear window as Alex ran and ran after them, never to catch up.

In college, she'd read a philosopher who had determined that the present moment lasted only three to twelve seconds, and everything else was memory.

Three to twelve seconds. The juicy sliver of orange you are slipping into your mouth, the sudden sour burst against the tongue. Then abruptly, the next thing. The phone's shrill ringing. Just that and only that until the next moment appears. An endless succession of brief intervals, always the present. Moments forever arising, and seconds later, forever lost.

But it was also within those three to twelve seconds that the past was recalled. So that every instant of the past was hostage to the vagaries of the present. Any story of yesterday had to be refracted and colored by the narrow lens of the moment. Even Darnel Flint did not exist except as Alex chose to revive him now. As if the past were not the past at all, but only a vast sequence of selective memory.

Accurate history depended on accurate journalism, good record keeping. But how could there truly be such a thing? As a child, how was it possible to know which things to pay attention to? What to store, what to let go. How many times because of a subtle shift of the viewfinder had Alexandra Collins missed some great streaking comet across her youthful sky?

The same long-ago philosopher had described the past as a palimpsest, that ancient tablet that was erased again and again so new directives could be recorded there, a tablet whose surface inevitably showed the traces of previous texts. New replacing old, but the old never completely disappearing. Shadows remaining, the faint scribbles showing through, year after year, layer after layer accumulating, until the present text was little more than a muddle, a confusion of imperfectly erased sentences from the past.

Jason returned a little after one in the morning. He was drunk and soaking wet, carrying his jeans and shirt and shoes in a waterlogged bundle, tiptoeing up East Ruskin in only his sopping Jockey shorts. He stumbled up the steps, banged himself in the nose with the screen door, roared with laughter, then pressed a finger to his lips and shushed himself.

He came over to her, dropping his soggy clothes in his wake.

He bent to kiss her, but she steered him away. He blinked, tucked his chin in tight, and raised a hand like a Boy Scout swearing an oath.

"I got waylaid," he said. "Not laid. Oh, no. Not laid. I'm a faithful fellow, but I admit, I was waylaid."

The acrid fog of his breath made her turn her head away.

"Maybe you should go to bed."

"No, I came to get you. To swim. There's moonlight on the water. It's great. You'll love it. There's people from Bud and Alley's, the chef and the waiters, and we shut the bar down, and then we went swimming. Skinny-dipping, actually. And I told them all about you and I said I'd come get you and bring you back, so here I am. They're all naked down there. It's great. You'll like them. They want to meet you."

"I don't feel like swimming, Jason."

"But there's moonlight. A whole lot of moonlight."

He was wavering over her; his mouth was rubbery, searching for a smile.

"No thanks."

"Okay, okay." He tried to straighten himself, get a serious look, control the bob of his head, but the booze wouldn't let him. "You're not a swimmer, then. Not a skinny-dipper. That's fine. No problem. So we'll go to bed instead. Now there's the ticket. Bed. Yeah. Some serious slumber."

"You go ahead. I'm not sleepy yet."

"Sure," he said. "Sure, yeah. You want to be alone. Right. I can appreciate that. A woman needs to be alone sometimes. Sort things out."

He stood there a moment more, then swung his head around and surveyed the porch as if he'd just materialized there.

"You should've been there, Alex. There was so much moonlight. I never saw so much in one place. Beautiful, just beautiful, dolphins rolling, it was spectacular. You're sure you don't want to go swimming? Just a stroke or two."

"I'm sure."

She led him to the bedroom. Helped him dry off and then shepherded him to the bed and eased him down. When he was inside the sheets, he squinted up at her and said, "Stop spinning, would you?"

"Okay," she said. "I'll stop."

"You're still spinning. Stop it. It's making me nauseous."

She went to the door and switched off the light.

"Is that better?"

But he didn't answer. He was snoring with such suddenness and fervor that for a moment she thought he must be faking.

In the morning, he shambled into the living room and with a groan sunk onto the couch next to Lawton, who was watching a fishing show on the television. Alex brought him coffee and aspirin and he thanked her with a contrite smile.

"Was I awful?"

"Not awful."

He swallowed the aspirin and massaged his temples.

"I was close though, huh?"

"Close enough," she said.

He sipped his coffee and watched with Lawton as a young sunburned man poled his skiff across the glassy flats of the Florida Keys.

"Shhhh," Lawton said. "All that talk, you'll scare the damn fish."

When the show broke for a commercial, Jason asked if Alexandra wanted to go for a walk on the beach, but she declined.

"I know it doesn't really work this way," Jason said, "but I've got a ton of toxins I need to sweat out."

"Go to it, then," she said. "Sweat away."

He gave her a chaste kiss on the cheek and marched off toward his penance.

After he was well away, Alex switched off the television, and when Lawton protested, she said, "Let's go meet this Grace."

He smiled and the light in his eyes powered up so quickly, it was as if she'd hit a switch that had been turned off for years.

"Oh, I forgot to tell you," he said. "Those people stopped by for the money."

"What people?"

"The ones with the pool company. I think it was the same ones."

Alexandra stared at him a moment more, then turned and went quickly to the freezer and flung open the door. The stack of cash was gone. Using a dining room chair, she climbed up onto the countertop and pulled down the large straw basket. Empty as well.

Her father was washing his face in his bathroom, lathering it up with the sliver of soap. She stood behind him, caught his eyes in the mirror.

"These people, Dad, the ones who took the money. They saw you?"

"Oh, yeah. They were right out there in the living room when I came up from the beach. I offered them some lemonade, but they weren't thirsty. We had a pleasant conversation. They weren't as bad as we thought. A little strange-looking, but basically friendly folks."

"Jesus Christ."

Lawton rinsed the soap away and patted his face dry.

"I don't like it when you take the Lord's name in vain, Alex. It isn't becoming to a young lady, that kind of gutter talk."

"We have to get out of here, Dad. Now, right now."

"Why?"

"Those people, they're the ones who killed Gabriella."

"Oh, they're long gone by now. They got what they wanted and now they're moving on down the highway. You can bet on that."

"They tried to kill us once. They must know we can identify them."

"I don't guess that bothers them much. They didn't kill me the other day. Had the perfect opportunity, too. Lots of guns, no one around. No, Alex, trust me, those people just wanted money. They aren't thrill killers or anything. They got what they want and they're gone. Trust me, I know my crooks."

"I don't know, Dad."

"What's your worry, Alex? You're so tense lately. There's nothing to be that tense about. Things always work out. One way or the other, they always do. Worst that can happen is you die. And hey, what's the big deal with that? Everybody gets old and frail and sick and everybody dies. It's the most natural thing in the world, next to getting born and having sex. So what's the worry? When you've got the dying thing sorted out, you begin to see there's just nothing worth fretting about."

"We need to get out of here, Dad. If those people found us, then Stan can't be far behind."

"Nope. I'm not leaving here, Alexandra. I haven't been happy for a long time and now I am. So that's that. I'm an adult, and I can damn well decide where I'm going to stay. And I've decided it's right here. So go on somewhere else if that's what you want, but it'll mean the parting of the ways for you and me. 'Cause I'm staying put."

In a yellow shirt with huge pink hibiscus blooms and baggy black shorts, Lawton Collins led Alex unerringly through a labyrinth of sandy paths directly to the front gate of a deep blue Cracker house with red trim. The plaque on the front gate said DOCTOR'S ORDERS.

In the front yard, working at a potting table, was the white-haired woman who'd checked them in two days before. She was wearing faded overalls and a loose-fitting red T-shirt and was planting small green shoots in tiny pots. Her face was slicked with sweat.

"Grace, I'm back."

She looked up and waved hello with her trowel.

"This is my daughter, Grace. She wanted to meet you, check you out. So be on your best behavior. No dirty jokes."

The woman came over to her picket fence, smiling into the sunshine.

"Yes, of course. Hello, Alexandra, hello. So glad to meet you again. I'm Grace Trakas."

She peeled off a leather glove and shook Alex's hand.

"I say *again*, because we met before, when you were a little girl. That summer—what was it, twenty years ago?"

"Eighteen," Alex said quietly.

Grace lifted her head and peered out toward the dunes as if those years were still lurking just beyond the horizon.

"Yes, well, I was living about a mile from here at the time and I remember you all very well. Your mother and I had some real heart-to-hearts that summer. I was going through my first divorce, and she was a great comfort to me. My first woman friend, really. We kept in touch for months afterward, letters back and forth. But you know how it is. One of us didn't answer a letter and it petered out. Very wise, your mother was, very wise indeed."

Lawton tugged on Alexandra's arm.

"Grace is my wife," he said. "I married her and took her to Miami. But we decided to move back up here to Ohio. Too much stray gunfire down in Florida."

Grace Trakas combed a sweaty curl of silver hair off her forehead and smiled at Lawton.

"My first husband had some problems with his memory, too. Started when he was only fifty."

"Grace is going to give me herbs. She's the light of my life."

He leaned across the picket fence and pecked her on the cheek. Grace gave him a gentle smile and patted his shoulder.

"I was a doctor," she said to Alex. "Retired now. But I was a GP for forty years, specializing in geriatrics. Now I've lived so long, I've become my own patient."

Alex smiled.

"But toward the end, I was having some success with conditions like Lawton's, using a combination of herbs. No side effects, mild benefits. But mild is better than nothing."

"You got any lemonade, Grace?"

"I do, Lawton. I have a whole pitcher right up there on the porch. Lots of ice, the way you like it."

He pushed through the gate and climbed the steps and Grace Trakas leaned close to Alex.

"He's very sweet. But I'm sure it wears on you."

"Sometimes," she said, and paused. Then she said, "Grace, I was wondering if you'd mind—"

Grace interrupted her with a wave of the hand.

"Of course not. You can leave him with me anytime you want. He's really no problem. No problem at all. Say the word."

"That's very kind," said Alex. "Very kind."

"I mean it. Anytime at all."

"I need to go back to Miami for a day or two. I know it's a lot to ask."

Grace dusted a honeybee away from her ear.

"No problem at all, Alexandra. I'm happy to help."

Alex leaned across the gate and kissed Grace on the cheek.

"Did your friends find you?" Grace said.

"Friends?"

"You're a very popular young lady."

"I don't know what you mean."

"Well, there were the three people asking about you Saturday night. And then the phone call."

"What three people?"

Grace described the large man in the bright yellow jacket and the small blond girl with the light eyes.

"The other one was a young woman of twenty-five or so, a tall, thin blond who seemed a little . . . I don't know, dizzy. To be honest, it's hard to picture them as friends of yours."

"They aren't."

"Did I do wrong to say that you were here?"

"No," she said. "Tell me about the phone call."

"Same thing. Some man wanting to know if an Alexandra Rafferty was staying at Seaside."

"When was that? Do you remember?"

"Saturday morning, early, nine-thirty, maybe. Not half an hour after you checked in."

"Did he say anything else? Give you any idea who he was?"

"No. But he seemed quite pleased to find you here. He said he was taking a wild stab. Those were his exact words, I believe, 'a wild stab.' He seemed amused, for some reason. A little smart-alecky. So did they find you, your friends?"

"I think they did, yes. I think they found me."

Lawton swung open Grace Trakas's screen door. He was holding a tall glass of lemonade and she could see he had a mustache of rind.

"Oh, Alexandra, hey. Don't forget about that blood. We don't want it to stain the woodwork."

"Blood?"

"The blood I showed you."

"What blood? You didn't show me anything, Dad."

"On the front steps of our house. Yeah, I'm sure I pointed it out as we were coming over here. Or maybe not. But I thought about pointing it out. You ever do that? Think something in your head and later you're not sure you said it out loud or not. You ever do that? I do it all the time."

"Do you mind, Grace? Taking him for just a little while?"

"Blood?"

"Please, just for a little while."

The woman touched a hand to her heart as if she were having pangs of doubt. She glanced at Lawton, then brought her eyes back to Alex. She shook her head solemnly as if she were overruling her better judgment.

"Go," she said. "He'll be safe here. Go."

There was the faintest sprinkle on the front steps of the Chattaway. Several smudges where she and Lawton must have trampled them, then a dozen distinct droplets leading out into the street and curving toward the beach. She stooped and dabbed at one spot and rubbed the gluey fluid between thumb and first finger. Had to be several hours old.

She followed the spatters a few feet down the street, then lost the trail and had to wander awhile before she picked it up again on the other side of the highway. It led to the whitewashed stairway that swept down to the beach and then it trailed out across a white stretch of sand to the still water's edge.

Just out of range of the tide, the spotty track led west toward the wild and unpopulated end of the beach. The blood was showing up in larger and larger patches, a clump, then, twenty feet farther along, another, slightly larger clump. As if he was worried that the sand might blow and drift and cover his handiwork.

Monday morning, the beach was empty, some gulls and terns standing stiffly and peering out to sea, but no human life. Farther on, she found a small blue crab tracking through a splash of blood, and she felt the flesh rise in patches along her shoulders, her sinuses flare open.

She spotted the twin humps of sand forty yards or so before the blood made its turn and led her to them. Two sand sculptures that seemed like no more than the standard reclining figures until she mounted the small embankment and stood a yard away.

The two sand figures were laid out side by side. The first one might have been mistaken for an archer's bow, while the second could be some headless running man. She swung around, but there was no one on the beach. Higher up the bank, the sea oats yielded to a feeble breeze, but she saw no one anywhere.

She looked back at the two sand sculptures.

It was *D* and her sister, *R*.

Alexandra knelt beside the first one and took a measured breath, then brushed the sand from the naked flesh until she found the young woman's face. The sky shook with a gull's boisterous laugh. And with the rhythm of an overheated pulse, a Jet Ski pounded across the washboard surf.

It was the tall blond girl she'd seen coming out of Stan's hospital room last Thursday evening. Jennifer McDougal, her body bent in grotesque service to the Bloody Rapist. On her face was the same bruise as the others, two fingers wide.

Viewing it in the morning sunlight, the purplish yellow print of the attacker's fingers, Alexandra knew all she needed to know. It was a bruise she had seen a dozen times before—on her own body and on countless others at the dojo. A *nihon nukite*, a two-fingered thrust, known as "a spear hand." It was commonly used on the softer, less muscled portions of the body, the neck, the gut, but the face would do nicely. A *nihon nukite* administered with enough force would stun an average man or woman, send them to the floor, docile and compliant.

Alex knee-walked through the sand and bent above the other figure and uncovered her face, as well. The dark-skinned girl with curly blond hair, her lips torn, her cheekbone gashed, a lime-sized knot on her forehead. This one had fought more viciously than any of the others, gone down flailing. Good for her.

Alexandra pushed herself to her feet and drew a breath.

Beside the dark woman's face, a large brown cockroach churned its legs in the sand, going nowhere, snagged by a green thread.

Alex scanned the dunes and beach. Only a pair of old ladies with net bags and matching white porkpie hats. Matrons of the seashells.

Alex lifted her foot and crushed the roach, ground it into the soft sand, then headed at a trot back toward the gorgeous town.

THIRTY-TWO

Dan Romano's voice was so hoarse, it sounded like he'd been gargling gasoline.

"I've got bad news," he said.

"Good, we can trade."

"Early yesterday morning," Dan said. "Florida Highway Patrol got a call. A passerby found Stan's body along the shoulder of a back road up in Escambia County. Ten miles from Panama City. Stan was shot in the back seven times with a large-caliber weapon. An execution. Yellow pool-service truck like the one you described was parked a few hundred yards up the road from the scene."

Alex sat down in one of the oak dining room chairs. She took a dry swallow and stared up through the transom window at a ragged fleet of clouds sliding past. They crossed briefly in front of the sun and the room dimmed to momentary dusk, its bright colors grown pallid.

"I'm sorry, Alex," Dan said. "Sorry to have to tell you over the goddamn phone like this. Stan had problems, I guess. But he always struck me as a decent guy."

"Then he fooled you, too."

"Okay, whatever you say. But I'm sorry anyway. It's gotta be a blow."

She heard the house creaking as the sun brightened and the timbers warmed. A purple slash of light stretched across the dining table, deflected by one of the antique bottles lining a high windowsill.

"Are you there, Alex?"

"Barely."

Out in the street, a young man pedaled by on an ancient bicycle. His chain clanked and rattled like a troop of manacled prisoners.

"What did you get on Darnel Flint?"

"Not a lot."

"I'm listening."

She heard Dan rustle through his papers; then he cleared his throat.

"Darnel Sampson Flint died about six months ago. A stroke. Body wasn't claimed. County had to dispose of it."

"About the same time the murders started."

"What?"

"Is that all you got?"

"Hey, come on, Alex. Where's the reciprocity here? Don't I deserve a fucking explanation? You got me digging through tax records and property deeds and insurance claims. All night I worked my ass off and you aren't even going to throw me a bone? Like maybe telling me what the fuck's going on."

"Reciprocity? That one of your new words?"

"Yeah, just so happens it is."

"I like it. It feels good in the mouth. *Reciprocity.*"

Alexandra stood up and stretched the phone cord out to its limit so she could reach the end of the dining table. She hadn't noticed the copper bucket till that moment. Something new.

She leaned forward and slid the wine bottle from the ice, turned it around and read its label. Lucere, the California chardonnay.

She drew a long, airless breath, then swung around and stared at the empty room.

"Alex? You still with me?"

She wasn't sure if her voice still worked.

"I'm with you, Dan." She screwed the bottle back into the wine bucket. The ice was still fresh. "But I'm under some time pressure. Speed this along, would you?"

"Okay, okay. The father left some small insurance policies to his children. From the Philadelphia Life records, we got an address for the two girls. Mollie and Millie share an apartment in Boulder, Colorado. Escort-service hookers is what it looks like."

Alex leaned out to peer into her bedroom. Vacant, as far as she could see.

"And the son? J.D.?"

"Yeah, well, he got ten thousand bucks from the same policy, apparently used it to buy a piece-of-shit house down by the Miami River. In the middle of a high-density crack neighborhood."

"Can you check out that house for me?"

While Dan cursed and ranted, she peeked in Lawton's room. Nothing.

When Dan was quiet, she said, "Is that all? No employment records, nothing else?"

"Christ, Alex, with what I had to go on, that's a pretty good night's work."

"The son's full name. Did you get that?"

"It's somewhere in my notes."

"Do you have them with you?"

"Yeah, yeah. Christ, I'm checking now."

Alexandra saw him coming up the stairs. Shirtless, with dark trunks, his coppery flesh gleaming, dark hair swept back and plastered down. He carried a red beach towel in one hand, his running shoes in the other.

"Is his first name Jason?" she said quickly.

"I'm looking, I'm looking."

Jason pushed open the front door and stood for a moment smiling at her. Then his eyes fell on the ice bucket and he gave her a quizzical look.

"Are we celebrating?" he whispered.

Alex shrugged a noncommittal reply as Dan spoke in her ear. "Yeah, yeah here it is. I knew I had it."

"What is it, Dan?"

"Justin David Flint."

"You're sure?" She watched Jason draw the wine bottle from the ice, check the label. "You couldn't have made a slight mistake with the first name?"

"Hell, I don't know. That's what I wrote down. Justin David. What's the big deal, Alex?"

"Later, Dan. I've got to run. I'll call you when I get a chance."

"Wait a minute. Wait a goddamn minute! Don't hang up on me."

Alex turned and walked to the kitchen and set the phone back in its cradle, cutting off the shrill bleating of Dan's electronic wrath.

"What was all that about?"

Jason stood at the head of the table. He pushed the Lucere back into the ice. The bottle was uncorked.

"Cop business," she said.

"Never stops, does it? Can't even go away on vacation."

"Killers and rapists aren't big on holidays."

"Wow, you're serious this morning."

"Oh yeah," she said. "I'm dead serious."

He took a step her way and she countered with a half step to the side. He raised an eyebrow, half-smiled, and made another experimental step, and she replied. A dream dance. A slow-motion waltz around the furniture. Keeping him at a careful distance, matching his rhythm with her own.

"What're we doing?" he asked. "What's the matter?"

"Did you bring that wine, Jason?"

"No, I've been jogging on the beach. I just got back."

"Where'd it come from? Have any idea?"

"What is this, some kind of joke?"

"I didn't put it there; you didn't put it there. So I wonder where it came from."

"Maybe Lawton?"

She wanted open space, room to maneuver, enough unobstructed area for a roundhouse kick, her strongest, most decisive weapon.

"Lawton's visiting a friend," Alexandra said.

"His new lady?"

He set his shoes on the floor beside the couch and slung the towel over his shoulders and drew it around him like a shawl, as if he'd felt a sudden chill.

"He's safe," she said. "And he's going to stay that way."

He looked puzzled, then shrugged it off.

"You're acting very strange, Alex. Are you still mad at me about last night? I mean, I understand if you are. But I certainly didn't go off intending to get wasted. I just sat down at the bar at Bud and Alley's, had a glass of wine, started talking to the bartender, and it turns out the guy is a stock-market junkie, of all things. So he starts picking my brain. Talking Dow Jones, bonds and mutual funds, global growth, and the guy's refilling my glass whenever it's half-empty. Next thing I know, I'm swimming nude with a bunch of people I never met before, and I looked around and realized you weren't there."

"I'm here now."

"I see that."

She had positioned her back to the kitchen so the rising sunlight was in Jason's eyes. Not much of an advantage, but all she could muster, given the situation. Her arms hung at her side, loose, relaxed, poised. She wasn't frightened, wasn't angry. Wasn't anything. There was a quiet buzz in her veins. A bee in a bottle. Just watching him. Knowing what she had to do. Ready for it. Way past ready. Eighteen goddamn years of preparation.

"Do you want me, Jason? Do you want to take me?"

"What?"

"How does it work? Do I have to say something to set you off? Some sexy abracadabra."

"What the hell're you talking about, Alex?"

"I bet you have to find a reason. Some little word or look or gesture that lights the fuse. Is that how it works? A sip or two of that Lucere, you cuddle with them. All the while you're getting more and more aroused, you're also secretly pissed off. Those are probably the same things for you. Your cock stiff with hatred and desire. You probably don't see a lot of difference, do you?"

Jason pulled the towel off his shoulders and dropped it on the dining table.

"Something's happened," he said.

"Damn right something's happened. A whole string of somethings."

He swallowed.

She saw the subtle shifting of his feet as he reset himself. An ambush was out of the question now. Element of surprise long gone. And that was as it should be. She didn't want to win by a sucker punch. She wanted this head-on. Down and dirty. Her outrage versus his.

"I don't know what you think, Alex. I don't know where all this is coming from. But you're wrong. You've made a wrong turn somewhere."

"I don't think so. I think you were in the bathroom eighteen years ago. You didn't go to the grocery with your parents and your sisters. You stayed at home with big brother. And a second or two after you flushed the toilet, there was a gunshot in the house. It was very loud and you were scared out of your mind. So you hid. You hid somewhere very good, because my father looked for you and didn't find you. And you were so terrified, you never said a word. Not ever. Not to anyone."

"This is nuts."

Alex came forward a half step, keeping her balance, hands relaxed at her sides.

"But that wasn't the end of it. Because that secret started to glow inside you. You kept thinking about how terrified you'd been, how impotent. Little by little, that terror turned into rage."

Three feet separating them now. His eyes had tightened. Stance focused on this attacker, this woman who had stepped inside his danger zone.

"And so you decided on a way to get even. Work your way through the letters of my name. Knowing I'd see the results, and maybe you could scare me as much as you'd been scared a long, long time ago."

"You're making a huge mistake, Alex. I don't know why you think I'm this guy, but I'm not. I swear to you, I'm not."

"Oh, come on, Jason. Don't back down now. You've come all this way, worked so hard. Been so diligent and creative. This is your reward, isn't it? Me, Alexandra Collins, the little girl all grown up. You're finished with the substitutes, you've perfected your ritual, and now it's time for the finale. Don't lose courage now, Jason. Not now."

He lifted his hands to a middle guard position. But he looked off balance, confused.

"Don't," he said. "Don't do this."

She flicked a right hand toward his face and he brushed it aside with an upward thrust. A half a second slower than usual. Wild static in his eyes.

"They didn't have a chance, did they? Just normal women. Not fighters, none of them black belts like you. They let you into their houses. You charmed them, seduced them, and when they were at their most vulnerable, you killed them. Just like you were going to do to me."

She snapped a front kick toward his groin, but he shunted it aside with an ankle block, then countered with an automatic left hand that was sluggish and only grazed her cheek. She feinted with another kick, and when he moved to block, she lunged with a chopping right to the side of his neck, which jolted him and made him hop back out of range.

"Goddamn it! What kind of game are you playing?"

"Come on, Jason. Let's get it over with."

His face went slack. He shook his head and lowered his hands to his side.

"Enough," he said. "This is insane."

She held her position, watched for the smallest shift of weight, the giveaway feint. But he didn't move. Just kept his eyes on hers, his stance soft and vulnerable. Hands loose at his sides. A trick beyond tricks.

It stalled her for a second.

"Look," he said. "Let's sit down and talk about this, Alex. Maybe have a sip of that wine."

He raised one hand toward her as if beckoning for a dance, then took a step her way, that hand moving toward her cheek.

Alexandra dodged to her right, planted her back foot, and snapped her right heel into his groin.

Jason doubled over convulsively, and she swiveled fast and drove her knee into his face, and it connected full and hard against the point of his chin, a charmed strike, and Jason hung for a moment, bent forward at the waist as if he were seasick at the railing of a swaying ship; then he tottered briefly and dropped backward to the floor, slammed his head against the oak. Eyes shut, breath filled with liquid guttering in his throat.

Stepping forward warily, Alexandra prodded him in the ribs with her toe, but he didn't move. He had sunk into a black stupor, as lifeless as a drowned man riding the departing tide.

She hustled into the kitchen and pawed through the utensil drawer until she found a paring knife. She marched into Lawton's bedroom and tore the top sheet from his bed and cut three long strips from the yellow cloth.

Back in the living room, she rolled Jason onto his belly and hauled his hands behind him and tied them with one of the yellow strips. She bound his ankles with the second, then used the third cord to double-tie his wrists.

When she rolled him onto his back, Jason's eyes were open, foggy and far away.

"My, my, that was quite an exhibition of pugilistic prowess."

Alexandra looked up.

"I certainly hope you didn't tire yourself out too much."

The brown-haired man who'd spoken was lounging in the doorway of her bedroom, arms crossed over his chest, a shoulder cocked against the door frame as if he were posing for a fashion shot.

He wore a tight black T-shirt and blue jeans and a pair of white tennis shoes. His gaudy biceps stretched the cotton sleeves. He had a slightly upturned nose and a broad forehead, and he was staring boldly at her with the caustic eyes of a rabid wolf.

"I see you got my little gift." He nodded toward the wine. "It's a tart, underachieving little chardonnay, but with some surprising complexity on the back side. I think you'll like it if you give it half a chance. It was one of my mother's favorites."

It took her a moment before she recognized him without his blue granny glasses and white hair net. She'd never seen his eyes before.

"Junior?"

"Oh, call me J.D. After all, we're practically family."

And then she saw it. The Flint bone structure, the knobby cheekbones of his mother, his father's heavy brow and slightly sunken eyes, that skin with its dull, unnatural pallor, as if he had sour milk coursing through his veins.

"We need to talk, Alexandra," he said, stepping into the room and looking down at Jason. "Before you die, I want to set you straight on a couple of things. Some small but crucial factual errors you made in that little story you just told."

THIRTY-THREE

Alex took a half step backward as Junior Shanrahan came out of his pose and sauntered into the living room. In his right hand, he gripped a five-inch shard of glass, holding it casually by his hip. He carried a heavy garbage bag in his left.

"You see, Alex," he said, "your father *did* find me that day. When I heard the gun go off, I hid in the linen closet, and he came into the bathroom and swung open the door, and there I was, sobbing, trying to be quiet, down on the floor, wedged in with the plumber's helper and the Clorox, and he squatted down and looked me in the eyes. You want to know what he did then?"

Alexandra glanced down at Jason. He was awake now, a thick smear of blood on his chin. His breath was noisy and irregular.

"Lawton Collins, this big tough cop that all the kids in the neighborhood were in awe of, he got in my face and he jammed the barrel of his hot, smelly gun into my mouth, and in this evil hiss, he said, "Kid, you either forget this happened or I'll come back in the night and murder you and your parents and your sisters."

"That's a lie. That's a goddamn lie."

He gave her a scornful frown.

"Of course you don't want to believe it. Daddy's a saint with a great golden halo hovering over him. Perfect in every way. No, no, he couldn't have done such an awful thing. Terrified a five-year-old boy. Not Lawton Collins. Dear, sweet Daddy."

Junior raised the mirror blade and slashed it back and forth through the air between them as if he were decapitating some ghostly recollection.

Then he stepped closer, two yards away. There was a chaotic spark in his eyes. Emotions shifting so quickly, it was as if he were listening to a dozen competing frequencies at once.

Alexandra's eyes were working hard, measuring angles, flight paths, trajectories. He was blocking her way to the front door, and behind her the back door was probably twenty feet away, impossibly far. She could leave Jason behind, take her chances through a window, risk the cuts, try to outrun him, lose him in Seaside's network of back streets and footpaths.

Or she could simply stay put and one way or the other be done with the horror forever.

Junior brushed the blade lightly back and forth across the bristles on his cheek as if sharpening it on a strop. Then he turned and tossed the garbage bag onto the couch. His sour mood abruptly brightened, shoulders lifting, eyes filling with reckless light.

"Two million dollars," he said. "Just sitting out in the open in one of your neighbors' houses. Imagine that. Nobody home, door unlocked. Two million greenbacks. That should get me a fresh start somewhere, don't you think? A condo on the water, a dog, a parakeet."

"How did you find me?"

"Followed the bread crumbs, dearie." His lips curled into an acid smirk. "Actually, it was more prosaic. I went over to your house. Kicked in the door. I was a little panicked I'd lost you. And there was a travel pamphlet sitting on your kitchen table. I got on the phone, called to see if you were here, and bingo."

"What do you want?"

"I think we both know the answer to that."

He ripped the blade through the air again, grinning as she stumbled out of reach. He took two more cautious steps her way.

"But come on, Alex, relax, don't be so morose. Let's have some wine, chat a little. Get to know each other. Catch up on all those missing years. We hardly ever get to talk around the office."

Alex was backing toward the kitchen, watching him carefully. Over the last few years, she'd seen Junior Shanrahan almost every day, but she had hardly noticed him. He was taller than Jason, probably outweighed him by thirty pounds. Heavily muscled in the chest, with arms covered in coarse black hair. Except for the narrow waist, he was his father's double. The same fierce brow, a back designed for heavy lifting. For such a large man, he walked lightly and with the limber sway of a cocky athlete.

He halted a foot from Jason's head and leered at her with his dark, chemical eyes.

The mirror blade in his hand was three inches wide, with one side beveled to a glinting edge and black traces of paint sprinkled across the silvery surface.

As his gaze drifted down to Jason, his leer evaporated.

Bubbles of red foam sparkled on Jason's lips. Bound as he was and in certain pain, he still managed a defiant glare.

Junior must have read his look, because the vessels surfaced in the edges of his face and he drew back his right foot as if he meant to boot Jason's head into the next room.

"No, Junior!" Alex shouted. "Stop!"

Junior dropped his foot and swung around to face her, the glass blade shimmering in his hand as if it were charged with electricity.

"Leave him alone, goddamn it. You want me, not him."

"You always were such a spoilsport, Alex. Little Miss Bossy, always making us play by the rules."

Junior gave her a choirboy grin, then abruptly drew the blade back and swooped down to slash at Jason's throat. Jason quailed away.

And Alexandra was across the room in one step and flinging herself into a roundhouse kick, but Junior was quicker than she'd imagined, quicker than Jason, quicker than anyone she'd encountered on the training mats.

With terrible efficiency, he ducked her leg, and her kick missed his face by inches. When she caught her balance, he was in front of her, and in the same instant he executed a strike so swift, she had no time even to flinch. Only caught the briefest glimpse of the two-fingered *nihon nukite* as it flashed through the air toward her face.

The daylight flickered. The blood in her ears roared.

As she was going down, she tried to roll, duck a shoulder, but there were chairs in the way and she clipped one of the oak seats with the back of her skull, lost a couple of seconds of daylight as she tumbled to the floor.

Above her, the ceiling was cockeyed; a lazy fan circled out of whack. Junior came into view, standing high above her, a wavering image.

"Now we know whose magic is superior," he said. "So let's don't have any more of these outbursts, shall we? Obviously, I trained harder at my dojo than you did at yours."

Kneeling down, he gripped a handful of her hair and held the silvery glass inches from her face. She peered at the reflection of her desperate eyes, at the careful black script hand-printed along the shard of glass: *Yea, though I walk . . .*

He tipped the blade out of view and teased its razory edge across her cheek, a stinging line, and down to her throat. He might've been drawing a thin trail of blood, but she was too woozy to tell.

With her hair clenched in his fist, Junior hauled her up and dragged her across the room and dumped her on the couch.

She squinted up at him, the light dazzling her eyes. A dizzy eddy of blood spun in her head. She took a measured breath, tried to blink her eyes clear, but a fine mist hung in the room, a dazed, uneasy rocking in her gut. She could feel a warm lump rising in her cheek, left eye beginning to squeeze shut, and Alex knew it was going to take several minutes at the very least for the fog to lift, for the blood to return to her muscles, before she would have half a chance against this monster. Every minute she stalled was a minute more to recover.

"You saw it happen, didn't you, Junior?"

"Saw what happen?"

He whisked the wine from the ice and stepped beside her and set it on the coffee table.

"You peeked in the playhouse that day and saw Darnel raping me. That was you, wasn't it, in the mirror? You were watching."

He reached across the couch and picked up the two wineglasses.

"Oh, yes, I was there. It was quite the enthralling scene."

He sat down beside her, a foot away. The blade burned in his right hand. With his left, he reached out with the bottle and poured two glasses.

"Oh, but come now, Alexandra, let's don't ruin our first date with a lot of psychoanalyzing."

He offered her the glass of wine. Kept it in front of her face until she took it. Then he clinked the lip of his against the lip of hers.

"To us," he said. "To our long, complicated past, our exquisitely tortured history."

She took a taste and watched him swallow deeply. He let out a gasp of pleasure, then settled back on the couch. His shoulders were wide, chest thick. Even his face seemed muscled. When he grinned or spoke, the sinews in his jaw and temple strained and twisted.

"Now what happens?"

"Just this," he said. "We luxuriate in the moment. Bask for a while in the beautiful symmetry of our lives."

Across the room, Jason groaned and twisted against the restraints.

Junior set his wineglass down on the coffee table and peered across at her as if trying to penetrate the haze of years. Bring the two images into alignment, the girl he remembered, the woman he faced.

She felt the spreading warmth inside her. A growing calm and sureness, as if that gaseous cloud that had escaped her so long ago as a child were finally sifting back, settling again inside her flesh, where it had once belonged. And her dizziness had mostly cleared, as well. A debt she owed to Jason, the morning training sessions with him, full-contact fighting, learning to process the pain more efficiently. To move past it, keep her focus as she fought her way back to clarity.

"How'd you work the fingerprints, Junior? Yours are on file in the AFIS. What'd you do, break into the files, switch someone else's prints for yours?"

"Always the cop, aren't you, Alex? Yes, yes, of course I removed my prints from the files. I'm not some idiot."

Outside the north window, a cluster of white bougainvillea fluttered like a thousand small white butterflies feasting on the branch. For a moment, Alex let her eyes rest on those quivering blooms.

"So tell me, sweetheart, where is he? Where did you stash dear old Dad?"

Alex watched a blade of sunlight inching across the hardwood floor.

"Might as well fess up. I'm going to find him anyway. If I have to go house to house through this entire silly little town. If I have to turn over every bed, dig through every closet, and kick down every door. I'm going to find him."

"You're going to have to kill me first, Junior."

His smile hardened.

"You don't understand, do you? You don't realize what the two of you did when you murdered Darnel. You destroyed my goddamn family; you twisted us into a festering mass of disease. You and that old man. The two of you caused the death of eight innocent women."

"Bullshit."

His eyes emptied and the blade jerked forward as if he meant to open her throat. Alex surged to her feet, flung her wine in his eyes, and shot a left jab at his chin. But Junior Shanrahan snatched her fist from the air, gripping it with such brutal force that she heard the gristle crack, felt the burning rip of ligaments. She couldn't breathe as he levered her back to the couch.

He glared into her eyes and wiped the wine from his face. But then his gaze strayed past her, out toward the porch, and he broke into a bitter laugh.

"My, my," he said. "Speak of the devil and up he jumps."

Alex twisted out of his grip.

"Dad! No! Don't come in here. Run, Dad! Run!"

But Lawton was on the porch and through the front door.

"I'm just here to get my camera," he said. "Go on with what you're doing." And he marched quickly through the living room, nodded at the two of them, stepped over Jason's bound body, gave him a quick, curious look, then strolled into his bedroom.

Junior reached out and pressed the cold edge of glass against her throat.

"If you so much as move, I'll open you up right now. I won't wait another second."

With his free hand, he gripped her by the jaw and peered into the depths of her eyes, a look meant to chill her into submission. The touch of his hands was so rough and careless, he might have been handling a chunk of broken rock.

"Okay, you two, say *cheese*."

Lawton was standing beside Jason, ten feet away. In his hands was the Brownie Reflex. He was looking into the pop-up viewfinder, aiming the camera at Junior.

"Come on, you two. Let's see a smile. Memories for a lifetime."

"Dad! Get out of here. Go!"

Junior rose and stepped around the couch.

"Hold still," Lawton said. "Don't want a blurry picture." He glanced up from the viewfinder and said, "Hey, I remember you."

"Yes, I'm sure you do."

"You're Frank Sinatra. The bastard who's been dogging our every move."

"What?"

Lawton dropped the camera and it smashed on the floor beside Jason's head. The old man brushed his shirttail aside and reached into the waistband of his shorts and drew out a black .38 revolver.

Junior held his place in silence, the insolent jut of his jaw still firm.

"Hands in the air, Frank. And you, too, pretty lady."

He sighted the .38 at Alex.

"Dad, it's me."

"Don't play games. Let's see those hands now. Both of you."

"It's me. It's Alexandra."

Lawton peered at her for a moment, then took a nervous swallow. He caught a glimpse of Junior inching forward, and he swung the pistol back to him.

"Don't think you can hoodwink me, you two. I'll shoot you both if I have to. I know what you're up to. A couple of thieves, here to steal our hard-earned cash. And you can't be my daughter. My girl's only eleven years old."

Alex stared into the dark barrel that was sighted on her heart.

"Dad. I *was* that little girl, but I got older, I grew up. I'm a woman now."

For a moment, Lawton's eyes flicked back and forth between

these sudden strangers. He licked his lips, working on the problem.

"And me, Lieutenant Collins," Junior said with cloying courtesy. "I'm the kid next door. The Flints' youngest child. The one you found in the closet. J. D. Flint. You remember me."

Lawton squinted hard at Junior, the pistol tightening in his grip.

"I don't have to remember any damn thing I don't want to remember. Now get your dirty hands up in the air, Sinatra, and cut the double-talk. Up, up, where I can see them."

Junior raised his hands, the mirror blade in his right fist, an overhand grip. He took a casual step forward, then another. Alex was on her feet, moving like a shadow toward Junior. In her right hand, she gripped her empty wineglass.

Lawton thumbed back the hammer and waggled the gun at Alex.

"Hold it right there, young lady. You wouldn't be the first female I had to shoot dead."

"Lieutenant Collins? Look at me. It's J. D. Flint. The kid you found in the bathroom closet." His voice had the quiet dreaminess of a snake charmer.

Lawton stepped back and stared at him.

"Sure, I remember you fine, kid. Nothing wrong with my memory. We had a conversation a long time ago, brief and to the point. I told you to keep your mouth shut and you did. And that's all there is to that story."

Junior moved closer and pointed down at Jason with the blade of glass.

"That's right," Junior said. "That's exactly right, Officer Collins. And do you know who this is, sir? This man on your living room floor?"

Lawton's eyes drifted down to Jason Patterson.

"This, Lieutenant, is the wretched fiend who raped your daughter."

"What?"

Lawton stared at Jason.

"He's lying, Dad. He's trying to fool you. Don't listen to him."

Lawton's head bobbed up and he focused the pistol on Alexandra. Then he swung it back to Jason.

"Is that right, son? You molested my daughter, did you?"

Jason groaned a "No."

"Yes, sir, he did. I witnessed the whole disgusting episode. This vile man trapped her in the playhouse, Lieutenant Collins. You remember that playhouse, don't you, sir?"

"Yes." His eyes stared blankly across the years.

"This man threw your daughter down on the plywood floor and he ripped off her underwear and he forced himself inside her flesh."

Lawton's eyes were drifting. His hand tightened on the .38.

"I knew something happened. She was so morose, so quiet. I knew, but I couldn't bring myself to ask her."

"I hate to be the one to tell you, sir. But here he is, the foul bastard who molested your daughter."

Lawton's pistol was wavering. He glared down at Jason, swallowing and swallowing again.

Alexandra angled out of Junior's line of sight, looking for her moment.

"Your beautiful young daughter fought this monster. She writhed and struggled; she bit this boy's finger deep to the bone and she drew blood. But this monster kept on raping her, Lieutenant Collins, plunging into her flesh, plunging and plunging. This twisted, depraved son of a bitch destroyed your daughter's childhood."

Junior gestured his silver blade at Jason.

"Pretty Alexandra, your fragile flower, bit this man's finger, and when he was finished raping her, the bastard walked across the lawn and all the way back into the house, and at every step he left behind a trail of his poisonous blood."

Lawton aimed the pistol down at Jason.

"You goddamn rotten son of a bitch."

"No, Dad, don't!"

But she was too late. Lawton's hand clenched and he clicked the trigger on an empty cylinder. And on another.

Junior laughed. "Fucking thing isn't even loaded. "

He drew back his blade and took a swipe at the old man's throat.

Lawton managed a quick side step out of range.

And Alex, despite her years of training in the orderly science of kicks and strikes and smashes, the cool, dispassionate art of self-defense, in that mad second abandoned everything she knew and threw herself onto Junior's back and snaked her arm beneath his chin, hard against his throat, and with her free hand she shattered the goblet against his cheek, ground the ragged edges in, held on as the man screamed and whirled and slashed at her with his blade. She felt the numb throbs as his blade gashed her flesh, but she held on.

Choking him with one arm, she jabbed and speared with the wineglass, broke all but the stem away; then as he howled and danced and tried to swing her off his back, she crammed that slender stalk of glass deep into Junior's ear.

And before he could slap it away, she made a fist and hammered the glass hard, drove it home through the tissues of his inner ear, deep into the doughy edges of his cranium, her own crude lobotomy, and rode the man's frenzy, his bucking, staggering steps, rode him with a throttling arm against his throat until Justin David Flint sank to his knees, wailing out his pain, and wilted, facedown, on the floor.

She lay atop his back, holding on until his breathing quieted; then finally, with a shudder, it tapered away to nothing.

When she got to her feet, Lawton was sitting on the couch, staring idly at the pistol that lay before him on the coffee table. Alexandra retrieved the paring knife from the bedroom floor, knelt beside Jason, and slashed the strips of yellow cloth binding his hands.

"Is he dead?" Jason asked.

"Guys like that don't die. They just change shapes and come back at you later from a different angle."

She helped Jason to his feet

"I'd feel better if we checked."

So Alex bent and held Junior's wrist and moved her fingers around until she felt the dull, soundless pulse of the dead.

"You need more work," Jason said, breath coming hard. "Rotten technique on that wineglass thing."

"We'll have to practice," she said.

She helped him to the bathroom and washed the cut on his chin and patted him dry. Jason helped her clean the gashes on her forearm. One near her elbow was going to need stitches. He rounded up Band-Aids and covered the worst cuts, then got ice from the freezer, and the two of them limped to the couch and eased down beside Lawton. Jason pressed the washrag full of cubes to his swollen jaw while Alex put her arm around her father's shoulder and drew him close.

They sat in silence for a while, Alex listening to the cries of distant gulls, a ball bouncing rhythmically in the street. She looked out a transom window at the moving sky, and when she brought her eyes back down to Jason's, his lips crinkled into a painful smile.

"You thought I was that guy. The Bloody Rapist?"

"I did," she said. "I'm sorry."

"Well, next time if you have a problem with me, please, let's try talking it through before you try to break my jaw."

"It's a deal."

Lawton slumped against her.

"I'm going to need a higher dose of those herbs," he said. "I still got a long way to go with this memory situation."

"It's going to be fine, Dad. Grace is going to help. She'll steer you the right way."

"I like that woman," Lawton said. "Lady's got spunk. I wonder what she sees in a broken-down old fool like me."

Alex hugged him close, lay her head on his shoulder.

"She probably sees what I see, Dad."

"Yeah, and what's that?"

"A warm, beautiful man. A treasure."

He studied the palms of his large hands, turning them to the light as if he were reading his difficult future.

"Maybe she'd like to take a little trip up north," he said. "Have a look at all those golden leaves, red and orange. I've heard Ohio's very pretty this time of year."